A C T OF
BETRAYAL

Also by Edna Buchanan

Suitable for Framing
Miami, It's Murder
Contents Under Pressure
Never Let Them See You Cry
Nobody Lives Forever
The Corpse Had a Familiar Face
Carr: Five Years of Rape and Murder

edna
BUCHANAN

ACT OF
BETRAYAL

HYPERION
NEW YORK

Copyright © 1996, Edna Buchanan.

This is a work of fiction. Any resemblance to actual events or persons, living or dead, is purely coincidental.

All rights reserved. No part of this book may be used or reproduced in any manner whatsoever without the written permission of the Publisher. Printed in the United States of America. For information address: Hyperion, 114 Fifth Avenue, New York, New York 10011.

Library of Congress Cataloging-In-Publication Data

Buchanan, Edna.
  Act of betrayal / Edna Buchanan.—1st ed.
    p. cm.
  ISBN 0-7868-6098-7
  1. Montero, Britt (Fictitious character)—Fiction.   2. Women journalists—Florida—Miami—Fiction. 3. Miami (Fla.)—Fiction. I. Title.
PS3552.U324A64 1996   95–38206
813'.54—dc20   CIP

Book design by Gloria Adelson

FIRST EDITION

10 9 8 7 6 5 4 3 2 1

For Renee Turolla, David M. Thornburgh,
and Peggy Thornburgh.
No writer could have better friends.

And, behold, there came a great wind from the wilderness, and smote the four corners of the house, and it fell upon the young men, and they are dead; and I only am escaped alone to tell thee.

—Job 1:19

ACT OF BETRAYAL

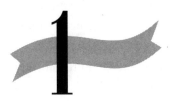

THE SWEET LITTLE old lady was dead, shot in the face by her Kenmore range when she opened the oven door to investigate the explosions inside. Baking cookies for her favorite grandson, she had no idea where he had stashed his ammo.

Her story was no more incredible than the backyard barbecue that had started my week. A patio bug zapper vaporized a mosquito, creating the spark that detonated a gas explosion in the outdoor grill. Still interviewing survivors, I was paged to go to a Miami Beach oceanfront resort. A makeshift raft had washed ashore with six boat people aboard. Only one, a sunburned and dehydrated six-year-old girl, was still alive.

Hours later an overloaded van crashed and rolled on a narrow stretch of U.S. 1. Like three others wrecked in the past four weeks, it was ferrying labor pools of Haitian workers to Upper Keys tourist havens. None of the vans had insurance or decent tire tread. The victims paid $25 a week for transportation to their minimum wage restaurant and hotel jobs. I had spent hours with the survivors and their next of kin and could still smell the haunting brew of green cachimon and vervine, a Haitian herbal tea used to sedate the bereaved.

Shell-shocked, I had escaped to unwind, catch my breath, and browse the new exhibit at my favorite cool and quiet place. In a small, vaultlike room, a powerful but solitary figure stood in shadows, a thick noose of nautical line coiled around his throat. My heels clicked on the cement floor as I stepped inside. Crudely drawn boats, small planes, and dark animal horns covered the walls. They seemed to close in like those of a prison, and the air grew dense. Suddenly claustrophobic, I fled out onto the sun-drenched piazza where pink pentas and demure hibiscus bloomed cheerfully under puffy clouds that cruised overhead.

Digging in my bag for the wrapped empanada bought from a street vendor, I sat in a shady spot near the sculpture court and nibbled my lunch in front of the most whimsical exhibit, a giant snowman built of tar, sweating dark tears in Miami's August heat. Public debate had raged around him. A symbol of white/good, black/evil, critics claimed. Symbolic of Miami's racism and prejudice, others pontificated. I simply enjoyed the incongruity of a tar snowman in the sizzling setting.

My tight shoulder and neck muscles relaxed as I stretched, soaking up the sun and the ambience. Wrought-iron gates surrounded the graceful Mediterranean arches and loggias of the piazza. The downtown skyline, towering glass and stainless steel sentinels, guarded the perimeter. My lazy thoughts drifted back to the man in the noose. The gallery notes said it was the work of an exile artist born in Havana during the Castro regime.

Time to get back to work. Reluctantly, I crumpled the greasy wrapping. As I stepped toward a wire trash basket, the ground shook. Walls trembled and sound waves rattled windows. For a millisecond I thought someone had fired the old Spanish cannon outside the Historical Museum. A dog howled somewhere. I stared up at innocent blue sky and with a growing feeling of dread knew what it was.

A pay phone hung on the wall a few feet away. Digging the ever-present emergency quarter from my skirt pocket, I punched in the dispatch number for Miami Fire.

"Hi. This is Britt Montero from *The Miami News*. I'm downtown. Where did the bomb explode?"

"Bomb?" echoed the operator.

"Yes. I just heard the explosion." Shifting impatiently, I eyed the walkway to the parking garage. Was the scene close enough to reach on foot? That might be faster and make more sense than driving.

"What makes you think it's a bomb?" The operator sounded slow and skeptical.

"This is Miami," I snapped. "I've been on the police beat long enough to know a bomb when I hear it."

"What was that location?"

"That's what I called to ask you." Frustration backed up in my throat along with my lunch, as I gripped the phone in a stranglehold, scanning the skyline. There it was, a swirling spiral of black smoke.

Suddenly she was serious. "I don't know what went down, but my nine-one-one phones are coming to life. Hold on."

I nearly hung up before she came back. "Don't have an exact QTH, but callers are all saying it's in the area of Northwest Second Avenue and Flagler. They say it's a car," the dispatcher added. "Have to go now, all hell's breaking loose." I hung up and ran.

Sprinting down the open stairwell from the elevated plaza at the Center for Fine Arts, I saw open-mouthed pedestrians staring in the direction of the smoke.

The location, two blocks away, didn't register until I saw the WTOP-TV tower. My heart pounded. Darn. Their reporters would be there first. Then it occurred to me that the television station itself, third in local news ratings, might be the target. Wisps of smoke wound up and around from behind the building.

Traffic was stalled. Sirens converging. People running.

As I caught my breath in that familiar suspended state of fearful anticipation, a thousand possibilities fast-forwarded through my mind. We have had car bombs explode under union officials, nightclub owners, drug dealers, double-dealing informants, federal witnesses, Latin political activists, and victims of mistaken identity.

Bombers have targeted police headquarters, the state attorney's office, the Justice Building, the Latin Chamber of Commerce, beauty salons, bingo halls, boats, trains, and planes, and the offices of the postal service, the FBI, and social security. Sometimes would-be bombers become the victims. A penis was all that remained of one bomb builder who made a mistake. Explosives have been planted in suspicious packages, booby-trapped television sets, and at Spanish-language newspapers. Cars outside various consulates have been blown sky high.

A bomb was even discovered strapped to a shooting victim during surgery. Found bleeding on an inner-city street, he had thirty packets of cocaine, two thousand dollars, and several bullet wounds. As he was transferred from a stretcher to the operating table, an explosive device equal in strength to a stick of dynamite was spotted, concealed in the small of his back. Had a bullet struck him half an inch lower, it and he would have detonated.

The hospital was evacuated as bomb squad experts gingerly removed the device and the surgical team fought to save the victim's life. He died despite their efforts. I mourned his passing. I wanted to hear his story but he took it with him.

Miami has had them all: letter bombs, pipe bombs, hand grenades, bazookas, missile launchers, remote control devices, and ticking time bombs. I hate their unpredictable nature, the impersonal character of their destruction. Bombs have no eyes. No soul. They will shred the flesh, blind the eyes, and end the lives of the innocent as well as their intended targets. Police are paid to face danger; innocent civilians entering a public building are not.

Journalists attract threats and scares, but we had never had a local TV station or reporter targeted by a bomb. My chest tightened. The reporters at WTOP-TV are the competition, sometimes friendly, some-times not. But they are fellow journalists and I know them.

Breathlessly, I pounded around the corner to the station parking lot.

Debris was everywhere but the heart of the blast was a late-model red Mustang. The tires were flat and smoking. Other parked cars had blown-out windows and shrapnel damage. Their alarms sounded in cho-rus, bewailing their wounds. The bomb had chewed away at the concrete parking lot where shocked employees now milled about.

Movie pyrotechnics, cars exploding in gigantic balls of fire and consuming infernos, are fiction. In reality, the initial flash and the blast wave subside almost instantly, followed by residual fire as gas and oil spew from fuel lines and slowly ignite. The Mustang's windshield and windows were gone. The hood, a crumpled piece of metal, now rested on the roof of the station's one-story building.

I thought I recognized the flashy little Ford with a blackened PRESS plate on the front.

An older woman stood dazed amid the debris. She appeared to be an office employee at the station. "Is that Alex Aguirre's car?" I asked.

"He was going home for lunch." She wrung her hands and I saw that they were burned, but she seemed unaware. "He goes home for lunch every day."

The mercilessly heated August air stirred against my skin like the hot breath of a wild animal.

"I tried to open the door," she said, her voice an odd monotone, "but it was too hot."

"He's still in there?"

"He just looked at me."

He could be alive. Heart thudding, I stumbled to the car, skirting metal fragments, stepping over broken glass—and instantly regretted it.

The figure in the still smoldering driver's seat in no way resem-bled the cocky, fearless, and loquacious commentator I remembered, a short, robust man who favored flashy suits instead of guayaberas and always meticulously combed his dark mustache before appearing on camera.

He was badly burned, clothes smoking, head arched back, mouth agape as though he had struggled for a last precious gasp of air. His right hand was missing. His right leg was wrapped around his neck.

Knees rubbery, I gulped deep breaths to settle my stomach and keep down my lunch. Turning away, nearly overwhelmed by the smoky, soupy mix of spilled transmission fluid, gas, oil, and the unforgettable stench of burned flesh, I remembered the family pictures of his smiling children that Alex had proudly displayed the last time our paths crossed at a press conference.

I wanted to warn away the growing crowd of gawkers, to block their view of what I would never forget. I know the dead have no privacy, but I didn't want strangers staring at him. Not now. Not this way.

I needn't have worried. Firefighters had appeared and begun hosing down the car. Police and homicide detectives arrived in droves. Cops began forcing everyone out of the lot, across the street and down the block, roping off a wide area. Bomb squad technicians in brown cargo pants and tan shirts argued noisily with the firemen, accusing them of washing away evidence.

More press was arriving. I saw my friend Lottie Dane and another photographer, named Villanueva, from the *News*. Lottie's fiery red hair, tight jeans, and camera are hard to miss. She is about five eight, but Villanueva towered over her at well over six feet. Both looked grim as they edged through the crowd.

"Is it who I think it is?" Lottie asked in her Texas twang. She was careful not to say a name.

"Alex," I whispered.

"Is he burned up?"

I nodded.

"A crispy critter?" asked Villanueva.

When I didn't answer, he shook his head and began rapid-firing a Nikon with a 300-millimeter lens.

A WTOP news van screeched to the curb, the last to arrive. The stunned crew leaped out to shoot footage but was kept at bay by police. Apparently every WTOP reporter had been out on assignment at the time of the blast. In the panic that followed, it had not occurred to the news editor to summon a team to cover the top story of the day in their own parking lot.

The station was evacuated as bomb squad techs began a search for a secondary device. Standard operating procedure. The chilling specter of another bomb primed to detonate after the first drew a crowd had not even occurred to me. The thought raised gooseflesh on my sweltering skin as I watched them cautiously comb the shrubbery, searching in and under cars.

"Too early to say," replied Bomb Squad Lieutenant Dave Yates when I asked what type of explosives had been used.

"We haven't even started yet." He glanced back into the parking lot. "We'll have to look at the metal, see if it's ripped or torn. Higher explosives like C-Four make clean cuts. Black powder explosives twist and rip metal."

He screwed up his face and asked a question of his own. "Was this guy controversial, or what?" Yates obviously didn't spend much time glued to a TV.

"He made a lot of noise in the Cuban community, liked to ridicule the pompous establishment with fiery commentary, but I don't think anybody took him that seriously."

"Yup," said Lottie, who had stopped shooting for a moment and joined us. "He wore a big hat but no gun."

WTOP, an English-speaking station, had tried to raise ratings among the predominantly Hispanic community by hiring Aguirre away from a Spanish-speaking station to deliver commentary three nights a week and to occasionally report on Hispanic affairs.

"He feuding with anybody in particular lately?"

"Ha," I said. "Try Fidel Castro, the President, our mayor, the city commissioners, Juan Carlos Reyes, *The Miami News*, the Mafia, the CIA. Alex is a"—I sighed and corrected myself—"was a gadfly, a Don

Quixote. He loved to tilt at windmills. He was super patriotic, hated Castro and communism, loved Cuba, this country, and controversy for the sake of controversy. He blasted anybody who didn't share his politics and played devil's advocate with those who did."

The possibility of a long list of high-profile suspects did not sit well with Yates. Cops always hope the answers will be simple. Usually they are. His expression grew more intense as he watched his men examine the crater under the front of the Mustang.

"Is that where you think the bomb was planted?"

He nodded. "Looks like the transmission and firewall and part of the engine are gone."

"Think it was remote control? That somebody saw him get into the car and pushed a button . . ." I squinted into the sun, scanning the crowd for a suitable suspect.

"It's way too early to know anything," he said irritably. "The way the metal is bent and the damage to the floorboard should give us some indication. It coulda been hooked in real quick with clamps and magnets to the undercarriage, or with alligator clips to the starter system, or to the ignition, or one of the spark plug leads. Or it could have been a time device."

"They say he went home for lunch every day," I offered. "Don't know if it was always at the same time. What will your guys do now?" I asked, jotting notes.

"Sweep up the entire parking lot, collect everything we can, then dig up the crater, put everything in bags, sift through it all with increasingly finer screens and examine each piece. We'll probably have to take some debris to Ford auto parts to determine whether it's a piece of the car or part of the device."

"Look there," I whispered. His eyes followed mine. Something hung high over our heads from the branches of a banyan tree. "What is that?"

He squinted up from behind his sunglasses. "Damn," he said. "Looks like one of the windshield wipers."

He called to a uniformed officer. "Move the crowd, including the press, back at least a block. We got pieces of evidence over here."

"Thanks, Britt," grumbled other reporters, irate at me, as uniforms began restringing the crime scene tape to close off a far wider area.

The WTOP camera crew argued noisily and unsuccessfully with police, who refused to grant them special privileges even though the victim was their colleague.

Bomb squad techs divided the entire parking lot into small grids. Homicide detectives canvassed for witnesses. Reporters clamored for answers. "Was it a high-tech, sophisticated device?" a radio reporter demanded, shoving a mike in front of Yates.

"Too early to tell," he repeated. "You don't have to be a rocket scientist to build a bomb, you just have to be careful. It's premature to speculate at this point. We've just begun our investigation."

"Was it high explosives?"asked a TV reporter.

"What do you classify as high explosives?"asked another.

"C-Four, TNT, Flex-X," Yates said patiently, as the crowd of reporters grew larger around him, like seagulls flocking to a food source. "As opposed to low-grade explosives like dynamite, gunpowder, or a reloading propellant for firearms."

I didn't remember smelling anything like gunpowder.

"Hell all Friday," Lottie muttered. "Everybody wants to know if it was high explosives or low, was it sophisticated? High, low, sophisticated or not, it don't matter when it kills you. Dead is dead."

"Here's what I've got," announced PIO Sergeant Danny Menéndez, who approached, notebook in hand. Drawn to the new source of information, the wave of reporters turned like the tide away from Yates, who seemed relieved. Homicide detectives had "ascertained," Menéndez said, in the stilted jargon apparently required of police spokesmen, that "the victim" had been the target of many threats in past months after his editorials on immigration, open trade with Cuba, and other controversial topics. Police had kept a watch order on his house because of threats. The dead man's name had not yet been publicly released, pending official identification and notification of his next of kin, but everybody in the press pack knew it. The victim, Menéndez said, had waved at a female employee, a secretary, the woman I had spoken to, as he stepped into his Mustang. He closed the door, turned the ignition key, and the car exploded. The horrified woman and other witnesses had seen dark smoke and flames. The car's hood had been hurled a hundred feet in the air before landing on the building's roof.

I left the crowd, trailing after Yates for one last question. "You think this is an isolated incident or the start of something?" The last wave of bombings had ended almost eighteen months earlier.

"How would I know?" he said, already weary of the press, including me. He paused. "I hope we don't see more. Last thing we need is another bomb boom. But this stuff brings out all the kooks, people who in the dark recesses of their minds always had the desire to do this type of thing."

Almost every organization or leader in the exile community had felt the sting of Alex's commentary. I hoped his death was unrelated to exile politics. I have no patience with people who think the way to free Cuba is to blow up South Florida. Their reasons are obvious. It's safer. My father would probably be alive today had he conducted his anti-Castro missions on Flagler Street instead of in the Sierra Maestra mountains of Cuba.

There was a flurry inside the roped-off crime scene. A bomb squad tech had discovered something in the rear seat of a car with blown-out windows, parked three slots away from the Mustang. Alex's right hand. It had to have been close to the bomb, I thought, shivering, to be torn off and hurled so far.

Back at the office, I settled in at my desk and checked the folder in my top drawer. Miami terrorist groups amuse themselves by issuing official communiqués sentencing their enemies to execution, then distributing the names to the media. Occasionally somebody on one of the death lists is killed or injured. Alex's name did not appear on any of them. Then I called a roster of Cuban exile leaders and politicians for their comments on his demise.

"A brave man," the mayor called him. "A martyr."

I called Juan Carlos Reyes, powerful leader of the *Grupo para la Libertad de Cuba* and a frequent target. An outspoken and macho veteran of Brigade 2506, the exile force that landed at the Bay of Pigs in 1961, he is now a highly successful businessman and a behind-the-scenes political power. I had to persuade a receptionist and then a secretary to be put through to him.

"His voice will be missed," Reyes said with resonance. "I did not always agree with Alex—but many voices are what makes this country great."

"A warrior, who died for his beliefs!" boomed Jorge Bravo. "Another martyr killed by assassins while trying to free Cuba from the tyrant's grip!" Bravo, an aging freedom fighter, had never stopped launching clandestine missions to liberate his homeland.

Recently he had been fighting not only Castro, but the FBI as well. Agents were constantly on his case for violations of the U.S. Neutrality Act, which prohibits military expeditions from U.S. soil against countries not at war with the United States.

The cops had trucked the shattered Mustang to the medical examiner's office, where Alex's body could be removed and the car examined in air-conditioned comfort, under high-intensity lights, away from prying eyes, crowds, and cameras. They said the bomber had apparently planted his deadly device beneath the hood in broad daylight in the station parking lot. Yet no one reported seeing a thing.

At sunset, I raced down to Dinner Key where Miami Fire was fighting a huge blaze that burned a forty-five-foot commercial fishing vessel down to the waterline. It was late when I finished the story, but I had promised to meet Lottie for a drink and a bite to eat at the South Pointe Seafood House. My appetite had died in the parking lot with Alex Aguirre and I was weary, but Lottie had stuck by me when I was in trouble and I had to be there for her.

Her troubles were not as frightening as mine had been. Hers, as usual, involved a man, or the absence of one.

I found her waiting behind the Seafood House, sitting cross-legged on one of the rocks overlooking the waters of Government Cut. She was stirring a frozen margarita and wearing a T-shirt that said SOUTH BEACH, WHERE THE WOMEN ARE STRONG AND THE MEN ARE PRETTY.

"What do you hear from Stosh, the Polish Prince?" I asked, joining her.

Stosh Gorski is a lawyer she had met in court while shooting pictures during a high-profile murder trial. His client was charged with fatally battering his wife and his mother-in-law with a ballpeen hammer. The jury didn't believe the defendant, and I suspected that his lawyer wasn't exactly credible either.

Lottie, long divorced and childless, yearns for a family. An award-winning photographer, she has worked all the hot spots of the world and shot history in the making. She has dodged bombs and bullets and fended off passes from lecherous foreign dictators.

Now she wants to settle down and play house, but the Polish Prince has problems committing and showing up when promised.

"Hasn't called me since last Friday," she said miserably. Out in the midnight-blue waters of the cut, the lights of a freighter moved east toward the Gulf Stream and ports unknown. "Last time we talked he said he was gonna break off with someone he had been seeing before me, said he had to let her down easy."

"That's good," I said.

She sipped her margarita, gazing at me balefully over the rim of her glass. "He's letting her down so easy that they spent the weekend at Sugar Loaf Key."

"That's bad. You sure?"

She nodded and got to her feet. "He wasn't home all day Saturday, or Saturday night, so I called his condo down there," she explained, as we wandered inside and found a small table. "A woman answered and I hung up."

"Oh, Lottie. I'm sorry. Maybe it was the cleaning lady."

She stared at me. "I heard Julio Iglesias in the background. Stosh's version of music for lovers only. He played the same CD on our big night, a real mountaintop experience, by the way," she added wistfully.

"If you can't trust him, it's better to know now."

A waiter interrupted, taking our order for another margarita and a glass of wine for me.

"I know, I know." She sighed. "You're right. But that man sure charged my batteries."

"You knew he had a rep as a lady killer."

"Yeah, but sometimes they meet the right woman and settle down. Look at Hugh Hefner." Her eyes were hopeful.

"Maybe," I said, "when he's sixty-two and has had a stroke."

She plucked her icy drink off the waiter's tray, took a large gulp, sniffed, and changed the subject. "Damn shame about poor Alex. Bombs are the worst, worse than snakes in the garbage. Hope all that Cuban crap ain't starting up again. I had a weird dream the other night. I woke up and everybody in Miami was named Raúl."

"That was no dream," I said flatly. "It's true."

She laughed like the old resilient Lottie.

"Whatcha hear from McDonald?"

"Got a letter from Louisville the other day." I paused to sip my wine. "Nothing that would curl your toes. I think he's afraid to put anything in writing."

My main man, Miami Homicide Lieutenant Kendall McDonald, was furthering his education at the Southern Police Institute for four months, a major career break for a man with his ambition. Our off-and-on romance, periled mostly by career clash, seemed on at the moment. We were *muy simpáticos*, a thousand miles apart.

"He said I should feel free to date others while he was gone," I added.

"Either he's cocksure of himself or he wants to cut a swath without guilt among the Kentucky belles."

"Thank you very much. I thought I came here to cheer you up, but now I'm depressed." I checked my watch. "I can't really stay. I've got an early start tomorrow, and so do you. Can you drive?" I asked, as she emptied her glass. "How many of those have you put away?"

"I'm okay. If a cop stops me, I hope he's husky and handsome."

We walked out into the starry night together. The late scene on South Beach was just getting under way, a Felliniesque sideshow of disturbed youth, drag queens, and go-go dwarfs, the unconcerned targets of a black-bearded, wild-eyed, Bible-clutching street preacher. He stood on a bus bench, legs apart, arms raised, railing to the open sky that God would soon destroy us all for our decadence.

I DROVE HOME, fed Bitsy and Billy Boots, then walked the dog around the block through the soft, moist summer air. Billy Boots meowed at us from the lighted front window of my apartment as we rounded the corner. Helen Goldstein, my landlady, cracked her jalousie window to call a greeting. Light and shadow flickered behind her in the darkened living room. She and her husband must have been watching TV from their twin recliners. "You won't forget your promise, Britt, will you?"

"Have I ever?" I sang back.

"We knew we could count on you. Good night."

I smiled and waved as she cranked the window shut. What promise? I tried to recall our recent conversations. At eighty, that good woman's memory was sharper than mine. Hell, I thought, whatever she wants, she's got it. Her homemade chicken soup and chocolate chip cookies had sustained me through more than one crisis.

Channel-surfing through late newscasts confirmed that every competitor in town had shot better bombing footage than WTOP-TV, the scene of the tragedy.

Trying to sleep, I wondered what went through Alex's mind the moment his world exploded. Did he have the time, even a split second, to think?

Did he know he was a dead man?

My alarm interrupted dark dreams before dawn. I slipped out of my apartment into shadow and trotted two blocks of deserted streets under a damp and streaky sky to where the sea foamed silver on a misty gray beach. As I jogged, my footsteps dull thuds on the boardwalk, the solemn predawn hush erupted in a sunrise that burst over the horizon like a brass band playing a John Philip Sousa march.

My spirits soared with the rush. So did my steps. More than ever now, I understand what a great gift each day is. I ran down the stairs to the sandy beach, stopped to catch my breath, took off my shoes, and combed the turquoise surf for shells tossed ashore by the dredging for a beach renourishment project. Sand oozed between my toes, sun-warmed water and the sea's insistent pull tugged at my ankles. Ships dotted the horizon beneath the sharply drawn edges of stacked clouds that could be signaling the tropical wave of thunderstorms and squalls predicted by forecasters. They had been monitoring the system's path as it drifted across the Cape Verde Islands off West Africa and traversed the Atlantic and the Caribbean, headed for the Gulf of Mexico.

The threat that such a wave will spawn tropical storms grows more ominous as summer wears on, but most of the seventy-five to one hundred twenty-five a year do not amount to anything and experts saw no danger signs in this one.

Treasure hunting amid the bubbling rollers and spin-drift, I tossed back shells still occupied and filled the pockets of my shorts with those that were vacant: sea-smoothed lightning whelks, shiny lettered olives, and fanlike scallops. I hated to leave, but now I was running late. Back at my apartment, I emptied my pockets, rinsed the shells, and left them on the drainboard to dry while I showered. I slipped on a cool cotton dress, swallowed some orange juice, marched Bitsy around the block, and made some quick calls to the cop shops.

A Miami midnight-shift detective about to go off duty disclosed an intriguing tidbit: a discovery a week earlier, west of the city, on a rutted dirt road in the Everglades. A car. Blown to bits. The county had handled it. Nobody hurt. No big deal at the time. Now it was. The shattered car was a stolen Mustang identical to Alex Aguirre's. The bomber or bombers had practiced.

Several years earlier, a union official had escaped a bombing, maimed but alive, because the device had been placed on the wrong side of his car's firewall. This careful killer wanted to be absolutely accurate.

Hopefully, the charred metal shell in the Glades would yield some clue. Police seemed to have no other promising leads.

After the phone checks, I drove directly to the office to work the bomb follow for the early edition. The medical examiner said Alex had suffered fatal injuries but did not die instantly. He had inhaled soot and smoke from the fire in his last moments. At thirty-four, he had seemed to enjoy good health. I learned something he never knew. The main artery supplying blood to the left side of his heart was almost completely blocked by plaque deposits. Alex was a prime candidate for a major coronary, or would have been had he lived long enough.

A reader interrupted, calling to complain about the crack addict who stole her checks, stripped clean her bank account, and pawned her television. She demanded to know why he had been released on bond.

I commiserated."Is he your only child?"

"Oh, no." My question seemed to please her. "He's only one of five. Let me tell you about them."

I regretted opening the door as she launched into her miseries. Her eldest, she said, was "a Jesus freak," devoted to an obscure wandering cult. Another suffered emotional problems because she was gay; number three was a skinhead unable to sustain a relationship or a job. The fourth, a compulsive spender, was divorcing, and the fifth, of course, was now free on bond.

"Maybe they're going through stages," I offered lamely, wishing my mother could hear this. She might appreciate her only child.

"The baby is thirty-three." Her voice was cold.

"My age," I commented, for lack of anything else to say.

"At least you have a job."

"That I do, and let me tell you, work isn't everything." Look who's talking, I thought, as I flipped through my Rolodex for the family counseling hot line number. I doubted she would dial it. She sounded as though she relished her soap opera life.

Then Lottie called, elated. Her suspicions about the Polish Prince were all "a misunderstanding," and we conferred about what she should wear on their date that night. I shuffled my mail as we talked, hoping without luck for a letter from Louisville. "If you wear the gauzy black one," I cautioned, "don't wear the cowboy boots." The lobby receptionist signaled me and I told Lottie I had to go. I had a visitor.

"I'm not expecting anybody," I said, irritated. "I'm working on a story for the street. Who is it?"

"Think his name is Randolph, third time he's been here. You weren't in before." She lowered her voice sympathetically. "I couldn't steer him to anybody else. Said he had to see you."

Was her sympathy directed at him or me? I made an impatient sound. "Tell him I'm too busy. . . ." Then I hesitated, put the phone back to my ear, and added, "To see him for more than a few minutes."

The best stories sometimes walk in when you least expect them, I told myself, hoping my visitor was not some madman who would need to be hosed down and hauled away by security. He stepped into the huge newsroom looking bewildered, glancing around uncertainly, a lanky hard-boned man with thinning light-color hair. He wore work pants, glasses, and a crisp white shirt with QUICKY LUBE embroidered in red on the breast pocket. My heart sank when I saw his eyes. Reporters know the look. The eyes are a dead giveaway: wide, brightly burning, darting in search of help. These people are easy to spot; they haunt the newsrooms of the world, clutching stacks of file folders and spilling dog-eared papers from worn manila envelopes.

Obsessed by lost causes, they fight city hall, the government, and their own families, and believe in elusive conspiracies. One brittle and aging mother remains adamant that her daughter's death decades ago was no drug overdose, as ruled, but a murder conspiracy. Another still sues her ex-husband, a former judge, for broken promises, twenty-two years after their divorce. Every newsroom has its regulars, steered by the savvy to the newest, unsuspecting staff members.

I steeled myself. This face was not familiar, but it wore the look. Sometimes a real story comes with the obsession.

He scanned the newsroom, his eyes focusing on me. I smiled and stood up, vowing not to spend a lot of time. I saw the folder under his arm as he eagerly approached and groaned "Oh, no," without moving my lips.

"Mr. Randolph," I said heartily, two-faced as hell. He hesitated as I extended my hand. His knuckles looked raw, an angry pink, as though scrubbed too long and too hard with harsh soap that had nonetheless failed to remove the permanent grime line beneath his fingernails. Hesitation past, his handshake was solid.

"Sorry," he said. "I just left work. They said I should ask for you."

"They?" I motioned to the chair next to my desk and he sat.

"My brother, Nick, and his wife." He leaned forward and lowered his voice. "He said you were the one who worked on that story about the little Rafferty girl."

"Mary Beth Rafferty." I nodded. Not only did I lose a friend while working on that story, I lost my car and nearly my life.

"The murder that was solved after all those years." He swallowed. "I'm hoping you can help me."

My phone rang and I scooped it up, smiling apologetically.

A Florida highway patrolman with details about an overturned truck on the Palmetto Expressway. Owned by a company that cleans septic tanks, it had dumped a full load across four lanes. I winced. A sticky situation on one of the summer's steamiest days.

As I took notes and asked questions, barely aware of my visitor, he sat patiently, hopeful eyes roving the vast newsroom, its big bayfront windows, and the wide sweep of sky and Miami Beach skyline beyond.

Finally I finished and turned back to him. "So, you have an old unsolved murder in your family?"

"I pray to God not." He hesitated, as though contemplating the possibility. One of the plastic earpieces on his eyeglasses was broken and held together by tape. "My son," he said, "is missing."

"How old is he?"

"Fifteen."

Every reporter hears this story a hundred times. "Did you file a police report?"

"Yes."

The misery in his eyes made me glad to be single and childless. How can kids break their parents' hearts like this? "What did they say?"

"They keep calling him a runaway. We know he isn't." His jaw tightened. "He had no reason, he isn't like that. He'd never . . ."

"How long has he been gone?" I asked, checking my watch, attention wandering back to the story on my computer screen.

"Two and a half years, the sixth of this month."

"What?" Startled, I refocused on his face. Did I hear right?

"Two and a half years," he repeated, his gaze steady. "Charles disappeared on February sixth, two years ago. It was a Saturday."

"Have you heard anything in all this time?" I swiveled my chair to face him.

"Not a word. Not a call or a Christmas card. This from a boy who never walked out the door without kissing his mother good-bye."

Punching some keys on my terminal, I saved my notes and opened an existing file. It's slugged MISSING. In it I keep the basics on the usual cases—wandering Alzheimer's patients, the diet doctor who disappeared after faking his own death at sea, the middle-aged couple who left a church supper eight years ago and had yet to arrive home. Miami's missing persons, all mysteries minus the last page. I don't know what preys on the minds of other people on hot, sleepless nights. I do know what haunts me.

"What happened?" I asked. "A family fight? Trouble at school? Did a girlfriend dump him? Were any of his friends with him? Where was he last seen?"

Something came alive in my visitor's eyes as he began to answer. Maybe it was hope.

Charles C. Randolph was an only child, a good and industrious boy, his father said. Tall and mature for his age, Charles had delivered newspapers, washed cars, and mowed lawns since sixth grade. He scored excellent grades and counted on college. His father whisked open his folder to display report cards dominated by A-pluses and glowing comments from teachers. A budding environmentalist, Charles loved reading books about sharks, aviation, and sports. Most prized was his modest baseball card collection and his best friend, Duke, a mixed-breed dog the boy had found injured and nursed back to health.

"Did he take Duke with him?"

The father shook his head. "That dog still sits by the front door at the same time every day, waiting for Charles to get off the school bus."

"How much money did your son have with him when he disappeared?"

"No more than twelve dollars, tops. He left some money at home and he had a small bank account. He worked cleaning boats, mostly scraping barnacles, for people in some of the big waterfront houses over on Fairway Island. It was something new he had started, his own idea."

I smiled. "Sounds like an entrepreneur."

He looked past me, out the window without seeing beyond his own thoughts. "I always wanted to go into business for myself. Always told him that was the way to go. I thought he'd make it."

He plucked a small school picture from the folder and held it in his work-worn hand, studying it solemnly for a moment before giving it to me. There was no earring, tattoo, or gang colors. Blond and apple-cheeked, Charles wore his pale hair neatly combed. Merry blue eyes regarded the camera with the innocence of early adolescence. His smile was engaging, with a hint of prankish humor.

"You're sure he's not staying somewhere, with a friend or a relative?"

"The only one who doesn't live here in Florida is his grandmother, Lillian, in New York."

"Has she heard anything?"

He shook his head. "She's elderly and ailing. We never told her. It'd be too hard on her."

"She doesn't know?"

"What could we tell her? We don't know anything. We drove up for three days last summer, said he was at camp. She's always badgering us for new pictures and wanting to know why he stopped writing her like he used to. We keep lying, telling her he's been real busy with school and baseball."

I glanced at the big clock mounted over the newsroom, hands rocketing relentlessly toward deadline. "Where do you work, Mr. Randolph?"

"The Quicky Lube at Biscayne Boulevard and Sixty-eighth Street." He fished a business card from his shirt pocket. It identified him as Jeffrey Randolph, Manager.

"Thank you. I'm on deadline right now, have to finish a story for our street edition."

He swallowed, closed his file, and began to get to his feet, face resigned.

"Then I'd like to come by and talk to you some more."

He reacted as though he'd heard a gunshot.

"I'll try to be there by four," I continued, ignoring his startled expression, "unless I'm sidetracked by a breaking story. I'll call you before I come."

Something that had been nagging me during our conversation suddenly triggered my memory. "Hold on a minute," I said, scrolling through the MISSING file, through "overset" left out of stories about misplaced

Miamians and lists with names, dates, and descriptions of others, handy for matching to the skeletal remains and unidentified corpses that surface all too frequently.

I found it. Blond hair, blue eyes, age thirteen. Virtually the same description. That had to be what I remembered.

"Does your son know a boy by the name of Butch Beltrán?" I asked.

Randolph squinted. "The name Butch sounds familiar. I don't know about that last name. Have to ask my wife."

"Probably no connection," I said, checking the date. "This Butch has only been missing since March."

Thousands of people become missing persons in Miami every year. Most surface quickly. Some wear sheepish grins and don't want to talk about it. Others can't. They are found in the morgue. A few stay lost forever.

I watched Jeffrey Randolph walk out of the newsroom. Where is his son? I wondered. Dead? If so, why hadn't his body surfaced? Corpses tend to turn up. If he ran off to hitchhike across America it was way past time for his adventure to end, for him to call home for a bus ticket or be picked up by the cops somewhere. Missing people are real-life puzzles.

I finished the bomb follow, wrote a short on the overturned septic tanker, and did cutlines for an aerial Lottie had shot of the traffic mess from a chopper. Then I called the medical examiner's office.

Unidentified corpses are buried in a trench dug by a backhoe, mourned only by jail inmates who perform the labor. They spend eternity in an unmarked common grave beside the poor whose bodies go unclaimed.

Unidentified skeletons are boiled in meat tenderizer to remove all remaining shreds of flesh. The bones are then stored in stacked boxes.

Photos and dental records are kept on all those unidentified. Occasionally someone is persistent enough to follow the trail of a missing person to the morgue.

The chief investigator was in. "Have you got any young John Does?" I asked.

"Have they got bagels in Jerusalem? Whatcha looking for?"

"White male, thirteen to fifteen. Slender frame, blond, blue-eyed, been gone—"

"Sounds familiar."

I caught my breath, heart thumping, as it always does when mysteries begin to unravel.

"Get calls about this one all the time. Family, I think. Last check I made was three, four days ago. No new Juans or Johns have checked in since then."

I sighed. Should have realized it couldn't be this easy. Randolph was way ahead of me.

"What about . . . ?"

"I checked Broward, Palm Beach, and Monroe as well. None that fit. Lotsa Johns and Janes but not this one."

"If one comes in . . . ," I said.

"You'll be the first to know."

Randolph said Coral Gables police had taken the report. The same detective, Wally Soams, handles both juvenile and missing persons. I left him a message, then called Quicky Lube to say I was on the way.

Now I needed to escape the newsroom before some roadblock loomed. Like Gretchen Platt, the assistant city editor from hell. She was stepping out of a meeting along with several executive types and the *News*'s lawyer, Mark Seybold. Wearing a nifty pin-striped power suit, she looked pleased to see me, which meant trouble. More deadly to morale than a speeding bullet, she is a known sniper, but occasionally lobs a grenade. White-hot ambition radiates from her statuesque, fashionably clad body, despite her chronic incompetence, which is matched only by her mean and officious streak. Making subordinates look foolish, with biting sarcasm or a well-timed roll of the eyes, is her specialty. She is, for reasons totally incomprehensible to me, on the corporate fast track. Eager to display her supervisory skills, she blocked my path.

"Britt," she said, her voice unnecessarily loud, "are you finished with your septic tank story?" Shooting sidelong glances at her colleagues, she wrinkled her nose and shuddered delicately.

"Yes, I am," I said. I smiled sweetly, wondering what it would cost to have the trucker dump another load next time she flipped the top on her flashy BMW convertible. Whatever the price, it would be worth it.

"Where are you rushing off to now? Has someone been killed?" Her tone was patronizing and condescending. Tossing her hair, cut in a sleek new style, she awaited my answer.

"Not yet."

She waited, an eyebrow arched, her glossy blond head cocked expectantly.

"I'm on my way to an interview."

"A story on tomorrow's budget?"

"No, a case I'm just beginning to look into."

"What kind of case?"

A troubling question. Missing teenagers are not considered bona fide news in late summer. With a new school term looming in their immediate future, some do make a run for it.

I pressed the elevator button desperately. "An old case, like the Mary Beth Rafferty mystery."

They all reacted. Mark, the lawyer, bit his lip, a nervous tic he displays when not gnawing his fingernails. My initial suspect in that case had been Eric Fielding, current resident of the governor's mansion. He was only a candidate when I accused him of murder.

The elevator doors yawned open just in time and I made my getaway, wondering what perverse quirk had made me say that. Gretchen always brings out the worst in me.

I drove north on Biscayne Boulevard, the main drag. The harsh glare of the afternoon sun seemed as merciless as the landscape. Once Miami's street of dreams, the Boulevard greeted travelers and tourists, refugees from the cold North. Now it is lined by shabby motels, laundromats, doughnut shops, and small Haitian and Cuban restaurants.

The Quicky Lube, a freshly painted, freestanding building, faced the Boulevard. The customers' entrance was at the back. Motorists formed lines to drive-through bays where fast-working crews changed the oil, checked filters, fluids, wipers, tires, and batteries, vacuumed the interiors, and washed the windows—all in ten minutes. The cheerful waiting room inside had a color TV tuned to a soap opera, a half-full coffeepot, a fresh newspaper, and a window to the cashier's cubicle.

Randolph was printing out a credit card receipt for a waiting customer. His somber face brightened when he saw me and he waved me into the small glass-enclosed office where we could see both the crews at work and the waiting room.

"Let's start at the beginning," I said, sitting in front of a metal shelf stacked with bold red and yellow cans of brake fluid and tune-up spray.

He nodded and settled into a chair across from me, manila folder in his hand, his look less desperate. Somebody now shared his lifeboat, or had at least acknowledged his cries for help.

"Charles was born here in Dade County?"

"Baptist Hospital. I was there. They let fathers in the delivery room. Two days before our seventh anniversary." He paused, then added, "My wife had had four miscarriages. This boy made up for all that, never gave us a minute's trouble."

Charles, in excellent health, he said, had left as usual on a sunny Saturday morning, dressed for work in a blue denim shirt over a T-shirt, blue jeans, and sneakers.

"Not his good high-tops, just a pair he used for working on boats," his father said slowly. "He usually came home by four. My wife felt a little uneasy by five, five-thirty. The three of us always ate supper together and Charles knew to call if he was late. When he wasn't home by six-thirty, we knew something was bad wrong, and we called the police. They wouldn't send anybody out or even take any information over the phone. Said it's not department policy to make a report until somebody is missing for more than twenty-four hours." He sighed. "We called all of Charles's friends. One had seen him 'bout ten-thirty that morning. Said Charles was walking along Garden Drive on Fairway Island, drinking a can of Dr Pepper, just beyond a house where we know he cleaned a sports-fishing boat. We never found a soul who saw him again. I went over to the place he'd been to last. The owner was out of town but the housekeeper said he'd cleaned the boat and washed down the dock. She had given him the soda pop before he left. I drove around there, looking for a couple hours, then went home to wait. That," he said, raising his eyebrows, "was one rough night."

His gaze made it clear that that bad night had stretched into many.

"We called the police again next morning." He smiled bitterly. "They didn't want to take a report on Sunday. A sergeant told me he had boys of his own, said this kind of thing is common. Not with my boy, I told him. He said to check with Charles's friends and give it till Monday morning."

"By that time," I murmured, "the trail was cold."

"Had I known then," he said, nodding. "What we needed was a search, with lights and dogs. . . ." He trailed off. "But they were the professionals, we had to listen to them."

"Did you know your son's next stop? Was he on his way to clean another boat?"

He nodded again, clearing his throat. "Went door-to-door ourselves. We didn't know exact addresses, Charles kept them in a little notebook he always carried. He must have had it with him. We just knew the neighborhood. Found two big houses where he should have been that day. People said he never came." He took a folded handkerchief from his pocket and blew his nose before resuming. "They all told us what a polite boy he is and what a good worker."

"You have the addresses?"

"Right here." He removed a sheet of lined paper from his

folder. "The first is the one we know he was at; he never got to the other two."

"Good," I said, studying them. "So we know that he disappeared somewhere in about a half-mile stretch of Garden Drive."

"The two he never got to was that Cuban singer, Vera Verela, and that other fella, Reyes, who's in the news all the time."

I nodded, aware of both. "And the one he left?"

"A doctor, some kind of scientific researcher, travels to Canada a lot. He was out of town at the time. Had a thirty-one-foot sportfisherman, a blue and white Rampage with a flying bridge. Too busy to use it much, he said. He sold it, not long after. I went back and met the man later. Said Charles reminded him of his sons."

"You think that maybe he arrived at the second house, started work, and then something happened? Was he a good swimmer?"

Bodies occasionally surface around local marinas, people who live or work aboard boats, usually partyers with a snootful who fall into the water unseen, usually at night.

"He's an excellent swimmer, knows to be careful around boats and the water. I'm not saying it couldn't have happened," Randolph said, rubbing his chin, "but if so, where is he?"

True. Bodies usually surface within thirty-six hours. Those trapped under docks or snagged on debris at the bottom are eventually freed by winds, wakes, and tides.

"Were the cops aware of anything unusual happening in the neighborhood that morning?"

"Like what?" Randolph stood for a moment to slide the glass window closed because of a distraction on the other side where an employee was explaining to a customer that if the transmission is not serviced at thirty thousand miles the "gasket on the pan could crack and the engine could seize up on you."

I shrugged. "Traffic accident? Film crews shooting a movie, bikers headed to a rally, a robbery, any kind of disturbance—even a stolen car, anything that might tie in somehow, anything that Charles might have stumbled upon or become involved in."

"I didn't hear about anything like that," he said, frowning, "and believe me, I combed every bush and turned over every rock in that neighborhood to the point where police were stopping me as a suspicious person. I would think that our detective must have checked that out."

"The Gables detective?" I hated to burst his belief like a balloon, but most missing persons detectives do little more than write reports. Sometimes they even slip up on that. Rarely do they leave the office. Unless foul play is obvious or an infant or small child is missing, nobody hits the street to investigate, and in those cases homicide usually takes over.

"No, our private investigator," Randolph said. "I hired him after the second week, when the police wouldn't do anything. The man said that for fifteen thousand dollars he could bring Charles home. We managed to scrape together seven thousand. He took it and did nothing. You're asking me more questions than he ever did."

I copied the phone number of the PI. "Hope you have better luck with him than we did. He stopped answering our calls," Randolph said.

I recognized the name, a shady ex-cop lucky to be fired instead of prosecuted, but didn't tell Randolph. No point in rubbing in the fact that he and his wife had been ripped off.

"What else have you tried?"

He sighed sheepishly. "Psychics. My wife and sister-in-law got into that. Word must have got around. They consulted one, and the next thing you know, half a dozen were calling. They all wanted money. Most of 'em did say Charles is still alive, but doesn't remember who he is."

I never buy amnesia. It only happens on soap operas. The few true real-life cases have a way of turning up. I could only remember one that might have been credible, and I even doubted her story. "What else?"

"We checked out the Hare Krishnas and some other cults, like the Coptics and the Moonies, any of 'em that were active down here. Charles wouldn't have been interested," he said with certainty. "He never had no inclinations, but it was something else to do, something else to rule out. I wanted to try everything. If he was with some group like that we could've

found him, brought 'im home." He leaned back and ran his fingers wearily through his hair, recalling the past two years.

"Went to the Youth Fair and a couple of concerts, the groups he
liked, just to look for him in the crowds. Did those alone. My wife could-
n't handle seeing all those kids."

We stared at each other, silent for a long moment. "Is there a dental chart?"

"It's available." He spoke without emotion. "The family dentist
knows Charles is missing. He has good teeth but he had a filling and
some work, an enamel cap on a front tooth. Chipped it when he was
twelve, in a spill he took water skiing. Had fliers printed up with his picture and description, posted 'em in laundromats, supermarkets, every-
place they'd let me. That's about it, except for our church group. They've
been holding prayer vigils."

"Publicity usually works faster." I sounded more cynical than I
intended. I thought of the private detectives, the psychics all smelling
money, vultures moving in for the kill. "Why didn't you come to the
paper sooner?"

His laughter held no humor. "Think I didn't try?" His scowl connected his bushy eyebrows. "Your security wouldn't even let me in the
building without an appointment with somebody upstairs. When I called
the newsroom some editor blew me off, said too many kids are missing
in Miami, when you write about one, you have to print 'em all in the
paper. Told me to buy an ad."

"That's ridiculous!" I exploded. Had to be Gretchen, I thought. It
sounded like her. When I started at the paper, anybody could walk in off
the street or call the city desk and speak to a reporter. What the hell happened? News gatherers in air-conditioned offices are now insulated from
the real world by security, voice mail, and recordings. Editors in their
ivory towers are blind to the realities of the street. Any two-bit terrorist
could infiltrate the building, but the average citizen jerked around by the
system and in need of help is stymied by security. I swallowed the frustration and disappointment I felt at the profession I love.

"Not many children are missing this long," I assured Randolph quietly. "This is a news story."

"They did put it in the *Gables Times Guide.*" His hands shook slightly as he presented me with a clipping from the small weekly. Folded and unfolded so many times, it was now Scotch-taped together. A brief account accompanied by the school photo concluded with phone numbers, police and the family, to call with information.

Our society is so mobile. Victims and suspects can quickly be a thousand miles away. This huge county alone is bigger than Rhode Island and Delaware, most of it far out of a neighborhood weekly's circulation area.

"Any response?"

"Nothing to speak of. A few crank calls, claiming to have seen him, but nothing checked out. I try to do something every day," he said. "I've been to the morgue, to the police station. I call the Adam Walsh center for missing and exploited children, go to the beach and playgrounds and show his picture. There's always somebody who's seen a boy who looks like him, but every time I track the kid down, it's another man's son, not mine." He shoved back an unruly lock of hair with his scraped fist.

"Had he been grounded just before he left? Any family fights?"

"Nothing more than the usual teenage stuff. Nothing that would make him run."

"What about sex and romance?"

"The boy was twelve and a half years old when he disappeared." He emphasized the number.

"Hormones are raging at that age."

He shook his head. "He hadn't been out on his first date yet. He was just learning how to dance."

"No sex, drugs, rap, or heavy metal." I was thinking aloud.

"That's why it's so bewildering." He put his head in his hands.

A frustrated employee interrupted with a problem. An expensively dressed woman customer, driving a late-model luxury car, was insisting they accept an outdated coupon for five dollars off her bill.

Randolph pointed out the clearly printed expiration date. She argued shrilly until he offered five dollars from his own pocket. Shamelessly, she took him up on it and drove off grinning.

"We run ninety, a hundred cars a day through here," he explained. "Repeat business is our lifeblood. It's worth it for customer goodwill."

I drove back to the *News* in a snit. Pissed off at people who prey on the wounded, annoyed at *News* security, and prepared to urge them to call me or some other reporter every time a stranger is seeking help. No uniforms were visible in the lobby. The receptionist said our security chief and his men were busy hunting down an irate reader at large in the building.

I rooted for the reader.

Apparently, a phone number in a daily display ad was transposed and calls for phone sex were going to the reader's home instead. When he pointed out the error, he was told that it's against policy to take corrections over the telephone. He called production. No one there was authorized to make changes, but somebody eventually promised to correct the problem. Nobody did. The ad kept running. Sex seekers kept calling.

Furious, the victim threatened to drive all the way from Homestead to throw a monkey wrench into the printing press. The first edition had hit the street, the number uncorrected, and a new wave of sex calls began. Now it was too late to correct the ad before Monday. All the weekend editions, more than a million newspapers, would carry his phone number.

When a stranger carrying a wrench showed up at the employees' entrance, a preoccupied security guard had waved him in. Now the manhunt was on.

Right on, I thought, wearing a smile to my desk. I had become a reporter to tweak, expose, and battle bureaucracy. How the hell did the enemy become us?

Wally Soams, the Gables missing-persons detective, was in this time.

"I always pegged that kid as a runaway," he offered.

"What made you think that?"

"Well, you know, kids that age." He sounded slightly irritated that I had asked. "We get 'em every day. Half the time they come home and the parents don't even give you the courtesy of a call to let ya know. I don't even know some of 'em turned up until the mothers call to report 'em missing again." He paused. "This is the kid who wuz hitchhiking on LeJeune, right?"

"No," I said sharply. "He was on Garden on Fairway Island, cleaning boats for rich people. What did you do in this case?"

I heard him shuffling papers. "Entered it in the county computer," he offered.

"Nice work."

"What's with the attitude, Britt?" he demanded. "You know how shorthanded we are, what we're dealing with."

"I just spent the afternoon with the father," I said. "How would you feel left in limbo for two and a half years, not knowing if your only child is dead or alive?"

"Here we go," Soams said, apparently locating his supplementaries on the case. "Okay. Yeah, this is the one. We had some reported sightings."

"Where?"

"Let's see, there was a story in some little throwaway and there were some circulars posted and . . . kid who went to school with him said he was pretty sure he saw Charles Randolph shooting baskets over at St. Patrick's playground the weekend after he disappeared. Then a woman, a former neighbor of the Randolphs, said she thought she saw Charles standing in front of the Pizza Hut at Dadeland Mall."

"When?"

"Same weekend."

"Wally, they're more than twenty-five miles apart. Any true sightings?"

"Some kid came forward after a PA announcement at his school, says he saw Charles at a video game parlor at Northside. Says he chased after him and the kid threatened him with big trouble if he mentioned seeing him."

"What do you think?"

"Ehhh, maybe a combo of being too eager to help, and an overactive imagination. At the time, though, it seemed like the kid could be out there playing cat and mouse. Now . . . who knows?"

"Anything lately?"

"Nah. This one's been gathering dust. We get new cases every day."

"He didn't run away," I said accusingly. "What happened?"

"All I know is a kid is walking down Garden in broad daylight, then poufff! You tell me. You got a good imagination. Could be he's some smart-ass still out there playing cat and mouse."

I made a derisive sound.

"Or," he continued, "for all I know the father walloped the hell out of the kid for sassing 'im, hit 'im too hard, buried his mistake in the backyard, and then reported him missing. It's been done before, ya know."

"Sure," I said. "That explains why he came to the *News* looking for help. Explains why they've given thousands of dollars to phony psychics and PIs trying to find their son." What I really wanted to tell Soams was that he couldn't find a fish at Sea World and was stealing his paycheck.

"Hey," he said affably, "if you turn up anything, let me know."

Cassie Randolph answered on the second ring.

"My husband said you might call. Thank you, Ms. Montero, for what you're doing."

"Well, I haven't done anything yet."

"We need to bring Charles home." Her soft voice had a razor edge. "Some people, even friends, say we should accept the fact that he's gone, that we'll never see him again—but it's not true. He's alive. Mothers know these things. He's out there somewhere and he needs us. We have to find him before it's too late."

"If he's out there," I foolishly promised, "we'll find him. Somebody must know something."

So I got carried away, but I meant every word, and we did have a good shot at it. *The News'* circulation is more than half a million. Wire services, radio, and TV pick up our stories, circulating them even more widely. If I reported this well enough, we probably could bring Charles home, one way or the other. I hoped her maternal instincts were right. I prefer happy endings.

The doctor whose boat he had cleaned on his last job was out of town. The housekeeper was new. Vera Verela was in New York cutting an album. I caught her at the Westbury Hotel.

Her memory needed jogging, but once she knew what I was talking about, she was effusive and quotable. "That beauuutiful boy," she trilled. "So quiet, so polite, and so hardworking. He still has not been found? *¡Dios mio! ¿Qué pasa en Miami?* People don't just disappear."

"This one did."

"How terrible for his parents. Tell them I pray for them and their beautiful son."

"Did he ever say anything to you about wanting to go somewhere or talk about anything that was troubling him?"

"Britt, I never really spoke to the boy. He comes once a week to clean my boat. I call it the *Sex Sea.*" She laughed, an earthy, show-biz sort of eruption. "Once I was sunbathing by the pool. He opened the gate, was afraid to look, so shy, blushing." She laughed again.

Juan Carlos Reyes was not as effusive. "Have they found who killed Alex Aguirre?"

"No," I said, "this is something else."

"So, Ms. Montero, I am sure you are aware that I am not on such excellent terms with *The Miami News.* Have you been instructed to call me every time you write a story?"

"Not at all. I'm just a reporter, on the police beat, calling about the disappearance of Charles Randolph."

"Who?"

I reminded him. "Oh, that one. I was not aware the young man is still missing. I remember speaking to the father some time ago."

"What was your impression of the boy? Do you have a theory?"

"Ms. Montero, forgive me. As you must know, my interests are international, and I am deeply involved with many matters of importance. I confess I have not given this matter a thought in three or four years."

"He's been missing for two. Two and a half to be exact."

"You see," he said abruptly, "my contact with the young man was limited. My houseman hired the boy as an employee to perform odd jobs on the *Libertad*. If the young man appeared at my door at this moment, I would not have the slightest hint who he was. I will instruct Wilfredo to call you if he recalls anything of importance."

The brush-off was polite but obvious, and I still had no quote worth using.

"Any message for the parents?"

"Why would I . . . ," he began. "Ah." He sighed knowingly. "A sound bite for your story."

"That's TV," I said, smiling. "I need a quote."

He paused for a moment. "I know what it is like to lose all that is dear to you. I lost my country. We can only hope that one day the boy returns, safe and sound, and that Cuba is soon free."

"How's that?" he asked.

I could have lived without Cuba as a metaphor, but it was usable. Though half Cuban myself, it exasperates me when Cuban-Americans relate everything to Castro.

I worked late on the story, dubbed it "one of Miami's most baffling missing persons cases," and used Soams's "pouff" quote. Gretchen had gone home, which was my good fortune. Bobby Tubbs was in the slot and needed a strip story for the local page, either mine or Ryan Battle's report on the county's classroom shortage. I wasn't ashamed to lobby for the spot.

"You're sure they won't find this kid before morning?" Tubbs asked anxiously.

"I promise," I said, crossing my fingers. Stranger things have happened. I definitely wanted Charles Randolph found, but not until my story landed on lawns in the morning. If he chose tonight to turn up and made the paper look foolish, it would be impossible to sell the next missing persons story to the city desk. "It'll be a great follow on Monday if we get some leads," I urged.

He bought it. Primo space, the Sunday paper, widest circulation of the week, when readers relax over coffee and their newspaper.

Home alone on a Saturday night with a frozen pizza, I was content. Lottie was out on the town with the Polish Prince, but I felt no trace of envy. I swept Billy Boots off his furry feet and hugged him, buoyed by anticipation. Miami's good readers never let me down. Somebody out there had to know something. One solid lead, that's all I needed. Reporters are often the last hope in a world full of red tape and bureaucracy. That is one of the joys of journalism.

Humming, I doctored up the pizza with a drizzle of olive oil, a sprinkle of oregano, and fresh mushroom slices, poured a glass of red wine, and drank a solitary toast to young Charles Randolph.

"Wherever you are, Charlie, we're coming for you."

IN MY DREAM I moved with the grace of a ballet dancer, leaping and whirling toward an elusive dream lover, a ghostlike boyish figure with pale shining hair. But as I slowly reached for him, he evolved into a stoic, solitary silhouette trailing a noose of heavy nautical line. The phone woke me and I sat up straight, dazed, until I remembered.

"Britt, *mi hijita*, little daughter. Is it well with you?" my Aunt Odalys asked.

"Sure," I said, sounding dopey, squinting at my clock radio. Five A.M.

"Something is wrong," she whispered.

"What do you mean?" I said fearfully, unconsciously lowering my voice to a whisper as I sat up.

"I don't know. The father of the spirits who live in the cauldron . . ." She sounded uncertain.

"Oh, no." I pushed the hair out of my eyes. "You haven't been sacrificing goats or anything, have you? Is the moon full?"

"Britt!" She sounded deeply offended.

I love my father's younger sister dearly, but Santería, a blood religion, a mix of Catholicism and African ritual from Cuba, is abhorrent to me as an animal lover. In my childhood her practices had created a chasm between her and my mother, the Episcopalian daughter of Miami pioneers. That, the matter of my Uncle Hector's arrest record, and, at the heart of it all, my father. His sin, in her eyes, was allowing his reckless pursuit of a free Cuba to widow her young. She never forgave him for throwing away his own life and our futures.

To his family, he is a martyred hero. They never forgave Fidel Castro, who ordered him executed by a firing squad.

I grew up in both Hispanic and Anglo worlds, never at home in either. What I do know is that this mercurial city of light and shadow, death and passion, is where I belong, as though we are bound by some secret destiny. My ties to Miami are stronger and more passionate than those of blood or family.

"Are you up early or have you been up all night?" I asked, sinking back on my pillow.

"You are wearing the beads and the *resguardo* I gave you?"

"All the time," I croaked groggily, trying to remember what I had done with them.

"Something is in the air, something terrible."

"I'm not surprised," I said. "There usually is. It's probably the Palmetto Expressway. Did you hear about that truck?"

"I am not joking."

"Everything is fine."

"That is not what the cowrie shells say. The orishas are angry. But I don't understand. I burned candles all night. The spirits have never been so agitated. You are in danger. You are a daughter of Changó, the god of fire, thunder, and lightning. Something terrible is coming, all around us, but I don't understand who, where. . . ."

"Everything will be fine," I assured her, then hung up and staggered into the kitchen to make coffee. No fan of the supernatural, I don't discount anything, either. I knock on wood, toss spilled salt over my left shoulder, and say my prayers. Nothing like covering all the bases.

As a reporter in a high-tech world at the tail end of the century I seek only hard facts. But on scorching streets and in the shadows during the pursuit of life and death, certain events and people defy explanation. The young cop who awoke in a cold sweat after dreaming he was shot—and was, hours later, exactly as in his dream. The woman whose searing vision of fire terrified her into staying home next morning—the day that fire swept her workplace, killing three co-workers. Active, healthy people who suddenly know they are about to die—and do, in freak accidents or random acts of violence.

In this magic place, at sea level, at the foot of the map, we are surrounded by water, beneath the tidal pull of a huge moon in endless skies that seem lower than anywhere else in the hemisphere. The temperature soars, the barometer falls, the full moon rises, and all hell breaks out. At one time in my life I sought logic in everything. Now I know better. We are constantly bombarded by unseen radio and television signals we would never receive without the proper equipment. Now I suspect that some people, for unknown reasons, become receivers, sensitive to other invisible signals.

A year ago, my Aunt Odalys warned me to wear the red and white beads and the *resguardo*, a talisman she had given me for protection. I ignored her and nearly lost my life.

As the smell of coffee filled my small kitchen, I scooped the newspaper off the front stoop, still in my nightgown. The sky was hot and pink as I slid the *News* from its plastic sheath and began to fillet it, flinging the advertising sections into the green recycling bin without a glance.

Charles Randolph's innocent smile greeted the world from the top of the local page. I smiled back. No late-breaking news had knocked my story off local. It read well. I love perusing my stories in the morning paper, aware that half a million strangers are reading them too. I imagined them, in hair curlers, bathrobes, fighting hangovers, over scrambled eggs or bloody marys, couples still in bed, swapping sections, families at breakfast tables. I hoped the right person was reading it and would talk. My bomb follow was at the bottom of the local, beneath the fold.

The phone startled Billy Boots off my lap. I answered eagerly, hoping for Kendall McDonald's voice.

It was Lottie.

"How'd your date go?"

"Just shoot me now," she muttered.

"What happened?"

Her romantic evening had never materialized. The Polish Prince failed to show up at the appointed hour so she had gone out to hunt him down. Cruised by his town house, his office, and prowled his favorite watering hole. No sign of the man.

"What would you have done if you spotted him?"

She paused. "Depends," she finally said, "on who he was with and whether or not he tried to make a run for it. But that ain't all."

When she finally gave up and went home, furious and sworn off the man for good, she found his business card in her door, along with a single red rose. She quickly called him, but he wasn't home.

"A damn cakewalk of musical chairs," she said.

"Oh, Lottie, I'm sorry. Why didn't he call to say he'd be late?"

"Dunno. That man has got me bumfuzzled for sure. At least he didn't think I was home waiting up for him. The question now is, who stood who up?"

We both laughed. "Did you see the paper?"

"Yeah, good story. Hope you find that young 'un. Think he's alive?"

"Common sense says no, after all this time, but his mother believes he is."

"Mothers always do. You see that story in the A section?"

"Which one?" I reached for the paper.

"Wire story. Some Harvard Ph.D. says seven percent of the population is pure evil."

"Only seven percent?"

"That's what surprised me. Hell all Friday, why'd they all settle here?"

"What's the breakdown on the rest of us?" I asked. "Fifty percent good and the rest undecided?"

"Don't say here."

I hate it when there's a hole in a story. I sipped my coffee, a wickedly rich, hearty brew that jump-started my batteries. "My Aunt Odalys called just before you did and said something bad is sneaking up on us."

"Maybe she's right. I feel something in my bones. Hope I git to shoot color."

I attended a nine o'clock church service on sun-splashed Lincoln Road Mall. As the congregation sang "safe and secure from all alarms," a violent thunderstorm blew up, triggering blinding bursts of lightning and a chorus of wailing, beeping, and honking car alarms. The sounds reminded me of Alex and the WTOP parking lot. By the time the service ended the air was radiant, with the only sign of the fast-moving storm the flower petals, leaves, torn branches, and water strewn in its wake.

I could feel my hair curling in the sultry heat. I drove home for a quick pit stop, parked the T-Bird, and got out. A stranger waited, seated on my doorstep. A boy, slim, blond, about twelve or thirteen, shifting nervously. He looked up, his blue eyes a shade darker than the short-sleeved cotton shirt he wore with twill trousers and sneakers. I swallowed, my mouth suddenly gone dry.

"Britt?" He leaped eagerly to his feet, gangly and long-legged. "Were you looking for me?"

I stared, mouth open.

He squinted suspiciously. "You know who I am, don't you?"

"Of course," I said weakly, mind racing.

"She said you wouldn't forget. You promised my grandmother you'd show me around the *News* and take me out on some stories with you. Well, here I am!"

He gave me the once-over with the incipient lechery of a would-be Groucho Marx. "Va va voom!" he said, stepping boldly forward to shake my hand. "Awesome. Real baaaad. I'm Seth."

"Seth?"

An Instamatic camera hung from a leather strap around his neck and a reporter's notebook jutted out of his back pocket. Three Pilot Explorer pens were clipped to his shirt pocket. He fished out his card.

"Seth Goldstein," he said, handing it over. "Assistant city editor of the Eastside Junior High School *Gazette* in Hopewell, New Jersey."

"Of course I didn't forget," I lied, and began to breathe again. "I was simply startled because you look so much like somebody I just wrote about." What was I thinking when I made this promise? What was I drinking? Manischewitz. At a Seder, at the Goldsteins' during Passover. A conversation began to come back to me. Smart as a whip, high IQ, a would-be journalist. Seth.

"Saw it. Today's paper. MISSING BOY A MYSTERY. Grandma sends me all your stories. We hang them on the bulletin board in our newsroom," he said, at my elbow as I inserted my key into the lock. Showing no signs of going away, he followed me inside, trailing behind me like a puppy. He declined my offer of a soft-boiled egg but wolfed three pieces of raisin toast and drank the last of my coffee.

Despite my warnings that it was a slow Sunday on the police beat and my suggestion that he might rather go to the beach, his enthusiasm knew no bounds.

"How often does a future journalist get the chance to go one-on-one and pick the brain of a Green Eyeshade Award winner for best deadline reporting?" he demanded, showing off that he had done his homework. "Why do you think I wanted to spend the last two weeks of my summer vacation with my grandparents?" He rolled his eyes. "This is my chance to see action with an ace street reporter for a big-city newspaper."

"Think we'll go to the morgue?" he asked eagerly as we drove to the office.

"Only if it's feet first."

One of the perks of working weekends is the nearly empty newsroom. Reaction to my story should have started coming in by now. I punched my personal code number into the phone, then, accompanied by Seth, all eyes, ears, and questions, went to the wire room where my messages were printing out. And printing out, and printing out. My heart swelled as the list lengthened.

I tore them off the machine, eagerly scanning the list, willing the solution to Charles Randolph's disappearance to be somewhere among these forty-eight calls.

One from my mother. I'd call her later. The Randolphs; perhaps they'd heard some news. Their line was busy twice. The third try was successful. Randolph answered, and Cassie picked up an extension. Surprised that I worked Sundays, they were grateful for the story and said their phone had been ringing nonstop since 6 A.M. No new information, just former co-workers, friends, neighbors, and total strangers, calling to offer support and sympathy.

"They all want to help," Randolph said. "They're asking what they can do. I don't know what to tell them."

A blinding flash of light stunned me for a moment and I continued to see spots, even after blinking several times. Seth was crouched in front of my desk and had just shot my picture with his little camera.

"They can be valuable," I told Randolph, one hand over my blinded eyes. "Take names and numbers. If no solid leads come in, maybe you can ask volunteers to distribute fliers, demonstrate, or conduct candlelight marches. Anything we can think of to keep the story alive. The more exposure the better."

"A reporter from Channel Ten wants to come over to talk to us and take pictures of Charles's bedroom. You think that's all right?" He sounded doubtful.

"Sure," I said, shaking my head in warning and glaring murderously at Seth, who appeared to be focusing on me again. "But don't let them touch anything. Now that there's publicity about the case, the police might want to come lift prints off Charles's books or belongings and try to take hair samples from his comb or brush."

"But I thought it was your story."

"All I want is to be sure that you tell me about any new developments first, right?"

"Of course, you're the only one who would help us."

"Any crank calls?"

He hesitated; obviously he had not intended to mention it. "A couple. Some kids called and were whimpering, 'Daddy, Mommy, come get me.' We could hear 'em giggling in the background. Then a young girl, a teenager, called and asked to speak to Charles."

Kids' cruelty amazed me, as usual. I could have cheerfully wrung their scrawny little necks. The scary part was that they may not have all been kids.

"How could they?" I murmured, as Cassie hung up to tend to something in the kitchen.

"It's all right," her husband said. "We can handle it. We're thrilled that other people care and want to help. Anything that will help find him."

"Right. That's what counts. Meanwhile, if you get any more prank calls, say: 'It's them, officer,' in a stage whisper, as though a cop is standing next to you. That'll give 'em something to think about."

Seth, wearing his pass from security, was pounding away on the computer terminal at Ryan's desk. "Be careful," I warned him. "Don't touch a thing."

"Man, is this system a dinosaur!" he said.

I began returning calls. A Broward County man was not interested in Charles Randolph. He had his own obsession. His mother had vanished without a trace when he was ten. Foul play was likely, his abusive stepfather long a suspect, but no charges were ever filed. I referred him to a reporter in the Broward bureau.

A Hialeah Gardens schoolteacher had no information about Charles Randolph either. She wanted me to help find her own missing person. At age forty, shy and never married, she had been swept off her feet by a handsome stranger. After a three-week whirlwind courtship, they married. Eight blissful months later he hooked his boat to his trailer and drove off for a day of fishing. That was a year ago. Unlike skeptical police, she believed he had met with an accident or foul play. I might have agreed, except that when she had tried to notify his family in San Antonio that he was missing she found that they were, too. Neither they, nor their addresses, existed. The man she married had no history, at least not in the name he had given her.

Scowling, teeth on edge, I began punching in the next number as Bobby Tubbs waved to me from the city desk. I saw the look on his face and moaned.

"They're shooting over at the Miami Dream Motel on Northeast Second Avenue!"

"Shooting? Again? Damn!" I snatched up a notebook and my purse. Whatever happened to quiet Sunday mornings in the Magic City? "You're sure?" I hate wild goose chases.

He shrugged. "Lottie called it in. She's out there."

"Shooting? Cool!" said Seth. He beat me to the elevator.

The Miami Dream Motel was wrapped like a gift in bright yellow crime scene tape, its rosy pink facade dimpled by large-caliber bullet holes. "Stick with me and try to stay out of the way," I warned Seth.

Traffic was blocked and the building crawled with cops. Their third shooting in two months, this could cost the Miami Dream its license. In a crackdown on violence, the city was enforcing a point system against occupational licenses, as states do against driver's licenses. Points are logged for each murder, shooting, prostitution arrest, drug bust, and SWAT team raid. When they lost their licenses to operate, of course, the vacant buildings usually converted to crack houses, presenting more problems.

The motel patio resembled a blood-streaked battleground, with one dead and four cursing, moaning, and whimpering wounded. Looked like another skirmish between embattled Jamaican sects, country boys from

Montego Bay versus city slickers from Kingston. Winners today were Miami cops, who had captured most participants too injured to run away.

This would give me a chance to review the players and update my scorecard. A Jamaican had staggered into county ER a week earlier, shot in the back and chest. He told police his name was Desmond Whitaker and that he was taking a walk, minding his own business, when a Rastafarian he knew as Dino drove by in a white Cadillac and shot him for no reason. He had survived surgery and gone to intensive care.

This could be related, I thought, scanning the street for a white Caddy.

"They're all Rastafarians, right?" I asked Cal Woodruff, a skinny detective in a dark suit.

He looked disgusted and stared at Seth, hovering behind me, notebook and pen in hand. "Jesus, Britt, bad enough I have to put up with you. Now you've got a shadow." He adjusted his sunglasses with a slight wince. Woodruff obviously would have preferred being someplace else, preferably air-conditioned, on this moist summer Sunday. "They look like Rastas, they talk like Rastas, but I haven't met a real Rasta yet," he snarled.

Woodruff could be right, I thought. The Jamaican Tourist Board insists that few real Rastafarians live in Miami and those who do are peaceful, artistic, and much maligned. Not everybody who wears dreadlocks is a Rastafarian.

"I fucking hate it when they get shot," Woodruff was griping.

"So do they, I'm sure." He ignored my remark.

"They're lousy goddamn victims," he said bitterly. "They never give their right names—ever. Most of 'em are illegals, but they claim to be from South Carolina. Now you know that ain't no southern accent." He slammed his clipboard onto the back of his unmarked car and took a pen from his pocket. "INS ain't worth shit. And if the bastards don't die, they disappear the minute they get outta the hospital and we can't find 'em again."

"A bummer when you have to hunt victims down like thieves," I said soothingly. His voice had the same frustrated edge I had heard in Lottie's when she recounted her pursuit of the Polish Prince.

I got to speak briefly to a sweating victim on a gurney. Bullet wounds in both legs had hampered his getaway. His name was Rat, he said, wincing, and he knew nothing. He was taking a walk, minding his own business, when he was shot. At that moment, however, a crime scene tech was photographing two guns, a mean-looking Walther semi-automatic and a Browning with a twelve-shot clip, lying where he had fallen. Each had apparently been fired until empty.

"Who were the guys shooting at you?" I asked him.

"Ah, mon, they sell smoke. . . . They just drive by and shoot at people." He batted bloodshot eyes at me, trying hard to sound virtuous. "I was just walking on the sidewalk and there comes this car down the street and they just start shooting."

"Are they mad at you?"

He stared straight up at puffy clouds overhead as he was bundled into the ambulance. "Probably." The medic slammed the door.

"Who the hell is that?" a cop shouted.

I spun around. The dead man in dreadlocks still lay sprawled flat on his back, arms outstretched. But now, inside the roped-off area, stood Seth, straddling the body, bending from the waist, snapping the victim close up with his Instamatic.

Cops bellowed. "No, no," I yelped. "He's just a tourist. I'll get him.

"Get away from there, Seth!" I insisted he step outside the yellow rope. He ignored me until he ran out of film. He was good. His face glowed. Bet his friends pay attention, I thought, when he whips out the snapshots from his Miami vacation. What would they think of us in Hopewell, New Jersey? What will his grandmother think of me?

He was everywhere, peering over the medics' shoulders, tailing the technicians, dogging the detectives. Never, ever give him coffee again, I told myself, as cops tried to determine which bullet holes were fresh and which had been left by the last shooting. I talked to witnesses, found

Lottie, and introduced her to Seth, who was instantly intrigued by her camera equipment. She had been driving out to breakfast when the shooting call went out on her scanner.

I tried to send Seth back to the paper with her, but he insisted on going with me to the hospital where Woodruff planned to sort everybody out. Reporters are barred from the emergency room, but if I simply breeze in with the cops, wearing press ID, which from a distance resembles police ID, I often escape detection.

"Wait here," I told Seth outside. Inside, a trauma team worked on the most serious victim, gut shot but still conscious. Woodruff hoped to talk to him before he went to surgery. I sidled up beside the detective and copied the name, Clement Blake, off the victim's driver's license in Woodruff's hand.

"Think this is related to that incident last week?"

"Desmond Whitaker?" the detective asked.

"That's the one."

"Could be," he said. "I been meaning to chat with him about the real Desmond Whitaker, a New York resident who lost his car and his wallet in a robbery two months ago."

"So, who is our Desmond Whitaker?"

"That's what I wanna ask him. Hey," he said. "Speak of the devil."

A gaunt man in a hospital gown was slow-stepping down the hallway. He carried his IV bottle and dragged a rack of tubes to which he was attached.

"That's him. The guy shot last week," Woodruff said. "Looks a helluva lot better." Desmond Whitaker, or whoever he was, stared at the wounded man being worked on.

"That's the man who shot me!" he screamed, pointing with an arm that still trailed an IV tube.

He lurched forward, still shrieking. A nurse blocked him, another called security.

"Hope they don't put them in the same room," I said.

"Hell, I gotta go talk to him," Woodruff said, as his walkie crackled to life. The true owner of the driver's license in his hand was in jail, the dispatcher informed him, and had been for two weeks. "You're sure?" Woodruff asked.

"That's affirmative," she replied.

A doctor signaled the detective that he could take a moment with the patient. "Who shot you?" the detective asked.

A shrug.

"What's your name?"

"Clement Blake," he muttered weakly.

"Clement Blake is in jail. You've got his ID. What's *your* name?"

The man sighed. "Clive, Clive Steadman," he said, and was whisked away to surgery.

The detective saw me scribble the name. "Not so fast," he said, frowning. "Clive Steadman was that homicide victim on the Interstate last month."

I remembered. Dead driver, careening car, wounded passengers who ran away.

Now I frowned. "But we have to straighten these IDs out by deadline," I snapped, "for my story and Lottie's pictures."

The detective covered his bloodshot eyes with his sunglasses. "When you do that," he muttered, "let me know."

A chubby cop named Peterson walked up and dealt out the driver's licenses of the other victims like playing cards on the counter at the nurses' station. "Lookit this," he said to Woodruff. "Two a these guys have the same name and DOB but the pictures are different. Whadaya make a that?"

Woodruff muttered curses as Peterson turned to me.

"Hey, Britt, seen your story today. You sure you got that missing kid's name right?"

"What?"

"Coulda sworn that was the same missing persons case I took the initial report on when I worked south. Same description. But that wasn't the kid's name."

"Cute," I said, and took off. Cops love to tease but I was in no mood to play.

The only people outside the ER were ambulance attendants unloading an elderly woman who had fallen at a nursing home.

"Dammit, Seth," I muttered, looking both ways. "Where are you?"

The ambulance attendants hadn't seen him. I trudged back to my T-Bird, annoyed. He wasn't there either. Had he been older, I would let him find his own way home. But he was only twelve, and a not-so-savory neighborhood surrounded the bustling hospital complex.

I marched back into the ER. Woodruff and two other cops were huddled over paperwork. "Did you see that kid I was with, the one with the camera?"

"You mean Jimmy Olson?" Woodruff said.

They had not seen him.

Neither had a security guard at the front desk.

Seth was gone.

Increasing alarm had replaced my anger. What would I say to Mrs. Goldstein? "Sorry, I lost your grandson"? Where could he be? He had promised to wait right there. I thought of young Charles Randolph. What did that Gables detective say?

"Poufff."

I dashed back outside. Nothing. The morgue, I thought frantically. He had talked all morning about going to the morgue. The medical examiner's office is right around the corner, at Number One Bob Hope Road. I piled into the T-Bird, hands shaking as I turned the key. I backed out of the space and was turning left when I caught sight of Seth in my rearview, a can of Coke in one hand, a bag of chips in the other.

"Hey!" He slid breathlessly into the seat beside me. "Were you gonna leave without me?"

"Damn straight." My knees were weak with relief and I fought the urge to hug him. "Don't you ever do that to me again, Seth."

• • •

I left him in the darkroom helping Lottie and listening to her police scanners. The phone at my desk was ringing. "Would have called this morning," McDonald said, as I settled back in my chair, glad to hear his voice, "but I had to go look for my car."

"The Cherokee? What happened? Was it stolen?"

"Nah, long story. One of my classmates is a Texas Ranger. Big, rugged, with hands like a blacksmith. Parties hard. Borrowed the Cherokee Friday night. Shows up this morning and when I asked where he parked it, he shoots me a blank. 'Jesus Christ!' he says. Did I have your car? Shit, I came home in a cab.'"

"Oh, no." I remembered many warm moments on hot nights in that Jeep Cherokee.

"Went downtown to look for it. Found it parked outside Jim Dandy's, a rowdy bar with sawdust floors. Not a scratch. This guy's a real character. Somebody asked in class the other day what they do down on the border when somebody runs from them. He said, 'You shoot 'im, right where the suspenders cross.'"

"Nice." I winced. "Maybe he could help with our immigration problem. Did you say Texas? Is he married?"

"Why?"

"Maybe I know just the woman for him."

"Lottie?"

"Why not?"

"Thought she was seeing some lawyer."

"Competition is healthy."

"Is that so?"

"Sure," I teased.

My description of the car bombing and the gun battle at the Miami Dream Motel made him homesick, or so he said. He sounded eager for local news and police gossip, so I filled him in and read him my Charles Randolph story.

"Don't know why, but that case seems to ring a bell."

"He'd never been in any trouble."

"Find out if Gables ever sent a tech to the house to try to raise a set of prints off his belongings. Be a shame if none existed."

"They didn't," I said. "Sounds like the detective did as little as possible."

"Miss you," he said, as romantic as he ever got on the telephone.

"Three months to go." I blew him a kiss.

"Maybe not," he murmured. "We may get a long weekend at Labor Day. Keep the dates open, I could fly down."

"Sounds good to me. I can put in for comp time."

I wondered later why I sounded so breezy when I really longed for the man. This time will be different, I promised myself. We'd work at keeping our jobs from becoming a conflict between us. He had never asked if I was seeing anyone else as he had suggested. Did he assume I was? Was he? Was that why he asked me to keep the dates open? Was there more than miles between us? Luckily, I had no time to box shadows.

Next on my list of messages to return was a woman whose only interest in the Charles Randolph case was that her son and his best friend were also missing. Long gone, presumed dead. A Drug Enforcement agent had unofficially informed her that the two were shot and deep-sixed during a drug-smuggling deal off Key West. That was twelve years ago but, despite her son's history of drug arrests, she could not accept it.

"Isn't there a chance," she asked, "that he's alive and has been working undercover for the government all these years?"

She didn't like my answer, though I couched it as gently as possible.

"I called about the Randolph boy," the next woman said. She sounded congested, as though she had a cold. "I'm sorry to bother you but I can't help it. I saw his picture this morning and . . ." She snorted and blew her nose. "I'm sorry, I've been crying."

"Do you know him?" I rolled my chair to my terminal to take notes.

"No," she whispered. "But it was such a shock when I opened the paper. He looks so much like my son."

"Oh." Disappointed, my eyes roved down the list to the next message.

"David has been missing for four years."

Something cold rippled down my spine.

"What happened?"

"His dad and I are divorced. He was spending the weekend with his father when they quarreled and he stormed out. It was over something stupid. You know how kids are. He had no money on him and he apparently tried to hitchhike back to my house in Surfside. We never saw him again."

David Clower was twelve, fair-haired, blue-eyed, and slender.

After we talked, I reopened my MISSING file and stared at the entry for Butch Beltrán. Fair-haired, blue-eyed, and slender, missing since March.

What the hell was going on here?

I woke up next morning still thinking about the missing boys. The early news reported that the third hurricane of the season, which had been barreling down on Bermuda, had veered away and was dying at sea. Weather watchers were already scrutinizing a new low-pressure wave that had spiraled into the Atlantic off Senegal, on the west coast of Africa. But that was thousands of miles away in the earth's atmospheric cauldron where the recipe—heated sea temperature, barometric pressure, wind direction, and other variables—must mix just so to spawn a storm. As many as a hundred and twenty-five tropical waves occur during a busy season. About ten become tropical depressions. Of the six that spin into tropical storms, about four escalate into hurricanes.

My mother called before breakfast. "What have you been doing, darling? Why are you too busy to return my calls?" Without waiting for an answer, she began bubbling over about the new winter fashions. What I yearn for this time of year is a bikini and a beach. Her spirited spiel about skinny belts, saucy patent mules, and forties-styled suits, which would be featured in the fashion shows she was coordinating, failed to interest me.

My own shop talk, when she did pause for breath, inspired the same nonreaction—until I mentioned the Alex Aguirre bombing.

"I saw it on TV," she said. "Those awful people, so brutal . . ."

"Did you see my story?" I sounded too eager, but if my own mother didn't read my stories, who would?

"You know how I feel about crime and violence," she said, skirting my question.

"I cover the police beat, Mom." I sounded like a child seeking approval, but couldn't help myself.

"When will you be promoted to something more positive?"

"That's not how it works. I love my beat," I explained, for what must have been the ten thousandth time. "That's where the best stories are, people stories. It's a gold mine for a reporter. You can expose the bad guys, change things, make a difference."

"Nothing changes, Britt. You can't save the world. I thought after what almost happened to you, when that other reporter was killed and you were wrongly blamed, you would consider yourself and those who care about you. Common sense says you can't keep courting disaster," she cautioned, for what had to be the twenty thousandth time to me, and to my father before me. Some things do not change.

She heard my sigh and abruptly switched subjects. "You'll be glad to know that the grunge look is out," she chirped cheerfully.

"What a pity," I said. "Grunge was me."

"Some of the new pieces are such fun!" she burbled, ignoring my sarcasm. "Flowerpot purses are going to be very big, they're clever and kitschy. So is faux fur and thigh-high vinyl boots."

I imagined whipping my notebook out of a flowerpot purse after making a grand entrance at police headquarters in faux fur and thigh-high boots. It would get their attention. I bit back a smart remark, suddenly overwhelmed by images of Cassie Randolph and the other mother, the stranger who had wept on the phone about her missing son, and the memory of how in my darkest hour my mother had been ready to mortgage all she owned and more, to save me.

"I love you, Mom."

She paused for a millisecond, then rushed on, as though she hadn't heard. "The new hemlimes are more realistic, right at the knee, but I have serious reservations about the white ankle socks with platform sandals."

"You're absolutely right," I said. "So do I." We promised to meet for lunch later in the week. There have been times with my mother when the thought of DNA testing crossed my mind, certain that I was somehow switched at birth—but I am so much like my father. Our simpatico is ephemeral, more a spiritual bond than direct knowledge. Whenever I am in danger or despair, he is with me. *Estamos juntos*. We are together. My real memories of him are few. I remember peering out from between bars, my playpen placed under a grapefruit tree in a sunlit yard, as he bent close to me, dappled light and shadow filtered through leaves dancing on his face and arms as he lifted me high and higher, up and away from my prison. I remember the warmth of his words, "*mi angelito rubia,*" and my mother laughing in a way I have never heard since. And there is a clear recollection of riding in a car snuggled comfortably between them in a world before child safety seats.

My mother insists that I was too young, that I couldn't possibly remember any such thing, but I do.

What little she says about him so conflicts with the stories told by my Aunt Odalys and other relatives that it is impossible to know now, nearly three decades later, who and what the man really was. But I sense that we are the same. Maybe it is simply that I long to be part of his committed and passionate world rather than that of haute couture and flowerpot purses.

No promising leads in the Alex Aguirre bombing, according to homicide. Nobody had called to claim responsibility, the motive remained unknown. I called Yates from the bomb squad to double check.

Bombers' signatures are as distinctive as fingerprints. The way they twist their wires, the components they choose, the tool markings they leave, the military or commercial explosives they use. "Haven't found it yet," Yates said. "We're still sifting through the debris, using finer screens now."

I had another story, a choice tidbit picked up during my phone checks. My first stop was the Miami Beach police station three blocks west of the ocean, on Washington Avenue. Until it was built, South Florida cop shops were formidable fortresslike structures. *Miami Vice* and the Art Deco renaissance changed that. Both influenced this gleaming white building with sweeping curves, glass brick, and a high inside balcony. The past was even respected, unusual in a city with a short history and officials with shorter memories. The new police headquarters stands behind the old City Hall built the year after the devastating 1926 hurricane. Unlike the sleek modern building that has replaced it seven blocks away, the original is a wedding cake, a show of faith erected in a time of disaster. A two-story base supports a nine-story tier topped by an arched confection garnished with balusters and urns and a red tile roof. It now houses courtrooms, offices, and a restaurant. The new Deco police station is connected by a plaza, a favorite location for fashion shoots and an exercise in psychedelia.

Glamorous long-legged models and famous foreign photographers mingle with rumpled detectives, handcuffed prisoners, battered victims, and sleazy bondsmen under a technicolor sky that smells of sea and salt. The giddy ambience creates an impression that nothing here is actually real, but all make-believe instead, created for the glossy pages of some slick magazine.

The chief scowled and ducked back into his office when he saw me, probably tipped off by the mayor, who was also evading my phone calls.

They had been too quick with the key to the city. Again. Forgetting the outrage last time, after another honored visitor was identified as a former Nazi.

Their latest honoree, a brawny German visitor, had wrestled an armed robber to the pavement, snatched away his gun and pummeled him until police arrived. After the negative worldwide headlines generated by the robbery murders of several foreign tourists, this was the answer to a publicist's prayer and cause for as much media hype as could be wrung out of it.

Police had awarded the hero a plaque, the mayor had presented the

key to the city, and he had been showered with accolades during a standing ovation at a full meeting of the city commission. Publicity pictures
were flashed around the world, revealing that the hero was wanted in
Berlin for child molesting.

In this world of scam artists and swindlers all drawn like magnets to
this city, the safest course is to honor only the dead—after thorough background checks. Miami city fathers now follow that route, burned too often
after renaming streets in honor of celebrities, civic leaders, and philan-
thropists quickly exposed as drug lords, tax evaders, or scam artists. They
should take the same precaution with proclamations, another kiss of death.
Shortly after city officials celebrated Yahweh Ben Yahweh Day in Miami,
the self-proclaimed God, son of God, was indicted in connection with
fourteen murders and a firebombing.

I cornered the chief for a comment, then dropped by the missing persons bureau. A young officer named Causey was in charge. Missing persons was once the exclusive province of women officers, but now the
women are more likely to be out on patrol, in uniform, fighting crime in
the streets while many male officers hold down desk jobs.

I asked to see the open missing-persons files, wondering how far back
to check. Some of the cases that filled two file drawers were older than
Causey, in his twenties and much more enthusiastic about his off-duty
security work for movie crews on location than in tracking lost people.

"Most of 'em are not lost," he said cheerfully, leaning back in his chair,
hands locked behind his head. "They know where they are, but we don't."

He laughed at his own joke, as I arbitrarily decided to go back five
years.

Seated at an empty desk, suspecting that this was a silly waste of
time, I flipped through file after file. Two possibilities: Samuel Lifter,
thirteen, and Derek Malone, eleven.

The Lifter boy: reported missing three years ago. The report on the
Malone youngster was a year older. Both were tall for their ages, fair-
haired and blue-eyed.

Lifter had threatened to run away because he hated to take his medication. He was epileptic. The day he disappeared he had been swimming with friends, over at Crandon Park Beach on Key Biscayne. When it came time to go home, they couldn't find him. The Malone boy had had an altercation with a teacher at Nautilus Junior High and hadn't returned home from school that day. There were no notations in the files that the cases had ever been resolved.

I dialed the Lifter number, wondering if the family still lived there. A woman answered.

I introduced myself. "I'm calling about your son, Samuel."

Her voice became cold. "Is this a joke?"

"No," I assured her. "I wanted to find out if you've heard from him, if he's come home."

She gasped. Samuel Lifter had been found, drowned in the surf, the day after he was reported missing. The official theory was that he had skipped his medication, suffered a seizure and drowned unseen during the beach outing. A strolling honeymoon couple had stumbled upon his body in the water the next morning. Samuel Lifter had been resting in the family plot at Shalom Memorial Gardens these past three years while still listed in the Miami Beach Police Department's active missing-persons file.

Apologizing profusely, I shot a look to kill at Officer Causey, oblivious at his desk, telling someone on the phone about how he had been thisclose to Sharon Stone during shooting for the big new action flick on location in South Beach.

I dialed the Malone home with more trepidation.

A teenager answered. "Hi," I said, "I'm calling from the Miami Beach Police Department. We're updating our files and I wondered about the status of Derek Malone. He was reported missing four years ago."

"Derek?"

"Yes, is he still missing?"

"Christ, no." The boy laughed. "I think I remember that. My brother got sent to the vice principal's office by his teacher, got scared, and took off. Hopped a bus to my grandmother's in Hallandale that night. She brought him home the next day. That was four freaking years ago. I love it! The cops are still looking for him! Duh."

"Thank you," I said sweetly, "and my regards to Derek."

I flipped both files onto Causey's desk, convinced that the only way he would spot a missing person was if one wandered across a movie set.

"You owe me," I said, picking up my things. "I just cleared two cases for you."

"Thanks, Britt." He put his palm over the mouthpiece and beamed boyishly. "Wanna stay and do a few more?"

I drove eight miles north to Surfside, a tiny eight-block-long oceanfront municipality that stretches from Eighty-eighth Street north to Ninety-sixth and from the Atlantic Ocean west to Biscayne Bay.

Huge equipment blocked Surfside's main drag, narrowing traffic to one lane. Signs warned that a twenty-mile-an-hour speed limit was strictly enforced. No problem. I crawled along at eight miles an hour, the top speed possible in bumper-to-bumper traffic.

The desk sergeant at the twenty-one-man department adjacent to the Town Hall did not recall the Clower case, but the lone detective in the building obligingly dug it out for me. Had it been a murder the county would be handling it, the file would be unavailable, and the cops tight-lipped, but missing persons are a routine nuisance.

I scanned David Clower's file. His mother had reported him missing on Monday, after calling her ex-husband to find out why he had not returned the boy. Assuming father and son were bonding, sharing quality time, she had been reluctant to interrupt sooner. David had been gone since about seven o'clock Saturday night when he slammed angrily out of his father's place in South Miami. I wondered aloud if there were independent witnesses to the boy's departure. Did the father have a record? Was he a drinker? Was there was a history of violence between father and son?

"Gawd, Britt," the detective said. "You're a suspicious woman." He knew nothing about the case. The file was sparse and had been referred to Metro-Dade because the boy had apparently disappeared in county jurisdiction. No way to know if he had ever made it back to the Beach or to Surfside.

There was a picture. His mother was right. David Clower was a dead ringer for Charles Randolph. They could have been brothers.

No other cases fit the profile. Most people who get lost in Surfside are ancient wanderers, confused senior citizens unable to find their way home because their memories have short-circuited, convincing them it is 1954 again and they are back in Brooklyn, or they are elderly desperadoes who march off in protest, angry at their current caretakers or living arrangements. Spunky, elusive, and evasive, they are eventually rounded up and trundled home, like it or not.

The Clower house was just a few blocks away. In Surfside everything is just a few blocks away. I rejoined the traffic jam to drive by on the chance someone would be there. The house was painted white, a neat one-story bungalow with a one-car garage.

I rang the bell and waited as a bright yellow front loader groaned by just a dozen feet away from the small front porch. A tarp covered what looked like an old metal love seat. After a delay, a masked woman inched open the door. She wore a mask.

Her nose and mouth were covered. The only people I have seen wearing similar masks, other than medical personnel, are homicide detectives dealing with badly decomposed corpses.

"Hi," I said uncertainly, introducing myself. "Did I interrupt something?" Was she performing surgery on her kitchen table? Or something worse?

She pulled down her mask. "Come in," she blurted, hustling me inside as though a posse were hot on my heels. "Quick!" She slammed the door shut behind us with a sigh of relief. "Whew!" She sucked in a deep breath and rubbed at her reddened eyes. "That roadwork coats everything with dust. They've been at it for three months now and my allergies are driving me crazy. It's impossible to keep it out of here. The dust and the fumes filter in through every nook and cranny."

She swallowed another gulp of air and smiled. "Thanks for coming." Like her missing son, Vanessa Clower was fair-haired and blue-eyed. In her late thirties, she was slim-hipped, wearing blue jeans and a paint-spattered, faded blue T-shirt. An artist. She worked at home.

The inside of the house shone, sterile and shiny, no rugs, doilies, or heavy drapes, as though she had cleared the decks to better combat the clouds of powdery dust and grit churned up by the equipment outside.

"The only relief is when it rains," she said, pinching the bridge of her nose. "There are still months to go, they're replacing the town's entire sewer system and not a minute too soon. You should see the standing water when we have a shower. Come on out here. I'll just be a minute. I'm working on something."

I followed as she padded barefoot to a Florida room at the rear of the house, far from the din in the street. Two large canvases rested side by side on the floor, a carpet of newspapers beneath them. One was blank, the other had been sprayed with glossy black enamel. She hunkered down over the black one and began to squeeze lines, blobs, and squiggles of rich, vivid color directly onto the canvas from big thick white plastic tubes marked Mars Black, Naphthol Crimson, Quinacridone Violet, Yellow Ochre, and Raw Sienna. I itched to try it. It looked like fun, like the fingerpainting I loved in kindergarten until I got in trouble for taking off shoes and socks and winding up with paint between my toes, on my knees, and all over my clothes.

She added shades of Burnt Umber and Permanent Green Light at the bottom, liberal amounts of Cobalt Blue across the top and Indo Orange Red, streaming like sunlight across the center. Then she carefully placed the second canvas face down on the first, took a heavy wooden rolling pin and rolled it out as colors squished out the sides, like mashing down a burger loaded with catsup, mustard, and mayo.

I watched, fascinated, as she expertly peeled apart the canvases, now fascinating mirror images of riotous color. She added a rapier-blade slash of white across the face of each, then picked up what looked like a large corrugated drop ceiling panel, a network of tiny open plastic windows, aligned it atop the first canvas, and, still barefoot, stepped carefully onto the panel. She walked back and forth several times, pressing it evenly onto the canvas. When she peeled away the panel, the canvas was imprinted with a mosaic-screen-like finish. She completed the same process on the second canvas.

"That's it," she said, smiling, wiping her hands on a rag. "You have to work fast before it dries."

"What do you call this?"

She cocked her head. "Abstract expressionism."

"No, I mean this technique."

She shrugged. "Just something I evolved on my own. Everybody has their own style. I'm getting these ready for the Labor Day Taste of the Arts show in Fort Lauderdale."

Nice, though my taste in art is more traditional. I never understand people who pay big bucks for canvases daubed by chimps or performing elephants who wield paintbrushes with their trunks. She must have read my look. "Several new office complexes are using these companion pieces together. They sell for about twelve hundred dollars a set," she said casually. "Seven fifty when they're sold individually."

I was impressed.

"Would you like a glass of orange juice?"

I followed her into the kitchen. The appliances were gleaming chrome, the only personal touch a child's drawings posted on the refrigerator along with a color photo. She, her son, and a little girl about four, their smiles captured at a beach picnic.

"My daughter," she said, pouring orange juice from a glass pitcher. "She's eight now, in school today. I always loved working at home when the kids were small. Now I wish I had someplace to go." We sat in her breakfast nook as she repeated the details of her son's disappearance.

"We've tried everything," she said softly. "We're absolutely baffled."

She knew exactly where I was going, taking no offense when I began to question her ex-husband's story.

"I believe him," she said simply. "For all his faults, Edwin is not a violent man. We broke up after he started something with the new secretary he'd hired. She knew we'd been having problems and moved right in on him. That was just the final blow to a shaky relationship. I blame him, as he does himself, for letting David walk out.

"He's a good father, but it was the macho factor. They are so alike, those two. Neither one likes to admit he's wrong. He thought David would be back. When he wasn't, he assumed he'd come home. The games people play." Her curly shoulder-length hair bounced as she shook her head.

"What do you think?" I asked.

She glanced at the happy photo on the fridge. "He's out there somewhere and I don't see how he could be alone. He's not a resourceful boy, he couldn't live off the land. It's been so long, now. Would you like some tea?"

She got up quickly, poured bottled water into a stainless steel tea-kettle, switched on a burner, and sat down again.

"I was struck by your story and that other boy's picture in the paper. The resemblance. And I admit that I was jealous that he got the press and the attention when nobody seems to care that David is missing."

"You should have called. I didn't know."

"I tried to contact the media. I called a TV station once, when they had all the publicity about that Miami college girl who disappeared in Atlanta. But if it's not a tiny child or a beautiful young woman, they're not interested."

"You think he hitchhiked?"

She shrugged and sighed. "He had no money with him. I think he may have done it before, although I had warned him."

"Is he street smart? Could he handle himself if somebody picked him up . . . and got weird?"

Gingerly, she touched her tongue to the corner of her mouth as though it was painfully tender. "To a degree, the way most kids are street smart these days. If the person was a criminal with a gun or a knife . . . no. My son was only twelve when he was taken."

"You don't think he ran away?"

"No," she said, as the teakettle began to whistle. She went to a shiny white cabinet, removed two mugs and a tin of tea bags. "Initially I entertained that possibility. He was disgusted and angry about our divorce. So was I. My husband had dumped me for the new secretary he'd hired. He was mad as hell at his dad that night—but he would never stay away this long. And he wasn't mad at me." She placed a steaming mug in front of me and resumed her seat. "He loves us, he likes his school, and he gets along well with his sister. And he likes his creature comforts, his bike, his video games, his own TV in his room, his favorite foods in the fridge. What's to run from?"

She looked at me, her eyes hopeful, as though I might provide the answer. I had none.

She stirred her tea and put her spoon down carefully. "It's a constant pain, like a knife twisting in my heart every time the phone or the doorbell rings. I always think it's him, or about him. It's odd, I developed all these allergies, at my age, since this happened. My work has become very dark." She gazed toward the Florida room.

"The innocence is gone," she decided, nodding, then raised her eyes to mine. "The worst possible truth is better than being left in limbo like this.

"I'll offer a reward," she said briskly. "Edwin and I have discussed it. We can offer five thousand dollars."

We finished our tea and her wide eyes followed as I got up to leave. "When are you coming back?" she asked matter-of-factly, as though it were a given.

"Soon," I promised, hesitating. "I'll call you."

I escaped the dust storm, traveling at a crawl until traffic began to move at Seventy-ninth Street, then drove west to the new Metro-Dade police headquarters near the Palmetto Expressway. There I found the case of Lars Sjowall, age fourteen, slender, blond, blue-eyed. A dozen Swedish exchange students had visited Miami for a week before returning home after a year in this country. The night before their departure, Lars wanted to see a horror movie playing at a multiplex within walking distance of their motel. None of his companions wanted to join him, so he went alone.

They never saw him again. Police theorized that he didn't want to leave this country and had run off to see more of America. He left behind his passport, money, clothes, his toothbrush, and all the gifts and souvenirs he had planned to take home to his family in Sweden. Neither they nor his host family in Indiana ever heard from him.

That was two years ago.

I also checked out Butch Beltrán. Still missing. The detective had recently spoken to a family member who had called for information.

Butch had run away before, but had always returned in days. This time it had been five months.

I made a pit stop at the office to write the German tourist story. The fugitive and his key to the city were long gone.

Then I went to Miami police headquarters and found two more. William and Michael Kearns, twelve- and thirteen-year-old brothers, missing for nearly a year. Both slender, fair-haired, blue-eyed. Went to a carnival in the Grove. Never came home. Runaways, the cops assumed.

Something prickled at the back of my neck as I looked at their pictures.

Dade County sprawls over 2,109 square miles. Two and a half million people live in Greater Miami, which has a vast unincorporated area and twenty-seven municipalities. Most have their own police departments. All take missing-persons reports.

I still had twenty-one police departments to check.

I PASSED THROUGH the guarded gate
and cruised the shaded stretch of Garden Drive where Charles Randolph
was last seen. Golden afternoon sunlight splashed through a lush canopy
of foliage. Serenity reigned behind the walled estates of the rich and
powerful. The only people visible were a uniformed nanny pushing her
tiny charge in a pram, and some yardmen at work removing coconuts
and cutting back the branches of top-heavy trees. The property owner
had probably been spooked by weatherman scare tactics. One tabloid-
style TV show even plays the theme from *Jaws* when reporting the formation of tropical storms. Every year forecasters solemnly announce
that South Florida is overdue for the Big One since we haven't been hit
by a hurricane since 1965.

I ignored my incessantly chirping beeper. Gretchen. That woman
did not know when to quit. She paged me again, over and over and over,
until I finally yanked the damn thing off my belt and flung it into the
backseat. Whatever she wanted could wait, I thought, hoping it was only
her usual annoying petty antics and not some major breaking news story
that I was missing. There was no urgency in the routine chatter on my
police scanner, except for an overturned truck that had spilled an entire

load of roofing nails across the fast lane on the big curve of the Palmetto Expressway. Another rush hour from hell.

The more I brainstormed about the missing boys, the more I kept arriving back at square one. Apparently they didn't know each other, attend the same school, belong to the same scout troop, or live in the same neighborhood. Charles Randolph was cheerful and industrious. David Clower was angry about his parents' divorce. Butch Beltrán apparently had a troubled past and a history of running away. Lars Sjowall was alone, six thousand miles from home. I knew little about the Kearns brothers.

But all they had in common so far was that they were slender, young, blue-eyed, and fair-haired, and the fact that they were gone.

Reluctantly, I drove back to the paper and walked into the newsroom, beeper in place on my belt. As I expected, Gretchen zeroed in like a heat-seeking missile.

"My beeper?" I asked incredulously, as she launched into a harangue. I removed it and stared at the device quizzically. "It's on," I told her. I tested it. "It's working." I gazed at her innocently. "Are you sure you dialed the right number, Gretchen?"

But she had the upper hand. "Did you hear about the truck on the Palmetto?"

"Yup," I said, "I'm right on top of it."

"And the press conference?"

Uh-oh. "Which one?"

She smiled malevolently, threw back her shoulders, and jutted her pointy breasts at me. Was that a Wonderbra? "On the Alex Aguirre case." She smirked and consulted her watch. "You're five minutes late for it right now. I didn't have anybody else to send."

Oh, God, I thought, stomach lurching. "Did they make an arrest?"

"That's the impression I got. I suggest you get yourself over there and ask them."

I lunged for a fresh notebook. During phone checks that morning they didn't even have a suspect. At least that's what they had told me.

"At the police station?" I headed for the elevator.

"No," she said, "at WTOP."

Odd, I thought, cops wouldn't announce an arrest or a break in the case at the television station.

Gretchen said something as I brushed by her. It took a moment to sink in. "From now on stay in touch with the city desk, Britt. Save your social life for your day off."

I was already on the elevator; she had turned away. "What?" I yelped in indignation. Did she just imply that I had spent the afternoon . . . ? The doors closed and I screamed all the way to the lobby.

As usual, Gretchen was a fountain of misinformation. No arrest, no cops. Station management had called the press conference to announce a fifty-thousand-dollar reward for information leading to the arrest and conviction of Alex Aguirre's killers.

Though twenty minutes late, I missed nothing but the bickering as station officials got their jollies by forcing all their competitors' news crews to move their equipment to inconvenient locations at the back of the room. TV people take forever to set up anyway. If Jesus Christ appeared to proclaim the end of the world they would interrupt, ask him to hold it until they set up their equipment, then demand that he start again from the top.

The widow was present, eyes swollen, dressed in black. The station had her tied up, refusing to let her answer questions from competing reporters. After their poor coverage the day of the bombing, they had had broadcast exclusives on every newscast since. Home videos of the happy family, footage of the bewildered fatherless children, the all-night vigil at the funeral home, the weeping widow pleading for anyone with information to call a special number at the station, or, as an afterthought, the police. The poor woman was caught in the clutches of the news director. The rest of the press corps grumbled, but I understood. Shocked, scared, and alone, she had kids to raise. WTOP-TV, her husband's employer, was probably the only security in her life at the moment.

I wondered what it had been like for my mother when she was left alone with me.

Lottie was there shooting art for the final. "Wait till you hear what Gretchen said to me," I told her.

"Let's go for coffee," she whispered.

"We can get it back at the office. I have a couple of stories to write."

"No, now."

"What?" She looked vibrant and excited; she had combed her hair. That could only mean one thing.

"I just passed La Esquina de Tejas. His car is parked outside. I wanna drop in for coffee."

I sighed. "You sure he's still there?"

"If we stop jawing and get over there, he will be. It'll be a surprise. He asked me to dinner but I had to tell 'im I was working. I felt terrible, poor thing really wanted to see me."

The restaurant was only five minutes away. We took my car, so if she decided to stay, Stosh could drive her back to her company Chrysler parked at WTOP.

Hungry, I decided as we walked in that I wanted a Cuban sandwich. I stopped mid-stride. The Polish Prince, jaunty as ever, sat at a secluded table. He was not dining alone.

"Lottie," I turned, hoping to detour her in time. Damn him, I thought. By now I really wanted a sandwich.

But she never missed a beat. She swept past me, to his table. Mouth open, I watched.

In intimate conversation, holding both hands of his companion, a striking young brunette in a red sundress, he did not see Lottie until she spoke. More a whine than a word.

"Ssstooooosh."

I had never heard such a sound come out of Lottie before. He looked up, with the expression of an escapee suddenly aware that the sheriff has got the drop on him.

"Ssstooosh. The kids are huungry, honey. When are you coming hooome? They keep crying for their daddy."

He swallowed. "Lottie." His smile was sickly, eyes pleading as he looked past her and saw me.

I smiled back, shook my head faintly, and sat at the counter to watch.

The young woman at the table dropped her napkin and stared at Lottie.

"Kristin," Stosh said anxiously. He got to his feet. "I want you to meet—"

"Don't feel baaad," Lottie whined at the woman. "It happens all the time, I'm uuused to it."

As I followed Lottie out the door, Stosh Gorski, face pained, was fast-talking Kristin, who had pushed away her plate and was picking up her purse.

"Damn, Lottie," I said admiringly. "That was good."

"That calaboose shyster," she muttered, climbing into my car. "He was all over her like a duck on a June bug. Let's git outta here. You was right about him all along, Britt. All I want to give that man now is a grenade with the pin pulled."

We laughed, as I drove off into the dusk.

I NEEDED MORE time to work on the lost boys and knew I wouldn't get it from Gretchen, so I confided in my city editor. A mistake. Fred Douglas leaned back in his creaky leather chair, fingers covering his mouth, heavy-lidded eyes inscrutable behind his bifocals. He might have looked distinguished except for the huge blue ink stain a leaky pen had left around the pocket of his pin-striped shirt.

"Nahh, Britt." His expression was that of a man who had just swallowed something unpleasant. "You know what happens with these missing persons stories. Remember that—"

"I know, I know," I said impatiently. Who could forget the virginal fifteen-year-old Catholic schoolgirl who left home as usual one morning but never got to her honor classes at Holy Name Academy? Shy and sweet, loved by the nuns who taught her, the girl had never been on a date or alone with a boy. Her mother, a widowed seamstress, was raising her only daughter in a sheltered and religious household. The cops and the press corps took the case seriously.

The mother wept on the television news for the girl's return. "We are more than mother and daughter, we are best friends." Savvy detectives and medical examiners all assumed the worst. The novenas, the publicity, and public concern mounted. By the fifth night a grim-faced anchor announced at the top of the eleven o'clock news that hope for the girl's safe return was all but abandoned. As footage of the search for her body aired, the missing teenager flounced angrily into the station.

"Leave me alone!" she demanded. "Quit putting my picture in the newspaper and on TV." She was not missing, she said, just sick of the nuns, sick to death of her mother, and had no intention of going home.

The damage she did to genuinely missing persons totally ignored by the press and police after her escapade is incalculable.

I am sure some died awaiting help.

"You're always seeing plots and patterns," Fred intoned. "I'm not saying you shouldn't," he added quickly, with a cautionary hand gesture as my face mirrored my indignation. "Your imagination and driving curiosity are what make you a great reporter. But this"—he spread out his arms—"sounds like coincidence. Everything that goes on doesn't necessarily have to be related or part of some gigantic plot. Shit happens."

"Listen, Fred." I leaned forward. "You know that Anglos are now a minority in Miami." He raised an eyebrow.

"In case you haven't noticed, blond, blue-eyed boys of twelve and thirteen are not all that common around here anymore," I continued. "At this rate they're becoming an endangered species. Don't you think that six or more missing sounds like more than a coincidence?"

"Not necessarily," he said. "Remember, it's over a long period of time."

"The missing boys are news," I said, trying my best to sound assertive.

"News is what editors say it is." The hard edge to his voice was unlike him, and made me wary. I didn't want to argue.

"Fred, remember when beauty queens and gorgeous models began disappearing? Christopher Wilder was using a camera to lure them into his clutches. He promised to make them cover girls."

Fred remained skeptical.

"Remember when young women with pierced ears and long brown

hair parted in the middle were vanishing from Seattle to Florida? Ted Bundy, another serial killer, was snatching them on a cross-country murder spree. Eventually somebody spotted a pattern."

"You don't know that any of these kids are dead, Britt," he said impatiently. "It would be totally irresponsible for us to suggest that a serial killer is stalking South Florida, preying on kids. You want to create a panic because some teenage boys ran away from home? We'd sure look silly if they started showing up."

"I'm not saying that any of the boys are dead or that there's a serial killer, that was just an example. But something is going on here. Printing the story will help find out what it is. If they are runaways we can probably flush them out. I just think it's a helluva story that all these missing kids fit a certain profile."

"I'm not saying you shouldn't keep digging. See what you come up with, but don't spend a lot of time on it. We've got the big special section on Cuba coming up and we need every warm body in the newsroom."

"I'm not working on that," I said quickly. "I've got my beat to cover. Just because I have a Cuban name doesn't mean—"

"Everybody is expected to contribute," he said sharply.

Rumors of Castro's demise and Cuba's collapse sweep Miami with regularity. I have heard them all my life, but lately the winds of change blow stronger and more persistently than ever. Real at last or merely wishful thinking? Perhaps the inevitable was imminent. The bearded one, however, has outmaneuvered and outlasted eight American presidents. I wouldn't count *el líder* out yet.

The paper was reacting to the growing evidence of instability and trouble in Cuba, determined, as usual, not to be caught unaware when it happened. Of course editors and reporters, many long since dead, retired, or senile, had been on top of this about-to-break story for thirty years.

"Things are happening in Cuba," Fred said vigorously. "We're gonna be right on top of them, the transition and its impact on South Florida. This isn't going to be another Watergate."

"I wasn't here then," I said defensively.

"I wish none of us had been. It was an embarrassment. *The Washington Post* beat us on every break in what should have been our story. The burglars were from Miami, the plot was essentially hatched here, and we wound up following the *Post* on everything." His jaw clenched at the thought of the humiliation. "We need to pull this special together in a hurry and the city desk will be spread pretty thin. I expect you to do your part, Britt."

How did this happen? I wondered, as I left his office. I had gone in there to ask for time off my beat to work the missing boys, and wound up arguing to stay on the beat to avoid writing for the special section. How did Fred do that? I had to work fast to come up with an enterprising idea with a Cuban connection, a good story that would take minimal time and research. If I waited until some editor gave me an assignment, it could turn out to be something tedious and time-consuming.

I try to generate my own stories and avoid Cuban issues. Because of my name and family history, people expect me to feel a passion for Cuban politics. I do not. My focus at the moment was on the lost boys.

I met Lottie for coffee in the third-floor cafeteria.

"He hasn't called," she said.

"I'm not surprised. Lottie, what did you expect?"

"I know, I know. But he had such pretty eyes and a great ass."

"I thought you were over all that."

"I am, I am."

She had been assigned to shoot photos for the special section and we brainstormed on what I could do.

She scrunched up her freckled face the way she always does when she's thinking. "How about," she drawled, "Can Cuba Be Saved? From bad architects and greedy developers. They're sure to be the first wave that lands once that island is liberated.

"Seriously, Britt, first thing they'll do is to replace all that great old Mediterranean and Deco architecture with strip shopping malls, fast food joints, and condos. They'll make the Malecón and Varadero into concrete canyons. I just know it. Lookit what they've done to Florida. They'll slice, dice, and pave over Havana till it looks like the Westchester Shopping

Center." She bit into a giant chocolate chip cookie, sharp teeth glinting in the fluorescent lights. "That will be our ultimate revenge on the Cubanos."

"Not a bad story idea," I said, "but I'd rather do something tied into my beat and I have to come up with it fast, before I get some cocka-mamie assignment."

"How about a trend story on how the Marielitos pushed up Miami's crime rate?"

"Politically incorrect," I said glumly, chin in my hand.

"Guess that rules out the Alex Aguirre bombing and other appar-ently politically motivated murders."

"You've got it," I said, then told her what I really wanted to work on.

She munched her cookie and sipped tea, listening intently. "Where in tarnation you think all them kids are at?" she finally said. "It's spread over so much time. You really think they could be related?"

"Don't know, but I sure wanna find out."

"Are they all Dead Heads, or rock star wannabes? Maybe every time some rock group or carnival hits town, kids leave with 'em."

"Don't think so, but it's worth checking." I scribbled a note to scan the papers at the time of the disappearances for local events attractive to teens.

"My big brother ran away maybe twenty, thirty times," Lottie remi-nisced. "I tagged along 'bout a dozen times, didn't want to miss nothing. Got as far as Hidalgo County once. We usually went home when we was hungry. Once we took my daddy's pickup. J.J. wasn't even big enough to see over the steering wheel. I was screaming at the top of my lungs. We landed bottom side up in a ditch, hauled ass, and didn't look back. Swore it wasn't us. My daddy went crazy and accused my mama of letting her low-life cousin Randy drive his truck. That man could wreck a one-car funeral. . . ."

"I don't want to hear about your dysfunctional family," I snapped. "I've got one of my own. I'm trying to think here."

She pouted, then asked, "Where you gonna start with those kids?"

"You tell me. The trouble is that they're at that awkward age. If they were younger, there'd be a nationwide child search. A few years older and we'd have driving records to check. Credit cards, bank accounts, utility bills, passport, marriage, divorce, social security, and phone records."

"And rap sheets, military records, and hunting licenses," she added, "and don't forget about boat registrations and titles."

"Everybody leaves a trail, but these kids haven't lived long enough. Twelve-year-olds don't drive, open checking accounts, or file W-twos."

"They fall right through the cracks. Some people are missing because they OD'd and their friends panicked," she offered.

I nodded, remembering the premed student who buried his teenage date after she overdosed. He eventually led persistent cops to her shallow grave. Most ODs are dumped by the roadside, in the woods, or outside hospital emergency rooms.

"Too young," I said, shaking my head. "And too many."

Trouble waited in the newsroom. Gretchen and Ron Sadler, the paper's political writer, looked far too happy to see me as I returned with a cup of coffee.

Ron, trim, studious, in his thirties, with wavy brown hair and dark eyes, underwent a major metamorphosis recently, transformed after becoming a "political pundit" on a local Sunday morning "Meet the Press"–style TV interview show. The owlish glasses he always wore were replaced by Giorgio Armani frames with nonreflective lenses, in order to make him look less nerdy on camera. His rumpled reporter look is gone. He now wears designer suits and power ties and no longer has his hair cut; he has it styled. He has arrived in the newsroom still wearing traces of television makeup on nights when they weren't even taping. Lottie swears he has become a star in his own mind.

They circled my desk like vultures. "Britt!" Gretchen trilled, relentlessly perky. "We were just talking about you!" This was bad.

"You are aware of the special section on Cuba, aren't you, Britt?" Ron boomed, in his new, hearty anchorman imitation.

"Like everyone else on Planet Earth," I said cheerfully. "I have some ideas about a piece I'd like to do for it." My scrambled thoughts broke like billiard balls and then coalesced. "The impact on Miami, the chaos when Fidel falls, the traffic, the street celebrations, rallies, car caravans, marches." I spit it all out while wondering where the hell it had come from. Panic triggers something creative in my brain cells. "City and county officials must be making contingency plans. I'll shoot you a memo this afternoon." I backed away, as though late for an appointment.

Gretchen waved it off, showing me her manicure. "Not necessary, Britt," she said, still perky. "Not a bad idea though." She pursed her bright red lips thoughtfully. "Maybe we'll assign it to someone. But we have something better in mind for you."

Oh no, exactly what I had feared.

"You're doing a profile of Juan Carlos Reyes," she announced.

"Reyes?" Are they crazy? I wondered. "That's up Ron's alley, isn't it?" I said. "He covers politics." I stared at their faces, didn't like what I saw looking back, and babbled on. "This is the busiest time of the year on my beat. You know how the hottest weather always brings more rapes, multiple murders, and bizarre crimes."

"This is a major piece, Britt." Gretchen spoke as though I should be honored. "We want you to do it."

"Why me? Ron has covered the man in the past, knows him better than anybody on the staff. Reyes hates me." I shook my head firmly. "It'll take a lot of time. Homicides are way up, hookers are being strangled in the south end, seven banks have been robbed in the last ten days. I have a missing persons project I have to finish for the weekend. . . ."

My voice trailed off. Their expressions said a thousand reasons would make no difference. "Why me?" I demanded again.

"He may be the next president of Cuba," Ron said. "He wants to cruise his yacht, the *Libertad*, into Havana Harbor with an entire new government aboard the minute Castro goes."

"And it looks like he's got Washington's blessing," Gretchen added.

"The Cubans may want to have a say in it after forty years of dictatorships," I said.

"Whatever," Ron said impatiently. "We can't do this section without including Reyes."

"You would do it better than anybody," I coaxed. "You've got the right touch."

"You know how he despises the *News*," Gretchen said.

"Right," I said. Reyes regularly bad-mouths the paper on Spanish-language radio and television, accusing the *News* of being pro-Castro because the paper refers to Fidel as Cuba's president instead of the Tyrant and fails to publish daily anti-Castro editorials.

"Well, he won't talk to me," Ron admitted, "or anyone else at *The News*, only you."

"What? He didn't say that. Did he? Did he mention me by name?" No way I believed it. "Why in the world would the man want to talk to me?"

"He doesn't *want* to talk to you, Britt. He doesn't want to talk to anybody," Ron said. "He apparently considers you the lesser evil."

"What the hell is that supposed to mean?"

"He knows we'll write about him, whether he gives us an interview or not." Ron pushed his glasses up on his nose, then folded his arms. "His ego won't let him refuse because he wants some input. . . ."

"But he'd rather not answer questions from a savvy political writer," Gretchen finished.

They exchanged glances. They had it all figured out. "Now remember, Britt," Ron said pompously, "this is no simple interview, it's an in-depth profile; you'll have to talk to his detractors as well."

"I know what a profile is," I snapped. First they force this assignment on me, I thought, then insult me.

"He must want you because you're Cuban," Gretchen said sarcastically. She had dropped the perky act once I was aware they were doing me no favor.

"You don't have much time to cram," Ron said urgently. "The interview is set for two o'clock tomorrow, downtown, at his office, the only time he was available."

"Thanks for the advance notice."

"Couldn't be helped, we've been trying to pin him down for weeks. Don't panic. I'll give you as much help as I can." He was becoming overbearing. "Watch out for Reyes," he warned. "The man is itching for a fight with this newspaper. He has a short fuse and explodes at the slightest provocation. Don't forget anything because you'll never get another shot at him. He's impossible to reach and doesn't return calls, at least to this newspaper.

"And don't forget to genuflect and mention how much you hate Castro at least ten times in the first five minutes or he'll throw you out on your ass."

Oh swell, I thought.

By the time they left me to my misery, my coffee was as cold as an editor's heart.

First I dialed the library. My friend Onnie was on duty and I asked her to print out all the stories she could find on Reyes. "Why you want him?" she asked. "Is he dead?"

"Unfortunately, no." I explained and she commiserated.

"That's not your beat, why doesn't Ron Sadler do it?"

"Long sad story. I'll tell you later."

"Okay, which ones you want?"

"All of them."

"You joking, girl? You got a hand truck? You wanna tie up every printer in here? We got 'em going back thirty years. That man's name has been in this newspaper more than the President of the United States."

"How about the last three years?"

"I'll start printing out," she said, as though I had no idea what I was asking for.

I dialed Lottie on her car phone to bitch and moan. She sounded cheery, giddy in fact, for somebody on the way to photograph a residential canal full of rotting fish killed by a chemical spill.

"Britt, you won't believe this." She had swung by her house to take out Pulitzer, her rescued greyhound. "And guess who drove up? With the most beautiful flowers on God's green earth! He delivered them himself."

"No."

"Yes! Did you ever hear of anything so sweet? What happened the other night was all a misunderstanding. Stosh explained everything."

"That must have been interesting."

"He is the absolute best."

"I hope you're right. Guess what assignment I got?" I told her my sad story.

"Hey, it'll be showcased, the centerpiece in the section and probably the best-read story in the paper."

"You don't understand, I don't want to miss anything on my beat. I don't want to get caught up in exile politics."

"Look at it this way, Britt, instead of standing over a dead body in the hot sun in some ghetto neighborhood surrounded by an unruly crowd and horny, hostile cops, you'll be sitting in Miami's premier luxury office high-rise in a posh suite drinking tea and making small talk with one of the richest, most powerful men in South Florida. Poor pitiful you. I know it's hard to take when you could be fighting off pit bulls, chasing purse snatchers, or joining me at a fish kill, but somebody's gotta do it."

Lottie had a point. Juan Carlos Reyes, savior or would-be dictator? Hero or potential tyrant? He was one of the few exile leaders who had continued to grow in political stature over the years. Who is this guy? The idea began to interest me.

Probably the only reason I had hated it from the start was because the assignment came from Gretchen. "Did I tell you that she said Reyes only agreed to see me because I'm Cuban? I hate that."

"Especially when she wouldn't have her job if she wasn't female," Lottie said archly. "Whatcha gonna wear?"

"What does that have to do with it?" I said irritably. "I have no idea. You sound like Gretchen or my mother."

"Hope I get to shoot the art. He's sexy."

"Sexy? The man is pushing sixty."

"So is Robert Redford. Power is sexy. Nothing I like better than making pictures of rich, powerful men. They may run their corporations with iron fists, but they sure love having their pictures made. I can make them do almost anything for the camera."

"Look who's talking power now." Maybe she was right, first impressions were important. "What should I wear?"

"You have to establish a chemistry to connect," Lottie said, "to get him to open up to you." The signal and her voice faded for a moment as she drove under an overpass. "You're Latin, what do Latin men like?" she was saying.

"Hell, I don't know." I laughed. "Plunging necklines, tight skirts, high heels, and castanets? This isn't a seduction, it's an interview. This is so weird."

"You have to look appealing," she said, "but not sexy, businesslike but not boring."

"This from the lips of a woman who lives in jeans and L.L. Bean blouses."

"That's different," she said smugly. "I make pictures. Oh, Lordy, I must be getting close to the canal I'm looking for. Great guns and little fishes! I can smell it!"

I looked up and saw Mark Seybold, the *News* lawyer, on a direct course for my desk. "Gotta hang up," I said. "To make this day complete, I'm meeting my mother for lunch."

"It could be worse," she said. "I'm there, and you would not believe this. I'm about to put on my hip boots. Your mama'll tell you what to wear."

Mark looked grim. "Hear you're interviewing Reyes tomorrow." He leaned over my desk and dropped his voice. "I'll be vetting your story. Watch out for this guy, he sues at the drop of a hat."

Ryan Battle, the general assignment reporter who sits behind me, stepped off the elevator as I left for lunch. "Heard about your story for the special section." His spaniel eyes reflected concern. "Reyes is macho, Britt. He doesn't like women. I saw him make one cry once at a press conference. How are you going to handle him?"

My mother looked cool, ash-blond hair slicked back, wearing white linen, a short jacket with gold buttons over a matching skirt. Why did clothes suddenly fascinate me? Had this assignment triggered some recessive gene?

She ordered a Caesar salad and a glass of chardonnay.

"What is that?" She scrutinized my skirt.

"Cotton."

"No, this." She plucked something from the fabric and held it up to the light between glistening manicured nails.

"Cat hair," I said, squinting. "Or maybe dog hair."

"Something wrong?" asked the impeccable waiter.

"No," I said, smiling. "I brought it from home."

I was about to make her day. "I need your expert advice about an important interview tomorrow, Mom."

"A job interview?" She perked up.

"No, a story. I'm interviewing Juan Carlos Reyes. What should I wear?"

She looked startled. "Why on earth . . . ," and knocked over her wineglass. The contents splashed across the tablecloth.

The waiter reappeared, murmuring reassuringly as he sopped up the spill.

"Are you all right?" I asked her.

My mother gazed up at him instead of me. "I guess I'm in shock." Her voice was shaky. "My daughter so rarely wants my advice."

"You must have thought this day would never come." I smiled. "What do you think? You're familiar with the contents of my closet."

"I'm sure you know better than I, Britt." This from the woman forever frustrated by my lack of fashion sense, and appalled by my attraction to clothes that I can toss in the washer and wear right out of the dryer.

"I'm serious, Mom."

She glanced at her watch and pushed back her chair. She hadn't even touched her salad.

"I forgot." She spoke crisply, face flushed. "We have a staff meeting at two. If I hurry I can just make it."

"But . . ."

"Sorry, Britt. I just forgot." She brushed my cheek with her lips and left.

I finished my club sandwich, then polished off her salad as well before paying the check. Frustration always makes me hungry.

The note Fred left on my terminal said *See me*.

"On the Reyes piece," he said. "Be sure you to talk to Ron first. Don't pull any punches, but be aware, the man has a hair-trigger temper." He rose from behind his desk and paced the small office. "Keep this under your hat. We never proved a connection, but the last time we ran a story that rubbed Reyes the wrong way, more than a hundred of our vending machines were stolen or trashed. The ones they found were totally destroyed."

"You think he did it?"

Fred's eyes widened and he shrugged. "He'd sue the shit out of anybody who suggested it. But I don't want you to feel intimidated, Britt."

Ron waited at my desk. What the hell is this? I wondered.

"I know how territorial you can be, Britt. But don't be upset if I have to come in and save the story." He smiled condescendingly as he placed a printout on my desk. "Here, I put together a list of tips and questions for you."

"You may have done all that work for nothing, Ron," I said, as I riffled through my messages. "Look at this. Reyes's secretary called. Betcha he's canceling."

"Damn it to hell." He stood there frowning as I punched in the number. I was almost disappointed myself, but now I could get back on the trail of the lost boys.

A receptionist transferred me to Reyes's appointments secretary.

"This is Gilda." The voice sounded competent and dressed for success. It sounded like a crisp snowy blouse and a well-cut suit. What the hell is this clothes thing? I wondered. "You had a two P.M. appointment with Mr. Reyes tomorrow here at his office, Ms. Montero. He's had a change in schedule."

Lifting my eyebrows at Ron, I nodded. He grimaced and punched a fist into his palm.

"The director is working at home tomorrow," Gilda continued. "He would like you to come to his residence." Her voice dropped, taking on a confidential tone. "This is much better, Miss Montero," she whispered. "He can give you more time and it will be much more private."

I WORE A dress I found still in the dry-cleaning bag, waiting at the back of my closet. Ice-blue with a jacket. I put on my antique gold earrings, a gift from my mother on my eighteenth birthday, and stuffed a small tape recorder and half a dozen tapes into my shoulder bag.

Another afternoon thunder boomer had been forecast. Thunderclouds mass daily over the Everglades this time of year. Grass turns to mush underfoot and gardens are drowned by downpours that raise the level of Lake Okeechobee, the Seminole Indian word for "Big Water." A rock levee eighty-five miles long and thirty-six feet high was built to protect the lowlands around the lake after it spilled over during a hurricane back in the thirties and drowned three hundred people.

The tropical depression was out there somewhere in the mid-Atlantic, but here sky and water looked serene. The bay was turquoise satin as I drove across the broad causeway lined by Australian pines and narrow sandy beaches to Reyes's Fairway Island home. Must be fun to come back to this place every night, I thought. Tile rooftops barely visible amid lush foliage gave it the impression of some exotic tropical island.

The gate of the guarded community was manned by armed security, this time it was an off-duty Metro cop whom I recognized.

"What you doing in the high-rent district, Britt? No action for you here."

"I was about to ask you the same question."

"Keeping the streets safe for the rich and famous. Doing my job, earning my pay."

"So am I. Juan Carlos Reyes is expecting me."

"Thought he didn't like newspapers." He shrugged, stepped into the guardhouse, and made a call. Moments later he pushed the button that lifted the security gate and dutifully recorded my tag number as I rolled by.

A more narrow bridge led to speed bumps, estates banked by flower beds, and royal palms and Venetian-style lampposts that added a feeling of Old World charm.

A civilian guard monitored the security gate to Reyes's walled mansion. His guayabera did little to hide the gun bulging in his waistband. He was steely-eyed, younger than I, with smooth olive skin, curly hair, and a military bearing. He asked in Spanish for my identification and did not smile when I answered in English and displayed my press card.

The gates ground open and he pointed me up the wide paved driveway.

Lazy bay breezes caressed my skin as I stepped out of the T-Bird. I could smell the water lapping against the teak dock where Reyes's sleek cabin cruiser, the *Libertad*, was moored. Bougainvillea and Mexican flame vines had crept across the walls. The house resembled a fortress. Lookout turrets faced the wide bay, and I imagined the original owner scanning the horizon for the rumrunners smuggling in his bootleg booze.

Fountains bubbled in a central courtyard surrounding a gigantic ficus tree, and carved stone benches sat in invitingly shaded nooks landscaped with dwarf palms, ferns, and bottlebrush trees.

Who would leave all this opulence to go back to Cuba, even as president? I wondered.

A fawning older man, apparently a butler, was waiting and motioned me to follow. A stroke of luck, I thought, to see Reyes alone at home instead of his busy office. This would all provide color and a richer atmosphere for my story. I hoped no pesky publicist would be present, hovering over his shoulder, primed to prevent his client from misspeaking.

I nearly gasped as we entered Reyes's large, high-ceilinged study. The room rivaled the Oval Office. French doors opened onto a terrace and a splendid bay vista with the Port of Miami in the distance. Heavy crimson drapes, the Cuban flag, and a life-size portrait of Cuban independence hero José Martí hung behind the immense mahogany desk, along with lithographs of old Havana like those I had seen only in museums. Framed photos signed with warm sentiments by politicians and celebrities covered one wall, a rogues' gallery of the rich and powerful. If this was designed to impress a writer who usually spent her time studying posters of America's Most Wanted at police headquarters—it worked. The President of the United States hugged Reyes in one frame. Reyes and Governor Eric Fielding golfed at Indian Creek together in another.

True buds and best friends, I thought with a reporter's cynicism. Since the early days of exile freedom fighting, Reyes had courted the White House and the party in power with major campaign contributions.

Security cameras were mounted in every corner. Were they being monitored? Was I being watched? Did I dare use a bathroom? Stacks of newsletters lay on an ornate glass-topped table. The masthead read *Cubanos Unidos*, "Cubans United," an oxymoron if there ever was one. Miami has more than a hundred Cuban human rights and dissident groups with personalities and strategies ranging from left to far right. They are consumed by passion and politics, *todo el mundo*, fighting among themselves ever more fiercely, their numbers growing as those eager to be major players in a post-Castro regime sense that the time is drawing near.

As I browsed the reading material, the man made his entrance. Tanned and fit, he wore a Savile Row suit of cream-color linen over a pale Egyptian-cotton shirt. The silk tie looked like Versace. His wingtips were soft Italian leather and his belt alligator skin. He moved with a quick assurance and presence, smiling confidently. Though soothing strains of classical music were being piped throughout the house on a central stereo system, I could have sworn the Marine band was playing "Hail to the Chief" somewhere in the background.

His grip was strong and warm, and he held my hand in his a moment too long. His bold eyes were deep-set and hypnotic.

"Ms. Montero," he said softly. "So we meet at last. Please"—he motioned—"sit down." I sank into a comfortable leather chair near his desk while he took his seat behind it.

My eyes swept the grand surroundings. I imagined the behind-the-scenes strategy sessions, the moving and shaking and political scheming that had taken place in this room. "What a wonderful place to live and work. If these walls could talk, what secrets they could tell."

He looked startled, then spread his hands, displaying the mono-grammed initials on the cuffs of his shirt, in a gesture of helpless embar-rassment. It was as though all this opulence had somehow been forced upon him despite his protests.

"I am a simple man, Ms. Montero. A *guajiro*. In my own coun-try I would be tilling the fields this day, a man at peace with Mother Earth."

Somehow I couldn't picture him plodding behind a plow in his two-thousand-dollar suit and wingtips.

He politely acquiesced to my use of a tape recorder and showed no objection to my initial questions. The man was surprisingly sim-patico, given his reputation and my colleagues' dire warnings. We dis-cussed the administration's plan for democracy in Cuba and the groups who advocate negotiations with Castro, ideologies, philosophies, and the work of human rights activists. Then he expressed his ideas regarding the situation at Guantánamo, the futures of Radio and TV Martí, and the embargo.

"It must be tightened," he said passionately. "I want the embargo tightened to the degree that nothing, not even air, reaches Castro. So he suffocates and dies." The heavy gold signet ring glittered on his clenched fist and dark fire danced in his piercing eyes.

He launched into his vision of the future. "The end of Fidel's dictatorial regime began with the failure of communism in Eastern Europe. East Germany, Poland, and Czechoslovakia all provide us with a glimpse of Cuba's future. The winds of freedom," he said, voice rising passionately, as though delivering an emotional speech, "will sweep away the Communists and Cuba will be rebuilt from the ground up."

"What about property rights?" I asked quietly. "Can the exiles who fled long ago reclaim property from those who have lived on it now for decades?"

"Ahh, a practical woman." He smiled, showing perfect, even white teeth. They must be capped, I thought. "That is a sensitive, very complex question, but I promise you that the issue will be settled fairly, in a most democratic fashion. Great change is coming, not only in Cuba, but here. Miami must expand its airport, highway, and port facilities to accommodate the resumption of trade with a free Cuba."

"And what will your role be in that free Cuba?" I tried to look innocent.

His expression became cagey, eyes shrouded, as though nudged by an invisible public relations adviser.

"Whatever role I am privileged to play," he said thoughtfully.

"Financial?" I prodded.

"Most certainly," he replied quickly. "I plan to invest millions when there is a free market in Cuba."

"What about the presidency?"

"I have never said I wanted to be the president of Cuba."

"You would refuse the job?"

He paused as though thinking, fingering a paperweight, a solid cube of polished wood.

"What if you were drafted?"

"The people must choose." He shrugged. "Whatever the people want. We all must make sacrifices for the cause of *Cuba libre.*"

He leaned forward. "I am Cuban first, last, and always. I do not want to be president, do not seek the presidency. I will serve only if the Cuban people demand it."

Maybe I was cynical, but I suspected that if they didn't, he just might kick the crap out of them.

The butler appeared at that moment to serve small, sweet guava *pasteles* and delicious *café cubano* in delicate bone china demitasse cups, far more elegant than the Styrofoam to which I am accustomed. I watched the butler, the same refined man who led me to Reyes's study, as he performed the task unobtrusively and efficiently. I held my question until he left the room.

"Why does your butler wear a gun in a shoulder holster?"

Reyes did not seem rattled by the question or impressed by my keen powers of observation.

"Exile has not been easy, Ms. Montero. For many years I was forced to wear a bulletproof vest at all times, to protect my own life. My name always surfaced near the top of the death lists circulated by Castro agents. Security is even more paramount today, now that Fidel has become a desperate man. All those in my employ are trusted members of my own security force."

I nodded. "On the more personal side, have you ever been married?"

"No." He smiled wistfully, leaning back in his chair. "My passion has always been Cuba," he said softly.

I sighed. Where had I heard that one before?

The most important questions had been covered and we were

chatting so comfortably that I could not resist treading on dangerous ground. Perhaps the jolt of *café cubano* made me reckless.

"I don't understand your animosity toward our newspaper."

"Animosity? On my part?" His face darkened. "I can show you documentation of the distortions, comments taken out of context, all part of your newspaper's campaign of attacks, plots, and attempts to discredit me and my work, a personal vendetta." His voice rose and he gestured angrily. "We who have been forced into exile by Fidel Castro's tyranny refuse to accept the tyranny of racism and bigotry promoted by your newspaper. Those who operate your newspaper scheme constantly to destroy my credibility. I denounce them."

I tried not to flinch as he rose from his chair, shook his fist, and picked up speed. "I denounce them! They try to destroy me because I repudiate them and their views. They choose to ignore the holocaust taking place ninety miles from these shores!"

South Beach's aging Holocaust survivors might think his use of the word a bit strong.

"Believe me, Mr. Reyes, no one at the paper has the time—or any reason—to plot against you." If he had me thrown out now, I still had enough for my story, I thought. "If you could only visit the newsroom on deadline, you would understand."

His smile was sardonic as he sank back into his comfortable chair. "My enemies at your newspaper are not those who work under the pressure of deadlines. You will find them in positions of power, in the boardroom. They issue the orders."

I sighed, remembering Reyes's marathon rants on Spanish-language radio, sipped my coffee, and wondered again about surveillance cameras in the bathrooms.

"You are very thorough. Obviously you will speak to others who know me."

I nodded, relieved that he seemed calmer.

"Who might they be?"

I shrugged. "Torriente, Masferrer, maybe Jorge Bravo."

He waved the last name away like a pesky insect. "*Viejo loco*, he has troubles of his own right now. He is nothing."

"He may well go to jail this time," I agreed, pleased that the conversation had taken a new direction. The Coast Guard had caught the aging would-be commando thirty-five miles off the Cuban coast in a fishing boat armed with machine guns, grenade launchers, assault rifles, and twenty thousand rounds of ammo.

Bravo was currently free on bond, charged with possessing six unregistered machine guns. "He could face a maximum ten years and a quarter-million-dollar fine," I said.

"The man is crazy." Reyes's index finger waggled in a circular motion toward his head. "Terribly misguided. He should stick to selling vacuum cleaners."

"Is that what he does?" Since being repatriated from a Cuban prison after the failed Bay of Pigs invasion, Bravo had spent most of his time organizing disastrous anti-Castro missions.

"Forget him," Reyes said disdainfully. "If you must speak to someone, why not the President? Is he good enough? Or Governor Fielding?"

I smiled nervously as the butler quietly cleared away the coffee service.

"This is the third time we have spoken recently," Reyes commented, changing gears. "What was that first call?" His brow furrowed in thought, reminding me of Ricardo Montalbán. "Ah, yes, the unfortunate departure of Alex Aguirre. Do the police know the bomber?" He folded his hands expectantly, awaiting my answer.

"I haven't spoken to the detectives today," I said. "But not as far as I know."

He shook his head solemnly. "How quickly the world forgets. And the runaway, the young man? Has he returned home?"

"No, but I'm working on new developments. There seem to be a number of missing teenagers who all fit the same pattern."

"Incredible," he murmured politely. "Your work must lead you down many fascinating paths."

"Including this one." I flashed a friendly smile. "Shouldn't Ron Sadler be sitting here with you? I'm not a political writer."

He looked slightly surprised and paused for a moment. "But we are connected, you and I." His voice dropped to a more intimate tone. "History binds us together. We have so much in common."

"Actually," I said skeptically, "we have little in common."

He shook his head indulgently. "You are so like your father."

I sat with my mouth open, stunned, wondering if I had heard right.

"Surely you knew." He reached across his desk and pushed the stop button on my tape recorder. "Tony Montero and I were boyhood companions in Camagüey. We served together as young men, side by side, guerrillas in the Sierra Maestra." His eyes took on a nostalgic look, as though steeped in memories. He pursed his lips. "We shared a prison cell at the Isle of Pines. We were *compañeros*."

I caught my breath, fumbling, trying to collect my thoughts. "I had no idea. . . ." A thousand questions crowded my mind.

He gazed at me intently, the softest of smiles playing around his sensual lips. "And Catherine. How is your mother? The beautiful Catalina. I see you favor blue as she always did."

"You know my mother?" The image of worldly journalist, the veneer of sophistication I had tried so hard to achieve, crumbled.

"Ahhh," he sighed, eyes alight. "No one could dance the *merengue* like your mother."

My pen fell to the floor and my eyes crossed as I bent to pick it up. *Merengue*? My mother? Were we both thinking of the same woman here? Reyes could not have flabbergasted me more had he announced that he had killed JFK.

"You have her grace," he continued. He perused me thoughtfully. "You possess so many of your mother's qualities. *Rubia, muy delicada*. But I have not heard you laugh. Her laugh always had a sound to it. *La música*."

I cleared my throat, puzzled. "She never mentioned you. I had no idea you knew my father. I was only three when he was killed."

He nodded, expression pained. "I was there. We were captured. He died for Cuba. A hero. A martyr. I was to be next, but managed to escape two nights later. I have not seen Catalina for years, but I know she is well. Friends keep me informed. And, of course, I have always followed your career with great interest."

"You knew who I was? That I worked for the paper?"

"*El mundo es muy chiquito.* There are no secrets in Miami. I see my friend Tony in you, too. A writer—what he always wanted. He would be proud. He always kept a journal."

"I've never read anything he wrote," I said eagerly. This was all news to me.

"A pity." He looked dismayed. "Catalina never shared his letters with you?"

"No." Why hadn't she? I wondered.

Reyes stared at the ceiling, as though trying to remember. "Now, do I still possess Antonio's diary or was it given to your mother?"

"What diary?"

Hand to his forehead, he concentrated. "I am trying to recall what happened to the diary of your father. He kept it faithfully, in prison. I may have it. It belongs to the people." Conviction strengthened his voice. "It should be published."

"You're sure it exists?"

"Without doubt. I was in prison with Antonio for many months. No day passed that he did not speak of you and your mother and write for hours in that book of his. It survived, passed hand to hand after his . . . execution. His words kept hope alive for so many. Why can't I recall its whereabouts now? Perhaps locked in an old trunk with other mementos of those times. In a storage room here, or at my office. I will have my assistant try to locate it." He snatched up a gold Mont Blanc pen and scribbled a quick note on a memo pad.

I was thrilled.

"Or"—he paused—"was it given to your mother?" He looked at me expectantly.

"I didn't even know it existed until now," I said, shrugging, bewildered.

"I'm sure I would have if my mother had it. She would have said. . . ." Or would she?

"I hope you can find it," I said with feeling. The book could be my bridge to the past, to the father lost so long ago. The possibility of seeing something written in his own hand, reading his words and learning his thoughts, thrilled me.

"He kept his diary like *The Gulag Archipelago* of Solzhenitsyn. When Cuba is free, the traitors whose names he wrote there must be tried for war crimes," Reyes exclaimed. "This book is prima facie evidence. The world should know their names. It must be published, if it still exists."

"I hope it does," I told him.

"Leave it to me," he said reassuringly. "We will find it."

Reluctantly I steered the conversation back to our interview, switched on the recorder, and cleared up a few last questions, but my heart and mind were racing. My mother's angry silence about my father had frustrated me all my life.

"Of course I will be available to answer any further questions," Reyes said. "And I will call you at once when I succeed in finding Antonio's diary."

He walked me to the arched entranceway and we shook hands again. His eyes were alert and intense.

"Your earrings," he commented.

"My mother gave them to me."

"Yes." He laughed with genuine pleasure. "Did she tell you where she got them?"

"No," I said. "I think they're antiques."

"Ask her," he said, reminiscing. "About the days when they were crafted for a beautiful woman by the finest jeweler on the *Calle de Oro* in Havana." His eyes were warm. "I am so proud," he said, "as though you were my own daughter. You may have been born in Miami, but your heart is Cuban. Never forget your *cubania*. Remember me, please, to dear Catalina."

"I'm sure she'll be pleased that you thought of her." I smiled serenely and strolled sedately to my car, aware of his eyes on my back. The setting sun, a scarlet disk, shimmered on an indigo bay. The view was spectacular but a whiff of something bad, a sewer smell, stung my nostrils. Something blowing in off the bay. I pulled out of the driveway and proceeded through the electric gate. The guards had gone. Reyes stood alone, still watching, in front of his magnificent home.

The tires of the T-Bird crunched out onto the road. I rolled around the corner past the stately royal palms, out of his sight into the gentle dusk, then floored it and roared into the twilight like a bat out of hell.

8

I CIRCLED THE parking lot, my frustration intensifying. My mother's convertible was not in its usual spot. No one answered the doorbell, so I pounded with the metal knocker until a door down the hall inched open and a reproving neighbor peered out. Where the hell was she when I needed answers? I slipped my card under her door and took the three flights of stairs down, too hyper to wait for the elevator. Disappointed and annoyed, I didn't want to go home. All that would make me feel alive was sex or work, and the only man I wanted was a thousand miles away. Thank God for the brightly lit newsroom.

Ron Sadler, who rarely worked late, was lurking.

He read the frustration on my face.

"I knew it! How bad was it?" he cried, scarcely concealing his jubilation. "He went crazy, right? Were you kicked the hell out?" He glanced at his watch. "Christ, where have you been all this time? Any way to salvage the piece?"

Ryan and two other reporters watched eagerly from their desks.

"Actually, Ron, I've spent the entire afternoon with Juan Carlos Reyes." I smiled sweetly. "Great interview. The man is absolutely charming."

Ron's eyes bugged behind his nonreflective lenses as his mouth opened in disbelief. "You're shitting me." I could have sworn he was wearing pancake makeup.

I opened my bag, spilling the used tapes onto my desk. "The man's a pussycat." I shrugged. "Didn't duck a single question."

"Reyes?" Ryan broke the silence. "The one who punched out that CNN reporter?"

"Did you ask the tough questions, Britt?"

"All of them, Ron," I said lightly. "I guess the police beat teaches you how to deal with people." I took that shot because he and Gretchen are among those in the newsroom who look down on my job. They are so wrong; it has everything any writer could want. People stories, true grit, and heroes.

Before he left for a television taping, the two of them huddled across the newsroom, heads together.

I tried calling my mother, but her phone rang unanswered. Her machine didn't even pick up. Where was she? A faint rumble, a vibration underfoot, signaled that the presses were rolling with the next edition. In an uncertain world, the newspaper is a constant, something to hang on to.

Before tackling the tedious job of transcribing the tapes, I called Mrs. Goldstein and asked her to take Bitsy out. Seth answered, eager to know if there had been any murders and asking when he could come to the office again. He promised to give Bitsy a good workout. "Remember, she has short legs," I warned. Then I checked my calls and found an urgent message from Lottie.

"You won't believe this!" she wailed.

"What?" I asked wearily.

"My flowers . . ."

"I know, I know. The most beautiful flowers on God's green earth. Lottie, I've got—"

"Listen!" she demanded. "I was adding some water and an aspirin today, you know, to give 'em a little boost and make 'em last longer. Guess what I found?"

"A snake?" Shoppers in several local garden departments had been bitten by poisonous snakes curled up in the potted plants, but I'd never heard of one in a florist's arrangement.

"Worse! I'd rather be snake-bit. It was a card. Guess what it says?"

"Lottie, I can't stand this. Just tell me. I'm hungry and frustrated. My life is passing before my eyes. I'm in no mood to play guessing games."

"Let me read it: *'With Deepest Sympathy for your loss. Good-bye Uncle Harry, we'll miss you.'* Signed, *'Tom, Adrienne, and the kids.'*"

"Who the hell are they?" My right eyelid twitched and I felt the early drumroll of a headache.

"The bereaved! The poor souls who paid for the flowers that shyster stole from some funeral home. They looked a little peaked when he gave 'em to me."

"Oh? I thought you said they were the most beautiful flowers on God's green earth. I could have sworn you said that. Maybe they fell off an ambulance he was chasing."

"Wait a minute," she said. "His office! That's right. His damn office backs up on Evergreen Cemetery. I'm so mad I could bite myself!"

I wanted to say I couldn't believe Stosh would do such a thing, but I didn't. In fact, I could picture him climbing the fence.

Lottie shot art of Reyes the following day, and I met her afterward for a late lunch in the *News* cafeteria.

An apron-clad chef looked bored behind a steam table of peculiar-looking tacos topped by wilted lettuce. He wore a giant sombrero. I blinked when I saw him, then realized it must be Mexican Day. The cafeteria operators had resorted to themes to lure back employees who persist in leaving the building to eat somewhere, anywhere, else. They never try the most effective theme, good food. I once discovered carrots in the spaghetti sauce on Italian Day. Even Lottie, who loves Tex-Mex and laces everything liberally with Tabasco, eyed the taco special with suspicion. "Wanna go halvsies on a grilled cheese and tomato sandwich?" she murmured.

"I'm gonna stick to the soup." I halfheartedly tossed some saltines onto my tray. "What's the word from the Polish Prince?"

"That sidewinder." She sneered. "It was the back end of bad luck the day I set eyes on him. Don't git me started."

"Sorry. How'd things go with Reyes?"

She looked pleased. "Made a great portrait of him on his yacht, the *Libertad*. Beautiful boat, but he's mad as hell at the city. Sewer pipe must have backed up and the smell behind his place is rank." Her eyes danced as she settled in the chair opposite me. "Reyes came on to you, didn't he?"

"Hell, no," I said.

"Well, that man is definitely hot to trot." She batted her eyes coquettishly as she sipped her tea. "All he did was ask questions about you. He wanted to know everything."

"Did he mention my mother?"

"Your mother?" Her freckled face screwed into a puzzled scowl.

I nodded. "He knew her and my father, years ago. The man practically drools at the mention of her name."

"Didn't know he was a friend of the family."

"Join the club. It was a surprise to me." I told her everything.

"Think he and your mama were sweeties years ago, a little hanky-panky? He had to be gorgeous then. He ain't bad now." She leaned back in her chair, eyes wide. "Lordy, Britt, that rich and powerful hombre might be your daddy."

"Oh, swell, thank you very much. My mother thanks you, too."

"Better than a sharp stick in the eye," she said, chewing. "What's to hate about having a real live politically connected millionaire in the family? You could be Cuba's first daughter or, if he has his way, the crown princess. Who would mind being a tadpole in that gene pool? You notice that strong jaw? Won't find no narrow-eyed, inbred young 'uns there." She bit into the second half of her sandwich.

"Be serious." I sighed, pushing away my soup bowl. "I'd give anything to read my father's diary. I've always felt we were connected."

"What's your mama say?"

"Can't even find her. I've been trying to reach her since last night."

"That's sure a turnabout," she said. "Who knows what happened all those years ago? What if it wasn't Tony Montero?" Once Lottie locks onto a subject she's as dogged as a pit bull with his teeth in a bone. "Your real daddy could be some furniture salesman from Atlanta—or the next *presidente* of Cuba."

"Come on, Lottie, you make my family history sound like some soap opera or one of those doorstop novels. I've just always wanted to know what happened to my father, what happened back then, and why my mother is so uptight."

"Ain't no future in the past," she said, blotting mustard off her lower lip with a paper napkin.

"Ignoring it is like running from your own shadow. I help solve other people's mysteries all the time but I've neglected my own, and it's important to me."

She nodded. "Gotcha. Photographers' kids have no baby pictures. Shoemakers' kids got no shoes. But hell all Friday, Britt, tons of folks have no clue who their daddies were and do just fine. At least most of 'em." She paused and looked pensive, probably recalling a recent high-profile case, a man, adopted at birth, who searched for his biological parents, tracked them to Miami, and beat them to death with a pipe wrench.

"It's hard to explain," I said. "Mine left a big void in my life, yet he's always there. As though he's trying to tell me something. Like we are one, always together."

"That 'ud give me the bijeebees."

"It's now or never," I said. "Time is running out. The world he lived in is disappearing fast. So are the people who knew him. They're not getting any younger."

"None of us are. But I'm with you, Britt, if there's any way I can help."

I smiled. I've always wanted a sister like Lottie.

• • •

I called the White House and was told by the political director that Juan Carlos Reyes was considered a loyal party member and fund-raiser and a valuable spokesman for the Cuban-American community. The President had met him during his first campaign swing through Florida. Now Reyes was a member of the Committee to Re-elect the President.

I also talked to the assistant secretary of state for Inter-American affairs, the former chief of the U.S. Interests Section in Havana, three Cuban-American congressmen from South Florida, and a spokesman for the Cuban-American Foundation. Despite pointed questions and prodding, the worst anybody would say on the record was that he seemed to have an ego problem. Don't all politicians?

I searched property, corporate, and court records. Reyes's holdings were vast, from a former upstate training camp for would-be freedom fighters, to shopping malls, a downtown arcade, office buildings, apartment houses, and supermarkets. All his business partners seemed legit, without criminal records. He seemed to sue more than he was sued, but the lawsuits he was involved in were no more than those generated by the average tycoon.

A rough draft of my story ran long, a hundred twenty inches, and I wasn't comfortable that Ron and Gretchen insisted on seeing it before I had time to tighten and polish. I had still had no feedback from them when Fred Douglas stopped by my desk.

"Good job, Britt. Your piece on Reyes will be the centerpiece of the section. Needs some trimming, but I've never seen Reyes so quotable. Seemed almost human. Lots of things in there I didn't know about him." He looked at me speculatively. "We should do this more often. Swap reporters around on different beats from time to time, bring in somebody with new eyes."

Oh no. "Once I wrap this up," I said quickly, before he got any ideas, "I have to get back out on the beat and finish my story on those missing teenagers."

He nodded absently, forgetting his former reservations.

• • •

Soon after, Ron Sadler sidled up to my desk like a crab. "Nice piece." He hesitated. "Reyes never talked for publication before about his plans to seek Cuban membership in the free trade agreement or his Bay of Pigs experiences. How'd you worm that stuff out of him?"

Lowering his voice, he gave me a smarmy grin. "What'd you do, sleep with the guy?"

I resisted taking a swat at him, didn't want makeup on my knuckles. "Ron, do you sleep with every woman you interview?"

"That's entirely different," he said self-righteously. "I'm a married man, with a family. You know, you're ambitious and unattached. These macho Latinos always go for younger women."

"Get away from my desk! Talking to you gives me whiplash." Heads turned as my voice rose.

He glanced around, embarrassed, aware we were being watched. "Don't get pissed. You know me, Britt. I was just kidding."

"You heard me! Beat it, before I slap you silly."

He slunk off and went to confer with Gretchen.

Later I told Lottie what he had said.

"I'll be go-to-helled," she said, "he sounds like a good ol' boy from twenty years ago. What's happened to him?"

"I dunno, Lottie. He used to be a nice guy."

"TV sure has changed that fellow. I never trust a man whose manicure is better than mine."

I took my transcripts and a printout home, to avoid further aggravation. No way. A stranger's car occupied my parking space. I unlocked my mailbox hoping for a letter from Kendall McDonald and found somebody else's mail instead. Mostly junk. Where was mine? Was some pervert pawing through my new Victoria's Secret catalog? Was my love letter from Kendall McDonald being held up to a light or steamed open by some voyeur? At least my darling pets would be glad to see me. I stepped inside and called warmly to them.

Bitsy had ripped Billy Boots's favorite catnip toy to shreds all over my freshly cleaned carpet. Billy Boots, obviously stressed as a result, had upchucked a fur ball and what looked like the remains of my spider plant. The sluggish room air conditioner seemed to be blowing hot air instead of cool and my bedroom was a furnace. Too late to disturb the Goldsteins. No repairs could be done at this hour.

I played my messages. No word from my mother or McDonald. I fed the animals and foraged in the freezer until I gave up and simply stood in front of it with the door open. The only cool place in the apartment. I would have remained indefinitely except for Bitsy, who brought me her leash and skittered around my feet, eager to go out.

The night air was a muggy slap. The depression had developed into a tropical storm somewhere between Africa and the Caribbean but nothing stirred here, not even a wisp of a breeze. Miami's late August is superheated, supercharged, an atmosphere in which people have been known to commit murder for the seat closest to the floor fan.

New York and Chicago have winter windchill factors but we have a summer discomfort index. Computed by the combined heat/humidity peaks, it currently hovered at 111.

The little red ribbon in Bitsy's topknot hung in tatters, probably from the skirmish in which the catnip mouse was decapitated. What was there between my mother and Reyes? I wondered. And where the hell was she?

When we got back, I tried her home and office numbers again unsuccessfully. My appetite gone, I skipped dinner. Instead I filled a glass with ice and a lime twist, poured in some tonic water and a tumbler of gin. I sipped it slowly, savoring the sweet, crisp taste on my tongue as I worked on the Reyes story under the ceiling fan in my bedroom. I cut about nine inches, but my heart wasn't in it.

I finished the drink, put the story aside, and slipped into a cotton nightgown. Hoping for a nonexistent breeze, I opened the windows wide, checked my gun, and slipped it beneath the pillow beside me, in the event that anything unexpected came through my windows in the night.

I dreamed I was aboard a sightseeing boat cruising Biscayne Bay after dark, music and laughter skipping across the water. Suddenly gunfire broke out and passengers hit the deck. The shooting stopped as abruptly as it had started. No one was hurt and the music and laughter resumed. Another Miami night. I strolled down a narrow ship's corridor when a boy tumbled out of the shadows and sprawled in my path. "It's me," he said. "I'm shot.

"No," he protested, as I reached for him, "you'll get blood on your dress." I gathered him up in my arms and began to run toward the voices for help. As we emerged on deck, the man with the noose was silhouetted in the moonlight. Surely he could save this bloody child, but ignorant people blocked my way, smiling and staring. My burden was staggering. I felt the blood. No matter how I tried, there was no way to push past or move around them in time. His face was in shadow. Was it the man with the noose—or was it Juan Carlos Reyes? I sat up in bed, wondering for a moment where I was. Laughter wafted through the open window from people passing. I twisted and turned on sweaty sheets until dawn.

NO INTRUDER CREPT through my window in the night. A Coconut Grove homeowner, the outraged victim of three prior break-ins, was not so lucky. When a thief climbed through his window at 3:30 A.M., he killed the man with an ax.

A second burglar escaped, with the irate ax-wielder, a thirty-five-year-old electronics engineer, hot on his heels. He shattered the driver's side window before the getaway car careened off. "He got some pretty good swipes in there," a detective said admiringly, when I arrived at the scene.

"I'd had it," the mild-mannered engineer told me wearily. I knew the feeling. His hair was straight and dark brown, his nose well formed, his eyes clear, with a hollow look at the moment. "I'm not a violent man," he said quietly. "But they'd wiped me out three times. They must have backed up a truck last time." He surveyed the carnage in his living room. "This wouldn't be such a mess if I'd only had a pistol. I need to buy a gun," he announced.

"Or a burglar alarm system," I suggested. "I've got a gun, but it's never been handy when I really needed it."

We stood in his bloody living room, this husky stranger and I, talking like old friends. He was right about one thing. Nothing would ever get that carpet clean again, and the walls and ceiling probably would have to be repainted. Even a guitar standing in the corner had been spattered.

"I'm Hal." He extended his hand.

"Britt," I said. His skin was warm, the fingers smooth and gentle. Hard to believe the damage they had wrought. Our eyes connected. Weird. It always is. Some women frequent singles bars or place personal ads; I seem to meet men at murder scenes. Tour boat captain Curt Norske and I met over the corpse of a long-missing person, still strapped behind the wheel when his rusted car was found in the bay. For that matter, I first connected with McDonald in a sleazy bar with blood on the floor as he tracked a shooter through a middle-of-the-night spree. No wonder my love life is a disaster. I should know better.

A proximity to sudden death feeds a basic, primal urge in the human animal for a life-affirming act, like sex. One of Mother Nature's little safeguards to insure survival of the species. Sex after death is great—so long as the death isn't yours.

"I'm sorry we had to meet under these circumstances," Hal was saying earnestly.

"I'm sure your living room doesn't always look like this," I said comfortingly.

Still barefoot, he wore blue-jean cutoffs and an open shirt, still unbuttoned. His eyes were brown; so was the curly hair visible on his chest. The pecs weren't bad. Hal was in excellent shape, as the hapless burglar had learned.

He rubbed his neck as though it was sore. "The cops aren't saying much. Am I in trouble?"

"Did you ever see the guy before?"

"Never. Not until he came at me in the dark."

Instinctively I believed him. "Sounds justifiable to me, but you never know. At any rate, there'll probably be an inquest. I'd bring a lawyer." The voice of my own bitter experience.

"A lawyer! Jesus. I was minding my own business, asleep in my own bed." He must have seen something in my expression. "Alone," he added. "Then this guy breaks in and I have to hire a lawyer."

Poor Hal, I thought, driving back downtown. The burglar's family will probably sue the hell out of him for loss of the dead man's future income as a thief.

I was eager to pursue the missing boys—and talk to my mother. We usually spoke every day. This was out of character for her. Could it be because of Reyes? Could she possibly have my father's diary? If Reyes had it, I hoped he'd come up with it before the special section ran on Sunday. My story was fair, not a puff piece or a hatchet job, but he already felt burned, right or wrong, by the press, and was gun-shy.

Such people often take offense at an innocent word or phrase. On my beat, a story may solve a crime, capture a fugitive, or make a cop look heroic. But are cops ever happy? No. Some high-ranking paper shuffler sees the name of one of his troops in the newspaper and is jealous. He chews out his lieutenant, who browbeats his sergeant, who bawls out the street cop, who abuses the reporter. Shit tends to run downhill and spread out.

A positive trait is that cops don't hold grudges forever. They know life is too short. What about Reyes? I wondered. All I usually worry about is fairness and accuracy. But if the story somehow pissed Reyes off, would he hold my father's diary hostage? Nonsense, I thought. No friend of my father's would do that.

Back at the paper I tried my mother again. She was out, a receptionist said, but expected back in the office shortly. So she was all right.

I dug into the story about Hal and his night visitor. The cops leaned toward justifiable homicide, but the State Attorney's office would make the final decision. Meanwhile, I learned that the dead burglar had a buck knife in his belt, cocaine in his system, and an extensive rap sheet. The largess of Florida's early-release program had recently allowed him to walk free after serving six months of a five-year prison sentence. Not a pleasant person to meet for the first time at 3 A.M. in your living room. I suspected that Hal would call me. I almost hoped he would.

I hit the SEND button, moved the story into the editing system, and called Charles Randolph's parents. After the print and television coverage, Crime Stoppers had offered a thousand-dollar reward and Vera Verela's manager had announced that the singer would post a five-thousand-dollar reward for information that led to Charles's safe return.

"Detective Soams called," Cassie said, excitement ringing in her voice. "He's following up some leads. He's interested in the case again."

Publicity does tend to spark official interest, I thought cynically.

The Randolphs recognized none of the names, parents, or addresses of the other boys. What I needed was a common denominator, a place, time, or individual the boys' paths had crossed. Establishing a link might start to make some sense of their disappearances—but I had nothing.

Eagerly I called Soams about the leads that had so excited the Randolphs. The tips he was checking looked lame, he admitted. There were unsubstantiated sightings from a number of people, mostly teenagers, who all claimed to know someone who had seen the boy since his disappearance. But when pressed to produce the actual witnesses each person would refer him to someone else, to another and then another and finally to nothing. The trails all evaporated, as though young Charles Randolph had become one of those will-o'-the-wisp urban myths never traceable to a source.

Edwin Clower expected my call and we arranged to meet. He sold and serviced business machines. His secretary greeted me and showed me to his office. I will never understand men, I thought. Why would he dump Vanessa for this round little woman with a dour mouth and sensible shoes?

Ruggedly handsome, with reddish-blond hair, gray eyes, and a firm handshake, Clower wore a short-sleeved white shirt and a tie. His suit jacket hung behind the door.

There was a framed family portrait of him, Vanessa, and their children, on his desk. Had he placed it there for my benefit?

"Let's grab some coffee," he said, and we strolled out onto the sun-blasted pavement and into a small luncheonette two doors away in the same strip center.

He ordered decaf as we slid into a plastic-covered booth.

"Drinking messed up my stomach for a while there," he explained, patting his midsection. "Got so I can't even tolerate more than two cups a day. I'm in AA now." His eyes fastened on the notebook I had removed from my purse. "What made you get into this now? I'm surprised you're interested after all this time."

"Your ex-wife. She called after the story on the Randolph boy."

"That's Vanessa," he said with a sad pride. "She refuses to give up on David. Gave up on me a long time ago, but she won't quit on him. She's one helluva good mother."

"She said you're a good father."

"She said that?" He looked interested. The waitress delivered our coffees and he stirred sugar into his. "What else did she say?"

"That David got angry and took off after you two quarreled. That his disappearance went unreported for two days because she thought he was safe with you and you thought he'd gone home to her."

"That's about it," he said grimly. "I had been promising him a canoe trip, a long weekend, just the two of us upstate, along the Peace River. We got into it when I told him we had to postpone 'cuz I had other plans."

"Doing what?"

He leveled a pained gaze. "Guess Vanessa told you I was seeing someone."

"Your secretary?"

He nodded. "Janine. We were planning a ski trip instead, to Colorado. David got really pissed. We had just gone through our first Christmas since the divorce. It wasn't pretty. The kids were having a tough time adjusting."

"Have you remarried?" He wasn't wearing a ring.

"Hell, no." He looked alarmed at the thought.

"Are you and she . . . ?"—I tilted my head back toward his office—"still . . . ?" One of the secret pleasures of reporting is that you can ask questions other people are too polite to ask.

"Hell, no," he said. "You thought—? That's not Janine. That's Sue Ann. Janine quit, got a job over at South Florida Motors. Last I heard she had a serious thing going with the owner. We busted up not long after David disappeared. The woman has no kids. Pity 'em if she ever does. Totally self-absorbed. Couldn't understand why I was so upset. Raised holy hell every time I talked to Vanessa. Even accused David and his mother of faking the whole thing to get my attention." He smiled ironically, shaking his head. "I would have given anything if she'd been right, that Vanessa and David had made the whole thing up. What a laugh. Neither one wanted any part of me at the time. I screwed up bad. Drinking, my business suffered, had to downsize."

I leaned forward, wanting him to focus. "Do you recall what David said before he left that night? Anything that might give us a clue as to exactly where he was going?"

"I've been back over it all a thousand times." He ran his fingers through his hair, teeth on edge. "It's all my fault. If it hadn't been for me, we wouldn't have been divorced. If only I had stopped him from leaving that night . . ."

"You can't keep beating yourself up."

"Why not?" He shrugged hopelessly. "Vanessa will never forgive me. I'll never forgive myself. I keep saying, keep praying, he's alive and that he will come home. Then maybe I can start to make amends. If we never see him again, if he's gone for good, so's my only chance." His face started to collapse in on itself.

I averted my eyes, pretending not to see his painful struggle for control. "There might be something you didn't pick up on at the time, some small thing he said that could be relevant."

Clower gulped a deep breath and cleared his throat. When he spoke his voice was strained but strong, with a hint of the irate. "Said I wasn't his father any more and he never wanted to see me again. And this was a kid—" His face colored with anger. "I had Dolphin tickets on the fifty-yard line for the two of us on Sunday afternoon. That's what he walked out on."

"Did you go to the game?"

"What?"

"Did you use the football tickets? Did you go?"

He stared into his cup. "Took Janine. She didn't like sports much."

"What did David take with him?"

"Nothing. He left everything, his overnight bag, his toothbrush. Even a schoolbook his mother had sent with him. He was behind in history. You have to understand, all this happened in the heat of an argument. He tore out the door, slammed it so hard the walls rattled. I was mad as hell, yelling at him to come back. Last I saw, he was crying, running toward one hundred and seventy-first street. We hadn't had dinner yet. We'd sent out to Little Caesar's for one of their giant combo pizzas. I figured he wouldn't want to miss that and he'd be back. After it came I kept it warm in the oven for a couple of hours. He never showed, so I assumed he'd caught the bus and gone home."

"You didn't call? It's a long trip back to Surfside. He would have had to change buses twice."

"I know, I know. It was a chilly night and he didn't even take his jacket. He was hungry. But he was a big boy and he'd made the trip over by bus once, with his sister, to surprise me. How was I to know he didn't have any money in his pocket? His mother didn't tell me until later. I shoulda called but I was in no mood. Vanessa had been after me to spend more time with the boy. It was another failure in my cap. I was in no mood to hear about it. Did Vanessa tell you about the reward?"

I told him she had. "She say anything else about me?" He looked like a heartsick teenager. His eyes had the appearance of someone whose constant companion was misery.

His ex-wife believed his story. So did I.

I drove down to Clower's house and parked the T-Bird in his

empty driveway. No one was home. I walked to the front door and stood there for several moments, then stepped off the porch and headed toward one hundred and seventy-first street the way the missing boy did that night, looking around at what he saw, trying to see through his eyes, except that he was tearful, angry, running through a dark and chilly night four years ago and I was squinting through scalding sunlight on a brilliant summer day. The street, lined with modest homes, looked as though it hadn't changed substantially in the past four years. No one would have heard the boy's cries if he had been dragged into a car on that cold night when most people had their windows closed. But he could have been accosted or picked up anywhere between here and Surfside. I wondered if the detective had canvased the bus drivers on duty that night. Probably too late to do any good now.

I gazed up at a sky full of low, fast-moving clouds as though for a sign. "Where are you, David?" I murmured aloud. "Where did you go?"

THE DRIVE TO Coconut Grove
took twenty minutes. Emily and Michael Kearns operated a small
plant nursery from their home. She was small and dark-haired, with
a nervous tic that reminded me of myself under deadline pressure.
Balding and overweight, with small mean blue eyes, he looked like
a beer drinker to me. Tension crackled across their living room. It
quickly became clear that Emily had interceded with her husband,
a strict disciplinarian, to allow their boys to attend the carnival in
the Grove the night they vanished. Now she had to cope not only
with the disappearance of her sons but with the enduring animosity of their father.

As we spoke she reached down to absently stroke a cat the color
of smoke who rubbed against her ankles as though sensitive to her
mood. When the animal warily approached, sniffed at my shoes, and
stared up with huge golden eyes, Kearns muttered, "Will you git that
rodent out of here? Can't you see he's bothering her?"

"Oh no," I said quickly. "He smells my cat, Billy Boots. It's all
right. I love animals."

Kearns looked disgusted and mentioned once more that his boys "never would have run off" had their mother listened to him. "She let 'em run wild. Spoiled, that's what they are," he said.

The older boy, Michael, thirteen at the time, was described as outgoing and friendly, and idolized by his younger brother, William, who was shy and close to his mother. They had left that night, youthful spirits high, ten dollars each in their pockets. When they failed to return by ten-thirty, as promised, their father drove off to find them. He had no luck, though he did locate some of their friends who had seen them earlier, hurling baseballs at one of the game booths. Willie had been determined to win a teddy bear for his mother. At 1 A.M. the parents called the police and were instructed to call again if the boys failed to return by dawn. At dawn, the cops pointed out that kids having fun often lose track of time, stay out too late, and fear facing the music. They suggested that the parents check with other relatives and the boys' friends.

The carnival had left town by the time anyone in authority took the case seriously, if they ever did. Official theory was that the boys had probably run off in search of adventure and would return in their own good time.

A missing-persons detective did catch the carnival in Atlanta, by phone. No one remembered the boys.

"My back's gone bad on me and there's nobody 'round here now to help with the heavy lifting," their father complained. "Know how much shrubs weigh in those twenty-gallon containers? We was planting a hammock under the canopy of that tamarind tree out back, gonna edge it with wildflowers. It's getting overrun now, still waiting till my back heals up or those boys come home."

The grim set of his jaw and a hint of malevolence around his eyes when he looked at his wife made me wonder if they had run away. If he was my father, I might.

Emily Kearns followed me out to the T-Bird and stood hugging her arms as though cold, despite the temperature simmering in the upper nineties.

"Do you have children, Ms. Montero?"

I said I didn't.

"When you do," she said, "never miss a chance to give 'em a hug. There is no security in this life, no way to know if you'll get the chance to do it again."

She studied the ground. "I keep thinking of so many things I wish I had told them that evening. Find a policeman if you get lost. Don't talk to strangers. When they talk to you, just turn and walk away. Horrible things pop into my mind." She looked embarrassed. "I've got a very vivid imagination."

She leaned toward the car, her eyes bleak as I turned the key in the ignition. The last thing she said before I drove off was, "My boys didn't run away."

Andrea Vitale was in uniform, ready to leave for work when I arrived. She lived in a southwest section complex called Bramblewood Park. A maze of small identical town houses surrounded a pool, playground, and tennis court. Each unit had its own tiny patio and two assigned parking spaces. What did they do when somebody threw a party? The narrow streets, with speed bumps, tight turns, and unexpected dead ends, were imaginatively named after letters of the alphabet. I soon realized, to my frustration, that the letters were not in sequence. Andrea Vitale lived at 402-B on D Street. But C Street was followed by G. Where the hell was D? Where the hell was I? There was no H, and I found myself rolling south on M. What a great hideout. No process server, stalker, or SWAT team could hunt down a quarry here. I drove around and around, gallumping over speed bump after speed bump, cursing the madman who had designed this maze and stopping periodically to plead with ball-playing children for directions. They shook their heads sadly and looked puzzled. They lived there. What hope was there for a stranger?

A woman, in white shorts and carrying a tennis racket, got out of a Subaru with two girls about eleven or twelve. I tried a new approach. "Do you know where Butch Beltrán lived?"

The youngsters stared, wide-eyed. "He's not coming back, is he?" The woman's voice rang with concern. Without waiting for an answer, she hustled the girls into the house. His neighbors did not seem ready to offer reward money for Butch Beltrán's safe return.

At long last, I stumbled upon D Street, purely by chance, and found 402-B. My relief was tempered by the fact that I had no idea how I had found it and prayed I would never have to come back.

Andrea Vitale was in her late thirties, attractive, solidly built, with warm, sherry-colored eyes and luxuriant light brown hair. She looked slightly worn around the edges but obviously possessed a smart-aleck streak. "Any trouble finding it?" she asked pertly.

"No, not at all," I lied. What I wanted to say was: No wonder Butch hasn't come home. He's scurrying around out there somewhere in the maze like a confused rodent, trying to make his way through the alphabet.

A framed photograph of the boy, missing since March, sat on a natural wood bookcase. T-shirt, baggy shorts, and a black baseball cap worn backward. Caught forever in motion, arms extended for balance, face set in concentration, he affected the scissored body language of a surfer, hurtling through space on a skateboard.

The smaller school photo excited my interest. Gleaming blond hair, blue eyes, so like the others.

I accepted her offer of coffee. She positioned our cups and a plate of oatmeal cookies on the coffee table between us. "His favorites," she said, perching on a beige tweed sofa. "I still buy them every week, and wind up eating them myself. I keep cooking for two. Force of habit. He better come back soon, my clothes are all too tight." She laughed, her eyes roving the empty room. "I miss him," she said flatly. "We don't always get along, but we're the two musketeers. We've been through a lot together. I've been both a father and a mother, by necessity. It's hard to be both a tough taskmaster and a loving mother to a high-spirited kid like him." She smiled fondly. "He's got a pure wild streak, like his dad, but I think he's smarter, or will be as an adult. If I can just get him through adolescence in one piece," she said, groaning.

"Any chance he's with his father?"

She shook her head, her look certain.

"He's on the NASCAR circuit, occasional driver, mostly mechanic. Two summers ago when Butch was driving me crazy I sent him to spend some time with his dad. An absolute disaster. Butch even appreciated me, briefly, after he came back—three weeks early, by the way. Sure messed up my summer romance. Butch is always good at that." She sighed good-naturedly. "I've spoken to his father, in Vegas, twice since Butch disappeared. He hasn't heard a thing. We divorced nearly ten years ago. I got married again right away but it only lasted about a year. Butch has never had a steady male influence on a regular basis. It's just the two of us."

"What happened when he disappeared?"

"I've been working nights at Coral Reef Hospital, in ICU. I took a late shift for the pay differential. We needed the money. Butch is your typical gimme, gimme, gimme All-American kid. I try hard to do right by him, you know, since he hasn't got a father and all. So it's always something, a one-hundred-seventy-dollar Planet Earth skateboard here, a hundred-dollar pair of Air Jordan Nikes there. I dread the day he's old enough to drive.

"I got home at one A.M. that night, as usual, but he wasn't up watching TV or in bed. I always bring him home a snack and we sit up and talk for a while. But he wasn't here." She shrugged. "After the fact, the neighbors told me that every night after I left for work, he'd go out, then scoot back in just before I got home. Had it timed right down to the minute."

"Where was he going?"

"Hanging out at Cutler Ridge Mall, at the video arcade, the movies, playgrounds, friends' houses. I found some kids and the manager who had seen him at about ten that night at the arcade. Nobody saw him leave. He just didn't come home."

"Would have been more neighborly if they had clued you in before he disappeared," I murmured.

"Well, we aren't too popular around here. He was in some trouble last year. I think they hoped he'd get in another jam before I found out what he was doing."

I thought of the woman in shorts and her reaction at the prospect of Butch's return.

"They wrote a story about Butch in your newspaper," Andrea said brightly. "But you couldn't use his name because he was a juvenile."

"What kind of story?" What was the name of this place? I thought. Bramblewood?

"They charged him with arson." She tossed out the word casually, as though it had been nothing more serious than a parking ticket. "But we got it all straightened out. That was more than a year ago."

"The bombs?" I said, with a sudden revelatory flash.

"He never intended to hurt anyone. He's a very curious boy, very bright." She went to the sideboard, rummaged in a drawer, and handed me a folded clipping. BOY BOMBER TERRORIZES NEIGHBORHOOD.

It was from the *News*. I had been on vacation at the time, on Florida's west coast, in the arms of Homicide Lieutenant Kendall McDonald. Another reporter wrote the story.

Butch had blown up a neighbor's air-conditioning unit on Fourth of July weekend. It was no mindless bombing; he'd had a reason. His mother had complained that it was too noisy and kept her awake. The unit was totally destroyed, as was one wall of the town house. When police investigated, neighborhood children tipped them about Butch's other incendiary concoctions.

The entire town-house complex had been evacuated. Bomb-sniffing dogs led their handlers to three pipe bombs in Butch's bedroom.

He was eleven at the time.

The news story quoted a neighbor who had forbidden her children to associate with Butch after she caught her six-year-old halfway out the door with a clock. The child explained that Butch needed it "to build a time bomb."

"The incident," as Andrea Vitale referred to it, "didn't make us too popular in the neighborhood, but Butch was adjusting very well."

"What happened in Juvenile Court?"

"We had to go to family counseling, group sessions at Jackson. After two or three times they said we didn't have to come back. He's been fine since," she insisted.

Sure, I thought, sneaking out every night to do who knows what, missing five months now, but otherwise, he's absolutely fine. The memory of Alex Aguirre's smoldering car made me see Butch's stunts as more than childhood pranks.

Her eyes had drifted to the photos. "I'm just so damn mad at that kid for not calling to let me know he's okay. When he does turn up, I'm gonna give him a humongous welcome-home hug, then shake him till his teeth rattle."

"So you feel he's all right? He has run away before?"

"Yeah." She bit her lip and tension crept into her voice. "But this time it's different. He's starting to scare me."

"How is it different?"

"There was no argument, like the other times, nothing to trigger it. Everything was fine. Things were good in school, they had put him in some classes for gifted students so he wasn't as bored. And he was in no trouble that I know of. What scares me most," she said, brushing cookie crumbs off her uniform, "is that I have no idea what he's up to this time. He was never gone more than a few days before. Even then, he couldn't resist calling or sneaking in and out, playing games, when I was at work. He'd always call, you know, 'Look at me, Ma.' What he's always wanted most is attention. He got none from his father. I gave what I could, but I was always busy supporting us. Every time the phone rings I expect to hear him say, 'Miss me, Ma?' But it's not happening and that's odd. Some people around here are probably glad he's gone. But nobody realizes that this boy is gonna *be* somebody some day." She smiled. "I wish you could meet him. This kid has really got what it takes."

She reached for another cookie. "One other difference. He didn't take any of his toys this time. The only thing he may have had with him was his Swiss Army knife. You know the kind, it's also a nail file, scissors, a can opener. He got it for his twelfth birthday and it's not here anywhere. He probably carried it during his after-dark adventures, for protection. He's totally nonviolent but he's savvy, aware of the danger out there. I was always straight with him about that."

She looked up at me, puzzled, as she munched. "Butch is not the kind of kid who simply disappears and is never heard from again." She sighed. "He should have come to somebody's attention by now, if you know what I mean."

She reached absently for another cookie and chewed thoughtfully.

It was easier to find my way out of Bramblewood than it was to find my way in. I didn't even notice the speed bumps. My mind raced, stringing the facts together in my head. When I got back to the office I checked my messages. None from my mother. Had she joined the missing boys in Never Never Land? I pictured her lost in Bramble- wood, with Butch.

Was she settling up with me for usually failing to return her calls promptly? I left her another message.

Phone checks of all the smaller police departments turned up no other cases. As I worked on the story, I thought about asking if the art department could put together a locator map marking where each boy was last seen. Had it revealed a pattern, it might have worked, but I tried it on the big map of Dade County mounted on the wall above my desk, placing pins at each vanishing point. Nothing. Then I tried a yellow pin at each home address, a blue at each school. Nada. No geographic pat- tern, rhyme, or reason. The carnival cases were on a Thursday night. Charles Randolph vanished Saturday morning, David Clower, Saturday night. Lars Sjowall walked off the map on a Tuesday afternoon, and Butch Beltrán sneaked out for the last time on a Wednesday night. No bodies or belongings found, no ransom demands made. No parents wealthy enough to pay any substantial sum. The only common link was physical appearance. That was what it boiled down to: age, general description, and the fact that they had vanished as completely as footprints in melting snow.

My doubting editors resisted. What sold the story was the pictures. The lost boys looked so remarkably alike.

Side by side, their young faces stripped across Sunday's local page, they resembled brothers, or cousins. WHERE ARE THEY? the headline asked. "No Trace of Missing Boys" said the subhead. The special section on Cuba, an insert, ran the same day. Lottie's color photo of Reyes at the helm of the *Libertad* was out front along with the first few grafs of my story, which jumped to the inside.

Not a bad day's work.

I SPENT THE early morning eluding
Seth Goldstein, who seemed bent on becoming my shadow, and pur-
suing my mother, who was apparently eluding me. Her machine now
recorded messages. If she ever played them she would hear half a
dozen from me, ranging from cute and coy, to hurt and bewildered, to
angry and demanding that she return my call. Then I covered a story
and my problems faded by comparison.

While I was fuming about my mother's failure to return my messages, a man named José Caliente was experiencing real live horror.
Bumper-to-bumper traffic ground to a halt, trapping his small ice cream
truck on the Florida East Coast Railway tracks. When signals sounded
and warning lights flashed, he leaned on his horn. Nobody moved. The
Cadillac in front of him was hemmed in. The bus on his bumper had no
way to back up. The train whistle shrilled. The bus driver screamed,
"Jump! Run!" Caliente hesitated, probably hoping to save his truck, his
sole means of support for his wife and four children. He did jump, too
late. The oncoming train hurled him seventy-five feet.

His overturned truck was dragged even farther. Strangers ran, but not to help. They swarmed over his truck, fighting over the cash box. Others stole all the ice cream. Those with stronger stomachs stripped what remained of José Caliente of his wallet, wristwatch, and the medal of the Virgin worn on a silver chain around his neck.

Age forty-five. He could have been any of us, caught in this urban jungle. Had I not been deadline pressed and impatient for reader reaction to my story on the boys, I would have been numbed. Instead, I barreled down the expressway like a battering ram, exceeding the speed limit. Striding into the newsroom, intent and focused, composing the lead in my head, I gasped. My desk was all but obscured by orchids, lavish, sexy white cattleyas, sprays of yellow cymbidiums and tiny oncidiums emerging like butterflies from a basketful of curling willow and bamboo. My mouth dropped. McDonald. How did he always know the right thing to do when I needed him most? McDonald. I did miss his square-jawed cragginess and gentle touch.

"Is it your birthday, Britt?" Ryan asked eagerly from his desk behind me.

"Nope." I smiled slyly. "There are other reasons for flowers." Every eye in a newsroom full of snoops was riveted on me. I was center stage.

"Britt's got a new boyfriend!" Howie Janowitz sang out.

A crowd clustered. "Who are they from?" demanded Barbara DeWitt, a no-nonsense reporter who covers the city commission.

"Yeah," Lottie said wistfully, "check out the card."

Gretchen and Ron Sadler elbowed closer.

I plucked the small square envelope from a slender branch. He spent so much, I thought, eyes swimming as I tore it open. He shouldn't have.

He didn't.

"You make the Montero name proud," it said. Juan Carlos Reyes had signed the card.

Stunned, I slipped it into my skirt pocket. Too late.

A cry of triumph from Ron Sadler. "Reyes! Juan Carlos Reyes sent them!" He cocked an expressive eyebrow at Gretchen as if to say, "I knew it."

"I can't believe he did this," I murmured, face ablaze, as Reyes's name rippled across the newsroom.

"It appears he liked your story," Gretchen said archly.

"He liked something," another voice crowed.

What could I say? Avoiding their eyes, I shoved the basket aside, along with a promising stack of messages I had no time to answer, and drew up my chair in businesslike fashion. "I'm on deadline," I said. "I've got to get this story done."

The curious began to wander away when I ignored them. The funereal fragrance of the flowers seemed eerily appropriate as I began to translate my notes about José Caliente into a story.

Had McDonald sent the orchids, I would have been thrilled. Reyes's taste, like his clothes, home and manners, was exquisite. There was no ignoring the breathtaking arrangement. Copy boy to publisher, all paused in passing.

"What's the occasion?"

"Birthday?"

"Somebody likes you."

And more directly, "Who sent those?"

I finished my story and tried to conceal the basket and its protruding branches beneath my desk. Faithful readers regularly bombard me with crank letters, hate mail, death threats, subpoenas, and Santeria curses. Flowers were rare. If this signaled a trend, I would know I had lost my touch.

"Told ya about Reyes." Lottie chortled. "That hombre's sure got the hots for you."

"Not you too," I groaned. "You should have seen Ron and Gretchen."

"Ran into him in the lobby last night." Her expression was quizzical. "Could have sworn the man was wearing blusher."

"I wouldn't doubt it."

She perched on the edge of my desk, wearing black Wrangler jeans, a ruffled shirt, and handstitched leather boots. "You've got admirers of all ages lined up and panting: Reyes, Seth."

"Sure, one old enough to be my father . . ."

"He might be," she said.

". . . and the other a twerpy twelve-year-old. You haven't heard about the ax killer yet." I told her about Hal.

"Sounds charming," she said. "Speaking of which, Stosh has a big trial coming up and wants to know if you'll cover it."

"Oh no. He's back?"

She grinned sheepishly. "The funeral arrangement was a misunderstanding, a mixup. He was so embarrassed and apologetic. In fact, he's buying me something. A big-deal present, top secret."

"What do you think it is?" What else could he steal from a cemetery? I wondered.

Smiling, she shook her head. "No clue." I liked seeing her happy. Maybe she could transform the Polish Prince. They were certainly a striking couple, he tall and blond, she tall and red-haired. But he'd have to be hog-tied and branded before I'd believe it.

"I told him you probably wouldn't cover it," she said.

"Why not?"

"It's a civil case. You wrote the initial story. Remember LaFontana Pierre? That Haitian woman who burst into flames on her birthday?"

"The one who survived." I nodded; who could forget? I had covered four identical cases in a year. "A civil suit?" I was puzzled. "Who is she suing, and for what? The woman accidentally turned herself into a human torch during a voodoo ceremony."

Lottie shrugged. "The landlord, the gas company, the stove manufacturer."

"But how . . . ?"

"Stosh says she lit her kitchen stove at midnight to warm up some milk and a defective burner spit out a two-foot flame that set her nightgown on fire. Burnt it right off."

"Lottie! She was taking a lucky bath! Everybody knows that."

The lucky bath, a ritualistic cleansing ceremony, is performed at midnight on one's birthday to guarantee good fortune in the year ahead. The celebrant chants a prayer, provided by a Haitian *houngan*, or priest, while bathing in perfume, surrounded by lighted candles. The flames, the chant, and the fragrance are to lure the spirits, who will answer prayers to win the lottery or a husband with a good job.

LaFontana Pierre had done as the priest instructed. Squatting hopefully inside a circle of candles, she poured perfume over her naked body at the stroke of midnight on her twenty-fifth birthday.

Instantly her luck changed—from bad to worse. Before she could even chant the magic words, she was enveloped in flames. The oil-based perfume was eighty percent alcohol, and the candles ignited the vapors. Alcohol burns at a higher temperature than most flames.

She ran screaming into the street. Burned over forty percent of her body, she was lucky. The first three victims had died.

Lottie shrugged. "She says it was the stove."

"Please. The stove happened to malfunction at midnight? On her birthday? What about all that candle wax on the floor? Lord, Lottie. How'd she get Americanized so fast? Where did she learn about frivolous lawsuits?"

Why did I wonder? The Polish Prince must have been drawn like a moth to the flame. Now he was trying to improve her luck—along with his own.

"Bathing in perfume on your birthday is a damn sight more civilized than decapitating chickens' heads and splashing blood all over. It might even work. Who knows? My birthday's next month," she said speculatively.

"Lottie, don't you dare!" I yelped. "Don't even think about it!" I ignored her obvious reference to my Aunt Odalys and her practice of

Santeria, something I had shared with Lottie after we covered the Miami murder of a South American drug dealer whose local stronghold resembled Satanism Central, littered with *palo mayombe* voodoo icons, buckets of blood, and animal entrails.

"I thought Stosh tried only criminal cases," I said.

"He knows the victim's family, represented her cousins on murder charges," she explained. "Wants to expand his horizons. Says if he can try complex criminal cases he can try complex civil cases. Nothing wrong with tackling new challenges." She sounded defensive. "He says it's a clear case of prejudice; nobody would even mention voodoo if his client were from Utah. Maybe there really was a defective burner."

Lottie's loyalty is a sterling quality, but misplaced in the case of the Prince. Love is blind. I almost wanted to cover the trial, to see him and his client try to sell that story to a jury of Miamians.

I was in a rush to return my messages. Would there be word from Charles, David, Michael, William, Lars, or Butch? We were now on a first-name basis. But first, the orchids.

Calling to thank Reyes would give me a chance to ask about my father's diary. I felt an anticipatory tingle as I reached for the phone. At that moment it rang.

"Somebody here to see you, Britt." The lobby security guard sounded like he was confronting some disreputable character.

"Oh shoot," I said impatiently, when he identified my visitor. "Does he know I'm here? Okay, send him up." I sighed.

Reyes obviously did not hate my story about him. But somebody did.

Jorge Bravo hobbled toward my desk leaning on a cane, his gait painfully slow. His right hip and leg had been shattered by a grenade during one of his abortive commando raids on Cuba. Typically macho, he always derided it as a wimpy, *maricona* grenade, because it failed to kill him.

His clothes were inexpensive, clean, and neatly pressed. He wore dark glasses. Balding, with a fierce mustache, he was shorter than the image he projected in pictures. But despite that and his handicap, he carried himself with a dignity belied by his simple work pants and cotton guayabera. He also wore an expression of outrage. He'd been wearing it since the Bay of Pigs invasion failed in 1961.

I stood to greet him.

"*¡Asesina!*" he shouted. "Murderer!"

I blinked.

"You killed them!"

Heads turned, jaws dropped. Newsroom busybodies were being entertained again, at my expense.

"I beg your pardon?"

"You are killing them again! *¡Asesina!* All the brave men who died. You are killing them." He shook his cane at me. "You are the *asesina!*"

"Mr. Bravo," I said coldly, "what are you talking about?"

"You are murdering their memories!" He slapped the top of my desk resoundingly with a rough-hewn hand that was missing two fingers. Several papers sailed off onto the floor.

"Stop shouting." I stood my ground angrily. "People are trying to work here. If you have something to discuss, let's discuss it rationally, like adults, but I refuse to be screamed at."

His lined and ruddy face grew redder, his voice louder. *"¡Muerte!"* He pointed a finger. *"¡La cómplice!"*

That did it. There was no way to reason with this man who, given his past history, might be armed. I turned to Ryan, who was wide-eyed, his hand on the telephone. "Call security," I said crisply.

"Reyes is a traitor!" Bravo shouted. *"¡Él es un monstruo!* You blaspheme the memories of those he betrayed! The heroes. You! The daughter of a patriot! Tony Montero must be turning in his grave!"

My patience was gone. For the first time I was relieved to see the two usually oafish *News* security guards appear with merciful speed.

I feared Bravo would fight, but he shook them off and limped out of the newsroom on his own, spewing a tirade over his shoulder.

"Write another story! Tell the truth, this time! You will hear from me." His shouts echoed from the hallway as they herded him aboard an elevator.

Trembling, I sat down. I'd been right, I told myself, furious and embarrassed. Writing just one story related in any way to Cuban politics is like stirring up a nest of yellow jackets with a stick. It makes them worse. Exile community fanatics will drag you kicking and screaming into their squabbles, schemes, and petty jealousies. No way would I become captive of my heritage and allow them to involve me in their battles with Fidel Castro and each other.

Reyes's secretary put me right through.

"Britt," he said warmly, as though delighted to hear my voice.

"Mr. Reyes," I said, speaking softly so my colleagues would not hear. "Thank you for the orchids. They are absolutely breathtaking, but you shouldn't have."

"Oh, but I should have. They are not good enough, but the best I could find. How can I thank you? For the first time, your newspaper published my name without including distortions and innuendos. There were a few things I was not so pleased with, but," he added quickly, "I am convinced they are no fault of yours. I know the people you work for."

"Have you found my father's diary?" I asked, ignoring his comment.

He sighed. "Did you remember me to the lovely Catalina, as I requested?"

"I tried," I confessed, "but she's been busy and we haven't talked."

He paused. "A pity. Family is so important. Ah, yes. I saw your story, also on Sunday, about the boys who ran away."

"I don't think they're all runaways," I said shortly. Why did he persist in polite small talk? Hadn't he heard my question? "It would be so exciting to read my father's diary."

"What makes you so sure?"

"I beg your pardon?"

"That they did not run away? The hearts of young men are bold, they yearn for adventure, to explore the world."

"Oh. I thought we were talking about my father's diary."

"You seem so certain they did not run away."

"Well, I may know more soon." I fingered the sheaf of messages on my desk. "There seems to have been a great deal of response to the story. I just haven't had a chance to check into it yet."

"A busy woman. Do you ever take time for yourself? You must do so. Has there been response to your story about me?"

Was he deliberately tormenting me by answering my question with unrelated questions of his own, or simply trying to prolong our conversation?

"As a matter of fact, there was some reaction. Hostile. From Jorge Bravo. I was unaware you two were at odds."

"So be it," Reyes said smoothly. "One is known by his enemies; therefore, I am flattered."

"I thought you were on the same side of the fight."

"Many years ago, we were all members of *la causa*. We spilled our blood and lost years of our lives in Cuban prisons. We endured the hunger strikes, the beatings, the threats. Adversity makes some men stronger. The weak are destroyed."

"The diary," I persisted.

"Ah yes, my assistant is conducting a diligent search but has yet to report back to me. I will inform him of your impatience and the urgency of this matter."

"Thank you," I said, slightly flustered. "Since it's been thirty years, I guess I can wait a few more days."

Gloria handed me a note. A detective, on another line. We said adios, but not before Reyes confided that he hoped to see me again soon, in a richly resonant voice that whispered of the dark and mysterious mountains of Cuba.

Still caught up in Reyes's lingering mystique, I failed to grasp the detective's name or that of his department. "Miz Montero," he drawled, "I'm wanting to talk to you about that article you did the other day on those missing boys. We've got us one that fits your profile to a T."

Another one? "What department are you with, detective? I'm sorry I didn't hear your name."

"Frank Burgess, the Oglethorpe County Sheriff's office in Georgia. We got us a young man missing 'bout eighteen months now, without a word."

Oh, Lord, would the trail of every missing teenager in the nation now lead to my doorstep? I wanted resolution, not more mystery. "What makes you think he could be connected to our disappearances down here?"

"Miami. That's where he was headed."

A cold feeling crept down my body, as though a stranger had just walked on my grave.

Todd Sutter had run off from Sandy Cross, Georgia, destination Miami. He left a note telling his folks not to worry. He hitchhiked. They got a postcard from Macon, another from a motel on the Georgia-Florida line. The last one came from Ft. Lauderdale. "Almost there, told ya I'd make it!" He was tall, slender, blond, and blue-eyed. Age thirteen.

That was nearly two years ago.

"Now we doan' know if he made it that far," the detective drawled, "but his folks seen your story in one of the papers up here. He resembles those other youngsters and, given the similarities, I thought I'd call to see if you knew anythin' more than what you put in your story."

I didn't.

By day's end I had three more. Robert Donovan from Chicago, Danny Harding from Tallahassee, and a lad named Watson Kelly from Gary, Indiana.

There was no proof any of them had vanished in Miami. There was no proof any of them had ever arrived in Miami, except for the Kelly boy. He had called his parents collect, said he was in Miami, and asked for money to come home. Mad as hell, they were practicing tough love at the time. "You managed to get there on your own," they told him. "You can come home on your own." They simply wanted to scare him, they said, and intended to wire the money next time he called. The call never came. That was three years ago.

I took notes on all the cases, spoke to the parents, and asked them to send pictures.

My count was ten and climbing.

It is not an unusual rite of passage for a teenage boy to run away, go off on a lark, or take to the road seeking adventure. It is unusual, however, when he is never heard from again.

I cleared my desk as I tried again without success to reach my mother. I hoped to surreptitiously smuggle out the orchids, which wasn't easy. When I lifted the arrangement I could barely see over it. I lugged my purse, my notes, and the giant orchid basket out to the T-Bird.

Dusk had settled across the parking lot with only streaks of crimson sunset still slashed across the western sky. Somewhere to the east a hurricane-hunting jet was in the air. A modified C-130, loaded with weather equipment, had been dispatched to check out the tropical storm. To anyone passing by I must have looked like a flowering bush on the move. I felt like something out of Macbeth, Birnam wood on the way to Dunsinane.

Something startled me, a sound, as a shadow emerged from behind a van I was passing.

I turned, trying to see between the bobbing white and yellow blooms.

"Juan Carlos Reyes is a traitor!"

The shadowy figure used a cane. Bravo.

"¡Basta! Vamoose! Get away from me!" I snapped, angry at being accosted when vulnerable and unwilling to replay the newsroom scene alone and without backup in a darkening parking lot. "Leave me alone or I'll call the police! They'll revoke your bond!"

Bravo shrugged. "So be it," he said dramatically, drawing himself up like a man facing a firing squad. "Summon them now. I have been to prison before."

Suddenly he looked small and old and harmless in the dying light.

I sighed. "What exactly is it that you want to speak to me about?" I said quietly.

"You must listen," he said, voice calm for the first time. "We must talk."

"Okay, okay," I said, eager to get it over with.

"Come." He waved me toward a car. "We will drink *café cubano*."

Was he kidding? No way would I get in a car with him.

"You can trust me," he said, grinning.

"I'll meet you somewhere nearby." Somehow I couldn't picture Bravo hobnobbing at the 1800 Club, frequented by journalists and cops.

"*La Cafecita?*"

I nodded. Brightly lit and always busy.

"Follow me," he commanded with the authority of a general.

I had to smile at his machismo. He climbed painfully into his old clunker of a car. Follow me, indeed. He would be lucky if it started. A vintage Oldsmobile Toronado with a bumper sticker on the back. "*En los Noventa, Fidel Revienta.*" In the Nineties, Fidel Will Explode.

I wondered how Bravo had accessed employee parking, attainable only by key card. A commando and guerrilla fighter, no matter how inept, I decided, would probably have no trouble circumventing the *News*'s parking lot security.

His old car needed a muffler and a paint job. I parked behind it outside the cafe on Calle Ocho. We sat at a small table in the back and ordered coffee. Drinking from a tiny paper cup, I looked around the shabby coffee shop, remembering the exquisite porcelain from which Reyes and I had sipped.

"You are Cuban too, you know the suffering . . . ," Bravo began.

"Only half Cuban," I quickly corrected.

"Better than none," he said, startled.

"Actually, Jorge, I know very little about my father or my Cuban roots. I was only three years old when he died."

"He didn't die. Never say he died!" He slammed his fist down on the table, eyes shooting fire. "He was executed! Murdered. You must never forget that."

Embarrassed, I glanced around. No one had noticed. Such passionate outbursts were not unusual here. His emotion, the smells, the music of Spanish spoken, and the Latin beat from a radio behind the counter awakened long-dormant memories of visits to my Cuban relatives during my early childhood. They were warm, volatile, and demonstrative, and I adored them. My mother cut off the visits when I was still small. She had a multitude of reasons. She did not like it when I came home speaking Spanish and talking about my father, and there were also the matters of my Aunt Odalys's rites in the night and my Uncle Hector's arrest.

". . . the tragedy we call Cuba," Bravo was saying. "I am a stranger, an outcast, an exile. My country is one of the last places on earth where people are not free. That shame burns my heart." He pressed his hand over his heart as men do when the flag passes. "We believed in a fiery young attorney who embodied the goals we believed in, or so we thought. We believed his loyalty had been pledged, like ours, to the ideals of José Martí, not to communism.

"Fidel's Twenty-sixth of July movement offered us hope for freedom and justice." His eyes grew dreamy for a moment. "Then Castro revealed his true nature and the Twenty-sixth of July became a mockery"—his voice rose—"a symbol of hypocrisy and deceit, and we found ourselves fighting again for liberty and justice. We were soldiers, and those of us who are still alive continue to be soldiers." His lined face sagged in the harsh light but his eyes and his words reflected passion and energy.

We sat, quiet for a moment. "You have the eyes of your father," Bravo said, studying my face.

The exile community of freedom fighters was small then, so I assumed they were acquainted.

"How well did you know him?"

"How well did I know him?" He smiled, eyes cast down, almost shy. "We blew up a sugar refinery together and sabotaged the bridge at Almendares, a major pipeline. Fidel was furious, he ranted for days.

"But you know all these stories." He shrugged, turning his attention to the door and passing traffic.

"No, I don't. I know so little, but I hope to see his diary soon and learn more about him."

Bravo drew back, as though stunned. "You know about Antonio's *diario*?"

"Yes," I said, surprised at his reaction. "I learned about it just recently, from Juan Carlos Reyes." I hoped mere mention of the name would not spark another tirade. "He's looking for it among his things. He suggested my mother might have it."

"Of course she does not." Bravo's expression was incredulous. "How would she?"

"How do you know? Have you seen it?" I stared at him.

He looked serious. "Reyes," he muttered, lowering his voice. "He is worse than Castro. Castro makes no secret of who he is. This man does his evil in secret."

"What do you mean?" Do not let them draw you into their feuds, I warned myself.

"We cannot discuss the *diario* here." Bravo glanced around as though we were being watched. "Too many ears. We will go to my home." He tossed down some money and sprang to his feet, or at least tried to do so, balancing precariously with his cane, his good hand grasping the table for leverage.

Ignoring the warning voices, I followed him to the clunker, leaving my T-Bird full of orchids parked on the street.

The interior of his car was in no better condition than the exterior. I tried to ask about the diary as we drove, but he placed a stubby finger to his lips to silence me, mouthing the letters FBI. The FBI wouldn't bug his car, I thought. Then I remembered the charges he faced. Would they?

I watched Bravo, his eyes alert, like those of the savvy street cops I have ridden with, checking the mirrors, roving the storefronts we passed, aware of everything around us.

His house was a small pillbox with peeling paint on a barren lot in Little Havana's heart. Some men played dominoes at a table under a harsh light in a side yard. Several stood and saluted as Bravo stepped from his car. He returned their salute, standing straight, trying to hide his limp.

His wife, Nerida, a tiny, small-boned woman, served us Iron Beer and disappeared quietly into the kitchen. A statue of the Virgin stood on the mantel in front of a Cuban flag and a blown-up photo of a much younger Bravo and about a dozen other men in military gear clustered in and around a jeep. Probably shot in the sixties. "Is that . . . ?" Another face caught my eye.

"*Sí*. There am I, and there is Antonio, and the others." He reached out, extending his good arm, as though introducing us.

I stared into my father's face.

He stared back boldly, chin tilted, one booted foot up on the running board of the jeep, what looked like an M14 rifle cradled in the crook of his arm.

"So many are gone now." Bravo sighed. "Antonio, Rolando, Angel."

"I never saw this picture before," I said, thrilled, unable to take my eyes off it. "Would it be possible for me to have a copy?"

"*Sí, sí*." He sank heavily into a chair and frowned. "I don't know where is the negative, but . . ."

"I have a friend, a photographer, who could come over now, tonight, to take a picture of it." Something told me not to miss the chance while I had it.

He shrugged. "Of course."

"I can page her."

While using the telephone I noticed something bulky under a canvas tarp in the corner. Machine guns? Grenade launchers?

Damn, I thought. Illegal weapons. Bravo was already free on bond on similar federal charges. With my luck the FBI would raid this place tonight. They'd seize everything, including me. How would I explain to the city desk? I hoped Lottie would answer her page promptly. The hour was late, she was having dinner with the Prince. She might not answer at all.

"Antonio and me," Bravo reminisced, "we were *plantados*, the political prisoners who stood firm. We refused to wear prison uniforms, refused to enter the government's rehabilitation program. In retaliation, we were brutalized, forced to labor in a rock quarry at the Isle of Pines. But we never stopped opposing the government, we organized secret resistance groups in Havana and Cienfuegos from our cells. Your father was a patriot, a noble man. His courage inspires me still. Like him I am prepared to do whatever I must to see Cuba free."

The phone rang and I heard the murmur of Nerida's voice. She came into the room. Yes! It was Lottie.

"Sorry to interrupt your date," I told her, "but can you come shoot a picture for me?"

"Sheet, you didn't interrupt nothing. Wait till you hear—"

"*Now*, Lottie," I said urgently and gave her the address.

"Whatcha working on?"

"No story," I muttered into the phone. "This is personal."

"I'm coming from North Miami, so it'll take a bit, but I'm on the way."

I took a seat in a threadbare chair, trying not to stare at the suspicious tarp in the corner.

"We escaped," Bravo resumed, as though there had been no interruption. "But Antonio, he and other brave men were betrayed, and captured again, in the mountains of Pínar del Río. Your father's trial before the Revolutionary Tribunal took twenty minutes. Twenty minutes! At age twenty-four he was sentenced to death by firing squad." His eyes returned to the picture. "He dedicated his life to bringing down the Castro regime. His death made us all fight harder."

"So he did keep a diary." Why was it impossible to keep anybody on track when discussing the diary?

"Of course," Bravo snapped. He struggled to his feet, leaning heavily on his cane. "We must find it before it falls into the wrong hands and is destroyed."

Were we on the same wavelength here? "What do you mean? Reyes probably has it stored somewhere."

"No, no." Bravo began to pace. "Reyes wants it, but we must pray that he has not seized it." His eyes turned to the statue on the mantel and he crossed himself.

"Wait a minute, let's start again. Why don't you think Reyes has it?"

Bravo stopped in front of my chair. "For years it was in the possession of the Castro government but it came to Miami recently, brought by a *balsero*."

"A rafter?"

"*Sí*, a former Cuban government employee. We expected it, we were waiting for it to be delivered to—"

"We?"

"Alex, Alex Aguirre." Bravo leaned forward, speaking passionately, with impatience. "You don't understand. Your father learned the name of the man who betrayed him and the others. It is there on those pages written before his execution. Alex said it would be the story of his lifetime. An exposé. He planned to read Antonio's words in a live broadcast." Bravo slammed his damaged fist into his palm. "Then Alex was assassinated! Now the *balsero* who was to deliver the diary to us has gone into hiding. He must believe that his life is also in danger. And it is true."

His eyes locked on mine, lips parted, awaiting my reply.

What a hell of a story. If true. That was my first reaction, *true* being the operant word. Obsessed freedom fighters are known for their grassy knollism, conspiracy theories, and for complicating simple matters. That lack of credibility rubs off on any luckless journalist caught in their web.

"But why? And why would Reyes . . ."

"Because," he spat, "Reyes is the traitor. I have always been certain that it was so. But we needed the proof."

I sighed. "Why would Reyes betray my father?"

"Reyes was a Castro agent."

"But he hates Fidel, he spent time in a Castro prison himself. . . ." I felt exasperated. "Do the police know this theory about Alex's murder?"

Bravo shook his head vehemently. "No *policía*, they are useless, corrupt. Many work for him."

Of course, I thought, they are all involved as well, conspirators under every bed. The doorbell rang at the right moment. Lottie was dressed for a date, except for the cameras slung from leather straps around her neck.

"You don't know the evening I've had," she muttered.

"Did you go to dinner?"

"Oh, sure," she said, "I went to dinner all right." Her evening had obviously not been all candlelight and roses. But she bustled in, all business, and charmed Bravo with her smile. She scoped out the picture over the mantel, snapped a short telephoto lens onto her Nikon, took the flash off the camera, and held it to the side to prevent a reflection on the glass.

Then she shot the picture, then one of me standing in front of the picture. Then she insisted on me and Bravo posing together, another of Bravo alone, then finally one of him and his shy wife. Bravo posed, chin held high, cane hidden from the camera's eye.

"We must find Antonio's *diario*," he muttered in my ear as we left.

"I'll check with Reyes," I said absently.

"No! Tell him nothing," he warned. "Use caution. The man is a monster."

"What the devil was that all about?" Lottie demanded as we piled into her car.

"The usual intrigue. Did you see my dad? Didn't he look dashing? So young. It's hard to believe that he was younger then than I am now. I really want his diary." I told her about Bravo's wild theories. "I also think the man has a living room full of illegal weapons."

"That stuff under the tarp in the corner? I didn't want to ask. . . ." Lottie glanced at me with concern. "You're not gonna start spending your time digging into old calamities, are you?"

"Not when you have new ones to share. What happened to your date tonight?"

"Stosh took me out for a fancy dinner at Mark's Place," she began.

"Not bad," I said, "a four-star restaurant."

"Outstanding," she said grimly. "It was awesome. Outta sight. I had the conch and green mango chutney for an appetizer."

"How'd they fix it?" I hadn't eaten all day.

"The conch?"

"Yeah."

"Grilled, skewered," she said, stopping for a red light. "I sorta suspected Stosh was watching the clock. Saw 'im check his watch during the main course." She cut her eyes at me. "Mine was sautéed yellowtail snapper with Oriental black bean and shiitake sauce."

"What did they serve with it?"

She sighed impatiently and accelerated on the green. "Scented rice with gulf shrimp and calico scallops."

"Twenty minutes ago all I wanted was a quarter pounder with cheese."

"His beeper goes off during dessert."

"Dessert?" I said dreamily.

"'Emergency,' he says, trotting back from the phone. A client just got busted on a murder-one charge. 'Who?' I ask and he spits out a name I don't recognize. Willy Santana. Has to beat feet over to the jail, he says, 'cuz the cops are trying to question his client illegally."

"Makes sense," I said. "But Santana doesn't ring a bell. Did he mention the victim's name?"

She shook her head. "He pecks me on the cheek. 'Can you take a cab home, Baby Face? Will you be all right?' Hell all Friday, Britt, I'm an understanding woman, right?"

"Definitely."

"He hands me a credit card to pay the tab and hauls ass."

"That's too bad, Lottie, but—"

"I'm fine," she interrupted, voice stressed, "I'm fine with all that. Lord knows we've run out on enough dates because of breaking news. It's the man's job. I understand. I'm okay. I finish my chocolate truffle terrine and my café calypso and ask the waiter to call me a cab. He brings the check and I drop Stosh's credit card onto his little silver tray."

She paused for effect. "That's when it happened."

The card was maxed out, I thought. I was beginning to feel like I knew Stosh well, and the more I knew the less I liked.

"The waiter says, 'Sorry, madam, we are not Sears.'"

"Sears?"

"He left me his dag-blasted Sears card!"

"What did you do?"

"Used my American Express." She stomped the gas.

"Stosh may have mistaken Sears for another card, the lighting is soft, he was in a hurry." I couldn't believe I was giving the Polish Prince the benefit of the doubt. "Although with his track record . . ."

"He went to the men's room right after the salad." She glanced over. "Organic baby greens with Gorgonzola cheese."

"Think he set up the page then?"

"One way to find out," she said.

"Yup. I'll check the jail, see if his so-called client was really booked. What was that name, Santana? Now, tell me all about that chocolate terrine."

The streetlights cast a greenish glow through the sweltering night and electricity crackled on the streets. I knew in my bones that bizarre events were happening somewhere out there in the dark, I could feel it.

"You tired?" Lottie asked when she dropped me at my car in front of La Cafecita.

"Nope," I said.

"Me neither. Let's go back to the office," she said. "I'll soup the film and print your pictures. While I do that, you call the jail and see who got busted tonight." She smiled. "And we can get you some Fritos and stuff outta the vending machine."

"Sounds good to me. What did that dinner with Stosh cost?"

"That man owes me a hundred and fifty-seven bucks. I tipped well."

We parked next to each other in the nearly empty parking garage beneath the *News* building just after midnight. I used my key and we entered the lobby through a back door. The lone elevator operating at that hour stood waiting. No security guards in sight. We stepped into the news-room, still brightly lit and cool, cursors winking on blank computer screens and silent TV monitors playing to an empty room. I love the office at this hour, no ringing phones, no pesky editors. I dropped my purse on my desk and Lottie turned to head for photo when we heard it. A muffled moan.

We exchanged glances and moved quietly toward the executive editor's glass-enclosed office. The blinds were drawn, as always. Holding my breath, I strained to hear. There it was again. Gasps. Another groan.

Chills swept across my bare arms and the hair on the back of my neck prickled. The door, usually locked at night, stood slightly ajar. More noises. A choking, gargling sound.

Lottie kicked the door open with the toe of her boot. Something red had pooled on the floor. Blood? And a bare foot.

Taking a deep breath, I barged in as Lottie hit the lights.

"Whoops!" I spun around, bumping into Lottie right behind me. We stumbled together trying to get out of each other's way.

"Great horned toads!" Lottie swept me aside and raised her camera. The flash caught flailing bare limbs and scrambling bodies. Another burst of light reflected off Ron Sadler's pale buttocks as he dove for his pants. Gretchen, eyes wide, mouth open, covered her bouncing breasts with both hands.

"Excuse me," I said stupidly, as Lottie fired off another flash.

"Stop them!" Gretchen cried, snatching a silky red half slip off the floor and pulling it over her head.

Ron, hopping on one foot trying to pull on his pants, mumbled something unintelligible.

"Whoa!" yelped Lottie, as we both backed out of the office, in a final explosion of light.

The door slammed behind us and we both collapsed, convulsed in laughter.

"Now we . . . know . . . what happened to Ron," I said, gasping for breath. "Remember . . . we both said he'd changed."

"I'll be cow kicked. I thought TV went to his head, got him all gussied up. It was Gretchen. You hear those moans? Like a pig stuck under a gate. Think his wife knows?" Lottie asked.

A muttered argument was under way inside the executive office.

"What chutzpa! I can't believe they did it in there. If the old man finds out . . ." I wiped away tears and sniffled. "I can't believe you shot pictures!"

"I didn't," Lottie whispered. "No film in that camera. But hell." She grinned. "They don't know that. Let's get outta here."

We high-fived and escaped back out into the night.

I CHECKED THE jail log from home that night. No Santana booked for anything from misdemeanor to murder. I decided to wait until morning to break the bad news to Lottie. I also called homicide about Alex Aguirre. A midnight-shift detective said they were checking a tip that Alex had been seen recently with a known drug trafficker. So far it seemed innocent. The two were old high school buddies and varsity baseball teammates, who apparently hadn't seen each other in years. They had had a drink and talked over old times after a chance encounter in a restaurant. Alex's financial dealings were also being probed in search of a motive. So was his relationship with his wife and the possibility that he had been mistaken for someone else.

The latter seemed highly unlikely, and the former had yielded nothing suspect so far.

"Anything to link it to Cuban politics, old feuds among freedom fighters?"

"Nah, Aguirre grew up here. Ain't seen no true political assassinations among our local Cuban brothers in years."

At one time it seemed as though every exile killed in Miami was a member of Brigade 2506. Had the death rate continued at that pace, Bay of Pigs veterans would be as rare as yellow-bellied sapsuckers. Fellow brigade members always blamed Castro agents, politics, and international intrigue for the slayings. But most were motivated by drinking, drugs, and love triangles, the usual vices most murder victims die for. Many men passionate about liberating Cuba turned to narcotics trafficking to fund the battle but soon became so caught up in that life that they forgot the cause and got rich, or dead, instead. When the motive really was political, it was invariably internal, the A team battling the B team over fund-raising and how the proceeds were being spent.

I slept little that night, my thoughts careening down strange highways at seventy miles an hour. I called Lottie early next morning. "He was running a scam," I said flatly. "No Santana arrested."

There was a silence and I heard her breathe deeply. "Then that's it," she said.

Ron, Gretchen, and their dubious judgment were a more cheerful diversion. Heads had rolled when the executive editor discovered late night high-stakes newsroom poker games. When you work for a daily newspaper, there is always somebody who will tell. Our business, after all, is disseminating the news. That scandal cost the night editor his job. How would the executive editor react to news of the workout on his office couch?

"Gretchen is so ambitious," I said, "on the corporate fast track. Why would she risk it all? It's not as if there are no motel rooms in this city."

"It's all connected," Lottie said flatly. "Sex. Power. Passion. Why do you think they were in the office, on the couch where the President himself has sat when courting the media? I'm surprised it wasn't on the old man's desk. That was probably their next move."

"But it's so stupid."

"Look at politicians. Why you think sex gets so many of them in trouble? Politics and sex: same kinda power trip. Lookit Gary Hart, the Kennedys, Packwood."

"Ron and Gretchen must be sweating it today," I said.

"No bout adout it."

"Probably expect to see their bare bottoms plastered on every bulletin board in the building."

"Or sent out on the AP wire."

"They probably have no idea that we wouldn't stoop to their level."

"We wouldn't?"

"Only if provoked." We both laughed.

My beat was relatively quiet that morning, aside from fowl play at the courthouse. Miami's criminal defendants rely increasingly on the occult to insure the outcome of their cases. That makes the Voodoo Squad, a special team of janitors, a necessity. Their job: to remove the decapitated chickens, roosters, and dead goats from the courthouse steps each morning.

Public relations geniuses dubbed Miami the Magic City many years ago. This was not what they had in mind.

The modern, high-tech justice system grinds on, with its closed-circuit TV, metal detectors, and computer imaging, while the Voodoo Squad sweeps up black pepper and vacuums away the white voodoo powder scattered in empty courtrooms. Papers bearing the names of the judges, lawyers, defendants, and witnesses are burned, and the ashes mixed with the white powder, which is sprinkled around the jury box to tilt justice in favor of the accused. Believers insist the black pepper will keep defendants in jail, and that cow's tongues bound with twine and dead lizards with mouths wired shut will silence snitches.

Smashed eggs are believed to result in the collapse of a prosecutor's case.

Some mornings, Voodoo Central, the narrow street between the Justice Building and the jail looks like a barnyard disaster. Now, after the hectic week of the full moon, their busiest time, the Voodoo Squad was on strike for beefed-up benefits, including hazard pay, before continuing to interfere with hexes and witchcraft. It was the first day of their walk-out, and courthouse employees were already complaining about the odor. Hot dog vendors usually stationed outside the building had been forced to relocate to new turf upwind.

Back at the *News*, the lovers' relationship seemed strained. They did not look at each other at all. Gretchen approached my desk after most people went to lunch and the newsroom was relatively empty. Fashionably dressed as ever, in a military detailed coatdress, she did not seem quite as overbearing as usual. In fact, she looked positively har-ried. Red undies, I thought, and grinned up at her.

The wire copy in her right hand quivered imperceptibly, but there was no tremor in her voice. "Britt." She spoke quietly, making sure we were not overheard. "I hope you and Lottie plan to be discreet."

I nearly felt sorry for her, well aware that there but for the grace of God . . . but then remembered all the times . . .

"What exactly do you mean, Gretchen?"

"Britt, try to put yourself in my position," she hissed.

"Frankly, Gretchen, I can't," I said, glancing back at Ron's desk. I reached for my ringing telephone as she stalked away.

A Metro-Dade missing-persons detective was on the line. He had been contacted about two more out-of-town cases that fit the lost boys' profile. Twelve and counting. Where would it end? I wondered, entering a runaway from Texas and a young wanderer from Boston into my notes.

Later that afternoon I slipped out of the newsroom and drove south to Little Havana. The small, well-kept house was shaded by a caram-bola tree heavy with sweet star-shaped fruit. The delicate flowers of a tabebuia had drifted down, carpeting the ground in soft pink. The Mexican heather and impatiens were looking a bit faded, however, and oddly in need of care. Her friend Berta answered the door and called over her shoulder to my Aunt Odalys, "She is here."

"She said you would come," Berta told me, smiling broadly.

"I wasn't expected," I said, stepping inside. My Aunt Odalys always did that to me.

The crude clay image of Eleggua, god of destiny and pathways, stared sternly from behind the door. Guardian of gateways, he is messenger to the gods, carrying communication between Santería priests and the orishas.

"But she knew you would come."

I squinted, my eyes growing accustomed to the half-light inside. Instead of the usual aromas of savory Cuban cooking, the air was heavy with incense and a smell I couldn't identify. I hoped it wasn't coming from the *nganga*, a large iron cauldron in the corner of the cozy living room.

"Where is she?"

"In the bedroom." Berta wiped her hands on a scarlet cloth that she carefully folded and placed in her pocket. "I will go now and come back later with the *palos* from the *botánica*."

Palos, twigs? Uh oh, I thought. "She's not sick, is she?"

Berta motioned me toward the bedroom and departed, her placid face unchanged.

"What's wrong?" She was stretched out on a chaise longue, dressed in white as usual. Her tawny skin, high cheekbones, and green eyes give my Aunt Odalys a slightly feline appearance. She looked beautiful, as always, but unnaturally still. In a cloud of incense, on a bedside table stood a statue of Yemayá, the Virgin of Regla, dressed in the blue of the sea.

My hand automatically went to my aunt's perfect brow, which was smooth and cool. But she seemed barely able to move.

"It will pass, *mi hijita*" she said, reassuringly. "It has not been so since I was paralyzed in the year the great storm struck Melena del Sur."

"Paralyzed?" This was the first I had heard about that. "That's the last time you had this problem?" I said. "Have you seen a doctor?"

"Then or now?"

"Either time." I pulled a chair up close to her side.

She smiled wanly. "Nothing can be done. This will pass. The gods are angry, Britt. There is great danger."

"Well that's Miami for you." I smiled, rearranging her pillows, to make her more comfortable.

Her eyes widened. "*¡El Mal!*" The evil! Where did you get them? The evil . . ."

"What?"

With effort she lifted a slim arm and with a long graceful nail, beautifully manicured in shiny platinum, she lightly touched one of the gold earrings I had worn daily since my interview with Reyes.

"Evil? No way. Gold is good." I smoothed her shiny dark hair, pushing it back from the small gold loops in her own tiny earlobes. "Diamonds may be better," I said, "but gold is good."

She didn't buy it, shaking her head woefully.

"My mother gave them to me when I was eighteen." Self-consciously, I fingered the gold. "I hardly ever wear them. But they're part of what I need to talk to you about. Why do you say they're evil?"

"Ask your mother," she murmured.

I sighed, took her hand in mine, and told her everything: my mother's odd behavior, Reyes and Bravo, my father's diary, and my questions.

"Your mother," she repeated, voice solemn. "Many years ago, she requested that I never speak to you of your father. It broke my heart but I gave my word."

"But why?"

"You must ask her, *mi corazoncito*. Antonio was a hero, a martyr. When we were children we were always together." She smiled fondly as she reminisced. "We played in the azure surf. He taught me to ride and to swim. Ah, *muy guapo*. My favorite brother." She paused and raised her eyes to mine. "Danger," she whispered. "The orishas will not be appeased."

"I'm taking you to the doctor," I said irritably, checking her pulse, watching the second hand on my watch. But she refused. "If you are not better tomorrow, you're going," I warned. "Do you know that my father's diary is supposedly somewhere in Miami?"

She turned to smile at the Virgin. "The sea and the winds have brought it. He wrote always. He wrote everything down. Always. Did you know he wrote poetry?"

A poet with an assault rifle, I thought. No wonder I am so screwed up.

"No I didn't know that. Why didn't you ever show me any of his poems? Do you have any?"

"Ask your mother." Her smile was sad. "She swore that I will never see you again if I speak to you of Antonio."

"For heaven's sake, I was a little kid. I'm over thirty now, old enough to see whomever I damn well please."

I brewed her some tea and as the water bubbled and roiled and began to boil, so did I. My life's work is communications. Why will no one I am close to communicate with me?

I intended to go right back to the office, but didn't. The T-Bird had a mind of its own and a lead foot on the gas pedal. Gotcha! I thought, as I wheeled into the parking lot. Her convertible occupied its space and I swung in right next to it.

When she did not answer the bell, I pounded with the metal knocker, my impatience fueled by anger and irony. I write stories about people's lives every day. What about my own? Why was the past so murky?

"Who is it!"

"Me." I sensed scrutiny from behind the peephole. "It's me, Mom." Did she suspect that some stranger was imitating her daughter? Would I need a SWAT team to get inside?

The chain rattled away and the door swung open. "Britt, what on earth . . . ?" Her pale hair was damp, a hand towel tossed over one shoulder as she tied the sash of a rose-colored robe. "All that pounding! I thought the fire department was evacuating the building!"

She brought the towel up to blot her hairline. "I was just getting out of the shower." She looked piqued, her voice husky. "You sounded like the Russian Army breaking down my door." She studied my face. "What's wrong?"

"Nothing." I brushed by, into her pastel living room.

"Look at you." Her voice was cajoling now. "You're out of breath, all windblown, your face is flushed." She stood back, giving me an appraising look. "You should really shorten that hemline, Britt. Legs are in right now. And yours are great."

I turned and folded my arms, lips tight, the posture of a stern mother. Barefoot and unaware, she looked the part of a vulnerable child.

"Why didn't you tell me you knew him?"

Her innocent blue eyes widened. "Who, Britt?"

"You know who. And that act of yours at lunch the other day. What *was* that?"

"How nice of you to visit," she said, voice frosty. "I don't have a clue to what you're talking about." She turned, flounced into her bedroom, and emerged wearing a pair of lace-trimmed scuffs that matched her robe.

I watched the graceful lope of her walk through new eyes. The luminescence of her still flawless skin, the lustrous hair exuding the scent of soap and rose water.

She was a fifty-three-year-old woman, but a damn good-looking one. What had she been like at twenty?

"Juan Carlos Reyes sends his regards."

She affected a world-weary look. "Now there's a name I never thought I'd hear again."

"Do you have my father's diary?"

"Your father's what?" She sounded irritated.

"His diary. I understand he kept one."

"Britt, that was thirty years ago. If there was such a thing I certainly wouldn't remember it now."

"Where are my father's things?" The few photos I have came from my Cuban grandmother and Aunt Odalys.

"Whatever there was," she said quietly, "is long gone."

"Why?" I cried out indignantly. "Didn't you ever think about me, that I would want . . . "

"I thought of nothing but you." Her cheeks reddened. "He's the one who didn't think! Of you, or me. He walked out on us both. What did he care?" She glanced toward the Waterford clock on a shelf. "I'm really busy right now. I wasn't expecting you. You should have called first, Britt." She tried to hustle me toward the door. Planting my feet firmly in the deep pile of her carpet, I refused to be hustled.

"I tried, but you ignored my messages. I'm not leaving without answers." We stared at each other like combatants thrust into the arena together.

"You barge in here," she said, voice rising, "spouting ancient history about which you know nothing, itching for an argument. . . ." Nostrils flaring, anger mounting, she ran out of words. For a moment I thought she might try to physically push me out the door. Instead she sank with weary grace into a wicker peacock chair. The fan back of the chair framed her patrician face, her robe draped just so as she reached for a cigarette in an enamel box on the end table. Always she had been just my mother. Would I ever see her that way again?

"Be careful, Britt," she said, her expression ironic. "You may get exactly what you want, and you may not like it." Her composure regained, she lit her long brown cigarette, then looked up. "I really must get to work. I'm coordinating plans for the fall fashion shows."

"I hate surprises." I spoke carefully. "How do you think I felt meeting a man like Reyes, never knowing that he knew me and my father, or you? I felt so stupid. I learn more about total strangers in twenty minutes on the job than I know about my own parents. I am not leaving until we discuss this." I plopped down on her soft flowered sofa.

She stood and walked to the window, staring out into the darkness that had fallen.

"It all happened so long ago." She spoke softly and I strained to hear. "I wanted to forget it. It was a different life, a different time, a different Miami. None of it has anything to do with you." She began to pace back and forth between the window and the sofa where I sat. Each time she neared the window she gazed out into the night as though searching for something that wasn't there.

"I had to put it all behind me. Why do you persist in opening old wounds? Why should you care about your father? He didn't care about us. He didn't give a shit about me or you."

"Tell me."

"What do you want to know?" she said flatly.

"What did you do with his things?"

"There wasn't that much. What I didn't toss I gave away." She shrugged. "I burned the letters."

"Why?"

"Britt, the son of a bitch abandoned me and my three-year-old daughter without a word. No note, no good-bye. For a long time I thought he took my life with him."

"Why, what happened between you?"

"That's what I asked myself until I hated him. He was the proverbial husband who went out for a loaf of bread and never came back. Not a hint. I had no idea where he was, if he intended to come home, or how I'd pay the bills if he didn't."

"Maybe he planned to be back."

"Sure," she said, her voice brittle. "I reported him missing, but the police didn't take it seriously when they heard who he was and who he ran with."

"And who was that?"

"Your friend Reyes, Jorge Bravo"—she drew on her cigarette—"and a man named Winslow who always seemed to be around in those days. All sorts of secretive, furtive people were in and out of our lives then. A pilot named Fiorini. I overheard them talk about covertly flying over the radar or under the radar, I don't know"—she shrugged impatiently—"dropping medical supplies, leaflets, weapons. Once they left on a boat. He said he'd be home that night, but didn't show up for three days and I was frantic. When they got back they talked about outrunning the Coast Guard on some mission and having to hide out in the Bahamas. Your father seemed to think that Cuba would be free soon and our lives would get back to normal." She sounded almost wistful. "Then he walked out the door on his way to some meeting and never came home again.

"Next thing I heard was that he was in prison in Cuba. He had always told me that if anything happened to him or if I had any problems, to call Winslow, but that phone number had been disconnected. Reyes and Bravo were nowhere to be found. I asked everywhere for help. None came. Then I heard he'd been executed. There were radio reports, a story in the newspaper. Bravo came by months later to pay his respects. I slammed the door on him."

"What about Reyes?"

She turned to gaze out the window again. "Oh, he reappeared as well. Courtly, suave, and full of secrets like the others. Adventurers," she spat. "People like them don't care who they hurt. Their lives are never normal, they are drawn to trouble. Danger is an addiction. They love it. As if there is not enough trouble and pain in the world. They made me sick, with their love of intrigue and egotistical dreams of making a difference." She stubbed out her cigarette, lit another, then lifted her eyes to mine through a haze of smoke.

When justifying my job to her I often talked about making a difference. Now I knew why she always took offense.

"It certainly made a difference in my life," she said sarcastically. "You have to understand, I was eighteen when we met and engaged to a young man my family loved. His parents and mine were best friends. Ironically, what attracted me most to Tony was his quiet strength and his strong sense of commitment. How could I know that what I interpreted as quiet strength was really secretiveness and that the commitment was an obsession that didn't include me? My family was furious when I gave up everything to marry Tony.

"They were right," she added crisply. "He left me broke,

betrayed, with a child. They never let me forget it. I never trusted another man. Why do you think I've been alone all these years?" Her blue-eyed stare was bold. "No matter, who would want you when you have a small child?"

So I am also to blame for her being alone, I thought. But I didn't object. She was talking at last. I wouldn't have interrupted for the world.

"So there I was, a widow, too stubborn to ask my estranged family for help. Never able to experience the closure of a final good-bye and burial. Do you know how important that is, Britt? More of those people kept being released from prison, coming back from Cuba or turning up, crawling out from under Lord knows what rocks. A steady stream of strangers, scary men dropping by at all hours. People who went by names like the Strange One and El Tigre. And then there were the FBI agents! They wanted to fill in their days and their time sheets and justify their existences by hanging around, sitting in my kitchen, asking me questions, even though they knew I knew nothing. It all replayed over and over again until I finally broke down. I was sick to death of it all and didn't want to hear anymore about it. I still don't." She paused, lost in thought.

"These earrings, the ones you gave me." I caught the smooth gold of one between my thumb and the knuckle of my index finger. "Where did you get them?"

Her eyes narrowed, focusing on me. "You wore them when you went to see Reyes?" she whispered.

I nodded.

"I should have known better than to give them to you! I want them back." Her voice rose. "Now! Give them to me!"

Lower lip quivering, I removed the earrings and dropped them into her outstretched hand. My hand shook. Hers didn't. The gleam of gold caught the artificial light for an instant. Then she dropped them into her pocket.

She went to her desk and began to flip briskly through some fashion layouts. "The only way I was able to hang on to my sanity was to try to forget it all." She turned and studied me over her shoulder, an odd look in her eyes. "I could have done it, if not for you. You're the only proof that it all really happened."

I stared back, her words scalding me. Like the scary strangers and the lazy FBI agents who had tormented her, I just wouldn't go away.

I lumbered to my feet, numb and clumsy. "I have a story to write," I murmured. She did not call after me as I walked out of her apartment and quietly closed the door.

I DROVE BACK to the paper on automatic pilot, feeling orphaned and alone, the familiar crackle from the police scanner comforting as it washed over me. Work, as always, was the best anesthetic. Taking a deep breath, I began returning messages. The boys' families had joined forces and had set their first meeting for Friday night. I promised to be there.

Lottie picked up the phone back in the darkroom and demanded to know where I'd disappeared to that afternoon. "Don't ask," I said. "I went to see my mother and my aunt. Separately, of course. God forbid they should ever find themselves in the same room. We are so dysfunctional. My mother has an elephant in her living room and pretends it isn't there. Trip over the trunk and she says, 'What? What elephant? What are you talking about?' Ask my aunt about the elephant and she says, 'Ask your mother.'"

"You can't belong to them," Lottie cooed soothingly. "You musta been switched at birth. At least you ain't blessed with all that many of the critters. You ought to try surviving one of my family reunions. It's like having a bowling alley in your brain. Some people ain't happy till they're miserable."

I told her about my encounter with Gretchen. "Are we the only people in the world who have no sex lives?" I sighed.

"What do you mean we?" she said smugly.

"Oh, no, Lottie, don't tell me? He's not back."

"Answer me one question, Britt. Just one. Could it be possible that Santana's name is not on the jail log 'cuz he's being held incommunicado, cooperating with cops who are arranging to put him into the witness protection program?"

"No. Shit. Is that what he told you? I mean it's plausible, but all his stories are plausible. He's a lawyer. He's always got some explanation that makes it seem possible that he is telling the truth."

"That's the hell of it," she agreed. "But this is absolutely his last chance. He swears he's a changed man."

"What's he gonna do, start cross-dressing?"

Silence followed. I'm dragging her down into misery with me, I thought guiltily. "Hell, it is possible," I said. "Anything's possible. But you deserve better. Did you get your hundred fifty-seven dollars back?" I asked accusingly.

"He didn't have any cash on him, left his wallet back at the office, in his briefcase."

"I rest my case."

"Maybe I shoulda frisked him," she conceded. "But he's making it all up to me. I'm seeing him tonight, and next week we're taking one of those day cruises to Freeport on the *Gettaway*. It sails at dawn, fab food, a casino, entertainment, dancing, swimming, sunning, with dinner and a nightclub show on the way back. No phones, no faxes, no beepers. I'm really looking forward to it."

What could I say? She sounded happy.

I returned Hal's call next, not expecting him to answer, but he caught it on the second ring.

An inquest had been set into the death of Ricky Mumper, the burglar Hal killed in his apartment.

"Will you be in court? Since you covered the story, I hoped you would be."

"I'm not the courthouse reporter," I said, "but I'll try. Are you hanging in there?"

"Sure," he said jauntily. "No problem, but you sound down. What's wrong?"

Did I sound that mopey? "Family stuff; you know, my mother." It sounded so trivial as it came out of my mouth. Hell, he was grappling with life-and-death issues, facing a court appearance that could brand him a killer.

"Want to have a drink later?"

"No, I'm working. . . ." I suddenly felt weepy. Work is my shield, my refuge from life's battles. Was I so bummed that a kind word from a stranger could disarm me and draw tears? She has finally done it, I thought. Her years of hard work have paid off. My mother has finally succeeded in turning me into a psych case.

"You can't work all the time. Maybe you need somebody to talk to."

He sounded sweet, but I was in no mood . . . I remembered the curling hairs on his chest and the lean belly . . . and his blood-stained living room. Did I want to date an ax killer? What would my mother think? Wait, I thought, who the hell cares what my mother thinks? Or my editors? Gretchen is one of my editors. Do I need her approval? I think not.

"Where do you want to meet?"

We decided on the 1800 Club, in an hour.

I blew my nose, visited the ladies' room, and dug out the cosmetics stashed in my locker. I mascaraed my lashes, daubed on some blusher, applied red lipstick in a shade called Torrid, and brushed my hair.

He was waiting near the door, seated at the bar in the dark, watching for me. "I was afraid you wouldn't show," he said, taking my arm and steering me with a comforting masculine presence to a table in the back. "That you'd get tied up on some story."

Handsomer, taller, and better groomed than I remembered, he was fully awake this time, fully dressed. And he hadn't just hacked up a stranger.

"Now," he said, closing his hand over mine across a small table in a dark room, as Sting sang "Fields of Gold" in the background, "tell me all about it." His smile was engaging, his eyes earnest. "Does your mom want to move in with you? Has she imposed a curfew? Or are you grounded?

"Hey, you're smiling. Can't be all that bad. Want me to write her a note on your behalf about what a good, beautiful, and talented daughter she has?"

"Let's not talk about my mother," I said wanly. "Tell me all about you."

He worked at an easy-listening radio station that played middle-of-the-road music. He told me about the new producer who spilled a thirty-two-ounce Slurpee into the control room console his first day on the job, the staggering cost of repairs, and the dreaded dead air. Small talk with him was effortless.

The place was nearly empty. We slow danced, and I fit easily into his arms. It was soothing, being held against his strong, warm body, moving effortlessly to "Because the Night" by 10,000 Maniacs. No awkward silences, or maybe I was too numb to notice.

Real life has a way of nipping at your heels. Nothing comfortable lasts. "I have to go home and walk my dog," I finally confessed, regretfully breaking the spell.

"Alone? At this hour?"

"Do it all the time." I waited for the words I knew would come.

"I'll walk him with you. I'm a pro. When I was eleven, I was in the business. Brushed, washed, and walked half a dozen pooches for our neighbors. Never met a dog I didn't like, except one. A black Chow named Mao." He shook his head and winced. "Mao the Chow. Whenever I turned my back he'd try to tear a piece outta my rump. God, did I hate that dog."

The image evoked thoughts of another schoolboy entrepreneur, young Charles Randolph with his boat-cleaning business.

I forced the phantom from my mind, at least for tonight. "How did you know my dog is a black Chow?" I joked.

Hal watched protectively as I got into my car, then followed me home to the Beach in his blue Nissan Maxima.

My landlords and neighbors had all retired. The security light must have burned out, and our two rows of garden apartments were enveloped in an inky sea of darkness. We spoke in whispers. Hal waited as I tossed my things inside and brought Bitsy out on her leash. The courtyard was as black as the bottom of a well. I grasped the leash with one hand and held on to Hal with the other as we made our way to the lighted street. Suddenly something lunged at us from the shadows behind the banana trees.

"What the . . . ?" Hal blurted. I gasped, heart pounding. Bitsy wagged her tail furiously.

"Hi, Britt! What were you working on so late?"

"Seth! You scared me. What are you doing up?"

"I was reading in my room, heard your car." He gave Hal a curious once-over. Seth looked even younger than twelve in the dark. "What are you doing?"

"Walking Bitsy," I said, putting my finger to my lips to shush him.

"Good, I'll go with you." He fell into step beside us.

Hal and I exchanged glances. Wide awake, full of youthful exuberance, eager for company and newspaper talk, Seth would be impossible to shake.

"Oh, no, you don't," I whispered urgently. "I don't want your grandparents waking up and finding your bed empty." I didn't mention the missing boys, but thought about them.

Seth was introducing himself to Hal and recognized his name. "Hey, you're the guy who whacked the burglar, right? Did you ax him what he was doing there? Heh, heh, heh."

"That's enough," I whispered furiously. "You get back inside."

Reluctantly, he went, and we strolled hushed South Beach streets under a silver sliver of a moon.

"Never took you for the toy poodle type," Hal said quietly.

"It was an accident. She's really a police dog." I explained how I inherited Bitsy from a close friend, a policewoman killed by a sniper during the riots.

"You are right out there on the front line," he said. "Maybe that's why I feel so comfortable with you after what happened. You're out there, you understand what the combat zone is like."

There was something in his voice. I looked at him hard in the soft glow from a streetlight.

"How are you doing, really, Hal?"

"Not the happiest of times." He tried to sound casual, watching a passing car. "You know it was different when that burglar was a frightening stranger in the dark, intruding on my space. Your only thought is survival. That and good old-fashioned outrage. Immediately after, you have this rush, relief that you got through it and nailed the bad guy. Then you find out he was a twenty-seven-year-old man with a name and a life and a family."

I squeezed his hand as we walked on in silence. "He put himself at risk," I said finally. "He made the choice. He took the chance. You were asleep in your own bed. Alone." I smiled. "You protected yourself and who knows how many future victims from pain and grief, or worse."

"I don't know whether that's true or not, Britt, but thanks."

Back at my front door, I fished the key from my pocket in the dark. He seemed reluctant to leave.

"Want to come in?" I whispered.

"You sure it's all right?"

I drew him inside, scanning the shadows for Seth, who I suspected was watching, and softly closed the door behind us.

He followed as I flicked on the lights and went into the kitchen. He stood in the doorway, eyes troubled, as I fed the dog and Billy Boots, who glared at the stranger from beneath a chair until I filled his dish.

"You see what people do to each other every day. How do you live with it?"

Pouring us each a glass of wine, I hesitated and studied his earnest face. "I don't know," I murmured, realizing that, at the moment, it was true. We took our drinks back into the living room and settled on the couch.

"When the cops emptied the guy's pockets," Hal said, "he had a grocery list and a card in his wallet, a reminder that he had a dental appointment. I know it sounds crazy, but I keep wondering if anybody called to cancel, like maybe I should do something. . . ." He shook his head, as though bewildered by his own thoughts.

"His record reflected a long history of rip-offs. That's what he did all his life. That's what he was gonna keep doing the rest of his life. What if, instead of you, it had been a young woman who encountered him in her apartment in the middle of the night? What would have happened to her?"

He traced the line of my jaw with a gentle touch, tilted my chin, and kissed my lips. My arms encircled his neck, drawing his face down to mine to prolong the moment, as though I was a Sahara wanderer quenching a desert thirst.

Wanting more, I settled for resting against his shoulder, his arm around me as we talked.

"My parents are embarrassed," he said sadly. "Because my name was in the paper, after it happened. I didn't expect that." He sipped his wine. "I didn't expect a lot of things. Since the . . . incident, the guys at work call me Killer or the Executioner. They think it's funny. People I hardly know slap me on the back and congratulate me—when this is not something to be congratulated about. It's a tragedy." He turned to look at me. "A girl I dated, nothing serious, is so turned off by it that she won't even talk to me. Another woman, at the station, is so turned on by it she wants to come home with me and have sex right where it happened. That's what she said." He raked his fingers through his hair. "Christ. I didn't want it to happen, Britt. I hit a rabbit once with my car, picked it up, and rushed it to the vet. I'm not some natural-born killer. How am I gonna live with this?"

He looked away, but not before I saw that his eyes were shiny with tears. This man was more wounded than I was.

"You did the best you could," I whispered, reaching for him. "If you weren't a good person you wouldn't feel this way. You did what you had to do. As for parents, we shouldn't ever let them hurt us."

I found his lips to comfort him, or was it me? He responded and our anguish became passion. Our bodies burned to comfort each other. His kisses heated whatever reservations I had into a molten need; our growing excitement swept us from the couch to the carpeted floor. My hair cascaded across his face as I was enveloped in his arms, sinking, his wordless murmuring in my ear. What began slowly became a fervent tugging, unbuttoning, unhooking, unsnapping, and unzipping as our bodies struggled to entwine. I expected a sizzle as our bare flesh met. I wasn't disappointed.

"No, no," I said abruptly, raising up on one elbow. Hal hesitated.

"Not you," I mumbled, pulling him to me feverishly. "Go away," I told Bitsy, who was slobbering a wet kiss on my left eye.

Hal laughed in relief and resumed his tender touching of my most secret places. This is right, I thought. The passion and the wine anesthetized the pain I felt for the missing boys' parents and for Alex, and the Haitian crash victims, José Caliente, and all of us dead too soon at any age.

Life's journey is so short, so solitary. We arrive alone and leave the same way. Sometimes, in a rare moment, we achieve a oneness with a fellow traveler. This was one of them. "Bedroom," I murmured. He nodded, breathing hard.

Like survivors of a whirlwind, we luxuriated in the soft comfort of my bed and each other. His tight shiny skin and the touch and smell of his hard body took my breath away.

He was skillful with his mouth and hands. We took all the time we needed and reveled in the warmth afterward. Sex after death is good.

"Do you want me to go?" he whispered, cradling me in his arms.

"Try it and I'll confiscate your car keys," I said, and kissed him soundly.

"Good." He sighed and settled into my bed as though he belonged there. At that moment, he did.

Too exhausted to sleep, we talked about the man he killed, about life, death, our parents—not typical pillow talk, but right for us.

"If only they hadn't released him early. If only he had been reha-bilitated or learned a damn trade . . ."

"Forget the if onlys," I murmured. "There is no justice, just us. His crimes were escalating. You saved somebody else."

I told him about my mother's rejection of me and about my father and his diary.

"I want to know," I said dreamily, Hal's heartbeat in my ear, "am I the kind of daughter he wanted me to be? Do I think like him? Walk like him? Talk like him?"

"If he was alive, he would probably kill me," Hal said, thoughtful-ly. "But you're right. Whatever he wrote belongs to you. You should find it, like the adopted children who track down their biological parents. It's a clue to what made you the wonderful creature you are." He kissed my left eye, where Bitsy had been licking earlier.

We slept like the dead, in each other's arms. He started awake once, disoriented, sitting upright in bed, fists clenched. The digital clock glowed 3:30 A.M. "It's all right. You're here with me," I said sleepily and reached for him.

"Jesus," he whispered, sinking back into my arms. "I've been doing that at the same time every night since it happened." Grazing his biceps with my teeth, I nibbled upward toward his throat. "As long as we're both awake . . . ," I breathed. He grinned as I straddled his body and we were lost again in each other.

14

I STARED GLUMLY into my pantry as Hal showered. The kitchen glowed with sunlight, birds chirped in the ylang-ylang tree outside, and all seemed right with the world—or would have if I had something besides stale bread for breakfast.

Hal loomed in the doorway, one of my blush-colored bath towels around his waist just below the tan line, running a comb through his damp hair.

"How does breakfast at the News Café sound?" In addition to his other talents, the man was a mind reader.

"Great. If only you had the right clothes with you, we could jog the boardwalk first." I ached to run beneath Miami's big sky, in front of the open sea and sand.

"I thought we already achieved our target heart rate." His voice was husky. He pulled me close, nuzzling my hair. "Best night's sleep I've had in a long time," he murmured in my ear.

We had been there for each other, paths crossing at a perfect moment in time. Synchronicity, coincidence, a gift from a benevolent God?

He drank coffee and read the paper while I showered.

"One problem," I said, as I finished dressing and brushed my hair. "Seth is an early riser."

"The jealous type, huh?" Hal grinned. "Should I climb out your bathroom window and crawl to the car though the hedges?"

"That may not be a bad idea. He may even have his camera," I worried, squinting through the blinds.

I took Bitsy out to reconnoiter and then we made a run for it.

We chose an outside table at the News Café on Ocean Drive, across from the sandy beach and sparkling surf, surrounded by drop-dead gorgeous models, tourists in shorts, habitués with their dogs, yuppie motorcyclists, wealthy retirees perusing their *Wall Street Journal*s, and beautiful people trying to hit on one another. Sleepy-eyed Europeans inhaled coffee with their cigarette smoke. The on-camera Hollywood types looked buff, well manicured and polished, while the off-camera specimens, artsy and creative, hunched at tables, hair in their eyes. The waiters and waitresses, mostly starving performers, wore shorts and T-shirts. Seagulls and in-line skaters flashed by, and a local character wearing a birthday-cake hat with real candles appeared to be selling something to passersby. Mere hours ago I was an unloved orphan. Now I laughed a lot while devouring a huge breakfast of yogurt and granola with Florida pecans, fresh strawberries, pineapple, watermelon, and honeydew. Hal drank fresh-squeezed orange juice and attacked his scrambled eggs and bagels ravenously.

As we lingered over café au lait, the sun climbing higher, superheating the salty air, my beeper chirped. The number was that of the city desk. "It's my day off," I said, and shook my head.

"Don't you think you should see what it is?" Hal said.

"I know I'll regret it," I predicted, and went reluctantly to an outside pay phone.

As usual, I wound up on hold. As I stood and waited, a booming voice rent the air behind me.

"*. . . and the sun became black as sackcloth of hair, and the moon became as blood . . .*"

The lean ragged street preacher from that night with Lottie at South Pointe was railing at the diners and passersby. "*And the stars of heaven fell unto the earth . . .*"

"Britt?"

"Yes, what is it, Gretchen? I'm off today."

"*. . . even as a fig tree casteth her untimely figs . . .*"

"Who on earth is that?"

"I'm on South Beach," I said, impatiently, blinding sun in my eyes, perspiration beading on my brow.

"*. . . when she is shaken of a mighty wind. . . .*"

"Apparently Jorge Bravo and his crew conducted a commando raid on the Cuban coast yesterday, and the FBI is looking for him. We're short-handed. Could you come in and handle it?"

"That crazy SOB." I remembered the bulky outline under the tarp in Bravo's living room and felt a stab of remorse. I should have tried to stop him. But he was so crippled, how could he . . . ?

"*And the heaven departed . . .*"

I turned to frown at the bearded preacher, intending to shush him, but his eyes were so wild and dark that I quickly averted my own.

"Are they sure it was him?"

"That's what we need to find out. And, oh, Lottie needs to talk to you. She's back in photo. Thanks much, Britt. I'll transfer you. When will you be in?"

"I don't get involved in Cuban politics. . . ." I sighed. "An hour." Amazing how polite Gretchen had become.

"*. . . as a scroll when it is rolled together; and . . .*"

Lottie came on the line demanding to know where I was.

"South Beach, having breakfast with a gorgeous man."

"*. . . every mountain and island were moved out of their places!*"

"That him?"

"No, it's that crazy street preacher, you've seen him."

"Not that I can recollect."

"Of course you have, what do you need?"

"Your buddy, Jorge Bra—"

"I know, I know," I muttered, "the feds are after him again."

She lowered her voice. "But didya know he's trying to reach you?"

"What?" I turned, and the street preacher was gone and there was only casual chatter and laughter from the café and the sounds of the Atlantic throwing its huge salty body onto the beach. I stared up and down the side streets but he had vanished.

"When he couldn't get you, he called me," Lottie was saying. "Said he needs to talk to you right away."

"Oh, swell." Wants to tell me his self-serving side of the story before he gets busted, I thought. "So he's back from . . . wherever he was last night. Give him my beeper number if he calls again. Is, uh, everything else okay?" Seeking nonexistent shade, I paced three tiny steps back and forth, as far as the phone cord permitted. The scalding pavement burned the bottoms of my feet through the thin soles of my sandals.

"Couldn't be better," she said. "I'm shopping for cruisewear later, if I can get a break."

"It's only a day cruise. For Pete's sake, Lottie."

"I know," she said happily, "but I'm in a mood to shop."

Lottie normally hates shopping and does hers by catalog. "I'm impressed," I said. Amazing what love does.

"Did you see where that street preacher went?" I asked Hal, back at our table.

"Who?"

"The guy with the beard, spouting doomsday stuff, making all that noise."

He frowned. "Didn't notice 'im," he said. "I was watching you."

• • •

"I'll call," he said, as he dropped me off at my apartment. "But I need your home number."

"I never share it with story subjects," I said briskly. "Bad policy."

I smiled at his expression. "But you're an exception. I have good news and bad news," I said, scribbling my number onto the back of a business card. "Remember why you called me last night?"

He blinked. The big breakfast, or maybe the busy night preceding it, had slowed his thought processes down to a crawl.

"The inquest. You wanted me to cover the inquest."

A shadow reappeared behind his eyes and I regretted mentioning it on this beautiful cloudless morning.

"Well, the bad news is that I can't report it because we now have a . . . personal relationship. But the good news is that I'll be there if you want me to, maybe bring my friend Lottie along, too, for moral support. Then we can go out for a drink or something."

"Deal."

Our good-bye kiss lingered.

The "war communiqué" issued by Jorge Bravo and his organization, A Free Cuba Regiment, was waiting at the office. Foreign tourists were ordered off the island and warned that future travel to Cuba would be at their own risk. Faxed to the newsroom at 2 A.M., the statement was addressed to the paper and marked to my attention. An accompanying press release announced an AFC raid on a "military target" in Cuba twenty-four hours earlier. Radio Havana had confirmed an attack on a Spanish-owned hotel in Varadero, Cuba's leading tourist resort in Matanzas Province about sixty-five miles east of Havana, on the north coast.

In an attempt to make up revenue lost when the Soviet Union collapsed, Castro focused on rebuilding the country's once thriving tourist trade. Spanish investors had poured millions into Cuba's hotel industry.

Hit-and-run raiders in a twenty-eight-foot boat had fired machine guns and lobbed grenades at the oceanfront Vista del Mar resort hotel. No deaths, but several security guards, a police officer, and a busboy at a poolside bar had suffered minor injuries.

The shapes under the tarp in Jorge's living room haunted me. The wires buzzed with protests from Havana, accounts from the State Department. My pager sounded. The number was one I didn't recognize. Taking a deep breath, I dialed.

"*¡Hola!*"

"Jorge?"

"*Sí, ¿Montero?*"

"Yes. Where are you?" I demanded.

He paused. "Little Havana."

"Where?"

"Little Havana is anywhere that two or more Cubans are gathered together in the cause of freedom."

I sighed. "Jorge," I said sharply, "are you aware that the FBI . . ."

"I cannot speak on this *teléfono*. It is too dangerous. Did you tell anyone?"

"No, Jorge, but I think the FBI wants to talk to you."

"I have nothing to say to them. It is you I must talk to."

"Talk."

"Face-to-face."

Why did I know he would say that? "Where?"

"The Torch of Friendship."

"In Bayfront Park? Isn't that rather public, under the circumstances?"

"I must hang up. This *teléfono*. . ." His voice grew distant. I could hear the din of traffic in the background.

The local cops probably couldn't trace a call successfully with six months' advance notice. I was not so sure about the FBI. They were probably better at it.

"I'll be there. When?"

"Now."

What am I getting into? I asked myself. Exactly what I swore I wouldn't, the murky undertow of Cuban exile shenanigans.

I found a parking spot on the Boulevard and walked across to the Torch, built in 1960 and rededicated in memory of President Kennedy in 1964. The eternal flame was not burning. The eighteen-foot-tall symbol of hemisphere solidarity and goodwill had been deliberately rammed by a huge rental truck ten days earlier.

A Cuban flag draped around him, a sixty-year-old refugee was driving the cargo hauler, fitted with a heavy-duty bumper, when it mounted the curb, roared through the flower beds and a black olive hedge, and smashed into the bronze torch. Gas lines feeding the perpetual flame ruptured. The symbol of unity buckled, and witnesses fled for their lives, fearing an explosion.

The driver didn't seem to care that his next stop was jail. He and several accomplices were painting "Cuba Will Be Free" on the memorial wall behind the torch and shooting snapshots of their handiwork when the cops arrived. The torch would be restored when the city figured out how to appropriate the money.

Jorge was nowhere in sight. I stood for a moment, sun beating down on my face, shriveling the ends of my hair into burned wisps. Sweat wormed its clammy way down the middle of my back. I needed a hat, I needed sunscreen, I needed my day off.

Nobody around but a few of the homeless who have virtually taken over the park. I checked my watch. A teenage girl in cut-offs and a black midriff top strolled by. She smiled persistently as I looked away, annoyed and impatient. Was she going to ask me for money?

"Britt Montero?"

"Do I know you?" No more than sixteen, she was slim, in straw sandals and mango-colored lipstick, her eyes concealed behind dark shades.

"Luisa, AFC *especialista*. The *comandante* asks that you join him."

"You're a member?"

"*Sí*," she said proudly. "Since I was born."

We strolled toward the Boulevard as I realized that an upper floor of the aging hotel across the street was an excellent vantage point from which to determine whether I had arrived alone or leading a phalanx of federal agents. I assumed, as we picked our way through traffic, that we would continue into the lobby and board the elevator to some small room overlooking the park. Instead an old Lincoln, black with rust spots, glided to the curb.

The girl steered me toward it as I resisted. "It is the *comandante*," she said. Sure enough the back door swung open and Jorge Bravo beckoned. He wore a military bearing, a white guayabera, and a sun-burned face. Like someone who's been out on the water, I thought grimly. A skinny middle-aged man with black shoe-polish hair and dark glasses sat behind the wheel. With major misgivings, I climbed into the backseat.

"*¿Estás loco?*" I greeted him.

"We are at war," he announced dramatically, as the car lurched away from the curb, leaving Luisa on the sidewalk.

"You can't wage war on tourists, Jorge."

"It was a military objective," he said, his jaw square.

"It was a resort hotel, for Christ's sake! Kill some tourists and see what happens. You want to create an international incident? If the feds prove you planned it here, you won't see daylight again."

"We must frighten them, so they stop traveling to Cuba, spending their tourist dollars, strengthening Castro and keeping him in power." He spoke matter-of-factly, as though explaining the only commonsense course of action to a child.

"I know what you're saying, but if you kill innocent foreigners, you only succeed in making Castro's position stronger. And what about you? What about the neutrality laws?"

Because the law forbids launching military expeditions from U.S.

soil, freedom fighters on missions usually make pit stops in the Bahamas in order to claim that their operations actually originated there. They don't fool anybody.

"This country cannot tell an oppressed people that they are not permitted to wage war on tyrants," Bravo said stubbornly.

"You know the Cubans will shoot you if you're caught. And you better hope they find you first. The Justice Department is already involved. You know what Janet Reno will do. She doesn't fool around."

"These are the same people, CIA, FBI, who gave us money and weapons to fight Castro. Now they say it is a crime." Bravo threw up his hands. "I was not a criminal then! I am not now. I am a patriot!" He shook his fist. "We are at war, it does not end because somebody is taken into a courtroom. I have no fight with the United States. My fight is with Fidel."

"This is loco," I said, looking out to see where we were. I wanted to go back to my car. This was hopeless.

"Some day, Montero, you will learn what your father knew, that freedom is more than the lack of bars around you. *Sí*, this is loco, so loco that if he still lived, he would stand with us."

He said it like he believed it. Was he right? Was my father this deranged?

"Are you going to talk to the FBI?"

"Of course not. I am underground. They will not find me."

Maybe I should just jump from this moving car now, I thought irritably, scanning traffic for undercover cars.

"You can't run around acting like a goddamn terrorist."

"Why not?" he said angrily.

"First," I said, "you are too old to run."

He smiled ironically. "I am too old not to run. I have spent my life fighting for Cuba. The spark never dies. That is how I will die. I want to be buried in a free Cuba."

He put his maimed and calloused hand over mine. "Our goal is to spark a rebellion among the Cuban people. That spark could be ignited by the words in Antonio's *diario*. We must find it before Reyes seizes it. If we can broadcast it to the people—"

"My father's diary?"

"*Sí*. It is in the possession of a man named Armando Gutiérrez. Reyes has his *criminales* searching for him now."

"Reyes is an international businessman, he is politically connected, why would he—?"

Bravo's ominous look cut me off, reminding me of the wild-eyed street preacher spouting doom and disaster.

He leaned forward. "If Gutiérrez contacts you, you must contact me at once. Luisa is my liaison officer. Here is her number." He shoved a scrap of paper at me and I stuffed it absently into my purse.

"How old is she? Shouldn't she be in school?"

Bravo ignored me, thinking aloud. "If the *diario* is lost, perhaps we could plant a bomb at the Morro lighthouse. *Sí*, extinguish the beacon that has burned for four hundred years. Perhaps that is the spark that would ignite the Cuban people."

"*¡Sí, comandante!*" the driver said enthusiastically. "*¡Explota el faro del Morro!*"

I rolled my eyes.

"When it happens and the people take to the streets, we will be ready. Our mission is twofold," Bravo said earnestly. "We will put an end to Fidel and prevent Juan Carlos Reyes from becoming Cuba's new dictator."

There is no stopping this madness, I thought. Just when I thought this day could go no further downhill, it did.

"*¡Comandante!*"

We had just run an amber light on U.S. 1 in Coconut Grove. A beige late-model Ford Crown Vic occupied by two men jumped the red and was rapidly closing in on us.

"*Eloy, ¿es el FBI?*" Bravo said.

"*No sé*." He shrugged.

Swell, I thought. How am I going to explain this to the FBI and to my bosses? I had told Gretchen I was going to lunch. I would have to display my press identification and explain to the agents that I was merely a reporter interviewing a newsmaker. I would have to involve Mark Seybold, the *News*'s attorney. I should have known this was a mistake.

Instead of pulling over, Eloy floored it. The old Lincoln leaped forward. "Wait a minute!" I cried. "Pull over!"

"*¡Rápido! rápido!* Step on it, Eloy!" Bravo said.

"*¡Sí, comandante!*" He spun the wheel, veering around a crowded jitney, as I looked over my shoulder in horror.

"You can't run from the FBI!"

"What if it is not the FBI?"

"Who else?"

"Castro agents or Reyes's men."

"That's ridiculous!" I cried, groping for my seat belt and finding there was none. Now, I thought, the situation can't become any worse. I was wrong. Bravo pulled a .45-caliber semiautomatic out from under his guayabera. And Eloy came up with a sawed-off shotgun, looking over his shoulder as we overtook a lumbering school bus at high speed.

Will my mother be sorry I am dead? I wondered. Probably not. But Hal will, and maybe even Kendall McDonald. Gretchen won't. Lottie will.

"Look out!" I screamed. "School bus!"

Eloy steered around it, two wheels on the curb.

"That's it!" I screamed. "Stop the car! I'm getting out."

Bravo and the driver ignored me, conversing in rapid-fire Spanish that I only picked up in parts. One thing was clear. They had no intention of stopping.

Taking both hands off the wheel, Eloy racked one into the chamber of his sawed-off. Bravo used his good hand to do the same with the automatic.

"You can't shoot at the FBI!" I screamed. My annoyance and anger had given way to true terror. The best I could hope for now was to wind up handcuffed, face down on the pavement with the barrel of an FBI semiautomatic Sig 226 to my head.

We hurtled south on U.S. 1. I watched frantically for a City of Miami patrol car. Only startled motorists standing on their brakes, leaning on their horns, and careening out of our way as we cut them off, ran red lights, and skidded through intersections. Broad daylight. Where are the cops? I glared at Bravo and Eloy, gritted my teeth, and held on. These were the same clowns who got my father killed. Now I was next.

"Don't worry," Bravo said. "You are safe with me." He opened a battered satchel at his feet, took out a box of shotgun shells, and tossed it into the front seat.

Traffic jammed ahead of us and Eloy took to the median, the big car mowing down plantings and young trees. Green fronds obscured the windshield. I prayed that a sprinkler head would puncture one of our tires. No such luck. The Crown Vic was gallomping over the median behind us, still in hot pursuit. Gaining, it swung around a line of traffic and came up alongside. I glimpsed the men in front, both wearing dark glasses.

The push-button window on the front passenger side rolled down and Eloy raised the sawed-off. "No! No! No!" I screamed, clamping my palms over my ears. The deafening blast created shock waves around me and I saw the huge front plate-glass window of an auto dealership disintegrate in slow motion. The car fishtailed all over the road as Eloy struggled for control. Why aren't they bleeding from the ears? I wondered. Their eardrums were probably already damaged from years of war games in the Everglades. The Crown Vic dropped back a car length but stayed right on our tail.

Oh no. A solid wall of traffic loomed ahead. Eloy swung into the parking lot of Coral Gables High School. "Not a school!" I cried. I could barely hear myself; my voice sounded as though I were under water. He skidded around the building into the big back lot. A driver's ed class was in progress. Rows of folding chairs occupied by about forty waiting teenagers. In the center seven or eight cars, two school kids to a car, maneuvered at slow speeds through lanes of orange traffic cones set up by an instructor.

"Look out!" I shrieked, ears still ringing, unable to hear myself. The Crown Vic spun out on a stretch of lawn behind us, then backed up and roared toward us. "Look out!"

We raced straight through the class in progress. The trainer cars scrambled, two collided. The instructor, several teens on foot, and the kids seated on the chairs all assumed it was a drive-by and instinctively hit the ground. Bodies flat, heads down, no running for cover, just as taught in their drive-by shooting drills.

We flew out the far side of the lot. Looking back I saw a folding chair bounce off the hood of the Crown Vic as it hurtled in reverse rather than try to navigate the obstacle course of kids flat on their stomachs all over the parking lot.

Eloy hit one of the quiet Gables residential streets, made several sharp turns, then slowed to a sedate speed. I eased down onto the floor, trembling, face in my hands. "Stop at the next corner and let me out," I said.

"*¿Qué?*" Bravo cupped his hand over his ear.

Would any of us ever hear normally again?

They insisted on taking me back to my car near Bayfront Park. I would have preferred a bus, a cab, hitchhiking, or shoe leather. I would have happily crawled. But in the time it took to argue the point we were nearly there, with me scanning traffic for the cops. There had to be a BOLO (Be On the Lookout) for all of us by now. I expected roadblocks, choppers, patrol cars. There were none. Perhaps it was luck, or some jurisdictional radio foul-up between the Gables and Miami.

Ears ringing, knees weak, I stepped out of the Lincoln onto sun-scorched Biscayne Boulevard. I wanted to drop to my knees and kiss the pavement in gratitude. It seemed so very long ago that we had left, yet by my watch it was less than twenty-five minutes.

Bravo said something before I slammed the door, looking furtively over my shoulder for police or the FBI. I couldn't hear what he said but it didn't matter. Had I answered, he couldn't have heard me.

I meticulously obeyed all the traffic laws as I drove carefully back to the office. My first reaction that morning had been to ignore my beeper. I was right. My hearing seemed to return a bit in the elevator.

Gretchen was waiting. "Have a good lunch?" She smiled sweetly. I liked the old Gretchen better, I thought. At least I knew where she stood.

"The FBI has been calling," she said, scrutinizing my face. "What's wrong, Britt? Did something you ate disagree with you?"

THE Y KNOW. THE Y saw. I'm dead.
Oh shit, I thought. Cops and crooks can be reasoned with, but the FBI scares me.

The message was from Don Farmer, the local bureau spokesman who often called in official press releases. Should I brief Mark Seybold or wait to see exactly what the FBI wanted? Lawyers hate surprises, especially unpleasant ones, so I called Mark's number. He was out.

I dialed Jerry, the reporter who mans our police radios in a claustrophobic cubicle off the newsroom. A cacophony of scanners chorused in the background, and I listened while he finished questioning a Coast Guard spokesman about the search for an accountant who had called his wife on his cellular phone to say his ship-to-shore radio was dead and his sailboat was taking on water three miles offshore.

"What's going on, Jerry?"

"Not much," he said. "Pretty quiet, in fact. Number cruncher lost at sea, a traffic dispute and chase on U.S. One, 'bout an hour ago. Shots fired, sounded like it would turn into something but they ran right through a driver's ed class at Gables High and got away."

"Anybody hurt?"

"Nope. Sounds gang-related to me."

I hung up weak with relief. Nobody hurt. No thanks to Jorge Bravo. I called Don Farmer.

"Got something for you, Britt."

"Yeah?" I said suspiciously, determined to stay cool and admit as little as possible.

"You know Jorge Bravo, the AFC honcho."

I squeezed my eyes closed, teeth on edge, stomach lurching. Why hadn't Mark Seybold been there when I called? "Yeah?"

"I'm sure you saw the press release he issued on that aquatic drive-by along the Cuban coast."

"The firing on the Vista del Mar."

"Right, well, we're about to execute a search warrant on Bravo's house. Thought you'd be interested."

"Why?" I said shortly.

"Well—" he sounded puzzled—"they said you were working on the story."

"Oh, I am." My eyelid had begun to twitch. Lucky I hadn't chosen a life of crime. I could never pull off a successful caper, I thought.

"Just thought you'd want the tip. The agent-in-charge appreciated your story on that bank robber, the one whose children turned him in after you put his surveillance camera photo in the newspaper."

"Thanks, Don. That's great." My enthusiasm sounded weak and phony even to me.

"Okay, here's the location." He repeated Bravo's address, which I dutifully wrote down. "The U.S. magistrate just signed the warrant, and agents from the terrorism task force will head out there in the next hour."

"He in custody?" I asked casually.

"No. If he's there they'll bring him in for a statement, but there's no arrest warrant yet. His bond may be revoked first. They're looking for weapons, evidence of illegal activity, contraband, that kind of thing.

"If you go out there, with a photographer," he added, "be cool, like some neighbor called it in to you."

"Sure. Thanks, Don."

"The FBI wants their picture taken when they toss Bravo's house," I told Bobby Tubbs at the desk, "probably to deter other groups Bravo might inspire to go south for a bite out of Castro."

The feds may just want to lure me away from the newsroom and the paper's lawyer, I worried, hoping Lottie was free. She was, and we rode together.

"Don't let on that we're familiar with the place," I warned her. "And if Bravo shows up, the operative word is *duck*!" I filled her in on what had happened, talking fast.

"Slow down." She squinted sideways at me as she drove. "We better git you some water afore you overheat. If what don't kill you makes you strong, you must be the toughest woman in town. Now tell me about your breakfast date. Did you go *out* to breakfast with him or did you meet him for breakfast? Big difference." She cut her eyes at me again.

I told her everything—almost. She was more interested in my romantic interlude than in my close encounters with death and/or arrest. Life-threatening occupational hazards are routine to Lottie. She has hiked through a jungle with Shining Path guerrillas in Peru, been caught in firefights in El Salvador, and dodged bullets in bombed-out Beirut.

"Great guns and little fishes, Britt. You mean we both have a personal life at the same time? Too bad you and Hal can't join us on the *Gettaway* in the morning." She read my expression. "You'll really like Stosh when you get to know him."

"It might be fun," I conceded. "I do love to be out on the water."

"You'd love the dancing and the gambling and the nightclub acts too."

"But no way, not on such short notice. Hal is working, and I have the parents' meeting tomorrow night."

"Just one favor, then. You're an early riser. Kin you drive me to the port to meet Stosh in the morning?"

"You're not going together?"

"He's working late tonight, preparing for some trial. The man is not an early riser. Always in trouble with some judge for being late. The ship sails at dawn. He's coming from south, I'm coming from the north. The port is in the middle. Imagine sailing into Government Cut at one A.M., beneath a blanket of stars and seeing the twinkling lights of the city, then disembarking from a romantic cruise and going home in separate cars. Puleeeze, Britt, you owe me one," she pleaded. "And I want this to be perfect. He's so gorgeous, so red hot, so . . ."

"Okay, okay, okay. What time do I pick you up?"

"Five," she said, beaming.

"A.M.?"

"A course."

"Oh man," I whined. "Deal. On one condition. Hal is nervous about the inquest. We have to be there for moral support. You'll like him."

A single Miami patrol car and several unmarked FBI vehicles, mostly white, a Dodge Aries or two, a few Chevrolet Caprices, were clustered on the gravel and in the street around Bravo's house. Much to my relief I saw no beige Crown Vic among them, or the old Lincoln. Half a dozen agents, four men and two women, from the terrorism task force were descending on the house. They wore jeans or cargo pants, sneakers, and blue baseball caps and raid jackets with FBI emblazoned on them in yellow letters. Two had gone to the back door. All had on the new bulletproof vests that fasten at the sides with Velcro and have handy pockets for shotgun shells. I remembered Bravo's words as I watched them. It is ironic that the federal government now targets exiles for doing exactly what it once trained, equipped, and encouraged them to do.

The case agent did not look surprised to see us, or perturbed as Lottie began shooting pictures. He was reading the warrant to Nerida, who stood submissively on the front porch in a simple cotton house-dress. Resigned and stoic, she was shrugging her shoulders, as though saying she did not know the whereabouts of the *comandante*. She had been through this drill before. A few neighbors had begun to gather, idly watching.

As the agents brushed by her, we joined Nerida on the porch. *"No está* home."

"Good," I said. Her eyes agreed.

She stepped back inside to watch and we followed. Agents were opening closets, pushing up ceiling panels. Our eyes went immediately to the tarp in the corner. It was still there. One agent approached and lift-ed the canvas. I caught my breath as he yanked it back to expose what was hidden. Lottie fired off a picture.

Vacuum cleaners. Half a dozen, ranging from the basic no-frills model to a deluxe top-of-the-line carpet beautifier with an automatic cord winder and all the attachments. Canisters, uprights, power nozzle connec-tors, flexible hoses, and disposable filter bags.

"Mi esposo es vendedor de vacuum cleaners," Nerida told them.

I remembered what Reyes had said. Bravo did demonstrate and sell vacuum cleaners.

One of the agents peered suspiciously down a hollow aluminum wand. "You attach that to the hose, then plug it in," Lottie said help-fully.

"I'll have to ask you ladies to step outside," the case agent snapped.

They searched for forty-five minutes. Wherever Bravo had stashed his arsenal, it was not at home. One agent even crawled under the house. They found no weapons, but did carry out some papers in a cardboard box. They left Nerida, who did not seem upset, with a copy of the search warrant and an inventory of what they had seized: some old maps of Cuba, bills and telephone records, a personal telephone directory, and "an eleven by fourteen framed photograph of several armed men." My father's picture.

The crowd of neighbors outside had grown. "*¡Cuba sí, Castro no! ¡Viva Bravo!*" they were shouting.

The agents were not happy as they departed. I knew the drill necessary for the warrant. First they had taken a detailed description of the premises and exactly what they sought to the U.S. Attorney's office and requested an affidavit. The case agent who signed it then took the affidavit to a U.S. magistrate, who issued the warrant. Agents had photographed the premises and scoped out the house and surrounding neighborhood for factors like small children and vicious dogs. They had checked out the phone number and the types of doors and windows and outlined a plan. A final briefing took place in front of a blackboard with sketches of the house, yard, and adjacent streets. Each agent had read the entire warrant. Radio channels had been set up and the route to the nearest hospital noted in case something went wrong. Miami police had been contacted and asked to send a marked patrol unit. The officer who responded had been filled in immediately before the warrant was served.

A great deal of effort had been expended. The FBI probably was not going to like a newspaper picture of its elite terrorism task force clad in body armor and uncovering—vacuum cleaners.

I called my Aunt Odalys later from the office, determined to carry out my threat to take her to a doctor if she was no better. No problem, Berta said, "No doctor. Hold on, she wants to talk to you."

"*Mi hijita.*" Her voice sounded weak. "The spirits in the caldron are weeping. They say that what you seek is gone forever."

"What does the heck does that mean?"

"Only you know, *mi hijita.*"

"My father's diary? The missing boys? Love? All hope of a raise, or a normal family life? Or my car out there in the *News* parking lot?" I was beginning to sound and feel hysterical.

"You will soon see, *mi hijita.*"

Deliver me, I thought. Whatever they meant, I didn't like it one damn bit. "Gone forever" did not have a positive ring. Overtired and stressed out by the ups and downs of this day, I was already depressed. Hal had not called. Had I been seduced and abandoned? Bummer. Although I, myself, was a major player in that seduction, which was one of the reasons I was short on sleep. I had to get some rest if I was going to pick Lottie up at 5 A.M.

I finished my story and went home, eager for a message from Hal, determined to eat something light and retire early. The heat hit me when I opened the door. The air conditioner was dead again. The Goldsteins were out. They had mentioned taking Seth down to Big Pine Key to visit a cousin. No message from Hal on my machine.

All I found in the freezer was a frozen cheesecake. As I stood in front of the open door, pressing it to my feverish brow, the telephone rang. I snatched it up, hoping for Hal's voice.

"Britt, you're home!"

I caught my breath at the unexpected sound of my mother's voice instead.

"I was hoping to catch you."

"Yes?" Tears welled as I sank into my armchair, orphan no more, clutching the telephone expectantly, the melting cheesecake in my lap.

"At Neiman's first thing in the morning!" she said. "Gloria Vanderbilt jeans marked down to half price. The ad won't hit the papers until Wednesday. The cut is perfect for your long legs and narrow hips. You must get there early before your size is gone. It's smart to pick up two or three pair at that price. You can always dress them up with a nice shirt and a blazer."

"Thanks." I spoke the word awkwardly, as though conversing with a stranger. "Thanks for letting me know."

"They have some nice pastel sweats, too. Marked down."

"Uh, it's too hot to think about sweatshirts," I said, moisture from the cheesecake pooling on my skirt and chilling my thighs.

"When it's cooler and you need them, they'll be full price," she warned. "Just trying to help."

Numbly, I thanked her again.

"Have to go now, dear," she said happily, and hung up as though all was swell between us. I sat for a long time, my hand still resting on the telephone, the cheesecake sodden in my lap, ignoring the TV weather and its color radar pictures of the storm far out at sea.

"You owe me," I croaked. Dawn was more than an hour away. Not even a glimmer of light cracked the eastern sky. Lottie's face glowed with anticipation. She wore sea green, striking with her red hair, and looked as happy as I've ever seen her.

We drove into the darkness on the soaring bridge to the port, the giant neon guitar atop the Hard Rock Cafe at Bayside a predawn beacon to our right, huge cruise ships to our left. I found the terminal, where passengers were already being welcomed by a steel band.

"There he is!" Lottie said, spotting Stosh as he parked his shiny black Jaguar. Tall and lean, he wore a slightly rumpled loose-fitting linen sports jacket, designer shades folded in the breast pocket, over a silk T-shirt and lightweight slacks. He did cut a dashing figure. But as he scanned the crowd for Lottie, he looked tense, as though he hadn't slept much, like a man burning the candle at both ends. His wit and quick mind that never ceased calculating the angles, coupled with his longish blond hair and intense pale blue eyes that grew hungry when he spoke to women, all gave him a certain fey charm. But his chin struck me as weak. So did his character.

We waved and he approached with a long-legged stride, his restless eyes inspecting the other arrivals. He kissed Lottie on the cheek, winking at me over her shoulder as he put his arm around her.

"Coffee, coffee," he muttered. "Take me to some coffee."

"They'll feed us a sumptuous breakfast right after we board," she promised, gazing at him as though he were the only man in the world.

"Bon voyage, you two," I said. "Have fun, the weather report says it's gonna be a great day out there." The storm was more than seventeen hundred miles to the southeast. Residents of Barbados and the French West Indies on the Caribbean's eastern rim were beginning to heed advisories and batten down the hatches, just in case.

The passengers boarded through an arch of bobbing red, blue, and green balloons at the foot of the gangway. The ship's photo concessionaire was shooting color stills to hawk later on the cruise. A splash of light bathed the happy couple as the camera's flash froze them forever in time. Would future grandchildren treasure it some day? It's the lack of sleep, I told myself as I drove west across the high bridge at first light, directly toward Freedom Tower. I was becoming as romantic as Lottie.

Instead of sacking out for an hour, I went to the beach and ran south along the surf toward Government Cut, the shipping channel from the Port of Miami to the deep blue Gulf Stream and the open sea. Summer clouds, low, white, and fluffy, banked the horizon and the smooth surface of the ocean sparkled with scattered diamonds.

Breathing hard and soaked with perspiration, I stood at South Pointe and watched from the jetty as the big white cruise ship glided east toward Africa. Of course it would make a U-turn after a stop at Freeport in the Bahamas and be back late tonight. I squinted at the ant-sized passengers clustered along the rails on the upper deck. With binoculars I would have been able to spot Lottie and Stosh. Those two would stand out in any crowd.

I waved anyway, then went home. Mr. Goldstein said he was giving up on my air conditioner and promised a brand-new one, installed by the time I got home that night.

I drank a glass of orange juice, showered, dressed, and studied the picture of my father with his old comrades before I left. The copy Lottie had shot was now simply framed and hung in my living room. If I was ever to read his diary of those times, I decided, I would have to find it myself. Bravo insisted it was in the possession of some newly arrived rafter who might or might not actually exist. Reyes claimed it was tucked away among his musty relics of the past. Like those associated with most Cuban exile factions, each accused the other of lying. Who was the liar, and why? If Reyes didn't have it, why would he have mentioned it to me in the first place?

After our wild ride the day before, I probably wouldn't be tête-à-têteing with Jorge Bravo anytime in the immediate future, if he had one. At least not if I could help it,

Luckily my beat was not busy, the only story that of a two-hundred-pound woman in trouble. After a night of drinking and arguing with her one-hundred-twenty-pound boyfriend, she had passed out and fallen on him. When she awoke she found him crushed to death beneath her. She told police it was an accident. Arrested for manslaughter and overcome by grief, she fell back in a dead faint, pinning to the wall the officer attempting to handcuff her. Four other cops fought to free him as he screamed, "Get her off me! Get her off me!"

I went back to the office, pounded out the story, then called Reyes. Gilda, his secretary, said he was out and would not be in the office all day. As I wondered whether I was being blown off, she added that he was addressing a luncheon meeting of Cuban business leaders at the InterContinental Hotel, and then had trade commission meetings scheduled with out-of-town associates at the Sofitel Hotel near the airport. His schedule was jammed until after an 8 P.M. interview with Telemundo, the Spanish-language television channel.

"If you really want to catch him," she confided, her tone warm and friendly, "your best bet would be at the luncheon, before or after his talk. You will find him in the Grand Ballroom."

"Think he'd mind?"

"For you, Ms. Montero? Not at all."

The InterContinental stands like a sentinel on the bay, at Chopin Plaza, once the site of a concert bandshell. Flags from a host of nations hung limp in the hot, muggy air as I searched for a parking meter. I hate leaving the T-Bird with a valet, even though that strip of meters delivers a notoriously fast count to hapless motorists, who pay a quarter for a scant fifteen minutes and usually wind up with eighteen-dollar parking tickets anyway.

Add this to traffic jams, voice mail, and the heat, and it's a wonder that more people don't buy high-powered rifles and barricade themselves in tall buildings.

I overfed the meter and walked through the huge lobby, airy, full of greenery and the vibrant work of Florida artists. The paintings made me think of Vanessa Clower, although none looked like her work. An entire wall of the high-ceilinged Grand Ballroom was glass with a view of Biscayne Bay and the port.

Before seeing him, I heard the mellifluous voice of Juan Carlos Reyes. He stood at the podium, in front of a microphone, addressing an overflow crowd seated in metal chairs, as waiters in an adjacent room placed breadbaskets, napkins, and water glasses on the luncheon tables.

I stood quietly near the draped entrance to listen. His dark eyes roved the room, adding to the intensity of his words. Before I could even pick up the gist of his comments, something about lessons learned in his youth in military school in Cuba, his eyes swept across my side of the room, then quickly returned, focusing his powerful gaze upon me. His white teeth flashed in an intimate smile and a few members of his audience glanced curiously my way.

"I must interrupt my prepared comments, *mis amigos*, for we have an unexpected and honored guest in our midst."

I looked over my shoulder. Nobody there. Flushed, I fought the urge to hotfoot it right out the door. I must have looked like a startled rabbit caught in headlights. Our eyes locked. He was talking about me, to me.

"Our brother Antonio Montero, who fought against the tyranny of Fidel Castro and communism and died for Cuba, has remained with us always, in spirit. Executed by Fidel's firing squad, he now lives on among us in the flesh." Reyes's deep and passionate voice picked up fire and volume as he gestured toward me.

"*Ésta es la hija de Tony Montero*. Because of Castro she grew up without her father. But he would be proud of her, as we should be.

"She is our daughter now," he boomed, arms outstretched. "*Ella es nuestra hija ahora.*"

I swallowed, as they began to applaud and cheer, louder and louder, as they got to their feet, standing to attention, some saluting, placing their hands over their hearts.

This was totally beyond the realm of my experience. Tears stung my eyes. Nobody cheers for police reporters. I am far more accustomed to running for my life from the good citizens of Miami when they are hurling rocks and bottles, or arguing with cops who threaten to arrest me at crime scenes.

The tribute seemed endless. I stared at the floor. Then, unconsciously mimicking my father's pose in Bravo's photo, I raised my head and stared boldly back at Reyes. He looked startled for a moment, but his voice gave no hint.

"His daughter," his electronically enhanced voice whispered over the din, "our daughter now."

I wished my mother could have been there, could have heard. I wished I had been more fashionably dressed instead of in my slacks, shirt, and old navy blazer. I retreated to the ladies' room to blow my nose and wipe my eyes. By the time I returned to the Grand Ballroom, everyone was being seated for lunch. Ripples of applause followed as I skirt-ed the tables and approached Reyes, now surrounded by local politicians and influential businessmen. I thanked him on behalf of my father; he smiled warmly and invited me to join him.

"I must get back to work," I said, declining. "I hoped for a quote on your feelings about the AFC raid on the Cuban coast."

"An unfortunate situation," he said solemnly. "The end is near for Castro, and emotions run strong in our exile community. But our actions must reflect intelligence and a respect for the laws of this country."

Those around him seemed to agree.

"And," I added quietly as the others found their seats, "I wondered if your assistant had determined whether or not he can locate my father's diary. Bravo insists it recently arrived in Miami with some rafter."

Reyes lifted his eyebrows, sadly shaking his head. "The ravings of a lunatic. You have seen the results of his handiwork. His motives are inexplicable. But I have good news. Wilfredo left me a memo this morn-ing. He has been studying inventory lists and believes that the files and boxes we seek are in the warehouse. It was used for storage during the transition when we moved to our larger offices." He glanced at his watch. "He planned to personally go there this afternoon."

My heart leaped. "Thank you," I said fervently. "This means a great deal to me." He kissed my hand, eyes boring into mine.

Still riding high, I found a message from Hal waiting when I got back to the office. I decided to call him after the parents' meeting that night, when we would have time to talk. Suddenly hungry, I ate a *News* cafete-ria tuna sandwich at my desk while writing the follow on Bravo's incur-sion into Cuban waters.

I answered some mail, reread my missing-boy stories and all my notes, then headed out to the Randolph house. The streets sweltered with shimmering heat radiating upward from the pavement. I envied Lottie and Stosh, cruising a calm summer sea surrounded by sky and clouds.

The Randolphs lived in Miami Shores, in a modest home with a flat roof, a lush green lawn, green shutters, and creeping vines on a latticework arbor framing the carport. A spacious screened L-shaped Florida room wrapped around the side of the house and was comfortably furnished in white wicker, but too hot to use this time of year.

The meeting took place in the living room-dining room area. Cassie had brewed a large sweaty pitcher of iced tea and there was an industrial-sized coffee urn that suspiciously resembled the one in the waiting room at the Quicky Lube her husband managed.

"Are you hungry?" Cassie asked. "I have cake and doughnuts for later, and Andrea Vitale is bringing cookies." I bet I know what kind, I thought.

Charles's dog, Duke, who must have claimed some golden retriever or Irish setter in his lineage, barked halfheartedly each time the doorbell rang, then padded dutifully to the door, claws clicking on the terrazzo floor.

He would sniff each new arrival, then return to his mat near the kitchen door, gazing at us balefully as if to say that no matter how many people arrived, the most important one was still missing. I wondered how long dogs remember. I was sure that Bitsy still grieved for Francie.

The Metro-Dade police department had sent a representative, a dapper, clear-eyed young detective named Simmons.

Vanessa Clower wore a figure-hugging white cotton jumpsuit and strings of multicolor beads. Her ex-husband, Edwin, arrived five minutes after she did and sat next to her on the floral cotton couch. He wore a suit, a tie, and a hopeful expression.

One out-of-town family, the parents of Watson Kelly from Gary, Indiana, was represented by the father's cousin, a postal worker in Holiday, a Tampa suburb. He had driven across the state for the meeting.

"They're grasping at straws," he said, speaking of the missing boy's parents. "They said to tell you all that they're willing to come down if you think there is something, anything, that they can do here."

That last collect call from their son had come from a pay phone at a downtown shopping arcade, a former movie theater, gutted and rebuilt into a mini-plaza with electronics and health food stores, card and souvenir shops, and fast-food outlets.

Emily and Michael Kearns sat in chairs six feet apart, rarely connecting with a look or a word. When they spoke it was to someone else, not each other. He looked fidgety and uncomfortable, while she appeared almost unnaturally chipper and eager. My guess was that he didn't want to be there and she had had to persuade him.

The Swedish consul had sent an aide to represent the country and the family of the missing exchange student, Lars Sjowall.

Andrea Vitale arrived last, fifteen minutes late. Probably had trouble finding her way out of Bramblewood, I thought. She planned to go right to work from the meeting and looked pretty in her nurse's uniform, but even pudgier than when we had first met. She was carrying a large platter of oatmeal raisin cookies on a paper doily covered with plastic wrap. Everyone was introduced, and Cassie Randolph poured iced tea.

I had expected the meeting to be awkward at first, with a somber or angry mood, but a spirit of instant camaraderie prevailed. Eager ideas and an air of optimism swept the room. Sharing lightens the load, I thought. It had to be exciting, after all their waiting, for something to finally be happening. Attention from both the media and the police validated their loss, an added bonus.

At times everyone spoke at once, comparing notes, dates, and pictures. They galvanized into action; Emily Kearns, a former secretary who now handled the business side of the family nursery business, took notes. The minutes of the meeting would be distributed to all the parents, particularly those unable to attend. Edwin Clower would provide unlimited use of fax and Xerox machines and a business phone number for tipsters. Vanessa would design a color poster bearing all the boys' pictures and combining the reward offers. "News of one could lead to all of them," she said.

Detective Simmons, clean-shaven, short-haired, and boyish,

though a twelve-year police veteran, took the floor to announce that the department was taking the investigation seriously and—based on the recently added cases, whether related or not—was forming a Missing Boys Task Force. The task force would include a detective from each local department with a case. Everyone applauded. An almost party atmosphere reigned. Cassie served the doughnuts, a chocolate cake, and Andrea Vitale's cookies.

Even Michael Kearns looked content, digging into his chocolate cake. Notebook in my lap, pen in hand, I studied them and knew the truth. Suddenly sick, I was afraid I was going to retch. The iced tea I had swallowed had turned to battery acid in my stomach. The only face in the room I could bear to look at was Simmons, who sat comfortably in his shirt and tie at the dining room table. My thoughts were reflected in his eyes, the look I'd seen in so many cops' eyes before.

They're all dead! I wanted to scream. Not one is ever coming back. Oh my God, I thought. They're dead.

Preoccupied with the Cuban business, my mother, my father, my own personal life, I hadn't been thinking clearly.

Each of the boys has probably been dead since the day he vanished. One person is responsible. Serial killers are nearly always loners. This one is still out there.

There are no coincidences. The smartest cop I ever knew once told me that. Nobody could hold that many kids. Any time this many are missing, they are all dead. I had been denying what my subconscious and my intuition had told me from the start, when I had mentioned both Bundy and Wilder to Fred, trying to spark editorial interest in the story.

The chatting and laughter and optimism in the room ebbed and flowed around me as though I were drowning. How many of them were also in denial?

I wanted to warn them: They are not coming home. Accept it now. Grieving is easier than being left in limbo, better than holding your breath when the phone or the doorbell rings, or searching the faces in every crowd of strangers. Hope ages fast. The most devastating truth is better than keeping life and emotions on hold forever. Better to grieve, close the book, and go on.

I took deep breaths to settle my stomach. The light hurt my eyes and my head throbbed. "What's the matter, Britt?" Andrea Vitale asked, concern in her voice. "You look pale."

Her son was one of the last to die, I thought. Only missing five months. All eyes turned to me now.

"Don't you want to try the cake? It's made from scratch," Cassie said warmly.

Her son, I thought, welcomed into the world after four miscarriages. The boy who never walked out the door without kissing her good-bye. My God, they're all dead.

"I have to go," I said, and stood so suddenly that my notebook fell to the floor. "Have an early deadline."

Simmons walked me out to the car, probably to be sure that I would mention his department's deep concern for these parents and their sons. "Who will the task force report to?" I asked him.

"Murphy."

"The homicide commander."

He nodded. "But that doesn't mean . . . ," he began perfunctorily.

I returned his nod, got into my car, and looked up into his boyish face. We both knew.

I drove back to the paper, a lump in my throat. How many? I wondered. How long has this been going on?

I called Onnie in the library to find me everything and anything she could on pedophiles. "Oh, Jesus," she said, "what happened?"

"Just research," I said wearily. "I'm trying to figure out what's going on."

"You don't sound good, Britt."

"I don't feel good."

Hal had left another message. I was in no mood for flirtatious happy talk, and he sure as hell would not be turned on by my current state of mind. How do you talk to a normal civilian about something like this? Only somebody in the business would understand. I wished for Kendall McDonald and his arms. He could hold me, we could exchange ideas. I could pick his brain and find warmth and comfort in his body. I missed Dan Flood, a street-smart detective, a source and a friend, now dead.

Lottie and I could have brainstormed, but she was at sea and in love. Having a wonderful time. She and the Polish Prince were probably cuddled in a chaise longue on deck under a romantic blanket of stars. I felt so lonely.

First I wrote the story about the meeting. The news peg, of course, was the formation of the Missing Boys Task Force, a smart political move. Before the parents' group could organize and publicly accuse the police of being unresponsive, uncaring, and slipshod, the department had defused the situation. Now that they had stepped in to the rescue, it would be nonproductive to ask where they had been all this time. I hoped the task force would be more than a token. We had to find the bodies. Once they were found, their families could join the Parents of Murdered Children, begin to heal, and focus on lobbying for victims' rights, tougher laws, and proper punishment. Simmons's assignment was a good sign. I knew him to be thorough, conscientious, and meticulously organized. The department has to do this right, I thought; they can't afford not to.

I turned in the innocuous story on the meeting and plunged into the research Onnie had brought. The divorced mother of two young boys, she had gingerly placed the print-outs and clippings on my desk as though eager to go wash her hands.

My headache worsened as I read through them. Five years earlier several small black boys, street kids from poor homes, had turned up in Miami canals. The first had been mauled by a gator. His head and legs were missing. Police and a medical examiner believed he was killed by the animal while playing on the canal bank, even though the canal was miles from the eight-year-old's home. The second was nude but so decomposed that it was impossible to determine his cause of death. He might have drowned while skinny-dipping, detectives theorized. The next two were found more quickly. The bodies were still fresh, one discovered by a fisherman, the other by snake hunters, ten days apart. The boys had been sexually assaulted and fatally beaten. The killer was never identified. In the hue and cry of publicity and the intense manhunt that followed, he had vanished. He either died, moved on, got into therapy, or was arrested for some other crime. There were no new cases.

The man responsible for the missing boys was obviously not the same. The ages and the profile of the victims were different. Serial killers usually select victims from their own race and these boys were well hidden, unlike the others, simply discarded, tossed down a canal bank when their killer had finished with them. Charles Randolph and the other missing boys, all tall for their ages, healthy and agile, could not all have been snatched off the street. They must have gone willingly with their killer.

The numbers were staggering as I read the latest research. I knew that the United States leads the world in the production of serial killers. But just two short decades ago it was believed that there were approximately twenty roaming the country at any one time, trolling for victims. Sociologists now estimate that there are as many as five hundred out there hunting other humans like animals. Either our reporting and tracking have become considerably more accurate, or our society is creating monsters at an accelerated rate.

My phone startled me. The newsroom was deserted, except for a cleaning man shampooing a carpet in one of the executive offices. It was after one o'clock in the morning. I answered, expecting a cop or a fireman with news of a late-breaking story.

"What are you still doing there?"

"Lottie? Where are you?"

"Down at the port, can you come git me?"

"Sure." It was only five minutes away. "But where's Stosh?"

"Come git me. I'll tell ya then. Everybody's leaving, it's dark as hell over here, and I'm loaded with money."

"I'll be right there." What the hell, I wondered, hanging up. I left my desk the way it was, grabbed my car keys, and took off. Didn't have to wait for an elevator, it was waiting for me. I love the *News* building when it is empty, and that dizzying high that comes after inhaling your first breath of hot, moist night air after so many hours in an over-air-conditioned, unnaturally frigid building. Head spinning, I slid into the T-Bird and drove with the windows wide open until my bones warmed and I began to perspire.

The other passengers had gone. Lottie stood alone, a tall silhouette in the dark under a sapphire sky. I didn't see the black Jaguar.

"Thanks, Britt." She settled in the front seat with an apprehensive glance behind us. "Thank God that woman's finally gone."

"What woman? Where's Stosh? What the hell is going on?" I demanded, and swung into a U-turn. "Is he swimming back from Freeport?"

"He didn't go." She spoke calmly and didn't look heart-broken.

We were sailing across the Dodge Island Bridge between the port and downtown. "What do you mean he didn't go? I saw you both board that ship."

"Yeah, but, as you know, even though you don't need a passport, you need to show two forms of ID, driver's license, birth certificate, voter's registration. When they ask us for it, Stosh pats his pockets. Whoops, he says, he left his wallet in the car and has to run back to the Jag for ID. He did, and the man did not come back. The *Gettaway* sailed without him. At first I thought he had to be on board somewhere, that he must be with the purser being processed."

"I don't believe it! What could have . . ."

"I saw the parking lot from the upper deck after we moved away from the pier. His car was gone. He hightailed it outta there like a lynch mob was on his tail."

"That's awful! What on earth would make him . . . Were you two having an argument?"

"Nope." She thought a moment. "Nothing. I did make a joke. When the captain greeted us, I asked him if he performed marriages on the high seas. He just laughed."

"But it was right after that?"

She nodded. "Not long. I'm surprised he didn't pass you like Mario Andretti as you was leaving."

"Do you think what you said could be the reason?"

"Don't know, and don't wanna know. Could not care less."

"It had to be awful. What did you do?"

"Wasn't half bad, Britt. I mean, it wasn't no transatlantic cruise. I ate till I thought I would burst. Played shuffleboard with a buncha young medical students and toured Freeport with a nice family from Austin. Bought some perfume and a bottle of duty-free rum. On the way back I tried my hand at roulette in the casino and won twenty bucks. That's when I started watching folks playing the slots. Never play those badger games myself, just watched. Some woman from Chicago had been playing one since morning. Never even went ashore. Eight hours she'd been feeding that machine, and nothing."

"Humph, like the parking meters down at Chopin Plaza."

"Exactly. Finally she takes a break to go to the ladies' room. Without even thinking I drop fifty cents in the slot and it belches up money, money, money! Red lights and sirens, just like a vice raid."

"You won!"

"Five thousand big ones," she said, speaking slowly, emphasizing each syllable.

"Five thousand dollars? Great! I love it! Oh, Lottie!"

We high-fived.

"That woman from Chicago comes back spitting fire. Real mouth on her. Coulda swallowed the devil with his horns on. Screeching like a stuck pig that I took her machine. Still at it when we docked, following

me down the gangplank yelling: 'That's my money! That's my money!'
Shoulda heard her."

"Did you give her any?"

"Nope. Not with her attitude. I'm quitting the game while I'm
ahead. No more gambling or Stosh Gorski."

"Good idea," I solemnly agreed.

"I shoulda done it before, but if I had, I wouldn't have won. Had he
come aboard and stayed, I wouldn't have won. I wouldn't even have been
playing, not a machine anyway. I should thank him. But I won't. I ain't so
bad off. He never was a plumb truthful critter, always full of balooey. Deep
down I knew it." She leaned back and sighed. "Greenbacks in my jeans
sure eases the pain."

"What are you going to do with it, after you buy me breakfast?"

"Been thinking about some white-water rafting, a painting by that
Haitian artist down by the river, some new camera equipment."

I told her what I believed about the missing boys.

"Glory, Britt, I assumed you'd figured that out. Ain't no secret
summer camp out there for lost boys. Little ones might git sold off to
chicken hawks, sent south of the border. Ain't no way big boys like that
could be controlled by anybody for so long."

We drove up the Boulevard, deserted at that hour except for the
hookers staring hollow-eyed from shadowy street corners.

"How come you're so good at judging character when it comes to
news but not in your personal life?"

"Ain't that true of all of us?"

She was right. I wondered about Hal and Kendall McDonald.

"Men give love because they want sex," she was saying. "Women
give sex because they want love. That's the difference between men and
women. Ever notice how when we talk about our love lives, it's always
about a man? Singular. All most of us want is one good man. But when
men talk, it's about women. Plural. They want as many as they can git."

"Did you really love him?"

"I guess I was in love with the idea."

I sighed. "All day long I was envying you and Stosh out there together on the water."

"Never take anything for granted, Britt." She leaned her head back on the seat and closed her eyes. "In this life nothing is ever really what it seems to be."

I CALLED DR. Rose Schlatter in the
morning. A bosomy blonde in her early fifties, she favors big dangly earrings, low-cut blouses, and outdated makeup. Her eyeshadow is thick and
blue, her lipstick bright and smeary. She resembles an aging barmaid
or your favorite waitress. She is actually a psychiatrist who directed a
once-praised treatment program for convicted sex offenders at the state
hospital.

The program lost its funding, shut down in a clamor precipitated by
an unfortunate incident involving hostages, escapes, and assault.
Currently she evaluates defendants in criminal cases, conducts a solo practice, and lobbies tirelessly for revival of her defunct program.

Rose Schlatter seemed pleased to hear from me. "Sure, I have time,
Britt, if you don't mind listening to me chew my breakfast while we talk.
Just let me get my doughnut and coffee."

"What kind of doughnut?" I hadn't even thought about breakfast.

"Jelly, sorry I can't offer you one."

"Me too." I was suddenly hungry.

"I have a jailhouse interview at ten. That handsome young weight lifter from the Grove, the fellow who chopped his girlfriend into little pieces last year because she was the devil? He's back from Chattahoochee. They say he's competent now. We'll see."

Her voice sounded younger than her years and had the slightly breathy, girlish quality of a Marilyn Monroe imitator. I waited while she lowered the volume on her TV and brought her breakfast to the telephone. She had read the stories and listened intently to my theory, that a serial sex killer had made the missing boys disappear.

"I was thinking the same thing myself," she said matter-of-factly. "Probably somebody narcissistically wounded in childhood, probably obsessive-compulsive. Since he's been successful this long, he must keep himself under control to some degree, rather than displaying an increasingly more apparent personality disorder dysfunction."

"You've interviewed so many sex offenders," I began carefully. "I just wondered whether you recall anyone obsessed with boys who might match that specific profile?"

She laughed gaily. "Nice try, Britt. But you know I couldn't reveal it even if I did. Doctor-patient confidentiality."

Even if it would save lives? I wanted to argue, but didn't. No point when I wanted her help. "So you think that the killer is sexually attracted to boys who fit the same physical description?"

She slurped her coffee, evoking the image of the thick pink smears that stained her cup whenever we chatted in the courthouse coffee shop.

"Power may be what he seeks." She cleared her throat and smacked her lips. "The exercise of power may be even more important to him than his sexual needs. Murder is the ultimate expression of power. How many victims did you say? At least twelve? I'd love to meet this man," she said, sounding like a schoolgirl yearning for an introduction to a rock star.

"Of course we'd want to do a complete workup: a neurological exam, electroencephalogram, chromosome count—all those good things—and see if any organic brain disease exists."

She stopped to gnaw her jelly doughnut.

"Based on what little we have, what can you tell me about this man?" I sounded like someone consulting a crystal-ball gazer or an astrologer. I hoped her reply would not be as nebulous.

"He must feel a great need to be loved and admired, probably can be very charming on the surface. God," she said, chewing hungrily, as though the thought had just occurred to her, "they're all charming." She swallowed. "If they weren't charmers they couldn't get away with what they do long enough to become serial killers. But underneath that charming veneer is a refrigerator that doesn't defrost. No guilt, no remorse. He somehow justifies his behavior. The only real remorse I've ever seen in any of them is that they're sorry, sorry they got caught. If what we suspect is true, the man we're talking about is apparently able to control and manipulate his environment. If he's married," she said thoughtfully, "he's most likely a wife-beater."

Married. That hadn't even occurred to me. "If he is, don't you think his wife must know?"

"She probably knows he's violent and off-center," she said, chewing, "but not the degree of his aberrant behavior. Life is probably more pleasant for her after a murder; it takes some of the pressure off her. The patterns of serial killers are cyclical, you know, like menstrual cycles.

"One other thing, Britt, he probably collects mementos, souvenirs. Anything from his victims' jewelry, to teeth, to body parts. He may take photos, videotapes, or recordings of their pleas for mercy for use in his masturbatory fantasies later."

My stomach churned as she masticated with relish, apparently devouring the last of her doughnut.

"The last victim I'm pretty sure of was five, six months ago. You think he's stopped?"

"Oh, this fellow probably won't stop until somebody stops him." She sounded cheerful. "He must pay attention to the news and he's probably not thrilled about the Task Force you wrote about in this morning's paper, but he won't quit. He may even enjoy matching wits with the police. I've got to run, even though Mr. Buff, the Body Builder, isn't going anywhere—not yet, anyway. You know how they are, these offenders get surly if you keep them waiting. They're so impatient. No impulse control. That's part of their problem. Anything else you need, Britt?"

"The killer's name and current whereabouts would be a big help."

She laughed. "Call me anytime, Britt, just remember whenever you attribute anything in print don't neglect to mention the program, and that I was the founder and director. I'm still trying to regain our funding. You know what a worthy program it was."

I remembered the nurse held hostage by the patients Dr. Schlatter was "rehabilitating," the mother and seven-year-old girl they abducted, and the fear generated in neighborhoods surrounding the hospital, but I kept my yap shut.

"And, Britt, if they should identify a suspect in this case, please call me right away. Day or night. You have my home and beeper numbers. I sure would love to get to know this fellow."

Why did I suspect that Dr. Schlatter enjoyed her job way too much?

The phone rang the instant I hung up. I half expected Dr. Schlatter, with a new flash of insight or some juicy tidbit she'd neglected to mention.

"Britt, is that you? Where have you been?"

"Hi, stud," I murmured, in my best try at sultry, embarrassed that I had neglected to return Hal's calls.

"I thought you dumped me."

"Are you kidding? It's been really hectic. I'll tell you all about it when I see you."

"What are you doing?"

"Just now? I was talking to a . . . a source."

"You didn't forget the inquest tomorrow, did you?"

"No way. Two o'clock, right? We'll be there with bells on. Lottie's coming too. I'll meet you outside the courtroom."

"Good." He lowered his voice. "I miss you."

"Likewise." Call waiting clicked in. "You have nothing to worry about. See you then." I pressed the button.

"Montero?"

"Jorge?"

"*Sí*. We have it! Antonio's *diario*."

"What?" My heart stuttered in my breast.

"At least we know the place to find it, the whereabouts of Armando Gutiérrez. Meet me at José Martí Park and we will go there together."

Oh, sure, I thought, frowning at the phone and the man at the other end. What kind of scam was this?

"Fifteen minutes," he said urgently.

"Wait, don't hang up, Jorge." What if Reyes was wrong? "You must realize that I wouldn't get into a car with you again under any circumstances." I'd rather sky-dive without a chute. "Ever."

"This *balsero* will be reassured if you are present, and you will see that I have spoken the truth to you and that the liar is Juan Carlos Reyes."

"How about if I meet you there?"

"To divulge his whereabouts over the *teléfono* would endanger his life."

"Give me a street corner"—I sighed—"within walking distance."

He conferred in rapid Spanish with someone else. "Okay," he said. "Meet me at Northwest Seventh Street and Second Avenue. Pronto."

I sighed. Why did I feel like a kamikaze pilot?

"I have to run out for a little while," I told Gretchen, as I passed the city desk.

"But Britt, the staff meeting is at two, to discuss hurricane assignments." The storm had stalled at sea, feeding on the heated water, picking up strength. Now officially a hurricane, it had swung slightly to the north and was whirling west like so many storms that barrel down the alley, a wide path through the Caribbean toward the Gulf of Mexico. Florida's peninsula juts out into the alley like a sore thumb. As a result, more than sixty hurricanes have slammed into the state with wild winds and storm surges that have killed more than 3,500 people over the past hundred years. Enough to excite editors and weathermen even though the odds were on our side.

"I'll be back," I said, not even slowing down.

I parked nearby, watching for *especialista* Luisa or a counterpart. I paced the scorching pavement, then stood there sweating and feeling stupid. If I missed the damn hurricane meeting I'd wind up with some assignment nobody else wanted, sitting alone in some Red Cross Shelter with ten thousand bologna sandwiches as the storm petered out over North Carolina or somewhere in the Caribbean.

Had this been a better neighborhood, I could have cooled my heels in the frosty draft escaping from some air-conditioned storefront, but the buildings here were old, un-air-conditioned, or abandoned. Several old apartment houses had been condemned, boarded up, then reclaimed by the homeless. There was a pawn shop that welcomed customers with barbed wire and steel shutters, a few boardinghouses, a couple of small hotels with laboring air conditioners, and rooms that rented by the hour.

I checked my watch, decided to give him five minutes more, looked up, and saw Bravo climb out of a blue Dodge across the street, a clunker I'd seen go by a few minutes earlier. The car rattled off; I couldn't see if Eloy was behind the wheel. I didn't care. I never wanted to see either one of them again. Did my father experience the same reservations every time he ran with this crowd?

Bravo beckoned impatiently as I crossed the street toward him. "*¡Apúrate!*" He jabbed at the pavement with his cane as I fell into step beside him. "Here."

We walked into the Bradley Hotel. If anything, the lobby was hotter and more sweltering than the street. A ceiling fan with a broken blade hung still and lifeless. The metal legs of the few pieces of vinyl furniture were corroded by the dampness. A few listless residents watched an old TV plugged into the wall with an exposed cord apparently gnawed by rodents. The picture was blurry, but the sound blared. Trailer-park types on some daytime talk show were divulging the intimate secrets of their bizarre private lives. They seemed entirely normal compared to some of the people I'd met lately.

A mountain of a man sat behind the desk sweating profusely. His grimy short-sleeved shirt hung open, exposing bristly hair and a raised red scar on his chest, either heart surgery or an old knife wound. Only his thick eyebrows acknowledged our presence, lifting slightly, as Bravo and I approached. He probably assumed we wanted the bridal suite.

"We are looking for Armando Gutiérrez," Bravo told him. "What is his room number?"

"He expecting you?"

"We are friends," Bravo said.

"Why don't you ring his room?" I said.

"Only phone's in the hall."

"We can just go up," I said. The less time I spent in public with Bravo, the better.

"Okay, but I can't let you go up alone. Too much happening these days. You know."

He continued to scrutinize us as he began to slowly lock drawers. Did he intend to protect his guests from us, or us from his clientele?

"We're not here to burglarize your guests or vandalize your halls," I said shortly. We would have picked a place with more class had that been our intent, I thought. Who would know the difference if this place was vandalized?

He mumbled something about liability, dropped the key in his pocket, and eased ponderously to his feet as I fidgeted restlessly.

I hurried toward the elevator, with Bravo following, but the manager moseyed toward the stairs. The smell of stale beer wafted around him as he moved.

"What floor is it?"

"Three," he said. "Elevator's out of order."

"Oh no," I moaned. I could use the exercise, but Bravo leaned heavily on his cane and the manager didn't look about to win any footraces either.

I wouldn't get back to the paper for an hour at this rate. "You sure it doesn't work?"

"Think I'd be taking these stairs if I didn't hafta?" He stared at me balefully.

We started the climb, the manager leading the way, Bravo behind him, and me, hyperventilating at the rear.

I'm sure Mt. Everest has been ascended more quickly.

"Room three-fifteen," the manager said, breathing hard halfway up the first flight.

So slow a pace in the heat made me groggy. I trotted past both and took the lead. The gloomy third-floor hall smelled musty. The few light fixtures had empty sockets or burned-out bulbs. The pay phone was near the landing. A chain dangled from the wall; the phone book that should have been attached was missing.

The manager, red in the face, was about to tackle the third flight. Bravo held his own, just behind him. I wandered down the hall to 315. No one in sight, but I could hear both Spanish and English radio or TV from several rooms.

When the manager was in sight, I knocked. "*Señor Gutiérrez?*" Not a sound.

Lord, I thought, after all this, he's not here. I rapped more sharply, then again. "*Señor Gutiérrez!*"

The manager and Bravo lumbered up behind me.

"He's not here," I muttered.

"I didn't see him go out," the manager offered. "He don't even go out to eat."

I didn't like a look that flickered in his eyes for an instant.

Bravo said nothing, leaning on the doorjamb and his cane, still catching his breath.

"Under those circumstances," I said, "you should probably open the door to check and see if he's okay."

He took his keys from his trouser pocket.

"When did you see him last?" I asked. Fingering the correct key, he wore an expression of mixed dread and resolve.

"'Bout an hour ago. He sent out for Chinese food. Came down to the lobby to wait for it just before the delivery."

Pizza and fast-food restaurants will not deliver to downtown hotel rooms. Deliverymen go only as far as the lobby, then get out fast. Otherwise they risk being robbed for the food on the way in and the money on the way out. And cops say *their* jobs are dangerous.

I expected to find an empty room, that Gutiérrez had stepped or skipped out.

The manager inserted the key and opened the door. I brushed by him into the room, Bravo behind me.

Two cardboard cartons of Chinese food were on the floor leaking into the carpet. So was Armando Gutiérrez.

"Oh, Jesus, Oh, Jesus," said the manager.

Bravo cursed, eyes searching the room. "They killed him!" He checked the closet and under the mattress. "Reyes killed him! Antonio's *diario* is gone!"

The pillow from the bed was on the floor, stripped of its case. Not many places to hide anything in a room that size. If something had been hidden in the pillowcase, it was gone. Or the empty case was used to carry something away.

"Don't touch anything," I warned. The manager still stood panting in the doorway. I did not need to warn Bravo. He pushed his way past the manager, nearly knocking him off balance, and burst out of the room like a racehorse out of the gate.

Moving pretty damn fast for a man with a cane, Bravo was halfway down the first flight of stairs before I ran out into the hall.

"Where are you going?" I shouted. "You can't leave me here! Stop!"

He never looked back. "*¡No policía!*" he shouted over his shoulder and tap-danced on down the stairs. The man could have qualified for the Olympics. I fought the urge to join him and turned back to what was in the room.

One lesson learned on the police beat is to never run away and leave a dead body behind. Cops hate that. They jump to conclusions and make your life difficult.

"I'm calling the cops!" the manager exclaimed and made for the hall phone.

They would arrive in minutes and when they did, the room would be off limits. I stepped back inside. The man on the floor had been shot, perhaps more than once, at the base of the skull. The blood in his hair made it hard to tell. He may not even have seen his killer. Probably surprised from behind as he carried the Chinese food back into his room. His knees had buckled and he had fallen forward. He looked bruised behind his ears, perhaps from internal hemorrhages. Taking a deep breath, I crouched beside him, trying to see his face. His nose had hit the floor and was flattened. Blood had poured from his nose and mouth but I saw no exit wounds. His eyes were open, their expression empty. Nobody home. Despite the laboring room air conditioner the blood had not congealed and the skin on his arm was still warm to the touch.

"What the hell happened?" I whispered. He didn't answer.

Sick to my stomach, I got to my feet. The commotion had attracted some of the other guests. A stringy-haired young woman in short shorts and a halter top stood horrified in the doorway, her hand to her mouth. Her nail polish was peeling.

"Did you hear anything? See anybody?" I asked.

She shook her head and made tracks for the stairs. A neatly dressed middle-aged man followed, buttoning his shirt. I decided to use the hall phone to call the paper, and Mark Seybold, once the manager finished.

He was gone and I saw why. The phone cord had been cut, neatly severed. He must have gone downstairs to call the cops, unless he had decided to make a run for it too, like everybody else.

I went back into the room. A toothbrush, but no paste, in a plastic glass in the bathroom. Towels and tub were damp, as though he had showered that morning. Few personal effects. A worn T-shirt and a pair of jockey shorts folded in an open drawer. A ballpoint pen and a half-finished letter on the dresser.

Without touching it, I tried to read the letter, which was in Spanish. He wanted his mother in Cuba to know that he was safe in Miami. He had made it, after leaving Higuero, near the eastern tip of the island, and enduring a hellish five days at sea on a crude raft. The raft flipped in strong waves on day three. The man who had accompanied him drowned and their supply of food and drinking water were lost.

God was with him, he had written. Fishermen found him ten miles southwest of Sombrero Light in the Keys, gave him food and water, brought him ashore, and drove him to Miami. Cuban Americans, they gave him some money and offered to help find him a job. But first, he wrote, he had a mission to accomplish and there had been complications. That was as far as the letter got.

Safe in Miami. I looked at Armando Gutiérrez, his brains blown apart in this fleabag hotel. In Cuba he was not happy, but at least he was alive.

Heavy footsteps sounded on the stairs, and I cleared out of the room.

"How the hell did you get here so fast? You're Britt, from the *News*, right?" asked an aggressive red-faced patrolman.

"She was here. She wanted to see him." The manager was pointing.

"She the one you were talking about?" The cop squinted at me. "You were here when the body was found?"

"She's the one who wanted me to open the door," he said, head bobbing, finger pointing, like a tattletale kid.

Sure, as though none of this would have happened if he hadn't opened the door. He should be grateful that we had found Gutiérrez now, not three days later. Bravo. I cursed his name. I had to speak to Mark Seybold before talking to the cops.

The manager was still pointing at me, so I retaliated.

"How many murders here at the Bradley so far this year?" I queried pointedly, pen poised over my notebook. I recalled a few right off the top of my head. The married accountant who had strangled his mistress on their lunch hour, accidentally he said, during rough sex. The dead hooker rolled under the bed by the room's former occupant, and undiscovered until the new occupant got down on his knees to investigate a rank odor.

The cop interrupted before I could get an answer, or maybe the manager was still counting.

I swore I had not touched anything. The cop stepped briefly into the room, then returned. "Slam-dunked right in the back of the head." He radioed for homicide.

Too bad Kendall McDonald was away, I thought wistfully. I would have gotten to see him. But then, again, one look at my guilty face and he'd know all about Hal.

"Wait downstairs in the lobby," the cop said, "and don't go anywhere. Homicide wants to talk to you."

I immediately obliged, eager to get to the lobby phone.

"What!" Mark Seybold demanded.

I repeated myself and told him that Bravo had split.

"Think he had anything to do with it?" Mark said.

"Don't know. Don't think so. Maybe. Probably. He claims Reyes had it done."

"Juan Carlos Reyes? Jesus, Britt."

"Am I obliged to tell the cops I was with Bravo?" The local police and the FBI are not on the best of terms and rarely share confidences, but the bureau would surely hear about this and I hated losing credibility with them and any possibility of trust in the future.

"How do you know Bravo? Did you go to him to obtain information for a story?"

I told him about the diary.

"Sounds like a personal matter. He's not a news source in this case, you're not obligated to protect him from an ethical point of view. You'd have a tough time claiming reporter's privilege and withholding information, especially in an investigation of this gravity. You say the dead man is an illegal alien?"

Two homicide detectives walked into the lobby. "Do me a favor, Mark," I said quickly. "Tell the city desk I won't be back for a while. I know the cops will want me to go to the station and give a statement."

"Wait, Britt. I want to be there when you talk to the police, even though you were not technically on assignment."

"Good." I was grateful, even though I knew he was more interested in protecting the paper's interests than mine. Something else I learned the hard way is to never be interviewed by homicide detectives without a lawyer present. That one would have saved me much grief the first time.

The detectives asked me to wait while they went upstairs for a quick look. I sat on a cheap vinyl chair in the lobby and wondered what the hell was going on. Did Gutiérrez ever have the diary? Did Bravo set all this up in some twisted scheme of his own?

A few guests, oblivious to the excitement upstairs, dozed in front of the blurry TV. I resisted the temptation to get up and try to tune in a better picture. An elderly wino was sprawled on the couch, either comatose or asleep. Crime-scene technicians and more cops streamed toward the stairs. The removal crew from the medical examiner's office would not be happy that the elevator didn't work, I thought, gripping the arm of my chair.

My fingers closed around something disgusting. Chewing gum, at least I hoped it was chewing gum, soft and sticky, left under the arm. Shivering, I tried to get it off. The wino on the couch sat up and began to gag. Trying to scrape the gob of goo off my fingers with a tissue, I nearly joined him. Could Cuba be any worse than this? I thought about Armando Gutiérrez upstairs, face down in his own blood. Of the mother who would never read his last letter.

This was no place to die. You were not safe in Miami, I thought. Tears stung my eyes.

I WOUND UP telling the cops everything. Not only is it my nature to be honest, this killer needed to be caught. The only detail I withheld was my wild ride down U.S. 1 with Mr. Bravo, and that was in no way related to the murder. Hell, they did not need me to tell them he had weapons and would use them.

The two detectives, a lanky, silver-haired veteran named Hanks and Billy Wogan, young, pudgy, and recently transferred from burglary, listened. They said they would check into the Bravo connection but seemed to write off Armando Gutiérrez's death as a robbery.

"Why would a robber single him out?" He had nothing, I protested.

"You know how it is, Britt," Hanks said. "You've seen people killed for a quarter, a can of Coke, or less. Happens every day. He musta pulled out his wallet when he paid the Chink who delivered his chow mein. Somebody in the lobby spots it, seizes the moment, and follows him back to his room."

"Why kill him?"

The detective shrugged. "Musta been somebody he woulda recognized. Somebody who didn't wanna leave a live witness."

"How come nobody heard the shots?" The assistant medical examiner who did the rollover at the scene said Gutiérrez had been shot at least twice.

The detective quickly wearied of my questions.

"You've seen the place. God knows we've all been there enough times. We haven't talked to 'em all yet, but they probably had their radios or TVs turned up loud, were otherwise occupied, or they're lying 'cuz they don't wanna be involved. The killer probably stays there and they're afraid of 'im."

It all sounded plausible, even to Mark.

Every time I spoke of the diary and thirty-year-old intrigues, their eyes glazed over and they would reach for mug-shot books of known armed robbers.

The manager was leafing through them with pudgy fingers as I left. It must have been like perusing his high school yearbook. From his expressions it appeared as though he recognized most of the faces.

Detective Hanks's final words to me were, "Don't try to make this into something bigger and more complicated than it is, Britt. You always do that."

That's what I always said about Cuban exiles, that they love intrigue, see conspiracies everywhere, and tend to exaggerate. Was it because I was a woman, because my name was Cuban? Did my heritage provoke that remark? Had I just encountered discrimination? I opened my mouth to argue, but Hanks was already talking to another cop about returning home to tie down his boat and put up hurricane shutters and asking to borrow a power tool for the job. As though Armando Gutiérrez, now lying on a plastic tray on wheels at the morgue, had never existed.

Maybe they were right about its being a random robbery. If my father's diary did indeed exist, I had serious doubts that it had ever been in the hands of Armando Gutiérrez. When his raft flipped in rough seas would he hang on to the diary of a man long dead instead of the food, water, and the companion he lost? Not likely. If Bravo was responsible for this killing, he should be tried. Perhaps I was being supersensitive, a characteristic I criticize many minority groups about. Mark wisely steered me out of there.

I expected to have to explain everything again to my editors back at the office, dreading the time it would waste to answer their questions. There were things I had to do.

But to my surprise I was not hustled into a meeting. The editors were all tied up, in meetings themselves, discussing logistics and making contingency plans in the event a hurricane watch was declared. Hurricane maps hung on every newsroom bulletin board, with copy boys updating them every three hours, as advisories were issued.

The hurricane, now a killer storm, had walloped Guadeloupe in the Leeward Islands. One-hundred-and-fifty-mile-an-hour winds had killed eleven on the butterfly-shaped island, ripped off tin roofs, destroyed the control tower at Pointe-à-Pitre International Airport, knocked out electrical power, and left four thousand homeless. Damage, deaths, and disorder are common when storms hit poor islands with lousy building codes. Guadeloupe, on the rim of the Caribbean basin, is frequently battered by storms. In the Virgin Islands and Puerto Rico emergency evacuations of thousands of coastal residents were under way.

I picked up the telephone book, made several calls, then dialed Don Farmer at the FBI. "I need a favor," I told him. "I was hoping you could help. I need to find one of your fellow feds. A CIA agent who was active in Miami about thirty years ago. Winslow. First name Frank. I don't have a DOB but he should be early sixties by now. Probably retired. I need to get in touch with him."

"What's this for, Britt? What are you working on?"

"A backgrounder on Bravo. This guy knew him back then." Not really a lie, though my fingers were crossed.

"How quick do you need this?"

"As soon as possible," I said. Before the bureau hears I was with Bravo today, I thought.

"Well . . ." He didn't sound convinced. "The best I can do for you is try to run this guy down and ask him if he is interested in talking to you. If so, I'll give him your number."

"Okay. Sure. Swell. I really appreciate it, Don. I owe you one."

"Well, let's see if I can find the guy first. You got a middle initial?"

"No, but there are only eight Winslows in the Miami phone book. No Franks, none related. I already called them."

"I'll see what I can do."

The rest of the staff was in full hurricane frenzy, churning out the usual stories: how to prepare your home, your boat, your garden, your windows and your pets for the big one. Same old stuff. Bring in lawn furniture and remove the coconuts from your trees to keep them from becoming cannonballs in one-hundred-mile-an-hour winds. Drain the pool, fill the tub, stock up on batteries, canned goods, matches, and candles. The same drill every year. Stock up, board up, lock up, and run for it.

I called the medical examiner's office to ask about Armando Gutiérrez. Dr. Sandra Lowe had already done the post.

"Was he in otherwise good health?" The answer to that routine question is often surprising. In this case it wasn't.

"A bit malnourished, an old arm fracture."

I thought about the lunch he never ate. Armando Gutiérrez died hungry. Alone in a strange country where somebody wanted to kill him—and did.

The ironies were not lost on Dr. Lowe. "Sad, isn't it," she commented, "that he risked so much to come here, only to have this happen.

"His skin looked like he was a real rafter," she added. "Leathery, with peeling sunburn."

Some so-called *balseros* are Castro plants, dropped a few miles offshore or refugees from elsewhere, their rafts set adrift from a smuggler's ship within sight of land. A major clue is when they claim to have been at sea for a week but arrive in good condition, well coiffed and neatly dressed, with no signs of sunburn or exposure.

"What about the bullet wounds?"

"Now, Britt, you know you have to ask the homicide detectives about a case under investigation."

"This one is different," I said. "I was there and saw the body and the head wounds. I've just come from talking to the detectives."

"Don't you get me in trouble, Britt."

"Of course not."

"What exactly did you want to know?"

What did I want to know? "He was shot twice?"

"Correct, but they probably wouldn't want you to put the exact number of shots in the newspaper. Only the killer knows that."

That's right, I thought, so it wouldn't tip him off to anything if we published it. But I didn't argue the point.

"Right," I said. "Was he beaten or anything first? He had bruises behind the ear."

"The bullets caused a fracture of the middle cranial fossa, the mid-part of the base of the skull. When there is a wound to the posterior it will look black-and-blue behind the ears. The bullets went through the cerebellum and midbrain and lodged in the front of his skull."

"Did he live long after he was shot?"

"Not at all. The wounds were immediately fatal, by the time he hit the floor. He fell in a face-down position, his nose was flattened."

"So maybe he never saw it coming?"

"Correct."

"How long?"

"He hadn't been dead long at all when you found him. Less than an hour, from the statement of the man who saw him accept the food delivery an hour earlier. As you know, Britt, witnesses who last saw the decedent alive are usually more accurate in helping to establish an approximate time of death than body temperature. He was lying only a few feet from the air conditioner. The cooler air stays down around the floor. There was no lividity. The cause is multiple gunshot wounds of the head, homicide. That's about all I can tell you."

I took a stab. "Wonder what kind of silencer was used?"

"You better talk to the detectives about that, Britt."

Aha, I thought. A silencer. I wondered about Bravo's leather satchel. I'd seen a few of the goodies he pulled out of that grab bag. A handgun, a box of shotgun shells. He probably lugged around an entire assortment of lethal playthings, including a silencer or two.

"Anything else?" I said. "Anything interesting in his pockets?"

"Talk to the lead investigator about that." She was getting hincty, probably concerned that she'd already said too much.

"Has next of kin been notified?"

"Apparently he had some relatives here in Miami; they were in the process of notifying his mother in Santiago de Cuba."

"Did anybody know his occupation, what he did for a living?"

"I understand that he was a minor government employee.   That's all I know."

Both detectives were out and did not return my calls. I turned in a brief story about the murder, then got captured by the city desk to do a hurricane story. A no-brainer on shelters and county-wide evacuation routes. I hammered it out after talking to the Red Cross and the county's Emergency Management Office.

Something nagged at my subconscious. A troubling something I had overlooked and could not quite remember. I ordered all the clips about Bravo from the library and took out the huge file I had compiled on Reyes when working on his profile. As I reread them, Andrea Vitale called. She was crying.

"What is it, have you heard something?"

"No." She gasped and caught control of herself. "It's just the hurricane. If it comes I'll be working emergency shifts at the hospital. And Butch, he'll be alone out there, alone in the storm."

I gazed out the big picture windows into bland blue sky and innocent fluffy clouds as she wept softly.

"Andrea, listen to me," I said sternly. "In the first place, the storm probably isn't coming. It's only a possibility at this point. It's almost fifteen hundred miles away, and it's a big ocean out there. Don't we go through this every year? Has the big one ever shown up? Not in decades. Weather patterns have changed. Remember the big panic back in 1979? They said the storm was on a direct course for Miami. It passed five miles offshore and never touched us. It was a sneeze. All we got was three days of rain. The only casualties were people who fell off ladders trying to put up storm shutters and got electrocuted trying to take down TV antennas. All for no reason. Don't panic."

She blew her nose. "You're right, Britt. I guess everything just hit me at once, the meeting and all. It made me afraid that he's really gone. Some of those boys have been missing for years and years. Butch isn't like them, he's smart, he's a survivor, he's a tough street fighter. It's just that we're—we're the two musketeers. We get through everything together."

"Andrea," I said softly. "Butch is smart and if he's okay, he'll get through this wherever he is. When he comes home, think of all the adventures he'll have to tell you."

"What if he never comes home?" she whispered.

"It's too early to panic or start to think like that," I lied. "You may be right. He may not be related to the other cases."

"It's too early to panic. Too early to panic," she repeated like a mantra.

What else could I say?

Action was heating up around the city desk, plans for a special Hurricane Preparedness Section. I escaped and went home.

Swirling rivers of humanity eddied and surged through the Richard E. Gerstein Justice Building. Outside, a crew struggled to install metal storm shutters over the tall lobby windows. Inside: cops and robbers, lawyers and victims, judges and defendants, good guys and bad guys, all interchangeable. The hallways were alive with desperation and tension where the depraved and deprived, overworked prosecutors, exhausted public defenders, career criminals, dazed civilians, shell-shocked survivors, and victims about to be revictimized all rubbed shoulders with rich lawyers, sleazy bagmen and bondsmen, paid informants, and protected witnesses. Shakespeare would have loved this stage.

Hal waited nervously outside the courtroom, handsome and serious in a dark blue suit and subdued tie. My heart skipped a beat. I knew how he felt. The law does not protect us. Neither does the justice system.

"That's the axman?" Lottie whispered as he saw me and smiled. She whistled long and low. "You can hose him down and bring him to my tent anytime."

"Lottie!"

"Okay, forget the hosing, just bring him."

He kissed my cheek and I introduced them.

At an inquest, less formal than a trial, the judge determines the manner of death and whether criminal charges should be filed. We sat in the spectator section as the police detective explained the circumstances. An assistant medical examiner testified as to the dead man's wounds. Hal looked pale as they were described.

He was not the only one affected. In the third row, a gray-haired woman with a frizzy perm caught her breath and pressed a flowered handkerchief over her eyes. Uh-oh, I thought. A relative, probably the dead man's mother. I hoped there would be no hysterical outbursts, floods of tears, or demands for retribution.

Florida allows homeowners to use reasonable force in defense of life and property. Reasonable is the operative word. My sole concern was that more than a single blow had been struck, indicating intent to harm. If one can actually form intent when confused, in the dark, roused from a sound sleep. I wasn't sure how sympathetic the prosecutor was in this case.

Hal was not required to testify, but chose to do so. The prosecutor asked him to tell the court what happened.

"I was asleep," he said, "alone in the house. I woke up, thought I was dreaming, heard something in the next room. I grabbed the phone but there was no dial tone."

"Who did you intend to call?"

"The police. I had had three burglaries in the past six months, all when I wasn't home. Now I thought they were back, in the house."

"What did you do then?"

"I had taken the ax from my camping gear and put it under my bed for protection after the last one. I reached down to find it. It was still there. Then I went to the bedroom door. I couldn't see anything. Then I heard a noise, like a drawer opening in the dining room and I yelled, 'Who's there!'

"The guy said something I couldn't make out and ran right at me. He knocked me back up against the wall and we grappled in the dark. I pulled away and swung the ax."

"How many blows did you strike?"

"Three, maybe four. Then I heard a door slam, and I ran out to try to stop whoever it was. He jumped in a car. I was yelling at him to stop. The car started to move and I swung the ax at the window. The glass broke and the guy took off.

"I went back inside and turned on the lights. I saw Mr. . . . Mr. Mumper on the floor. I found that they had taken the phone off the hook in the kitchen. I got a dial tone and called nine-one-one for the police and an ambulance."

"Was Mr. Mumper still alive?"

"He wasn't moving, or saying anything."

"Did you try to give him assistance? First aid?"

Hal shook his head, face white. "I was shaking, in shock. I just sat there and waited for the police. It seemed like forever but they said later that they got there in four minutes."

They played the 911 tape. Hal's voice, breathing hard.

"There's a burglar in my living room! I think he's dead."

The woman with the gray hair had buried her face in her hands during Hal's testimony.

The prosecutor entered Mumper's rap sheet into the record and the date of his recent early release from prison.

The judge asked if Hal had any record of violence.

"Nothing, your honor," the prosecutor answered. "Violent or otherwise."

"Is that all you have?" The judge looked around the courtroom. "Is there anybody else present who would like to speak in this matter?"

The woman in the third row raised her hand, then got to her feet, trembling.

I braced for the worst.

"I am the mother, sir. Ricky Mumper was my son." My heart sank. "I just want everybody to know I'm sorry. I did everything I could. He wasn't the man I tried to raise him to be. He's in God's hands now. I don't hate anybody."

She sat down again, heavily.

I almost wished she had ranted and raved and threatened to sue instead of exposing her broken heart and breaking ours.

Hal pulled out his handkerchief and wiped his eyes. I took his hand.

"The finding of this court is that the death of Ricky Mumper was justifiable homicide during commission of a crime and that there is no cause for criminal charges in this matter."

Outside the courtroom, Mrs. Mumper hugged Hal. "I'm sorry," she said, weeping. "You did what you had to do."

Did he? I wondered. He could have run out the door or climbed out a window. He could have barricaded himself in his bedroom while Ricky stole everything he owned. I knew Hal was asking himself the same questions. When is it right to draw the line and take a stand?

"I've got to call my folks," Hal said, clearing his throat and turning away so I wouldn't see his lip quiver. He groped in his pockets for a quarter.

As I opened my purse for change, a high-pitched scream echoed from a courtroom down the hall, turning all heads in the crowded corridor. Some miscreant just slapped with a stiff sentence, I thought. In this building, screams are not unusual. Gunfire is. The sound of two shots in rapid succession was unmistakable. Pandemonium erupted. People were fleeing courtroom 4-2 in a panic. Lawyers, witnesses, and clerks stumbled and shoved each other out of the way. The crowded corridor turned into a mindless stampede as the panic became contagious. Somebody fell on the escalator, knocking others down like tenpins. Handcuffed defendants seized the opportunity to run. Cops drew their guns. People dove for cover, scrambling in all directions.

"She shot him!" screamed a ponytailed court reporter who had run from the courtroom. "She shot him!"

My first thought was that a judge had been hit. I grabbed her hands as she kept screaming. "Who?" I asked her. "Who was shot?"

"Stosh Gorski, the lawyer. He's shot!" She jerked away and ran for the escalator. Her words resounded up and down the hall.

The Polish Prince. Lottie and I exchanged looks. "Oh, my God," she said.

We ran toward the courtroom.

"Wait, wait! Somebody in there has a gun!" Hal shouted. "Don't go in there!" He reached for me, too late.

As we burst into the courtroom, I saw Lottie's face, intent, focused.

Oh, no. Poor Lottie, I thought.

The scene inside was chaos. The judge cowered behind the bench. Half a dozen cops and bailiffs were scuffling with a woman they had wrestled to the floor. She still clutched the gun but it was twisted from her fingers as she shrieked and struggled.

On the floor in a puddle of blood in front of the bench, the Polish Prince whimpered and thrashed like a wounded animal. "She shot me!" he howled. The front of his expensive trousers was bloodstained. Clutching his upper thigh, he rocked in pain.

He looked up, eyes wild. "Lottie!" he cried pitifully.

She ran toward him—and began shooting his picture from all angles.

The bullet wound did not appear life-threatening. The shooter, disarmed and handcuffed, was his client, LaFontana Pierre, the lucky-bath burn victim.

While paramedics worked on the Polish Prince, cutting his exquisitely tailored trousers to expose the wound, she wailed about how "he promised me . . ."

The judge appeared on all fours, crawling out from behind the bench. "How the hell did she get that pistol in here past the metal detectors?" he demanded.

Nobody was killed but it was still a big story, exposing the fact that the high-tech, expensive, and sophisticated security system at the Justice Building could not deter anyone truly intent on smuggling in a weapon.

"These are great," the photo editor said later, examining Lottie's pictures.

"Yeah, ain't they," she said.

Thank God for small favors, I thought. She's really over him.

Ryan winced as he scrutinized a print of Stosh as the medics worked on him. "Was he circumcised before the shooting?"

Lottie didn't say a word. She just rolled her eyes.

HAL UNDERSTOOD THAT the shoot-
ing story, with a sidebar on Justice Building security, forced postpone-
ment of our evening. He kissed me good-bye and left to help his parents, who had panicked about the storm and were bringing their boat up
the Miami River to safe harbor.

"They want to do it before boat traffic jams up waiting for bridge
openings, and land traffic gets crazy because of people trying to evacuate," he said, shrugging.

Some Miamians' idea of storm preparation is to throw their most
valuable possessions in their cars and speed north, inland, or across
state. Problem is, you can't outrun Mother Nature. No place to hide.
Hurricanes are so erratic and unpredictable that not even the scientists
who track them from their inception can precisely predict exactly when
and where they will make landfall.

This one, still far to the south, in the Caribbean, was not even a
threat to South Florida at the moment. But as José Martí wrote, "Man
needs to suffer. When he does not have real griefs, he creates them."

I had not read Martí since I was a schoolgirl, yet his words came back to me now. Perhaps I am more Cuban than I thought. More likely it was because of my thoughts of my father and the fact that the storm might be headed for Cuba.

I worked the shooting story, learning that Stosh had apparently caused LaFontana Pierre grief, both personally and professionally. She seemed to believe they were engaged at one point, but had caught him with another woman. He had stopped returning her calls, but she knew where to find him. She had shown up packing a pistol as he represented another of her cousins, held on robbery charges. When she whipped out the gun, the defendant had leaped eagerly to his feet in the belief that she had come to break him out of there. Much to his disappointment, she gunned down his lawyer instead.

When I returned home, to the delicious luxury of my efficient new air conditioner, Mr. Goldstein and Seth were lugging out the hurricane shutters, numbered aluminum panels for each window and door. The young boy was already an inch or two taller than his granddad, and his back was certainly a lot straighter.

"Hey, Britt, we gonna have a hurricane party?" Seth was obviously thrilled by the idea.

According to the latest advisories, the huge storm had nicked the southern tip of the Dominican Republic's Barahoma Peninsula. There were reports of flash flooding in hillside barrios, crops and fishing boats had been destroyed, and airports were closed. Hurricanes are rated on a scale of one to five, with five the most fierce. This was a three, with winds of 111 to 130 miles an hour, but reports were that the storm was picking up speed over open water south of Jamaica and had veered to the northwest, toward Cuba.

"Hate to tell you this," I said, "but last I heard, the storm may hit Cuba. That should slow it down and then, most likely, it will die in the Gulf."

Seth looked crushed at the prospect.

"You can't be too careful, Britt," Mr. Goldstein said, a screwdriver in his hand. "There's nothing like being prepared." He mopped his forehead with an oversized handkerchief, his expression concerned. "I've been wondering if we should send Seth back home early."

"No way!" his grandson cried. "I've never seen a hurricane! I want to write a first-person account for the *Gazette*. I'll be the first staffer on my school paper to do an eyewitness account of a killer storm!"

They were still debating as I took Bitsy out for a walk.

By morning the storm had escalated to a four, with winds of between 131 and 155 miles an hour, and slammed into the Isle of Pines, off Cuba's southwest coast, site of the prison my father had once escaped. The hurricane had hit the mainland's narrow neck at La Habana Province and was roaring north toward Havana leaving widespread destruction in its wake.

Reports out of the country were sketchy with communications down, but the damage was apparently severe, with casualties high. Havana, where most houses and buildings are old and in poor condition, was sure to be hard hit. The mountains of eastern Cuba, where there is much more land to cross, will destroy a hurricane but this storm had struck at the narrow neck to the west.

A note on my word processor directed me to see Fred, the city editor, in his office. "Sit down," he said, looking grave.

Uh-oh, I thought. Something had caught up to me. The U.S. 1 caper with Bravo?

I smiled, mind racing, and tried to look innocent.

"Britt," he said reluctantly. "This is a sensitive matter." He arose, stepped outside, spoke quietly to his secretary, then returned, closing the door behind him, another bad sign. "Normally we wouldn't ask you something like this," he said, settling in his chair, "but we've had a complaint. . . ."

My stomach churned.

"About me?" I said, quick on the defensive.

"No." He looked startled, as though wondering why I would think such a thing. "The, eh, spouse of one of our staffers has made allegations, stating that they have experienced marital difficulties," he paused—clearly uncomfortable—"because of a situation here in the newsroom."

"A love triangle?" I said.

He nodded. "It's said that you might know something about it."

"Me? How?" Possibilities flashed through my mind. Had Lottie told someone?

"Evidently the aggrieved spouse suspected there was a late-night assignation here in the building last Wednesday and was outside, somewhere, watching. Claims she saw them leave together but that shortly before they emerged, you and Lottie Dane arrived, then left. The two individuals deny the allegations and claim both were here in the newsroom working late on individual projects. I might add that the couple involved is seeking counseling in an effort to repair the marriage, but the spouse appears to want some sort of disciplinary action on our part. These are valued employees, this could factor into their futures. Careers are involved here." He looked up at me expectantly.

I stared back, hating to be caught up in this. He misread my expression.

"What adults do should be their own business," he conceded. "Normally that's the way it is, but you know the old man. He has always adhered to high moral standards and insists that we do the same. After all, we are in the daily business of scrutinizing and reporting the behavior and the ethics of others and, I might add, this aggrieved party has called him a number of times demanding action."

"You've talked to the two people?"

He nodded.

"These are valued employees, and you don't believe them?"

"We want to cover all bases. Did you observe anything out of the ordinary Wednesday night?"

"People could lose their jobs?" I leaned back in my chair, crossed my legs, and smiled wickedly at the thought.

"Now, Britt," he warned, "I know you and one of the individuals involved may have experienced some difficulties in the past, but I expect you to be absolutely candid with me."

I sighed. "Okay. I was here that night, with Lottie. I came in to check out an arrest, and she had film to bring in."

"Did you see anyone?"

"Yes," I said casually.

"And?"

"I didn't see anything that looked unusual to me."

The "individuals involved" were fools to do it in the newsroom, but it's not that unusual, I reasoned. I know two cops who claim to have done it on the fifty-yard line at the empty Orange Bowl after dark. Lottie has confided about a steamy encounter in a hot air balloon, and though any sexcapades of mine probably pale by comparison, I thought that it was really gross for him to spy on employees' sex lives for the executive editor. Had their positions—professional positions—been reversed, if a male editor had indulged in sex with a female reporter, would there be prurient corporate interest? I thought not. I'd have to warn Lottie.

As though reading my mind, Fred said, "Ah, here she is now."

I glanced up and saw Lottie approaching, apparently summoned from the photo department.

"Thanks, Britt," he said, motioning her in as I left.

I tried to give her a subtle high sign as we exchanged looks in passing. It would not be cool if our stories didn't match.

Ron was nowhere in sight, but Gretchen was at the city desk and watched me return to my terminal. She had to be aware. First me, then Lottie called in for questioning. This is like the Kremlin, I thought. She looked sick. I could have given her a reassuring smile, but, hell, I'm not that nice.

Glancing back at Fred's glass-enclosed office, all I could see was Lottie's profile, lips slightly parted, eyes wide in an expression of studied innocence.

She emerged a short time later and walked past my desk. "Coffee?" she asked brightly.

"Sure," I said. We did not speak again until the elevator doors closed behind us. I punched three for the cafeteria.

"You see anything?" she said, leaning casually against the back wall, arms folded.

"Nothing unusual," I answered.

"Me neither."

"Good," I said with relief. "I hoped you'd say that."

"I saw that old fish eye you gave me as you left Fred's office. Don't it suck that they're investigating private lives?"

"You see Gretchen's face?" I said, as we stepped off. "She's worried."

"Good." Lottie grinned fiendishly and grabbed a tray. I poured a cup of coffee while she ran boiling water over a tea bag.

"Wish I'd finished putting Bahama shutters on my house," she said, as we settled at a corner table. "They're so expensive that I've just been adding a couple a year. Still have four windows to go. Sure hope that storm don't head our way. If it don't, that's what I'll spend my slot-machine money on, afore the next one stirs up out there. It's only a matter of time before we get hit."

"Hey, we always manage to dodge the bullet," I said confidently. "It's over the west end of Cuba right now."

"Nice if it just blew Mr. Castro the hell outta there." She sipped her tea. "Ain't the delicate balance a nature amazing? A little butterfly flaps his wings somewhere in Australia and that teeny tiny waft of air snowballs, somersaults, and spins around until three weeks later we got us a hurricane boiling up the Caribbean."

I blinked at the image.

"I don't think that's exactly how the meteorologists would describe it. Although, to tell you the truth, that makes more sense to me than some of the jargon in their forecasts."

I tried to call the detectives in the Armando Gutiérrez case, but when somebody finally did answer I was told they were out. Farmer from the FBI was out of his office, too. What the hell was going on here? A little storm hundreds of miles away and everybody disappears.

My Aunt Odalys did not sound great but insisted she was okay. "Britt, *mi hijita*. Listen to my words," she muttered weakly. "The spirits are with you always. But remember, one can never escape *la mala hora*."

The bad hour of one's life.

"Okay," I chirped cheerfully. "Just wanted to be sure you're all right and that if the hurricane does come this way you have somebody to help you."

"*Sí*," she whispered. "Beware *la mala hora*."

On that sunny note, I called my mother.

"Britt! Do you still have that little London Fog trench coat I got you at a discount? It will be perfect if the storm comes. Will you be coming to my place?"

I smiled. The last real hurricane to slam South Florida came when I was a toddler. I remembered us huddled together in her small apartment, wind howling around us. The power was out for a week.

"I'll be working, Mom. If the storm comes, I'll be covering it. I need to ask you something."

"Yes," she said guardedly.

"Winslow, from back in Dad's days, remember him? He was CIA. Do you recall him ever saying where he was from, or where he planned to retire to?" I asked, pencil poised over a blank page in my notebook. "You wouldn't happen to know his exact age, would you?"

She hung up.

I stood, fuming, and reached for my car keys as Ryan, working the weather story on the phone at the desk behind me, yelled to the city desk, "Hey, we may get it! It battered the hell outta Cuba, now it's standing still in the Straits, hasn't moved in three hours, but it could head northeast for the Keys."

The National Hurricane Center in West Dade, a big gray brick shoebox built like Fort Knox, with ten-inch-thick walls, rooftop satellites, wind gauges, and rooms crammed with radar and tracking equipment, was on red alert.

Oh swell, I thought, and stalked out of the newsroom. I knew what my reception would be, but didn't care. Fueled by anger, I stormed out to my car. Enough was enough. How dare she hang up on me? I have endured a lifetime of her fashion crap, her embarrassing attempts at matchmaking for me, her moods, lousy temper, cigarette smoke, secrecy, and evasiveness. But never once did I hang up on her.

I rapped once and she threw open the door, a garment bag over her shoulder. A suitcase beside her on the floor.

Her mouth opened in surprise. For a moment she said nothing. "I thought you were the doorman."

"Where are you going?"

"Emma, from the office, invited me to stay with her. She lives on high ground, in the Grove. So I'm evacuating early."

"This building is perfectly safe, Mom. It's only a hurricane watch." Was she running out on me or the coming storm? "Weren't you even going to let me know where you were?"

"I planned to call you."

She was lying. I closed the door behind me and stood with my back to it. "Mom, I can't believe you hung up on me."

She watched me warily.

"You've got to help me. Don't you realize that the more evasive you are, the more I want to know about my father?"

"I told you everything," she said, indignantly, "the last time we talked."

The doorbell rang. The doorman. "I have to go now," she said briskly. "I'll call you later, dear."

"No," I said, opening the door. I smiled at the middle-aged man in uniform. "Sorry. She doesn't need you now. I'll help her downstairs with her things." I closed the door before either of them could object.

"Because you refuse to help me and keep playing games," I told her, my rage mounting, "I wound up nearly deafened, within an inch of being arrested or killed, running around with Jorge Bravo, trailing after Juan Carlos Reyes, finding a dead body, and being humiliated in front of cops I have to deal with every day, and even falling into the arms of a man I scarcely know—all because of you!"

Her expression softened. "There's a new man in your life?"

"That is not what this is about." My voice shook. "If you ever want to see me again, you'd better start answering some questions!"

"Ask!" Her eyes glittered with anger.

"What the hell was your relationship with Reyes?"

"How dare you pry into my personal life!"

"And what's the story on the earrings?"

She jerked her chin up stubbornly. "They were a gift."

"I gathered that. From whom?"

"I don't know." Her eyes searched the room, as if for a means of escape. "Reyes gave them to me, saying they were from your father. Supposedly Tony slipped them to him in Cuba, asking him to deliver them to me if he didn't get out. I never believed it for a moment."

"Why?"

She raised her neatly penciled eyebrows. "For one thing, they're for pierced ears. Tony knew my ears aren't pierced—and that they were not the sort of thing I would ever wear." Her classic nose wrinkled delicately.

Typical, I thought. I loved them.

"I just assumed that Reyes felt sorry for an abandoned widow with a child and was being kind, or trying to ingratiate himself for some other reason, such as seduction. You know how men move in on women who seem vulnerable. And why would Tony Montero send a gift to a woman he had left?"

"Perhaps because he intended to come back," I said quietly.

"That's the sort of naive remark that turns my stomach!   Why do you keep making me miserable by dredging up the unhappy past?" she lashed out furiously. "I'm out of here." She swung the garment bag back over her shoulder.

"Did you have an affair with Reyes?"

She glared at me. "We had dinner a few times. Danced. I was young, lonely. No."

"Did my father work for the CIA?"

She looked startled, then shrugged. "Not that I know of, but of course I was the last to ever know anything."

"Winslow was an agent. When was the last time you saw him?"

"Thirty years or so ago," she snapped. "I really have to leave now." She took a step toward the door that I still blocked.

"Did you ever see or hear from him again after my father's death?"

She thought for a moment, then erupted as though agitated by whatever she remembered. "No, I don't think so, but I don't care! I don't give a shit about any of this. Your father was a bastard and it's a pity you take after him. I'm out of here! You can stay if you like! Just lock the door when you leave."

She pushed by me, red in the face. I didn't try to stop her. I didn't help with her luggage either. She picked up the suitcase and left, dragging the garment bag behind her.

She didn't even say good-bye.

When I was sure she was gone, I turned the deadbolt, checked her address book, and rummaged through her neatly kept desk. Then I checked her bedroom closets. Nothing from the past. The gold earrings were in a junk jewelry box on her dresser. I scooped them up and slipped them into my pocket. They were mine. My eighteenth-birthday gift. I wanted to call Hal or Kendall McDonald, or somebody, for a kind word. Instead I drove back to the paper.

The newsroom was hectic for this time of the day. Stalled over the straits and fueled by the warm water, the storm had built and was now a category five and on the move, according to the latest advisory.

Barreling north, with winds exceeding 155 miles an hour, it was skirting the coast and bypassing the Keys, which were being hit by outer edge gales, rain bands, and tornadoes. The big news was that the storm was traveling at nearly twenty miles an hour, twice the normal speed of a storm that size, and was accelerating.

The hurricane watch had been hurriedly upgraded to a hurricane warning, meaning that a storm is expected within the next twenty-four hours.

"If you have to, go secure your homes and your families, then get back in here as quick as you can," Fred told the staff in a hasty newsroom meeting. "I'll be calling in everybody who's off. This thing could reach here a lot sooner than anybody expected."

I had no messages from Farmer or the detectives. I called the FBI office. Farmer was in.

"Hey," I said, "find out anything?"

He sounded harried and in a hurry. "Good news and bad news," he said. "The good news is, I found Winslow."

My heart beat faster. He had to talk to me.

"The bad news is, he's dead."

"What happened?"

"Retired early, apparently an alcohol problem he couldn't control. Five years ago he was coming out of a bar in Alexandria, Virginia, and was shot to death. Apparently a robbery. Never solved. His daughter still lives up there."

"What's her name?"

There were noises and voices in the background. He seemed distracted. "You need that?"

I said I did. "What's going on there?"

"A storm's on the way," he said irritably. "We're trying to secure this place and move all the files to upper floors."

"The daughter's name?"

"Okay, don't tell her where you got it. Meredith Jessup, at, uh . . .

Sorry, I tossed it. She's listed under her husband's name. Simon. A Worthington Avenue address."

I tried the detectives again, without any luck.

"You still here?" Fred said, pacing by my desk and looking impatiently at his watch.

The usual drive home took forty minutes instead of ten. Bridges were opening, bringing road traffic to a standstill in order to let high-masted boats through. The roads were becoming a nightmare, and it had only just begun.

I thought of my hurricane supplies, left untouched from year to year, bottled water and a few outdated cans of tuna. I had plenty of pet food but needed to stock up on candles, batteries, bread, and ice. The Publix parking lot was full but I found a space on the street nearby when another car pulled out.

I walked into my supermarket and stood still in shock.

Bedlam reigned. Most counters were already empty. The bread was gone, the bottled water and batteries were gone. They were already out of ice. Frantic shoppers, panic buyers, carts piled high with anything and everything, were rushing through the store, several fighting bitterly over the last few cans of soft drinks.   I wanted to grab half a dozen ten-pound sacks of Kitty Litter to sandbag my front door just in case, but it was too chaotic. I'd never get out of there.

I turned and walked out with nothing. Car horns blared, tempers flared, and there were two fender benders in the parking lot. Several drivers were jockeying for my space as I pulled out. I didn't stay to referee.

Mr. Goldstein and Seth had nearly all the hurricane shutters in place. Seth was practically giddy with excitement.

"It's really coming, Britt!"

"Not necessarily," I said calmly. "It could still veer off and bypass us altogether."

"Are you going to evacuate?" I asked his grandfather. Miami

Beach, a narrow island, has no storm shelters. One must go to the mainland and then rely on the "authorities" to decide when and if you can return home. That might be days, if the storm did hit.

He nodded. "If the next advisory doesn't show some big change. My wife is packing up some things now. What are you going do about Bitsy and Billy Boots?" he said.

Shelters do not admit pets.

"I don't know." If there was a crisis, I wanted the animals with me.

"We're not going to a public shelter," Mr. Goldstein offered. "We have a niece at Country Walk, in the southwest section. That's pretty far inland, a relatively new development. It should be safe. We can take them with us."

I hated to send them, but as he had said, it didn't hurt to be prepared. "I'll put their carriers by the door along with their food," I said gratefully.

I did so, adding Billy's new catnip toy and a chew bone for Bitsy. I still believed it would not happen, that this was all a drill like every other hurricane season in my memory. South Florida would breathe a sigh of relief at the next advisory and then go on as before, except that the people who sell batteries and bottled water would be a bit richer.

I filled the bathtub and some water jugs, set the freezer and fridge at their coldest levels, and unplugged all the other appliances. I tossed my flashlight, portable radio, the few batteries I could find, my toothbrush, toothpaste, soap, deodorant, a change of underwear, a pair of jeans, a T-shirt, socks, and a granola bar in a canvas bag. My fire department boots and another pair of Reeboks were already in the trunk of the T-Bird. Bitsy watched, subdued, from beneath a chair but Billy Boots was pacing, agitated and meowing.

How annoying this whole damn thing was. The timing couldn't be worse. I wondered about Winslow, the only person who could have filled in the gaps, who could tell me what I wanted to know. Damn, why did he have to be an alcoholic?

I kissed the Goldsteins, fought off Seth, who begged to go with me, and tossed the bag in my car. This didn't seem real. I detoured to South Beach for a look at the ocean, as though it could tell me what Mother Nature planned. Perfectly peaceful and placid. As beautiful as always. People were playing Frisbee on the sand as usual. The bearded street preacher ranted on a street corner, arms outstretched. Nothing seemed different or ominous in any way except that something didn't seem quite right. Something missing. I stood next to my car, squinting in the sun. What was wrong with this postcard-perfect picture? The usual afternoon thunder squalls, a line of low dark gray clouds, lay offshore, to the east, instead of over the Everglades, to the west. Then I saw what was missing. No sea birds, no birds at all. Not a gull in sight. They had all gone.

The damn thing is really coming, I thought in awe. Shit!

Reality suddenly sank in. I started the car, made a sharp U-turn, then switched my police scanner to the weather channel. The storm had gained speed and strength in its northward sweep. Drawn by a low-pressure area, it had changed course, veering to the northwest, on a relentless course for Miami. At five, the most deadly category, it was currently 185 miles offshore, with wind speeds clocked at 160 miles an hour and gusts approaching 200.

Not now, I thought. Dammit. I'm not ready for this.

Bridges would no longer be raised for boat traffic. Women in the final trimester of pregnancy were being urged to go to the nearest hospital because the extreme low pressure of a hurricane induces labor. Family members, however, could not accompany them because the hospitals were already overcrowded with heart patients and diabetics. Forecasters were voicing concerns about the residents of coastal counties. Ninety percent had never experienced a major hurricane. The last one was in 1965. We were way overdue. Exactly what Lottie had been saying. Shit.

My assignment was to spend the hurricane at the Dade County Medical Examiner's office. My job would be to provide the paper with an accurate casualty count. I was issued a cell phone by the city desk and told to tally the storm victims as they arrived. Not as bad a job as some. The brick building is solid, secure, and elevated, adjacent to the county hospital, directly across the street from the trauma center, and equipped with emergency generators. The morgue can hold 350 bodies and is the last place county officials would allow to go without power. Before leaving the office, I called Alexandria, Virginia.

Meredith Jessup answered.

"You don't know me," I began, introducing myself. "I'm calling about your father."

"You know he's dead," she quickly responded.

"Yes, that's why I'm calling you."

"Finally," she breathed. "You've learned something?"

"No," I answered, puzzled. "I wanted to ask you about his work, in Miami, with Cuban exiles, the freedom fighters, thirty years ago."

"Oh." She sounded disappointed. "I really didn't know him that well. He was never around, always away on assignment, when I was growing up. Florida, Haiti, Central America, Mérida in Mexico. He and my mom got divorced." She sighed. "I was just beginning to get to know him when he was murdered. That's what I thought you were calling about. You're a reporter, so I thought . . ."

"What?"

"His murder. I never believed it was a robbery. Just a fantasy of mine, I guess. I thought maybe you'd uncovered something."

A kindred spirit, I thought. Another woman caught up in the mysteries of her father's past. "What happened?"

"He moved back up here after he retired. My mother had died. I was getting married and asked him to give me away. He did, and we really hit it off. He had a drinking problem but he stopped. He was getting his life together. He had a lot of regrets. You know, about his work. You're not writing about any of this, are you?"

"No, I'm trying to find out what happened to my own father. They knew each other. My father was killed when I was three."

There was a moment of silence.

"The past is always with you," she said wistfully.

"No way to shake it," I agreed.

"He had a lot to live with, from his work over the years. I'm sure I don't know the half of it. He had to do things in the line of duty that haunted him later. Contributed to his drinking problem, I'm sure."

"Do you know much about what happened in Miami?"

"I know he was there for several years. When I was in the first and second grade he used to send me postcards."

"Anything else?"

"A lot of regrets. He would never even vacation there. He wanted no part of Miami."

"Did he leave any files, records, journals?"

"No, when I got his stuff there was nothing. You wouldn't think he had a past."

He should have met my mother, I thought, then I remembered: he had. "It is funny, though. Just before he was killed he mentioned something, just in passing. He'd come over for lunch with me and the baby. He was so happy he had a grandson. He mentioned that he'd seen somebody from the past that he hadn't seen for many years. I got the impression it was someone from Miami."

"A friend?"

"No, no friend. He didn't seem upset, just depressed."

"What happened?"

"Two nights later he was shot on the street outside a bar downtown. I was surprised at that. He hadn't been drinking anything stronger than iced tea for six months, as far as I knew. The police said it was probably a robbery. But they gave me his wallet. Had two hundred dollars in it. And his watch. They said the robber must have been scared off. I never bought it. I thought it had to be something out of his past. The detectives talked to somebody at the Agency, only after I insisted. But they never really looked into it."

"Where was he shot?"

"Twice in the back of the head, just below the ear, as he was about to get into his car on a side street. Small-caliber. I think they said a twenty-two. Never knew what hit him, they told me."

A chill rippled across my shoulders, raising goose bumps on my arms.

"Any witnesses? Anybody hear the shots, see the killer?"

"No. He'd been dead for a while when he was found. A taxi driver saw him lying there and called it in."

"When did this happen?"

"Five years ago last May. May twenty-seventh. I really resented it," she said. "I never knew him all those years growing up. I was finally get-ting to know my father, and then he was gone again. This time, forever."

"At least you had him for a while," I said gently. "Some of us aren't that lucky."

"You're right," she said sadly. I could hear a child playing in the background. "How did your dad die?"

"Executed in Cuba, by a firing squad. Apparently he was on an anti-Castro mission."

"At least he died for a cause and you know why. Good luck. Call me anytime. Aren't you having a hurricane down there? I thought I saw something on TV."

"It's not here yet," I said.

A crowd was clustered around the bulletin board reading the latest Hurricane Center advisory. The television monitors overhead were broadcasting infrared satellite pictures of the storm, giant counterclock-wise spirals of angry red, the eye pulsating at the core like the beating heart of something alive.

Lottie strode by wearing a yellow slicker. She would be out in the teeth of the storm, shooting pictures. I was sorry I wouldn't be with her, in the middle of the action.

She paused by my desk. "Hell all Friday," she said. "It looks like this is it. The big baboomba!"

"Watch yourself. I hope this damn thing blows over before the Vera

Verela concert," I fretted. The benefit for the missing boys was only two days away.

I dialed the homicide detectives. They weren't in. I could try again from the ME office. My phone rang as I gathered up my things to leave.

"Montero?"

"*Hola, Jorge.*"

"You must leave that place, a storm is coming. A bigger storm is soon to follow."

"What?"

"The same winds that swept across Cuba have brought us the truth. Antonio's *diario*. We have it!"

"Oh puleeze."

"Reyes's own hired *criminal* came to us after he saw what Antonio had written there. Reyes was a Castro agent. He betrayed all of us."

"I hate to interrupt your usual routine, Jorge, but did you know that Frank Winslow is dead? Murdered."

"*Muerto. Dios mío,* I did not know."

"You didn't know he was blown away, up in Virginia, in a murder quite similar to that of Armando Gutiérrez ?"

"No, my word to you. Who killed him?"

"I thought you might know."

"Reyes! Winslow knew the truth. So Reyes had him killed."

"Sure, and Reyes shot J.R., put the cyanide in the Tylenol capsules, and blew up the Federal Building in Oklahoma City."

"*¿Qué?*"

"I can't talk to you now, Jorge. I'm busy."

"*Sí,*" he said quietly and hung up.

The wind was already gusting as I drove to the medical examiner's office at Number One Bob Hope Road.

The Cuban capital had been devastated, the radio said, with hundreds of lives lost, buildings collapsed, mass destruction. The minor damage Bravo had inflicted with grenades and gunfire in his speedboat drive-bys was a trifling annoyance compared to the devastation wrought by Mother Nature.

Cuba, so close and yet so far away. I remembered my Aunt Odalys saying that Cuba is everywhere: in the food we eat, in our prayers, in our hearts, in our daydreams. Why does this small island no bigger than Pennsylvania forever obsess this sprawling and complex city of exiles and contradictions?

I parked and trudged past the fifteenth-century Spanish cannon up the stairs to the entrance, lugging my bag and a fistful of notebooks.

The lobby, with its raspberry-colored furniture and soft-patterned carpet, was empty. The chief was not in, but there was "a skeleton crew," according to Miriam, the motherly chief investigator, who emerged from her office cracking one of her usual morbid jokes. She settled me in a small conference room near the morgue.

"Anybody attributable to the storm come in yet?"

"One dead, two wounded, in a family fight over whether to evacuate, one electrocution." She ticked them off on her fingers like a housewife with a shopping list. "Homeowner was trying to knock the coconuts off his trees. He touched a hot wire with the metal pole he was using."

Ouch. People were already dying, and the storm hadn't even arrived. Miamians cannot seem to do anything without killing off themselves or each other.

"And I hear we have two traffic cases on the way. Oh"—she brightened—"here are the detectives on the electrocution."

Hanks and Wogan appeared in the doorway and did a double take when they saw me. They wore boots, their hair windblown. "Hey, guys. Just who I wanted to see."

They rolled their eyes.

"Did you get my messages?" I asked.

"Mucho messages, Britt. Don't you ever give up?" Hanks said.

"No."

"That's what I thought."

"I wanted to ask you about Armando Gutiérrez. What kind of silencer was used?" The detectives exchanged glances as Billy sat down at the conference table to write the report on the electrocution.

"Who you been talking to?" Hanks demanded.

"Nobody," I said quickly. "He was shot execution style, two right behind the ear in the middle of the day. Nobody heard a thing. You don't have to be a genius to think it was a professional hit, with a silencer. . . ."

"You're not gonna print that?"

"Not until you say it's okay."

I had not seen raw potato chunks around the body, ruling out the cheapest, most popular silencer. Firing a pistol through a potato is messy but effective. They may be bulky to carry around, but they have their advantages. Possession of a potato is not a federal offense. Yet.

"Okay, so there was a silencer," he conceded, "but I don't want to read about it in the newspaper."

"How do you know for sure?"

"He had a contact wound. There was so much blood in his hair that we couldn't see it at the scene. But when the ME cleaned off the wounds the muzzle mark was bigger, larger in diameter, than the barrel of any weapon that caliber. Had to be a silencer, probably a reworked lawnmower muffler with a few extra baffles. Turns the sound down to what sounds like the thud of a car door. Takes the crack right out of it."

"The gun was a twenty-two?"

"Listen to me now, Britt." Hanks took a seat at the conference table and began to pry the plastic lid off the Styrofoam coffee cup he'd been carrying. "You can't be printing this."

"You know better."

"Yeah, a twenty-two. Smaller caliber has less noise to start with, and the barrel can be easily machined to screw on a silencer."

Billy looked up from his paperwork. "You got the name of that cousin, the next of kin?"

"Uncle," Hanks said. He put down his coffee, opened his small black notebook, and spelled out the name.

"What did Gutiérrez have in his pockets?"

"Nothing much," he said, closing the book.

"What?"

"One thing you might find interesting. I know we did." Billy grinned.

"What?" I looked from one to the other. "I can't stand it. Tell me. I'll trade you some information I guarantee you don't have. Tell me."

"You first," Hanks said. He was grinning now, too.

I told them about Frank Winslow. Neither changed expression. "So?" Hanks said.

"Same MO, same connections."

"In goddamn Virginia, five freaking years ago." Hanks looked skeptical.

"That's not all that unusual an MO, Britt," Billy said.

"It wouldn't hurt to check it out."

"A pro probably wouldn't keep a piece that long," Billy said.

I shrugged. "I thought it was interesting."

"Maybe it's worth a call or two," Hanks said.

"Now you tell me."

"I dunno," he teased. "You think that was good enough for a trade, Billy?"

"Give the girl a break."

"You promise you won't . . ."

"Yeah, yeah, yeah."

"Tucked in his shirt pocket, close to his heart," he said, speaking deliberately, excruciatingly slowly, "the late, unfortunate Mr. Armando Gutiérrez was carrying the late, unfortunate Mr. Alex Aguirre's business card with his home number and his beeper number written on it."

I stared, mind racing. Could Bravo have told me the truth? No way. Maybe. "So you think they're related?"

"Now *that* is something worth checking into." He pointed his index finger at me. "That's exactly what we plan to do once this freaking storm blows over." He pushed his chair back. "Come on, Billy, we've gotta get back out there."

"Was the card new, like he got it here? Or did it look like it came with him from Cuba?"

"Dirty, dog-eared, had been wet and dried off." Hanks looked to Billy, who nodded in affirmation as they went out the door.

How can I reach Bravo? I wondered. I called Reyes. He answered his home phone himself.

"Mr. Reyes . . ."

"Juan Carlos," he corrected. "I tried to reach you, Britt. First and foremost, I am deeply concerned. WQBA radio news reported that you and Jorge Bravo were present, together, when a murder took place in a hotel downtown."

Drat, I thought, now the FBI will know for sure, unless they're too busy boarding up to listen to Spanish-language radio.

"I cannot emphasize enough my grave concern," Reyes was saying, "for your safety, for your reputation. Bravo is a madman. Dangerous. He will stop at nothing. I strongly suspect that he is a Castro agent."

Hell, was everybody in Miami a Castro agent?

"Why would you say that?"

"Many reasons, among them his constant efforts to malign and slander me and my organization. You are aware that I am a threat to Fidel as his economy and his leadership falter and weaken. Fidel knows this. Of course you understand all that. The other reason I attempted to contact you was that Wilfredo, my aide, did as promised and I now have the diary of your father."

"You have it?" I blurted out. "Jorge Bravo claims he has it."

"You see, he is a madman. I am looking at it at this very moment. Here at my desk. Holding it in my hand. Fragile, dusty, but definitely intact. At this moment, I am preparing to leave. The island neighborhoods must evacuate, as you know. But when the storm has passed I will personally deliver it to you and Catalina."

Now that would be a scene.

"No, I'll come right now. I'm on the way."

"Impossible." he said. "I'm sure the police will no longer allow traffic onto the island. Out of the question. I will be in touch with you later."

The connection broke.

I upended my purse onto the polished conference table, pawing frantically through the contents. Did I have it? What had I done with it? It had to be here.

A scrap of paper fluttered to the floor from the inner lining. I snatched it up. The contact number Bravo had given me for *especialista* Luisa.

Nothing else seemed to matter. Other goals had come first all my life. I followed through on every story, always put my job first, but had never done for myself what I had so often done for others. This one was for me. This time I would follow through, for my father, for myself. The storm was nothing. I had lived in the eye of a storm all my life. Nothing could stop me.

I grabbed my bag, punching the number into the cell phone as I ran up the stairs to the lobby.

"Britt?" said Miriam. "You're not going out there?"

"I'll be back," I said. "Something I have to do."

"Answer, answer," I muttered at the phone. I had trouble pushing open the front door, surprised by the force of the wind that buffeted me as I stepped out. It nearly knocked me off my feet. Head down I fought my way to the car.

"*Hola.*" Someone answered at the other end of the phone as I slammed the driver's side door.

"Luisa! Is that you?"

"*¿Sí.*"

"I must talk to Jorge Bravo, right away," I said, identifying myself, turning the key in the ignition.

"*¿El comandante?*"

"*Sí.* It's an emergency."

"*¿Emergencia?*" I heard her speaking to someone else. "Give me your number." I did. "He will call you."

"Now!" I said. "As soon as possible."

The call came almost immediately, as I pulled out onto Tenth Avenue. "I don't know what's going on, Jorge. But I just talked to Reyes. He said he had the diary in his hands. I am going to his house right now, to see for myself."

"Wait! It is not true. He lies! It is too dangerous. Wait, I can prove to you . . ."

"I don't know who or what to believe," I said. "This whole thing is weird and I intend to get to the bottom of it."

"The storm . . ."

"Fuck the storm!"

"I will meet you."

"No, I've tried that. It never worked out."

Garbage and an entire garbage can blew across the street in front of me. I swerved to avoid it. Miami looked like a ghost town with boarded windows and deserted sidewalks.

"I beg you, Montero, do not risk this."

Did he ever say that to my father?

"What about Alex Aguirre?" I said. "Was he really on a story?"

"The information I gave you was correct. Armando Gutiérrez was bringing the *diario*. . . ." A burst of static and we lost the connection.

As I approached the causeway, a lone Miami patrol car inched through the residential waterfront neighborhood. The driver was broadcasting over a public address system.

"You must evacuate. It is the law. You must evacuate. If you do not have transportation, we will assist you."

Oh sure, I thought, heart sinking. *We are from the government and we are here to help you.* That is when you know you are really in trouble.

Oh God, I thought, as turbulent skies closed in overhead. Please let Reyes still be there. I might have just enough time to get the diary and get back to the morgue.

THE GUARD SHACK stood empty. The wooden arm barred the entrance but the exit side was open. As the T-Bird wobbled and wavered on the wind-blasted bridge, I heard the latest advisory. A storm surge of fifteen to twenty feet was predicted across Miami Beach from the ocean to the bay. Those who had not evacuated were told it was too late and warned to stay off the road and hunker down where they were. Were my mother, the Goldsteins, and my pets in a safe place? *Was* there a safe place?

Darkening clouds masked the sun, and the sky glowed an eerie shade of maroon red. Palm trees bent in the wind, pliant fronds thrashing like warning flags in the gale. As I approached his home, I saw Reyes's electronic gates wide open. The *Libertad* danced on black waves at its moorings behind the house, despite more than a dozen lines that tied it down. His Range Rover stood in the driveway. He was closing the lift gate.

I pulled up behind his car. He frowned. "You shouldn't have come here," he shouted, above the wind. "It's time to leave."

"I want the diary!" I followed him as he darted back into the house. The huge hallway seemed eerie with all the windows now shuttered.

"I packed it in the trunk," he said impatiently. "We must leave."

"No, I want to see it."

"Don't you understand, have you heard the reports? The storm is nearly upon us!"

"I'm tired of being put off," I said stubbornly. "I want the diary."

"Are you crazy?" He snatched a stack of files from his desk and threw them into a valise. "Hand me those," he said, gesturing impatiently toward several small silver-framed photos on a shelf behind his desk. I picked one up, of a small blond boy astride a pony. Another boy, with Reyes's eyes, stood solemnly beside the animal, holding its lead.

"Is that you?" I had not seen it before.

"Yes." He glanced at the photo for a moment. "My boyhood in Camagüey."

"The other boy?"

"My American cousin. He was visiting."

"I didn't know you had relatives here."

"Is there a Cuban who does not have American relatives?" He reached for the photo of him and the President.

As he did so, I saw he wore a gun in a shoulder holster. That, or something he had said, reminded me of the elusive detail I had been trying to remember. What was it? Out in the main hall the front door blew open, and the wind found its way into the house.

"We must leave," he said.

"I want to get out of here as much as you do," I said. "Please, just give me my father's diary and I'll go."

Then I realized it was not the wind in the front hall. Reyes heard the sounds at the same moment I did. A cane.

In the process of removing a commercial-size checkbook from a cabinet, Reyes swiveled toward the door.

Bravo stood there, one hand on his cane, a gun in the other. "What are you doing?" I asked him.

"You!" Reyes said.

"Give her Antonio's *diario*," Bravo said and grinned. His smile had no humor. Rain drummed against the shutters.

Reyes glared at him. "Get out of my house!"

"Call the police," Bravo said gleefully.

Reyes continued to glare.

"Give her the *diario*." Bravo turned to me with a little bow. "He cannot. Why? Because I have it here." His teeth gleamed in a wide smile. He used the barrel of the gun to lift his guayabera, exposing a weathered book stuffed in his waistband.

"I told you, Montero. You would not listen to me. Just like your father. I could not save him, but I will save you from this would-be tyrant. He would have killed you."

"You are in league with Castro," Reyes said, his face twisted in rage.

"Perhaps Castro sent Antonio's words to Miami to stop you." Bravo shrugged. "So be it. Perhaps for the only time, Castro has done something for the Cuban people. The *asesino* you sent to kill Armando Gutiérrez and steal the *diario* read Antonio's words and would not deliver it to you, even though he knew he would not be paid. He is Cuban first, that is what you misunderstood."

He turned to me. "When you publish your father's words, the world will know—and Reyes is finished. Ask him what happened to the young *rubio*, the boy who joined us in Camagüey. They told the parents he died in prison." Bravo shook his head slowly.

"Pervert!" He spit out the word.

And that was when I remembered. Ohmigod.

"Watson Kelly, one of the missing boys, called his parents from a pay phone in the downtown arcade, the one you own." Reyes, eyes half closed, lips working, said nothing. "Charles Randolph was last seen coming here to work for you. You know what happened to them, don't you?" I remembered the questions he had casually raised about the investigation. His attitude change when the task force was appointed.

"He is a pervert!" Bravo said.

"Where are they?"

Reyes ignored my question, his eyes deep wells of darkness.

"You are both crazy," he said, and glanced toward the shuttered windows, resounding with pounding rain. "I suggest we save ourselves from the storm first and continue this discussion when it has passed."

The lights flickered and went out. The power was gone.

"You see!" he said angrily. He was barely visible in the shadows. The only light filtered through the thick glass of two decorative porthole windows high on the wall. Bravo shoved his gun back into a holster clipped to his waistband. He pulled out the book and presented it to me.

"For you, Montero. The truth, a legacy from your father."

I held it in my hands. At last. I wanted to take it and run but where? The wind might tear it from me. I wanted to go to my car for my bag, my flashlight. But when I cracked the door, it took the three of us to close it against the storm.

We were trapped. The bridge would be impassable.

"We need candles, a lantern," I said, clutching the diary. Reyes led us through his huge kitchen into the pantry. He found some candles and a powerful beam flashlight, a big one encased in plastic.

We returned to his office where he stood the flashlight straight up on the bar, pointing to the ceiling, its beam illuminating the room in a soft glow.

Gravel, stones, and tree branches barraged the house. My mind was racing, full of questions. Reyes seemed strangely calm, almost suave. He offered us something from the bar and, when we declined, selected a bottle of Scotch from the shelf and mixed himself a drink. I sat on the arm of a chair, fingers curled around the cracked leather of the book held next to my body. Bravo took a chair nearby.

"We are together for the duration," Reyes said, raising his glass. "As politics makes strange bedfellows, so does the storm. We should be sociable."

The house shuddered in the scream and boom of the wind. Walls shook and reverberated. "Do not worry," Reyes said. "There is no reason to be alarmed. This house will withstand anything." He tuned in a battery-powered radio. The storm, indeed, was upon us. The house was being battered now by flying debris.

As we sat in semidarkness, a newscaster interrupted the storm coverage with a warning.

"All emergency personnel, police and fire, have been ordered to seek shelter for their own safety. No calls for assistance will be answered. I repeat, no emergency calls will be answered.

"Miami," he added, "you are on your own."

The voice of authority had just informed us that there was none. The words filled my heart with dread. What about accidents? Sick people, heart attacks, those injured and bleeding in the storm? We were alone. Reyes finished his drink.

"Britt," he said calmly. "Give me the diary."

"What?" I was startled. "It's mine. I've waited all these years."

Bravo struggled to his feet. "This is the man who betrayed your father!"

The house rocked. I remembered that at its height, the hurricane of my childhood screamed with the high-pitched shrieks of a thousand women. Yet this storm rumbled with a deep-throated roar, like a freight train. Each storm must have its own distinctive voice.

"If you fear that your home is becoming unsafe," the newscaster was saying, his voice compassionate, "hunker down with your family in an interior closet or bathroom. Use mattresses for cover." I prayed that those I loved were safe.

Reyes snatched the flashlight from the bar with an abrupt move. I thought he was leaving the room. Instead he stepped swiftly toward me, shining it in my face. I couldn't see. Was this how it was in a prison interrogation?

"You will never read this book," he said. I shrank back, blinking. "You were stupid to come here, stupid and naive like your father. Let me tell you about your father; he was a worm."

"I trusted you."

"So did your father. Only fools trust."

Something heavy crashed upstairs and the house began to shake, as though pounded by a bulldozer. As Reyes reacted, directing his light toward the stairs, Jorge stepped forward, gun in hand.

"I will not permit this. This history must not be repeated. I cannot allow it to happen again. Get behind me, Montero."

Reyes cursed and flicked off the flashlight, plunging us into a black well as the house rocked and moaned. Bursts of gunfire lit up the dark, four, five shots almost drowned out by the bricks and roofing tiles slamming the outside walls like machine-gun fire. I hit the floor. Glass shattered and I heard Jorge draw in a shuddering breath and fall. The wind whined and whistled, finding cracks in the metal shutters.

He lay near me somewhere on the floor. I reached out to touch him and felt the warm blood on his shirt.

"No, no," he whispered. "I want to die in Cuba."

The flashlight beam blinded me before I even thought to grope for his gun. Reyes kicked it away, standing over us, unhurt, breathing hard. "Loco old fool!" he said.

"Montero," Bravo mumbled.

"I'm here," I said.

"Antonio . . ."

"Call an ambulance," I muttered to Reyes.

"There are no ambulances, no police, no doctors. Remember? Just us."

"How could you do this?" I said tearfully.

"You saw," Reyes said, indignantly. "He tried to kill me."

Jorge's body quivered, he was gasping. I found his maimed hand, caught the other, and held them both. "Give me some light," I pleaded. "I have to stop the bleeding."

"Too late," he said coldly. "The old fool is dead."

He was right.

Jorge Bravo was a poor man compared to Reyes and his riches. Like my father, he spent his energy, his health, and finally gave his life to free Cuba. But quick death by firing squad had to be easier than thirty years of frustration, heartbreak, and defeat. Bravo had no political plans. He did not feign patriotism to make money. He did not talk about freedom, he struggled for it, not on the streets of Miami, but in Cuba. He did the best he could.

Green lightning flashed outside the porthole windows, illuminating the trees as they twisted, writhed, and toppled. The house shuddered. Wood ripped and splintered.

I ran to the front door. Reyes followed with the light. Rivulets of water were creeping in over the top. "Don't open it!" he shouted. The door buckled in the wind. We pushed a heavy bookcase against it, but the roaring gale began to move the bookcase, inching it toward us.

I ran back to Bravo, stumbling across his body in the dark. I tugged at his shoulders, trying to move him into a sitting position, hoping to somehow drag him onto the sofa. I didn't want him wet, exposed. But he was too heavy and the front of my blouse grew sticky with his blood.

One of the small round windows exploded. Rain and debris peppered the air like bullets. Metal shutters were snapping off.

"The bathroom," Reyes said urgently from behind me. I picked up the radio, following the beam of his light as we fled to an interior bathroom with no windows.

"Mattresses," I shouted, "we need mattresses!"

He ran to another room and returned dragging a twin-size mattress. "Help me!" he said.

I followed him to another small bedroom at the back of the house. His light skimmed the ceiling. It was sagging. Reyes cursed wildly as we tore the mattress off the bed, pushing and pulling it out the door as the ceiling split open like overripe fruit. We hauled it into the bathroom and slammed the door.

The burnished gold of the lavish bathroom fixtures glowed in the flashlight's beam. From the other side of the door came the unearthly sounds of shutters being ripped away by an angry, scratching, howling beast.

My ears kept popping from the pressure.

"*¡Dios mío!* This cannot be. This cannot be." Reyes was hyperventilating.

"We have to keep the door from opening," I muttered. Like a wild animal, the storm was loose in the house, crashing, smashing, and tearing. He kept his shoulder to the door. I lay on the floor, braced against the sink, feet pressed against the door. The wind pushed and we pushed back. I listened, ready to scramble into the tub and crouch beneath a mattress if the ceiling gave way. "We may not live through this," I cried. "What about the boys? Where are they? Did you betray my father? Tell me the truth about what happened to him!"

He grunted, turning the other shoulder to the door. "Truth? That's all your father wanted. He did not see the big picture: politics, countries, governments, survival. You are like him. You miss the big picture." He laughed, a vile sound that mingled with those of the storm. "You babble on about truth while the storm of the century rages around us, when survival is all that is important. He did not survive.

"But I will! I am a survivor. Always," he ranted. "The Bay of Pigs, the cold war, business and politics. I survived them all. I have Secret Service clearance! I occupied the podium with the President when he last visited Miami. I have been to the White House!"

"How will you explain Bravo's body?"

I strained to hear as he lowered his voice. "People disappear in a storm like this. They are never found. Swept away. This is a perfect time for somebody to disappear."

Despite the suffocating heat in the small room, I felt chilled. Did the barrage seem to be subsiding? The pounding wind and the roar were no longer as loud. The eye of the storm must be approaching: my chance to escape. My only chance. I could make it to my car and across the bridge before the second half of the storm hit. I could find a safe place to ride out the rest of the hurricane.

I got to my knees, in a crouch. Reyes stretched and stepped away from the door.

More terrified of him than of the storm, I flung the door open and ran out. The darkness was pitch black, the water ankle- and then knee-deep. Splashing. He came after me.

"Wait!" he shouted. I him heard crash against a wall. I groped in the darkness. The shutters were gone. The windows were out, the storm was in. Green lightning flashed again, in the distance. The roof had peeled away and one wall was gone. It was raining inside. "Wait, stop!" Reyes shouted, lunging after me.

The stench was horrible. Water was rising. The sewer lines have ruptured, I thought, nearly gagging as I kept moving, his flashlight beam dancing behind me. Lightning flashed again, and I saw another face, in front of me. A skull, grinning. I recoiled, screaming.

Reyes stumbled over a fallen timber and his flashlight fell into the water. Floating and bobbing, driven by the wind and storm surge, its strong beam illuminated horror after horror like a macabre light show. I was hallucinating. Was I dead? Bones, skulls, bodies in various stages of decomposition and mummification. Staring up in terror at the shattered walls, I saw limbs, arms and legs, dangling from the crawl space beneath the broken roof.

Oh God. I was alive. They were real.

He saw them too. With a cry of anger and despair, he caught my right arm and ripped the diary from my waistband. I fought to keep it, thrashing off-balance in the stinking water, the horrifying tableau still playing all around us at the whim of the spotlight's wavering beam.

He hit me in the face, so hard I saw an exploding sun and fell back onto a water-soaked chair. Dazed, I heard him at the splintered front door. "No! What have you done?"

Sobbing, gagging, I lurched to my feet and chased the bobbing light, caught it, picked it up, and stumbled toward the door. I heard the engine of the Range Rover. I saw it, covered with tree branches that fell away as it rolled slowly out of the driveway, picking up speed. I had to stop him. Knees shaking, I tried to find my car but couldn't see it. Branches, debris, and fallen trees were everywhere.

Taking a deep breath, I steadied the light and slogged through water to where my T-Bird should be. Instead there was an impenetrable thicket, a mountain of green branches as high as a house. My T-Bird was beneath the fallen ficus tree that had stood sentry in the courtyard, flattened like a smashed toy.

The Range Rover was gone, its four-wheel drive somehow navigating the obstacles, downed trees, water, and floating lumber. The wind was receding to a whisper, the sky awash in stars, more than I had ever seen before, because now there was no other light to diminish them. Suddenly I became aware of the sound of high-pitched wails. Panic swelled in my chest. The storm was returning. Only after several moments did I realize that it was the sound of burglar alarms from other houses on the island.

But the storm would be back.

I struggled through the branches to reach the cellular phone in my car, and my gun, in case he came back. Bruised and cut, my knuckles bleeding, I managed to reach the bag with the phone. Nothing. Only static. Then I realized that even if I could call for help, none would come. I cut myself on broken glass but wrestled my portable radio out through a broken window. No way to reach the gun in the glove compartment.

The starry sky and the water were absolutely calm now, with an unnatural beauty. I clutched the radio, my only link to the world. I would have to conserve the batteries, I thought, wading through water and wreckage, alarms sounding around me, the entire island empty.

The *Libertad* was splintered wreckage, scattered by wind and water. Poles and power lines were down, roof tiles everywhere.

The thought of reentering Reyes's house of horror made my skin crawl, but the radio warned that the second half of the storm was about to strike and would be just as vicious. The sky began to close in again. The night grew darker, the stars vanished, and the wind stirred ominously. Where to go? Back to that bathroom? I would rather die. I shuddered convulsively. But I must survive this, I thought, to tell what he has done.

The house across the street, away from the water, on higher ground, had a collapsed patio structure but looked otherwise intact. I knocked hopefully and tried the doorbell. No one there. Locked and shuttered. I checked under the mat for a key. Nothing. As the wind picked up, something at the side of the house began to slam back and forth.

I skirted the house. Across the street the bay seethed and began to rise again. The slamming continued as I trained the flashlight. Something moving. A dog, a golden retriever, whining, running in and out of his doggie door as the winds began to regain their strength. His owners must have left him behind when they evacuated. I called out, hoping he was friendly.

He gave a small bark and came running, tail frantically wagging, as glad to see me as I was to see him. If I can get inside with the dog, I thought, I'll be safe. On hands and knees, I crawled in through the doggie door. He followed and I secured it from the inside.

He wore a red scarf and a collar with a tag that said his name was Waldo. We sat together on the kitchen floor, both whimpering.

Sick at heart, I thought of Charles Randolph, Butch, and the others. Resisting their images, I forced myself to my feet.

There were matches and candles on the kitchen table. I lit one and put it carefully on a china saucer. No time to be careless with fire, with nowhere to run and no fire department to respond. Rummaging in the kitchen cabinets, I found some cognac and drank straight from the bottle. I thought of Jorge Bravo and drank some more. I found dog food but no manual can opener, and the electric one was useless. Everything would spoil anyway, so I fed Waldo sliced turkey and cold cuts from the refrigerator. Then I drank more cognac. The storm howled and shrieked around us, as Waldo and I climbed up onto the big formal dining room table and went to sleep.

By dawn the storm had gone and the alarms had died, leaving an eerie silence. I stepped outside to a city changed forever.

THE UTTER DEVASTATION evoked an almost mystical quality. More than one hundred fifty thousand people were left homeless. Hundreds more, dead or missing. One condo complex lost an entire wall, exposing ten floors of apartments like an open-ended dollhouse. A blind woman safely rode out the storm in her seventh-floor apartment, then plunged to her death when she reached to close a window in a wall that was gone.

Reyes was apparently still trying to make his way across the causeway when the second half of the storm hit. His wrecked Range Rover was found overturned and partially submerged. His body was not recovered, though forty-one others were. The diary disappeared with him.

The horrific story of Reyes's crimes, which would have dominated front pages for weeks, took a backseat to storm coverage, to the survival of a city.

Large housing developments had been obliterated, wiped off the map, as though by a nuclear blast. County Walk, where the Goldsteins had sought shelter, was devastated. They and Seth barely escaped with their lives. They managed to cling to Bitsy and Billy Boots, who were saved from the terrible fates of thousands of bewildered pets lost in the storm or abandoned by owners left homeless.

For thousands of people who scrambled from room to room in order to survive as their homes disintegrated around them, the drenched clothes they wore were the only possessions they had left. Those trapped inside by fallen trees had to cut and tunnel their way out. Mobile-home parks were reduced to acres of torn sheet metal.

Miamians had no power, no ice or food, no police, fire, or emergency medical service. Tap water was contaminated. Epidemics were feared.

The storm had wobbled slightly at the last minute, deviating from its once head-on course for Miami Beach and downtown Miami, and slammed ashore ten miles south instead. If not for that, the toll would have been far worse.

My mother's shuttered condo went undamaged. But at her co-worker's home, windows shattered and the garage blew away. They huddled under blankets in a closet after the front door blew open and rain blasted into the living room and bedrooms.

Miami looked like war-torn Beirut with exploded storefronts and shattered glass. Huge highway signs had crashed to the streets, and thousands of traffic lights were knocked out. Florida Power and Light crews worked to the point of exhaustion, but company officials said it would take weeks to restore power to Miami Beach, and the hardest-hit areas would have no electricity for at least six months.

Miamians lost their homes but not their spirit. Good and decent people do not change, nor do those who are neither.

Thank God so many Miamians are well armed. Had they not been, what little they had left would have been taken. Gutsy gun owners fought off looters. Crude signs appeared, spray-painted on buckled walls.

YOU LOOT, WE SHOOT.

LOOTERS WELCOME. WE NEED TARGET PRACTICE.

Government could not protect them. Overwhelmed police and fire-fighters did what they could, but many were homeless themselves.

Some looters took only what they needed from damaged convenience stores and supermarkets, others emptied entire shopping centers, then swarmed over Tamiami Airport, stripping expensive electronic equipment from damaged planes.

Twenty thousand Florida National Guardsmen were called in to maintain order. Unfortunately, a local newsman broadcast the fact that the guardsmen had no arrest powers—and no ammo. Within an hour, guardsmen carrying empty guns were being robbed at gunpoint by punks with loaded weapons, and the wrong people now had M16s.

Relief efforts were totally disorganized. Disaster plans had focused on evacuation and shelters, not the aftermath. As bureaucracy floundered, lives were saved, not by government, the Red Cross, or the Salvation Army, but by the Jaycees and the Kiwanis and Lions clubs. They and heroic private citizens mobilized, rolling south with truckloads of food and water.

Even the simplest tasks were impossible. Lines stretched for blocks in brutal heat to use the only functioning telephone for miles. Mail could not be delivered; mailboxes, houses, and entire communities were missing.

Jorge Bravo was not buried on the island where he had hoped to die but two hundred fifty miles away, in Miami. Though he remains forever in exile, his heart was true to Cuba.

His coffin, draped in a Cuban flag, was surrounded by members of his wretchedly small band of Sancho Panzas. He was laid to rest in a cemetery full of fallen trees and broken monuments, like broken promises. Eloy and *especialista* Luisa saluted *el comandante* for the last time. His wife cried. So did I. For Jorge and for Cuba.

I found my Aunt Odalys conducting her own relief effort. The woman, frozen into near paralysis, barely able to function before the storm, was vital and vigorous, helping the elderly, boiling water for the neighborhood, and distributing candles. Her house was unharmed, her stove was gas operated, and Lord knows the woman had an endless supply of candles.

"You're all right!" I said, hugging her.

"*Sí, mi hijita*. It was so after the storm in Melena del Sur."

"You were right about the *mala hora*," I said weakly.

She held my face in her hands and searched my eyes solemnly. "It is yet to come," she whispered. "The most difficult hour still lies ahead."

Lottie's house, in El Portal, to the north, sustained only landscape damage. Pulitzer, her rescued greyhound, was frantic and hyper but he's always that way. She shot unforgettable pictures throughout the storm and its aftermath.

The walls of houses left standing were stained green by the chlorophyll from pulverized foliage pounded against them during the storm. Trees still upright had been defoliated. Once-shady neighborhoods were left naked, exposed to the merciless late-August sun.

Without refrigeration or air conditioning, ice became a precious commodity. Entrepreneurs sold it for five and ten dollars a chunk. People waited in line for hours and were turned away when supplies ran out.

Andrea Vitale had been in the auditorium at Coral Reef Hospital with two hundred fifty pregnant women when the storm hit and the power went out. While she delivered four babies singlehandedly—three girls and a boy—Bramblewood was demolished, sweeping away her home and all the photos and mementos of her only child. The Kearnses lost their house and the nursery. Vanessa Clower was flooded out of her Surfside home. Her ex-husband's business suffered severe damage. The Randolphs lost their spacious L-shaped Florida room and their carport, but the rest of the house and the Quicky Lube came through fine. For all of them the devastation of the hurricane was overwhelmed by the grief and horror of the truth. The storm they all survived had brought back their sons, in plastic body bags, with cops as pallbearers.

They were all there, Charles Randolph, the Kearns brothers, David Clower, Butch Beltrán, Watson Kelly, Lars Sjowall, the Swedish exchange student—all of them and others who may never be identified. A total of twenty-one bodies.

In various stages of decomposition, they had been concealed in an attic, in the crawl space, and the walls. The storm had done much of the work for the cops, excavating Reyes's own private boneyard.

Detectives sifted the wreckage of the house piece by piece. Despite the chaos around them, the cops and medical examiners excavated the site as meticulously as an archaeological dig. Wearing protective charcoal-filtered masks, they crawled on hands and knees and unearthed gruesome finds in the upper crawl space and beneath the house, under air-conditioning ducts, long depressions covered with cracked coatings of dried gray lime. The heat and the noise were horrendous. Because of the water table, they had to use pumps and generators. Their shovels unearthed rib cages and spines, knee caps and lower leg bones. The fresh excavation smelled like a sewer and resembled a scene from a horror movie, with flies, gnats, and maggots, and puddles containing thousands of tiny writhing worms.

Reyes had wrapped the bodies well, using lime and acid to mask the smell. Those under the house were buried beneath eighteen inches of earth. Their clothing and personal effects were missing except for the few souvenirs that police found: Charles Randolph's ring, Butch Beltrán's Swiss Army knife. Dr. Schlatter had been correct: the killer did collect mementos.

Detectives also confiscated books on pederasty, erotic films, handcuffs, and a police badge. Reyes may have posed as a police officer to persuade the boys to accompany him.

Charles Randolph was the first positively identified through dental records. Aware that Charles was missing, his dentist had made a point of keeping the model he had made for the boy's enamel cap.

The biggest story of my career was overshadowed by the storm's wake of looting, crime, lawlessness, and misery.

The *News* published. The presses rolled, powered by emergency generators. There was no air conditioning for the staff. Some had lost their homes, Fred among them. He moved his family in with friends and, like all the others, never missed a day of work.

For many Miamians their newspaper's arrival was the first sign that life might be normal again someday. Editors, delivery men, and even reporters climbed over downed trees and rubble to hand them out in otherwise inaccessible neighborhoods.

They were welcomed. Many people cried.

Our Miami Beach apartment house withstood the storm with only minor roof damage. My bank opened after three days, but allowed only two-hundred-dollar withdrawals because the money supply was limited.

A rash of deaths, not directly attributable to the storm, were related nonetheless. Heart attacks, stress and grief, fatigue and heat, a lack of medication and medical help took a deadly toll on the frail, the elderly, infants, and the chronically ill. Accidents soared: amateurs wielding chain saws, others trying to patch their own roofs or clear heavy debris.

We all worked to exhaustion. It was hell. I yearned for ice and luxuries such as a glass of water or a cup of hot coffee. Brushing my teeth with Pepsi got old fast. I yearned for a hot shower or even a cold bath, but we were warned not to bathe in the contaminated tap water. Heavy rains, humidity, and ravenous mosquitoes compounded the misery.

As I slept fitfully on the hot and muggy fourth night, a damp washcloth draped over my feet to cool me, I was jolted awake.

The sheets felt sticky in the sweltering darkness. Dazed, hypnotized by the heat, I wondered numbly what it was that woke me. Pounding. No doorbell without electricity. No digital clock either. It had to be two or three in the morning. Must be the Goldsteins, I thought. What could be wrong now? I groped for an oversized cotton T-shirt, pulled it over my head, picked up my flashlight, and plodded to the front door.

Wearily, I threw it open, expecting my landlady or Seth, and looked into the silver-blue eyes of Kendall McDonald.

I caught my breath, stomach wrenching as it always does when I see him.

"Britt, I'm so glad you're all right." He smiled, stepping forward as I heard a sound behind me.

His eyes lifted, staring past me into the dark where a battery-operated lantern had just bloomed.

I swallowed hard and turned. "McDonald, this is Hal. Hal, Kendall McDonald."

Hal had pulled on his jeans and was bare-chested, much the way I had first seen him. McDonald, all class, reached past me to firmly shake Hal's hand.

I saw the pain in his eyes.

"I would have called first," he explained. "But the phones are out. . . ."

". . . along with the electricity, the water, and the roads," I said, knowing I must look as miserable as I felt.

"It's good to know you're okay." He studied me for a moment, then turned and disappeared into the night, leaving me standing there.

"Think he knows where to get ice?" Hal said, wiping his brow with a kitchen towel.

"I don't know," I whispered, gently closing the door. "I forgot to ask him." We could have chipped it off the icy stare in his eyes.

REYES'S SURVIVOR SPEECH began to prey on my mind. No trace of the diary was found in the Range Rover. I despaired at my own weakness that had enabled him to wrench it from my grasp. It was in my hands at last, then I lost it. Nightmarish visions plagued me, my father's words caught in the maelstrom, torn from the book's spine page by page, spinning into the whirlwind, gone forever. Twice I put on my fire boots, went to the scene where the Range Rover was found, and slogged through the area in ever-widening circles, searching for a trace, a page, a scrap of paper. Nothing. Not so significant when freighters riding out the storm two miles at sea were hurled half a mile inland. But still, I began to wonder: could Reyes have survived?

Seth stayed on to assist his grandparents, at least until power was restored and repairs to the building done. Each time I saw him, sturdy, strong, and sunburned, eyes alight with enthusiasm, uncomplaining and eager, I imagined the others and what was lost forever.

Lottie had been so right when she talked about sex, power, and politics. Ted Bundy and John Wayne Gacy were among the serial killers once considered politically promising, but their lust was for power, not politics. Reyes never loved Cuba; he loved power. Had I pieced it togeth-er sooner, Jorge Bravo would still be alive and Reyes would be bound for prison or the electric chair.

The President and Governor Fielding came, donned boots and hard hats, took tours, and declared that South Florida was indeed a disaster area. They promised aid and left. The media mob was such that I never had the chance to ask them about their former fund-raiser and compadre. They were both probably relieved that the storm coverage had eclipsed his story and that Juan Carlos Reyes was dead with no high-profile pros-ecution in the offing.

But was he dead? If not, where would he hide? His was too famil-iar a face to remain in Miami, even a Miami in chaos, confusion, and despair. He would have found it simple to vanish following the storm. He had said it himself as we held the door against the winds: "This is a perfect time for somebody to disappear."

He would have to go into hiding until he could flee the country, lose himself, and create a new identity. But people who run away take themselves and their demons with them. I remembered Dr. Schlatter's comment the first time we discussed the case. The killer, she had said, "won't stop until somebody stops him."

I called her again after sporadic phone service was restored. Rose Schlatter was busy applying for federal funds, to conduct a study of the storm's effect on the sex crime rate. Included in her proposal, of course, was funding for a sex offender treatment program that she would direct while conducting the study. The woman was persistent.

"His conscience function must have looked like Swiss cheese with big holes in it," she said, as we discussed Juan Carlos Reyes. She seemed to be his sole mourner. "We could have learned so much," she said. "It's too bad, his kind are usually survivors."

The National Guard erected a tent city where at least eighty thousand people left homeless by the storm would live shoulder to shoulder for months. The military shipped in half a million plastic-wrapped Meals Ready to Eat (MREs) left over from the Gulf War.

Scam artists poured in from all over the country to file claims for loans and grants from disaster aid; strangers moved into abandoned houses and applied for federal assistance. Lawyers recruited clients to sue for shoddy construction and prosecutors pledged to investigate the building inspectors. Nearly a thousand looters and curfew violators were arrested. Legal fallout from the storm would surely grind on for years.

The bruise Juan Carlos Reyes left on my chin was fading fast, my cuts and scratches had healed, but my heart was an open wound. I worked for six days with little sleep and felt like a zombie. Must have looked like one, too. The desk ordered me to take a day off to rest. I neglected to say I might take two. Maybe Reyes was dead, but I felt no sense of resolution. If the man was alive, he should not be. If the diary still existed, I wanted it. It was mine.

First I needed a car. I cornered Lucas Taylor, one of the owners of Double Eagle Towing, behind the bulletproof glass in his well-fortified office. Hard-boiled and husky, he is in his mid thirties, sun-bronzed, and as tough as the business he operates.

"I'm desperate, Lucas. I need something, anything with wheels."

"What happened to the new T-Bird?" He hung a clipboard on the wall and grinned. People were waiting outside. "Lost another one, huh, Britt?"

Lottie and I have had some bad luck with cars but it was never our fault. Who knew our car would be hit as we covered a crash on the expressway? Or that a mob would demolish our car during a riot months later? Or that my last T-Bird would settle to the silty bottom of a deep Everglades canal, nearly taking me with it?

Lucas loves to rub it in.

"Only me and ninety thousand others," I said, "which is why I can't find a rental. You've got to help me, Lucas," I pleaded, "for old times' sake."

He stopped in mid-stride and looked puzzled. "What old times?"

"You know," I said lamely, "all the cars I've watched you haul out of the water, the swamp, airport parking lots, and the woods, sometimes with bodies in the trunk or still strapped behind the wheel."

"Oh," he said, nodding. "I thought I would've remembered."

"You would have," I said.

He came up with a dented 1987 Camaro, half coated with primer, the other half painted electric blue. I didn't want to know its story, didn't even ask about what looked like a bullet hole under the driver's-side window. I just wanted to drive it.

"The frame is a little bent and it pulls to the right, so watch it, Britt. You got to have it back here by Friday, in one piece." He winked and handed me the keys. "Then we can talk old times."

I drove it home, sat in my kitchen, and opened a room-temperature Coke that fizzed all over my last pair of clean jeans. I needed help but had no one to turn to. Reyes was the story of a lifetime, but nobody wanted to listen and there was no room in the newspaper. It was like trying to report a local story in the middle of Hiroshima after the bomb.

Too much was happening; we were in the middle of a national disaster. I was the only one who still considered Reyes more deadly than the hurricane. If he was out there, he had to be found. There was nobody else.

McDonald was working around-the-clock shifts and nursing his own wounds. The dead boys' parents were grieving and planning funerals. Hal was too gentle and too busy as well. His station had gone to twenty-four-hour-a-day emergency public service programming, broadcasting where food, water, medicine, ice, generators, and aid could be obtained, where facilities were being set up for the homeless, reuniting families. He, too, was working nonstop. Everybody else was either trying to cope, to heal, or was occupied with the relief effort. I tried to reach Simmons, but the Missing Boys Task Force had been disbanded and he had been appointed liaison between guardsmen and the local police. When I asked for the homicide captain, no one was there but an overwhelmed clerk who took my information and said somebody would get back to me in a few days.

I couldn't wait. I had to know. I checked my gun, took another box of ammunition from my dining room closet, and loaded it in my car, with some toiletries, in a nearly empty overnight bag.

I consulted my Florida map, made a few calls, stuffed some dirty clothes in a paper grocery sack, put on a pair of cutoffs, a T-shirt, and my Florida Marlins baseball cap, and left an upstate motel number with Seth in case of emergency. Then I took the two hundred dollars I got from the bank and a credit card, locked my apartment, and drove north.

Traffic was madness. Rush hour was all day, in every direction. Designated lanes were reserved for emergency vehicles and convoys of supplies, thousands of portable toilets, plastic sheeting to cover broken roofs, insect repellant, and troops.

The interstate looked like a giant demolition derby. The majority of cars on the road had blasted-out windows, missing windshields, or smashed roofs. Peppered and pockmarked by barrages of roof tiles, damaged by falling trees, signs, and poles, they looked as though they had been caught in a war-zone cross fire.

The landscape was barren, without trees, the sky even bigger than before. Would Miami ever be back to normal? I mourned.

As I drove farther north, into Broward County, the freakish misshapen cars began to disappear from the road, though Dade plates passed frequently, running scared at high speeds, headed due north, away from the chaos: carloads of hollow-eyed adults and grave children, the few possessions they had left, salvaged household goods, mattresses, and furniture, tied to the tops of their rolling wrecks.

Near the Palm Beach County line I took an exit, filled the gas tank, checked the oil and radiator, then stopped at a small coffee shop. I drank glass after glass of ice water while they filled my thermos with steaming coffee. Not as strong as I like it, but my first hot coffee in seven days tasted delicious.

I picked up the turnpike at Stuart, Florida's Treasure Coast, where

Spain's ill-fated 1715 treasure fleet still lies scattered in submerged graves. Though exhausted, I did not worry about dozing off while driving through shallow wetlands surrounded by tall slash pines, saw palmettos, and wax myrtles. My adversarial relationship with the Camaro kept me awake, as I fought to keep it from veering off to the right. I yearned for my T-Bird and its excellent radio. This one emitted mostly static with occasional bursts of country and western.

I couldn't find any news at all.

My destination was located on the fringe of the Ocala National Forest near the small town of Mount Dora in central Florida orange country. A former labor camp for itinerant fruit pickers, it had gone from migrants to militants in the sixties when the CIA began trucking in busloads of would-be commandos for training. Property records showed it was in Reyes's name.

Four and a half hours after leaving home, I exited the turnpike north of Orlando. The next twenty-eight miles were the longest of the entire trip, on winding two-lane roads, as it grew dark in the kind of country you don't want to break down in, isolated and marked by small-town speed traps.

I stopped at the Golden Gem citrus packing house in Tangerine for directions. Twenty minutes later I checked into the Comfort Inn in Mount Dora, population 6,200. I locked the door behind me, turned up the air conditioning, reveled in a hot shower, and washed my hair with the tiny guest bottle of shampoo the management provided. Then I walked to the twelve-block downtown area carrying my grocery bag of dirty clothes. The streets were lantern lit and the homes quaint with New England–style tin roofs, cupolas, and gingerbread. Spanish moss dripped from live oaks and the somnolent setting seemed light-years away from Miami's madness. It felt good to stretch my legs. I found a laundromat, then searched for a meal while my jeans, nightgown, and underwear were washing. There were no fast-food restaurants but I found a small café and ate a light supper, then stopped in the Silver Oyster Gift Shop and bought a Mount Dora T-shirt.

As I watched my clothes spin in the dryer, I thought about closure for all of the victims. Distance did not dispel the strong sensation I had had in Miami, that Reyes was alive, out there somewhere, not far away.

This is my last chance, I thought, the last place I can think of to find him. If he is not here, I promised myself, I will go back to Miami and work dutifully on storm stories, but I will stay alert, keeping eyes and ears open for Reyes. He was out there somewhere in the world. I felt it and was too weary and numb to do more than trust my instincts.

I folded my clothes thinking about Jorge Bravo, who never stopped trying to liberate Cuba with his little ragtag group of misfits. He lived in a sweltering little pillbox, drove balky old cars, and appeared to be threatening, but he was a hero—while Reyes, the smooth, well-spoken patrician with his mansion and high-placed friends, looked heroic but was a monster.

Members of Reyes's organization had trained at this upstate camp for years, plotting secret commando operations. It shut down after federal agents raided the camp and seized the exiles' weapons. They had become an embarrassment. Several would-be warriors had shot themselves or each other in training mishaps, and during a mock invasion of Ocala National Forest, all the rifle-toting commandos had been captured by park rangers.

Reyes had turned to politics to accomplish his mission, but he still owned the property, supposedly a hunting camp. What better hideout? It was only a few miles from where Ma Barker and her boys shot it out with the FBI back in the thirties.

My plan was to drive to the camp at dawn, after a good night's sleep, taking the element of surprise with me. Back at the motel I engaged the dead bolt, propped a chair against the door, and slipped my gun beneath the pillow. This was not Miami, but the possibility of Reyes's presence in the vicinity made me queasy. My body ached with weariness. The room was cool, my bed comfortable and clean, so why couldn't I sleep? It had to be almost dawn, I thought, then sat up and stared at the clock. It had only been twenty minutes. Strangely energized, beyond exhaustion, I slipped out of bed and dressed quickly in the dark, in jeans and an oversize cotton sweatshirt. No way could I wait until morning. I had to know.

I stuck the gun in my belt, clipped to the inside of my jeans, pulled the sweatshirt down over it, took my flashlight and scribbled directions, and left the room. I walked to the car as though in a dream, the fragrant night soft and misty around me.

There was little traffic. In the center of town, a shadowy figure caught my eye, staring from the sidewalk. I tapped the brake and turned to look but he had disappeared. I could have sworn it was the bearded street preacher from South Beach. No way he could be here, I thought. My mind was playing tricks on me. My Aunt Odalys's words came back to me. "Beware *la mala hora.*" The bad hour of one's life. I shook off the thought.

I drove slowly past the rutted dirt road that led into the camp. It looked dark through the pines and cypresses. No lights. I pulled the car off the pavement, cut the engine and headlights, and sat watching. Nothing.

The night sounds quickly resumed around me. I stepped out, searching for any movement, then walked back to the dirt road, sailing solo through a sea of night. A heavy chain stretched across the entrance, secured by padlocks. As I slipped beneath it, a small creature skittered, an owl watched, eyes glowing. Stumbling in the dark, I moved slowly, carefully, toward the only building in sight, a wooden barracks.

And then I heard it. The hum of a generator, and the faint sound of a radio, a Spanish-language program. I stood frozen, listening to a station out of Miami. There was an antenna on the roof. Heart beating wildly, I crept closer, senses acute, skin tingling, then peered around the corner of the building. There was a light, not visible from the road because the windows facing it had been covered. There was a car, also hidden from the road.

Through a screened window I saw that the barracks was a far cry from a luxurious bay-front mansion or a presidential palace. But still too good for a man who murdered children.

The radio sat on a wooden table at the far end of the room along with several open newspapers, a dirty plate, a glass, and a bottle of Scotch.

Where was he?

"Britt Montero?"

Startled by the familiar voice, I spun around with a gasp.

He stood behind me, no longer the suave, immaculately tailored man who had shared a podium with the President. Unshaven, he wore rumpled dark trousers, a dark shirt, and an empty shoulder holster.

The gun was in his hand. It looked like a nine-millimeter Glock.

"How did you find me here?" He was genuinely puzzled.

"I knew you were alive," I said softly. "I knew it."

"You came alone." It was more statement than question.

"No," I lied. "The cavalry is right behind me."

He knew it wasn't true and smiled, listening to the night, head cocked like a wild animal sniffing the air.

"Come visit my humble abode." He gestured with the gun and we stepped inside.

Some papers and documents lay on a chair. "My new passport," he said, following my eyes.

"Jorge Bravo told me from the start that you were a monster. I should have believed him." Totally without fear, I was full of questions. I wanted to pick his brain. How did he become so evil? Was he born that way?

I sat at the wooden table.

"Did it start with your American cousin?" I said. "The boy in the picture."

"He died in an accident," Reyes replied offhandedly. "They said it was an accident." He smiled and took an opposite seat, watching me intently. I could see that he was wearing a bulletproof vest again. He had good reason for paranoia.

"What about all the other boys, why . . . ?"

"They were out on the street," he said, shrugging. "They did not belong there."

"So that justifies what you did to them?" My voice rose shrilly. "Charles Randolph wasn't out on the street. He was taking care of your fucking boat!"

"I am not a homosexual," he said.

"Oh?" I said sarcastically. "What about the Swedish boy and David Clower . . . and all the others?"

His eyes took on an almost dreamy look in the dim light. His voice softened.

"That one, David. Beautiful. A beautiful *niño*. Fine features. Like a little girl, perfect in every way. Delicate fair skin."

I shuddered but he appeared eager to talk. Isolation was so unlike his usual lifestyle. The gun remained in his hand, the barrel resting on the wooden table.

"They were all beautiful. Only one was difficult. He had a knife, a Swiss Army knife. When I tried to handcuff him, the little bastard struggled and tried to cut me." He looked incensed, indignant that a victim had tried so hard to fight him off.

"He was the one five months ago, wasn't he?"

"Very good," he said, nodding.

"You kept the knife. They found it." Way to go, Butch, I thought. You should have cut his throat.

"Most people don't understand," Reyes was saying, "but the Greeks, they had a philosophy. Women are intended only for procreation. They used boys for birth control.

"You know"—he leaned forward, voice fatherly and persuasive, as though seeking my approval—"it is all part of a plan in human nature."

I shook my head. Was he trying to convince me or himself?

"What about murder? Is that part of a plan? I don't recall that part of Greek history."

He rocked back impatiently, eyes threatening, so I changed the subject. "How did you find Armando Gutiérrez ?"

"The obvious." He waggled the gun, making me nervous. "I had the home of his relatives in Miami watched. He was cautious enough to stay away but he could not resist calling. My contact with the telephone company cooperated with a tap on the line and traced it back to his hotel." He looked pleased at his proficiency.

"Did you destroy the diary?" I held my breath.

He smiled. "I have been reading it while waiting for other plans to fall into place. You and Catalina would have found it most interesting. Too bad you cannot leave here." He sounded almost regretful.

"But it is impossible." He rose, the gun in his hand. "If Catalina had given Tony Montero a son there might have been a contest here. Reyes versus Montero, history repeating." He smiled. "Thirty years ago I stopped him. Now this. But I assure you that I find no joy in killing a woman."

"Perhaps if I was a little boy . . ."

He slapped me then, almost knocking me off my feet, his heavy ring bruising my cheekbone.

"Enough," he snapped. "We will take a stroll in the woods. You can carry this." He tossed me a shovel with a wooden handle and shook his head sadly. "You should have stayed in Miami." We stepped out into the night.

The moon spilled silver across the treetops as it emerged from cloud cover, big, ripe, and full. News had to be breaking on the streets of Miami, I thought, despite the curfew.

I entertained the idea of swinging the shovel at him as hard as I could, but his gun was at my back. No way could I move faster than a bullet.

"Was it on a night like this that you betrayed my father?"

He did not answer. Instead, he stopped in a stand of slash pines. "Dig here."

The sandy ground was matted with pine needles that resisted the shovel. I bent to scrape them away, then cried out and fell back.

"Rattlesnake!" I screamed.

He danced backward, the gun in both hands, training it from left to right, seeking the reptile. I slammed him in the shins with the shovel. The blow was not solid enough to knock him down.

His gun fired, the bullet went wild.

He was off balance, face contorted, as I swung the shovel again, bashing his gun hand. The weapon fell into the palmetto scrub as he lunged toward me, cursing. He caught me in a headlock, a choke hold, and began wrestling me toward where his gun lay.

I managed to reach down to my waistband and wrench out my gun. I don't think he ever saw it in the dark. Grunting, he continued to drag me as I tried to dig in with my heels. Awkwardly I lifted the gun behind my neck, tried to aim in the general direction of his head, closed my eyes, and squeezed the trigger.

The explosion hurt my ears. The flash lit up the night around us. Reyes's grip on me relaxed and I fell onto my back, wriggling away, lifting the gun again.

Smoke still trailed from the barrel as I held it in front of me, steady in my hands. He drew in a ragged breath of surprise and toppled sideways into the palmettos, then rolled onto his back. In the bright moonlight, I stared at Reyes's empty eyes and the blood leaking from the corner of his mouth and felt nothing. Not a thing.

Killing him had been so easy.

It did not seem necessary to check his pulse. Although I am not squeamish, he disgusted me, even in death.

History might have repeated, I thought, if my mother had given Tony Montero a son. Reyes surely would have frisked a man. I brushed the pine needles off my clothes, then walked back to the barracks, where I searched methodically until I found what I wanted: the worn leatherbound volume with my father's initials on the cover.

I put it in the trunk of the Camaro, then drove to a truck stop and called the police.

I WAS AFRAID it would be like a bad movie, that we would tramp back into the woods and the corpse would be missing. But Reyes was still there, just the way I had left him.

One of the two officers on duty stayed to maintain the scene until daybreak. The other took me to police headquarters, located on the first floor of a small modern building. The fire department was upstairs, on the second floor. I found it curious that the dispatcher-receptionist who greeted us on an intercom in the tiny lobby was seated snugly behind bulletproof glass. The chief, furious after being roused from his bed in the middle of the night, had all but convinced me that his community had no crime rate, at least not until I arrived.

"You have a lot of 'splaining to do, young lady," he said, reiterating once more that this was their first murder in three years.

I kept telling them that the dead man was a serial killer from Miami, that I was a reporter from Miami, and that he should call the Miami police.

"Might know," he muttered. "Nothing good ever comes up here from Miama."

"I think it's probably the full moon," I said wearily. "At least that's been my experience."

"I thought that whole damn town down there just got blowed away."

"Almost," I said, yawning.

"You on drugs?" he said suspiciously. "You are pretty damn cool for somebody who just shot a man down on his own property."

I assured him that I was only very tired and asked him again to call Miami homicide.

As it happened, Miami called him first. My second call from the pay phone had been to the homicide unit. A beleaguered midnight-shift secretary had finally answered, recognized my voice, and assumed I was calling about the national guardsman who had run amok and killed three hurricane survivors who had been taunting him, or the woman who was holding a baby and threatening to jump from an overpass.

"No," I had told her, my voice wan. "Don't tell me about them now. This is long distance and I don't have time." I gave her the short version of where I was and what I had done.

My own calm surprised me as I sat alone in the small interrogation room. I had always believed that killing another human being was a wrenching emotional experience. I had met combat veterans who never recovered and knew cops who required psychological counseling to deal with the trauma after taking a life even under the most justifiable of circumstances. I remembered the tears in Hal's eyes. I had always pitied those who carried the burden of such remorse. But killing Reyes had been so simple, so natural.

What would always haunt me was the lost boys, all of them, and the lives they would never lead. I would never forget their parents. The enormous guilt that led to Edwin Clower's drinking. The allergies his exwife, Vanessa, acquired after their son vanished. The Kearnses at each other's throats. Cassie Randolph, whose only child never walked out the door without kissing her good-bye. And Andrea Vitale, eating compulsively for two, still buying snacks for her missing son.

The chief returned from the phone with a new attitude. Miami was sending people up to sort things out, he said. I could go back to my motel room if I agreed not to leave it until morning. He would pick me up then to return to the scene for a walk-through of what had happened, for him and the local prosecutor.

I drove the Camaro back to the motel, trailed by a police car. "Git some rest," the officer said. He waved and drove off as I closed the trunk, walked inside, and nearly ran to my room. Sleep played no role in my plans. I had no trouble staying awake. I had waited all my life for this moment. I curled up in a chair beneath a lamp and opened my father's diary.

> *June 10, My Angels, my dearest wife and daughter. How can I express how tenderly and respectfully I love you both and Miami, the home that is ours.*
>
> *My only solace here in this place that is always night, where candle flames are snuffed out forever, is that you are both safe in the land of flowers and sunshine. By now Winslow has kept his promise and you know my situation and why I was sworn to secrecy about our mission. . . .*

My Spanish is not terrific, the letters were faded in some places, and at times tears blurred my vision, but it was all there.

The secret mission that the CIA had prevailed upon him to carry out. The insistence that he tell no one of the plan, the promise that his wife would be informed after his departure, and that the government would provide for his wife and daughter should anything go wrong.

First Juan Carlos Reyes betrayed my father, then it was Winslow, the CIA, the government. One act of betrayal after another.

> *I know the monster,* he wrote of Reyes. *More dangerous, depraved, and treacherous than Fidel. Had it not been for this traitor among us, success would have been ours. When we took to the hills, the people joined us, patriotic Cubans all filled with a passion*

for freedom and dignity. Now we are all scattered, dead or in prison. But others will carry on in our names. I know that Jorge Bravo, if he still lives, will fight on forever.

I am doing my duty here. Our spirit is one. Endless kisses to my beloved wife and our golden angel. I have two countries now. The one I die for and the one where my heart lies.

I may disappear but my thoughts are with you forever.

Put my ashes in the stars, not in the ground.

I cried for my father and for Jorge Bravo and all the others betrayed. And for my mother, who was betrayed perhaps the most of all. Like Bravo, she too had lost thirty years of her life, he in an impossible crusade, she to bitterness.

Odd that an act committed by Reyes so many years ago had resulted in his death here in this place, that justice ultimately overtook him, with my finger on the trigger.

I walked through the reenactment in the morning. The bullet had caught Reyes at an angle near the top of the head and slammed into his brain, a lucky shot. Lucky for me. Not him.

La mala hora had been his. Not mine. The chief was sending out for sandwiches when the detectives from Miami arrived.

Lieutenant Kendall McDonald found me sitting in the police station drinking coffee. He asked if I was all right.

"Fine," I said too loudly, smiling cheerfully, startled as always by the silver-blue depths of his eyes.

He frowned and went off with the chief. They wrapped things up in a few hours.

"Come on," McDonald said. He put his arm around me. "I'll take you back to Miami."

I had to make one call first, to my mother.

"Mom," I said, excited. "I can't wait to get back. I have something to show you."

"Where are you, Britt?"

"On my way home," I said. "I love you."

She can grieve at last, I thought. Her life will change.

Detective Simmons, from the Missing Boys Task Force, had come with McDonald. He followed in the Camaro.

"Watch out," I warned him. "It pulls to the right."

I sat beside McDonald in a city car, headed south, the diary in my lap. It is my history, I thought sleepily. One of the relics of my life. All I will ever have of my father.

McDonald understands such things, so I told him how easy I had found it to kill Reyes.

"It is easy to kill when you have a reason," he said, skillfully passing a slow-moving citrus truck on the two-lane road, "but it's hard to forget. You have the rest of your life to think about it."

The afternoon light hurt my eyes and I was already dozing off. I woke up once, when we stopped on the turnpike for coffee.

"How's Miami?" I said, sleepily, as though I had been away for a long time.

"Don't ask about last night," he said, and grinned. "We had to call in extra teams from home."

I became wide awake as we got closer, into Broward County. I thought of Jorge Bravo, who would never again walk on his native soil. One day I will do it for him. And I will bring back a handful of Cuban soil to sprinkle on his grave. Then I can whisper: "You can rest now, Jorge. Cuba is free at last."

Strangely battered cars began appearing in traffic and I knew we were nearly home. The sun was setting as we reached the Dade County line. "Take the flyover," I told McDonald, and he signaled for the right lane.

The flyover is a forty-million-dollar boondoggle that tied up motorists for years while it was being built. Its purpose was to end the traffic jams at the Golden Glades interchange. The result is a single lane, a nightmare that has worsened the problem because of poor engineering, lousy signage, and cars that crash and burn. But, rising high over the rest of the traffic, it has a great view.

There it was. Miami. All purple and rosy, the golden fingers of dying sunlight curling around its skyline. I caught my breath, as though glimpsing a passionate lover after being gone too long. My heart beat faster. I do love this place. The city glowed, like hope overcoming the misery, the recovery to come, the pain of rebuilding.

"It's beautiful, isn't it?" I whispered.

"Yeah, it is," he said, and held my hand.

ACKNOWLEDGMENTS

I AM GRATEFUL to Homicide Sergeant Jerry Green and Lieutenant Robert Murphy, Miami's best and brightest; to Lieutenant Greg Terp and Officer Dan Eydt of the Metro-Dade Bomb Squad; to Mount Dora Police Sergeant Arthur Beck and Paul Miller of the FBI; and to Dr. Stephen T. Nelson. I am indebted to *Miami Herald* star staffer Arnold Markowitz and to Sam Terilli, Tom Fiedler, and photojournalist Bill Cooke. Karen McFadyen, Diana Montane, Joel Hirschhorn, and Mike Baxter generously shared their brilliance and expertise, as did the Miami Beach Public Library staff. My friends Ann and D. P. Hughes never fail when it counts. A tropical wave to Lixion Avila, to my agent Michael Congdon, and to Leslie Wells, the talented editor who shares my vision. The steadfast support of Ruth Ann Cione and the generous spirit of Marilyn Lane, my cheerleader and confidante, keep me on course.

My life has such a sterling cast of characters.